Send 'Em to the Deep

To Ed

By Keith R. Kirkwood

Keith R. Kirkwood
7-18-09

PublishAmerica
Baltimore

First printing

All characters in this book are fictitious, and any resemblance to real persons, living or dead, is coincidental.

ISBN: 1-60836-648-0
PUBLISHED BY PUBLISHAMERICA, LLLP
www.publishamerica.com
Baltimore

Printed in the United States of America

Out of sight and mind of the American people, the war on drugs goes on. A team of unknowns takes the fight to the Cartels to stem the flow of Colombia cocaine into the U.S. through Cuba. This is a fictional account of how the war might be won had this method been used.

INTRODUCTION

This is a story of a group of courageous men who signed onto dangerous missions to aid the United States Government in combating the War on Drugs. The government had found that routine methods of law enforcement were not working. A recruiting was begun to find men who loved excitement. Risk takers and loyal Americans. The job was a dirty one that would take guts to pull it off. It was to be an uncover, secret operation with government sanctions. They would be working outside the law and could expect help from no one. This is a follow up to my two earlier books, The Cuban Connection & Thrown Undercover.

The assault from the Mexicans was getting worse as millions poured across our borders. With them came terrorists and billions of dollars worth of drugs. The harder law enforcement tried the worse it got.

The congress was sitting on their butts and not doing a thing to protect our border. They were actually in favor of the flood of cheap labor under the Bush Administration. The Mexican government was actually assisting in getting wet backs across the borders. American money was leaving the country by the billions of dollars. Medical services to the illegals were draining the resources of our hospitals and several hospitals were forced to close. One item appeared on Television confirming the illegals were being give free bus tickets north by the border patrol.

Not being able to reduce the demand for the drugs inside the states a small group decided to take drastic action to kill the supply coming out of Colombia.

This is the setting in which this story is taking place.

-1-

It was dark as the hubs of hell in Cartagena, Colombia, on this April night. It was a moonless night as Nate Armstrong stood in the shadows. He was in a seedy part of town where murders were common. Drug cartels still operated and it was rumored this end of town was under their control. The police would never admit to this but the citizens knew. Decent people did not go into this area. He sucked on a cigarette as he peered across the cobblestone street. His attention was directed to the bar across the way. He knew he must enter that place to make his contact with a woman named Katrina. As he stood looking around to make sure this meeting was not a set-up, his mind drifted back to what brought him here.

Four months earlier, there had been a meeting in the Central Intelligence Agency in Langley, Virginia. It had been a very hush hush meeting even for this agency. Only four men were present beside him.

He recalled he had been enjoying a peaceful time in Portland, Oregon. He had a nice apartment and a couple of girl friends. Life was good. He had a nice bank account courtesy of the C.I. A. This was money earned while doing covert operations during the Viet Nam War. He knew that his funds would be running low and in a year or so, he would have to look for work. *That is fine he thought but for now it was the good life.*

Nate prided himself in not worrying about the future. After all death might take us anytime, so why worry.

He was a tall man of forty-nine years of age, had never married mainly because he loved living on the edge. He could never expect a woman to contend with that. He was ruggedly good looking but had one of those faces that could blend in to a crowd and not be recognizable. In his past line of work, this had saved his life several time. He was well built and weighted two hundred pounds. Women found him attractive and enjoyed his sense of humor. He had

7

picked up the nasty habit of smoking when in Viet Nam. It seem to quiet his nerves and allowed him to think more clearly. He had found he could take it or leave it. This could be accounted for by the fact he did not inhale. He just liked the taste and the bite of tobacco to the tongue. When he was with a woman who did not like him smoking, he simply quit. He would begin again when she would try trapping him into marriage.

Why should I marry, he often thought, *when I get from them what I want without all the pain?* This way when with a woman it was for a happy, rewarding experience. Never an argument, only enjoyment.

At the meeting, he remembered how when he walked into the building in Langley being impressed with its beauty. However, a chill came across him as he moved across the seal of the agency. He understood the need for spies but felt uncomfortable around them. As he crossed the seal, a man came out of a booth set a little further inside and just down the hall.

"Are you the one expected tonight?" he asked. Funny he was not asked by name. When General Scofield called, he had been told not to give anyone his name and if asked for one, he was to report it at once.

"Yes, I'm expected in room six," I told him.

"Follow me," the guard said turning and starting down the hall.

Nate fell in behind him and had to bite his tongue to keep from asking what was going on. He realized that this person would not know as this was to be kept very secret. He wondered what waited within. That eerie feeling came over him again. He could hardly believe he was in harms way. This was America and this agency was on his side. *Well time will tell,* he thought.

The guard opened a door marked with a six. Nate noticed this number was a different color from others he had passed. He wondered what the significant of this was. He stepped through and the door was closed behind him. The guard had not entered with him.

Nate looked around and finding himself in a standard looking office. No one was here. He looked at his watch. He was on time. He walked further into the room when the back wall opened up and a three star General stepped forward.

"Hi, Mr. Armstrong. Nice of you to come. Sorry, I could not tell you more on the phone. It was not safe to say any more. No line is safe. Even our computers are taking fifty hits a day by hackers trying to get into our secrets. Come lets go into this next room, some folks are waiting to meet you." He extended his arm in a jester indicating Nate was to go first.

Hell, I have gone this far. Might as well go the rest of the way. Besides, he was curious about all this cloak and dagger stuff.

He moved forward into the room. The back wall opened and he saw three men were seated at a table. They were dressed in business suits. The General was the only military man present. The wall closed behind them. *Strange,* Nate thought the room had no windows or doors. The moving wall was the only way in or out.

"Come in Mr. Armstrong. Nice of you to be on time. Please be seated. I would like to introduce you to these men but I cannot. At least not until you accept our proposition. We have invited you here on a matter of national security. Every thing that is said here tonight must stay here. If word gets out about a plan we have, the government will move to stop us. Don't misunderstand, Nate; by the way can I call you Nate."

Nate nodded, he really did not care. It was his given name so people might as well use it.

"As I was saying don't misunderstand, we are loyal Americans with a great concern on how our homeland security is being run. We are not here to plot the overthrow of the President. We just do not think he is doing enough to protect us. The Mexicans are streaming across our borders by the millions, yet the president and congress does nothing to stop it. President Fox of Mexico has refused to place his troops on the border to stop his people from leaving. I fact we have proof he is doing just the opposite. His troops are actually helping them to get to the border. We know that terrorists and billions in drugs are riding this wave into America," he hesitated to catch his breath. Nate could see the beads of sweat of concern on his brow.

"I agree General; this is happening and any day now dozens of strikes of terror will befall this nation. The war on terror will be fought on our soil. But I'm just one man and have no way of stopping this migration of Mexicans," Nate stated.

"We know that Armstrong, but we think you would be the right person to interfere and greatly reduce the amount of drugs coming into this country. Drugs have eroded the moral fiber of our people. Americans do not seem to understand the gravity of the situation. Every time one buys an illegal drug, they are supporting organized crime. Millions have fried their brains and no longer care. Voting is a national disgrace. About fifty percent of them no longer vote. We are going to hell in a hand basket. Some one with guts has to step up and try. We have others working on the migration. We want you to concentrate on killing the drug trade. You can speak freely and we will honor that. This room is sound proof and nothing is being recorded. Are you interested in helping us?" he said. Somewhat relieved he leaned back in his chair and waited.

Every eye was on Nate as he turned this conversation over in his mind. One of the men asked if he wanted coffee and leaving his chair he walked to a table along the wall where a pot was plugged in. He picked up a cup, filled it and sat in front of Nate. He nodded thanks for the coffee as the man filled all the cups on the table. *That's one thing about being a spy; you drink a lot of coffee,* he thought.

"I need to know more about your plan before I would commit myself. You have had me checked out so you know I am no security risk. If I were, I would not be here. Lay all your cards on the table, gentleman, then we'll talk," he stated. *Damn now, they have me even more curious and a little intrigued,* he thought.

The group around the table looked at each other. They nodded their heads to the General, their representative.

Nate was sizing them up as he waited a response. The three men in suits were all in their late fifties and early sixties. They looked to be congressional representatives or high-ranking members in the C.I.A. If they were either, they were the ones behind scenes. The ones you never see in public or on T.V. They were all wearing a large ring; each ring was the same with some sort of emblem in the center. He wondered if this was a form on identification. You never know when you enter the world of spooks.

Nate never really thought of the C.I.A. as spooks. It was a much-needed organization to protect our freedom. They may use unorthodox methods overseas to uphold our country's needs. So what. The dirty bastards coming after us know no rules. Murder, torture, kidnapping and any other method they could think of. No rules just craziness.

From the look on their faces they believed in the program they were about to lay out for Nate. As he looked at them, he felt they were part of the front line in our battle to repel our enemies. It was obvious from the looks on the faces, this was serious business. He did not smell any fear in the room, but he did feel determination. It was quite possible these folks were putting their careers and perhaps much more on the line. He was curious now.

"Ok, here's what we have in mind," started the General. "We need to cut

10

back on the supply lines of drugs coming into this country for the reasons I've told you. The only real way to do this is to sabotage the vehicles of transportation and murder the top people in Colombia. Ninety eight percent of the drugs coming in through Cuba come from Colombia. The plan is simple. We train a small group of men to scuba dive off fishing vessels and plant explosive devices to the bottoms of ships carrying the poison. We do not need men that are affiliated with the government nor have military service. This would make them untraceable to any agency of our government. These men can be renegades and cutthroats but with a strong patriotic belief in the U.S. They must be loyal and tightlipped. They do not have to be murderers now, as that will come when the first boat goes down. The boats must go down in deep water, leaving no debris behind. If pieces of wreckages are found, then the cartels will know what we are up to. The men we send must realize it is a dangerous mission and they could be killed. If captured they are to have no information, verbal or written that would point back to us. If caught they will be at the mercy of their captors and can expect no help from us. As far as the world knows, the group will be just a few renegade anglers. The catches will be taken into ports in Colombia and sold at their markets. We are willing to pay each man fifty thousand dollars in tax-free money for every vessel they make disappear. You will be in the same boat. You must never say a thing about this mission. If you or any of the men you must recruit do then they will be killed. Understand. No trail leads back here. This is a must."

He finished talking and Nate felt all eyes boring into his very soul.

"God, this is heavy stuff you're laying on me. I have a question for you. Why me?" Nate asked.

"Because of missions you had in Viet Nam. We contacted the one man who handled your payments for work. You were not an agent of the C.I.A. but a private contractor. You were paid in cash and there is no record of you doing anything for us. We would never have known about you except one of our agents knew of covert missions in Nam. He knew the man who paid you but knew nothing else. We found this man living in Oregon and asked for the name of the man who was so successful in Nam. We had to convince him that we had similar missions for you if we could find you. He finally gave your name. Checking you out we found the only thing that could be used against you is you are an American citizen. That is of no concern because many Americans like the free and open life on the sea. Many do so to get away from wives and families, responsibility, to escape punishment for crimes committed. You sir, are the perfect man for this job," he finished saying.

"You're talking about murdering several people on each boat we blow up. Some may be innocent. I don't know about this," Nate said with concern in his voice.

"We know you killed in Nam. This is no different," said the General.

"Yes it is. We were at war with the Viet Cong and it was killing or is killed. This doesn't look like it to me," Nate replied.

"We are at war Nate, with an enemy that is more destructive than all the weapons of all the wars we've fought. They are destroying our nation from within and the politicians are afraid to move. To damn many pussys on the hill," said the General.

"Ok, I'll give you that one. I agree we are not fighting this war any better than we did in Nam and we are losing. I see other problems with your plan," Nate said with firmness in his voice.

"Let's get everything out on the table and I'll answer all your questions. Go ahead you have the floor," said the General.

"In the first place we would need explosive devices that would only blow in one direction and make a hole. If you have too much of an explosion, you spread debris all over the water. Someone would see this and after a short time, as you said, figure out what is going on and we are dead. The only device I know of that could do that would be an anti-tank mine. They are too damn heavy to even consider for this type of work. How do we get around that," Nate explained.

Sensing he had Nate coming his way, the General stood up and walked to a blackboard. He took a piece of chalk and began drawing.

"We have that problem solved. We have taken the anti-tank mine and redid it to fit our purpose. At the CIA. Labs we have redid it in a light plastic with the same amount of power. On the smaller boats, it will blow a four-foot hole in the bottom. The explosion is under water and is muffled. If two are placed on each boat, they would sink live rocks and this would sink-em deep. The plastic is made of material that will dissolve in seawater in two days. No evidence left. When placed on a metal bottom boat they would have the same effect. The only problem we have not worked out yet is how to silence their radios. On the smaller ones, we do not believe there is a problem. They would go down in two minutes flat. We have tested them. Large vessels pose a problem. We do not intend for you to sink ocean-going vessels. Most of our information says small yachts and six men fishing boats. A tug boat or two also. You would make the decisions on which ones to sink," advised the General.

His drawing on the board illustrated how it would work.

Nate was silence for a couple of minutes. To himself he throught *boy these people were serious and had figured things out.*

"You've forgotten one thing General," he began, "what about the bodies. They will float to the top and could easily be spotted. How do you suggest we dispose of them?"

"That's the easiest but most disgusting part of this whole business. It would be your decision but we would suggest you find them, cut them open and let the sharks have them. Of the seven man-eating sharks in the world, five are located in those waters. If for some reason you are close to shore, says Panama, you might want to chance a landing and burying them. Your choice," said the General.

"Disgusting is right," Nate, answered, "I don't know gentlemen. Sounds messy to me. How do I go about recruiting men for such a mission? How can I find men I could trust, etc?"

"Your problem, Armstrong," one of the suited men said

A hush fell over the room. It was deadly still in there. Nate was thinking fast and furious. He felt these men were getting impatient.

"How many of these gallant heroes do you think it would take to pull this off," Nate asked.

"At least four and six would be better," answered the General, "we have outfitted two smaller fishing boats and three men to a boat would be just right. Do you still know where your team from Nam is? They would be perfect for this job. If you don't know and would trust me with their names, I could locate them for you."

"Suppose I take the job, we would need someone on shore to feed us information on what boats were carrying so we'd know who to hit. I don't want to kill innocent people if I don't have to," said Nate.

"That's been taken care of. We have had an agent on the ground there for eight months. It is a woman. She works in a joint called the El Toro. It is in a bad part of town controlled by the cartels. She is experienced and very trustworthy. She is living under discussing conditions. This El Toro is where the drug lords hang out. She tells me they keep their hands off her because of the owner. He is in love with her and I guess a real tough bastard. She has nothing to do with him outside the bar but he protects her. In this bar, the men speak freely of their business and how easy it is to get into the U.S. with their poison. She is in her early forties and lost a younger sister to drugs a couple years ago. That is her motivation. She hates them and their trade. She is willing to die to help slow this trade," spoke the General.

"What's her name," Nate asked.

"You won't know that until you've finished training and are on you way there," the General responded.

Nate took a sip of the hot, black coffee and considered what he had heard so far. It was quiet in the room and again all eyes were on Nate. He got the feeling that they wanted this so bad and that he was their last chance.

"Tell me more about the explosives before I commit myself," Nate asked.

At the blackboard, the General explained the devices and how they would work.

"In the labs here the techs found they could shape plastic explosives into a cone. Make it wide at the bottom end and narrower at the top. Depending on the size of hole, you wanted to blow would determine how wide. We have found that the right amount of the plastic would blow the hole, leaving sawdust remaining. No other part of the boat would be affected and the sawdust from the material would soon disappear. The sea would carry it away. Nothing floating except what floated out of the boat itself. Once you sink the boat, you stick around a while and retrieve floating garbage. You will have to decide how to dispose of that material. The bodies will soon be pulled under and eaten by sharks. It is a good plan. All we need are dedicated Americans who like to live on the edge and do this work for maybe a year. Sooner if anyone catches on to you. If they do catch on to you, will be required to get the woman out. It would not take long for them to find out she was getting the information out. Her life would not be worth a plug nickle. What do you say," explained the General.

"Can I see one of these devices?"

"No, not yet. You will see them during your training. It is a good way of sinking boats without leaving any debris. I will tell you that on the top end or what you might call the funnel end, we have attached sticky glue. It is covered with a thin plastic that you peel off to use. It will stick for a twenty-four hour period. This would make it possible for you to even attach one in port. Of course, you'de never does that unless you know when the boat was sailing. Salt water would eat away at the glue and cause it to fall off. It has been tested and the max time is 48 hours. We believe one should never expect it to go over 24 hours. The movement of the boat causes a strain on the attachment and could pull it loose. No harm done, as you know, it would just drift to the bottom harmlessly and dissolve," advise the General.

"This training you mentioned," Nate asked, "how long will it take and where is it to take place?

"You're familier with the Pacific. Do you know a group of islands called the Marshalls," the General asked him.

"Yeah, they're about half way from Hawaii to Viet Nam. I believe there is a missile range there. Right?" Nate answered.

"Well you and your crew will be sent there for a two week training course. The course will consist of swimming with oxygen tanks. Scuba diving the main course. You will learn to plant the devices on a fishing vessel we have made available. There will be a study of sharks and equipment to combat attacks. Shark repelent will be supplied. When everyone masters the swimming, etc. you will then be sent to Colombia. Your crew must understand that this is top secret. No one must know. You will be given a couple phones that are scrambled so we can talk without anyone else listening in. This will put you in touch with me. Your two boats can converse over these. All orders and reports are for me only. Everytime you send a boat to the deep, I want to know. The same day, I will deposit fifty thousand dollars to your account and each of your men. It is important we move quickly. The crop is being harvested now and soon boats with tons of cocaine will be on its way to Cuba. Warehoused there and later smuggled into the U.S. Billions of dollars worth of human misery. What do you say Nate, will you take the assignment? Asked the General.

Nate looks around the table. Every eye was on him. The expressions on their faces told him they were dead serious about this program. There was a sense that he was their only chance of pulling this off. He sat a couple minutes without saying a word. His thinking was *it would strike a blow for justice and the money they could make would secure his and his men's retirement. This was tax-free money, a chance of a lifetime.*

"Ok, I do it," Nate spoke up, "but there is a condition. My people would need money up front to accept this sort of deal. They have bills, etc. to pay. $50, 000.00 to each as soon as you get the account numbers. There will be six of us. My team from Nam. If you agree, I will give you their names and an idea of where they may be. At least the state I believe their in. Agreed?"

15

The general looked around the table. Nate also watched for a reaction from the suited men. Both noticed a sign of relief appear on their faces and all nodded in agreement.

"Gentlemen, you can leave and I'll work out the details. Leave the building one at a time so as not to be noticed as a group. Thank you and I'll keep you informed," the General addressing the others.

A button was pushed and the wall opened and the suits all left the conference room, to the outer office. The wall closed behind them.

"Have some more coffee, Nate, and lets take a couple minutes before you give me the information on the where abouts of your team," came from the General.

Both relaxed, poured coffee sitting back and chatting about minor things.

"You know, Nate, I was also in Nam and still believe that if the damn politicians had stayed the hell out, we could have won that one. Having the dredge keeping, the harbor open at Hanoi, off limits to our bombers, was the dumbest thing I ever heard of. All the war supplies from China, etc. came in through that port and Washington knew it. We did not have enough troops there to win. Thousands of our men died for nothing." said the General letting off steam.

Ten minutes passed quicky and he soon pulled out a pad and prepared to write.

"Go ahead Nate, I'm ready," announced the General.

"Well most of the crew, if not all of them and living in the Northwest. At least one is in Idaho a couple in Oregon and maybe Northern California. One mentioned Seattle, Washington several times. That should help you. Their names are for your eyes only. Understand," Nate began.

The General nodded and motioned him to continue. Nate gave him the names and settled back to listen to further instructions. This is the way it is in the military. A major Kennedy will meet you up your arrival on Kwaj. He is a navy seal. He does not know why you are getting this training and he does not need to know. Ok.

Nate nodded he understood.

"Oh, I almost forgot," said the General as he passed a business card to Nate.

"I'm a little confused. This card says Brown's Realty. What the hell does that mean," Nate said.

"Keep that card on you at all times. If you are searched or fall into the wrong hands, that is my cover and the way I will answer when called. Ok," advised the General.

Nate gave the General the following names: Delbert Osborne, Carl Brooks, Don Hopkins, Bradley Jacobs and Ed Chaney.

"The names look good Nate. Now you take a cab back to Hilton Hotel and wait for my call. It could be three or four days. A reservation has been made for you and everything is on the house. You will hear from me as soon as I have the addresses ready. Enjoy the treat on the government while you can. I know this is dirty business but necessary," said the General.

A button was pushed and the wall opened again. Nate left through it, opened the outer door and stepped into the hallway. Making a left turn, he went out through the lobby. The guard was still on duty and Nate stopped at his station for a moment.

"Can you call me a cab," Nate asked.

"Yes sir, if you'll just wait outside, it will be here shortly," advised the guard. He went back into his little office and picked up the phone. Nate walked outside to wait.

In five minutes, a cab pulled up and he got in.

"The Hilton downtown," he instructed the driver.

The meter flag went down and the cab pulled away from the curb.

It was a nice ride through a nice section of town and he was soon at his destination. He passed a bill to the cabbie and dismounted. Walking to the desk, he was impressed what a nice hotel it was. The lobby was filled with some of the nicest furniture he had ever seen. There were chairs and couches and a couple of love seats. All quality stuff.

He approached the desk, gave his name and was registered. He was handed a key card and informed his room was on the fourth floor. Room 4036 to be exact. In his room, he deposited the one piece of luggage he had brought, pulled out his clean shirt. He showered and dressed and was ready to go down to the restaurant or bar to eat. A good stout drink would be good so he stopped at the bar.

The bartender greeted him as he sat himself on a stool. Ordering a straight shot of tequila, he looked around. The bar was magnificent. Very plush furniture right down to the bar stools. Three chandeliers hung from the front to the back of the room. They were brightly lit and showed off the entire bar.

The walls had rich red wallpaper, the kind that felt like a fuzzy cloth. The bar itself was black with a light brown top. The side next to the customer was padded in leather, which was a darked red than the walls. The bar was not that long but was laid out so it was bartender friendly. Glasses hung from over the bar. Hundreds of all types of glasses. More than Nate had ever seen in all his travels. Nate guessed this was one of the bar/restaurants that congressional representatives hung out in. He noticed it was quiet with mabe a couple dozen people sitting around tables and talking. There were two cocktail servers dressed in short skirts with a kind of black panties on. The kind that looked more like tight rounded shorts. Their tops were a little revealing and were white in color. The mini skirts were red. This made them very attractive. Both were pretty girls in there thirties, Nate guessed. He looked forward to a quiet evenng after a couple of drinks and a good dinner. He had had enough excitement for one day. The meeting with the General kept playing through his head. Quite a mission he was about to embark on. He hoped it was worth it.

After a couple of drinks, he noticed the place was filling up. An attractive middle-aged woman sat down next to him and immediately started talking to him.

"Hi stranger, how are you tonight?" she asked.

"I'm fine, how are you?" he replied.

"You new in town? I've not seen you here before," she asked and made a statement at the same time.

"Just passing through," he said, "thought I'd stop here a couple days for a rest before going back to Oregon," he said.

"Oregon, you say. I have never been there but from what I hear it is beautiful. What do you think?" she asked.

"Best part of the United States," he answered, "we don't have the huge floods or storms out there. Some snow but just right to provide us with some of the best drinking water in the country. It rains quite a lot in the Willamette Valley in the summer. This keeps it nice and green all summer long."

"Well it's nice to meet someone from that part of the country. I could never leave Washington for such rural country. I must have a city with the shows, opera and all the things you do to keep life interesting," she said, "I'm Irene," reaching out to shake his hand. "What's yours?"

"I'm Nate," he replied as he extended his hand to shake hers. He had been sizing her up while they were talking. He figures she was a rich but loney woman. *She was probably looking for some excitement and maybe a man for the night,* he thought.

Well he was alone and she was very attractive. *Why not,* he asked himself.

"Could I buy you a drink," he asked.

"Why, yes you can," she answered, "A vodka martini would be nice."

Nate held his hand up to get the attention of the bartender. The bartender looked up and saw the hand a started down the bar towards them.

"What can get you," he asked Nate.

"Get me the same and the lady a vodka martini, please," he replied.

A couple drinks later Nate mentioned he was hungry and looked over at the woman beside him.

"Would you like to join my for dinner?" Nate asked.

"Why, I'd love to," she answered.

Nate again got the attention of the bartender.

"Could you get us a waitress? We would like to have dinner. When we get settled, send us two more drinks," he instructed.

Nate laid a ten-dollar on the bar when the bartender said he would get the server.

"Show these folks to a nice table," the bartender told the server as she stepped up to the bar.

"Sure follow me," she said, "do you have a preference."

"Just a nice table back aways but one that looks over the dance floor," Nate replied.

The server seated them at a very nice table and headed back to the bar. Momentary she returned with their drinks and menues.

"The dinner is on me," Nate said, "so order anything you want."

They took a couple minutes looking over the choices. The server returned to take their order.

Irene ordered a lobester with all the trimings and Nate a T-bone steak. He told the server to put everything on one check. *After all Nate was thinking, the government was actually paying.*

They chatted about the weather, each other and places they have been in the world. Nate found out that this woman had traveled extensively. She told him she had been married for several years. Her husband had died four years earlier and being alone, she just had to get out of the house once in a while.

Dinner arrived and they dined in silence. Both being hungry made food the main attraction. Time for other things would come later. Thirty minutes later, they finished and pushed back their plates. The server came to clear the table.

"Would you like a nice wine to wash the food down," Nate asked Irene.

"That would be nice," she said "and that will be all the drinking I will do tonight."

"I agree," Nate said and ordered the wine.

When the server left for the bottle, Irene leaned over and kissed Nate on the cheek, near the mouth. Nate turned his mouth to where it was facing her.

"You can do better that, I'd bet," he said.

Again, she leaned over and kissed him. This time he felt her tongue entering his mouth and they french kissed. When they broke away, she spoke.

"How's that?" she asked.

"Great," he replied "and I hope you saved some for later."

This was his way of saying he would like to go to bed with her. Most women understand that. Irene did and answered.

"I always have more for later."

"Would you like to dance? I'm not very good but it's fun to try." Nate asked and explained all a one time.

"Yes, I'd love to. Just let me hang on to you and we'll get through it," smiling, she replied.

Once on the floor they discovered that they could dance well together. They glided across the floor several times. She was nice to dance with because she would press her body against his very tight. He moved his right leg so that it would fit right against the inside of her left leg. When they turned, he would slide the leg against the area containing her pubic hairs. Everytime he did this, she seemed to hold her body closer.

Returning to the table, she expressed her feelings.

"I love the way you dance," she said, "you are actually seducing me right in front of all these people."

"I can stop if it offends you," he said.

"Oh, no. Don't you dare, I love it and no one is paying any attention to us. It's fun and a little bit exciting.

Nate could relate to that. He himself was feeling like she was seducing him. He knew his equipment was ready and she would move her body against him, making a tingling through his body. He guessed she loved exciting a person. Damn he was ready for all she had to offer.

They returned to the dance floor and holding her very close, whispered in her ear.

"Let's go to my room and quit teasing each other. I can have a bottle of wine sent up a little later if you'd like."

"No, I don't need any more to drink but I'd love to see your room. Let's go," she said with a big grin.

They went back to the table and he asked the watress for the check.

"It's been charged to your room. My instructions," she announced.

Hand in hand, they marched to the elevator and in a couple of minutes were inside his room. No more than had the door closed than she turned and wrapped her arms around him. Pressing her lips against his, the French kissing began.

As they kissed, their hands roamed their bodies, finding the sensitive areas. In a matter of a few minutes, they were undressing each other. They were in a hurry it seemed.

The last article of clothing to hit the floor was her panties. When they did, Nate picked her up and carried her the few feet to the bed. He laid her gently down and lies down beside her. They were kissing passionately for moments. His hands were on her breasts and she squirmed with delight. His lips found the nipples and he gently bit at them. They were hard and she muttered for him not to stop. Rolling over on top, he placed himself between her legs and began kissing downward. As he neared her bellybutton, he spoke.

"You can stop me by saying no if you don't want this," he said.

"God, no I would never tell you stop. By the time you reach the place you want I will have my first one. Don't stop. Oh God you make me feel like a woman again,"she said in a gasping manner, breathing hard.

-2-

All this seemed like months ago and yet it had only been three weeks. Peering across the cobblestones, he decided it was time to go. His information was that Katrina would be working tonight. He must make contact with her as soon as possible. To start the mission her information was needed.

Nate ran across the road and into the bar. The smoke lay heavy through out the room. It was so thick it caused his eyes to burn. It took a couple minutes for his eyes to adjust. When they were clear, he noticed many of the patrons were looking at him.

He noticed a table against the back wall that was not occupied and he walked to it and sat down. He sat so he faced the crowd. His butt had barely hit the chair when a woman server arrived.

He ordered a beer and waited for her return. He didn't have to wait long. As she sat the beer on the table, Nate was looking her over. Looking close he noticed she had on way too much makeup. He figured if she scraped off a quarter inch of the stuff, she would be a nice looking woman. This had to be Katrina. He was sure she was American.

"Are you Katrina?" he asked.

"Yes and you must be Armstrong. I'm glad you're here. I'm not sure I could I could continue living like this without some good reason," she said. Leaning closer to him, she spoke again.

"Pay me with a ten or twenty always with enough to get back a five. My information to you will be numbers on a five in change. The information will be the date and time only. Good luck," she whispered.

Shore enough there were ink numbers on the five he received in change. He tucked the money into his shirt pocket and put his attention to his beer.

As he sipped it, his mind returned back to Washington and the woman Irene he'd met there.

It was eight am before anyone stirred. Irene was the first to awake and she slipped from the bed and walked to the bathroom. She tried not to wake him but because of his type of employment, he heard every noise and he felt the lifting of the mattress as she rose. She soon returned to find him propped up with pillows looking at her.

"You're as pretty this morning as you were last night. My turn for the bathroom and don't you dare dress while I'm gone," he jokingly said as he pitter-pattered to the bathroom.

Soon he returned and as he lie back on the bed she rolled on top and began kissing him and occasional his chest.

"Now you just relax, it's my turn to return a favor," she announced as she slide her body down his body, kissing as she went. He just closed his eyes thinking; *this is going to start out his day just right.*

The two appeared in the restaurant for breakfast at 10am. Both starved from the workout of the night before and this morning.

They ordered the usual, eggs, bacon, sausage, toast and hot black coffee. They talked quietly, enjoying each other's company. Fifteen minutes later, they pushed back their plates, finished.

The server brought the check and Irene picked it up.

"If you like another good evening tonight I'll come by. If not I'll go home with a big smile," she said.

"God, you were great last night and yes, I'd like some company. I may get a call and be gone tomorrow. Please come by and bring that smile. Perhaps we can improve on it," Nate replied.

"I doubt that," she said as she rose from her chair, kissed him on the cheek and left for the day. She had said something about shopping.

Nate watched her walk away. She had a nice tight little butt that swayed so naturally. He was quite sure it was natural. Most women who swing it on person over do it. They swing then becomes too much and is quite obvious to those watching. They only do it to catch the attention of men. Nice looking women don't really need to do that. Most of the time they spoil themselves by trying too hard.

He walked outside and walked around the block to get some fresh air. It was a beautiful day and was to be in the seventies for the day's high temperature. He stopped and brought a pack of Swisher Sweets cigars, the small ones. Lighting one up, he puffed on it for the remainder of his walk. He was thinking about what he had himself into with the General. He was interested in slowing the flow of narcotics into this country. He had known people who lost children, wives and husbands, etc. He also knew, from TV news networks that one out of three people were either addicted or at least using dope. Why in the hell people were so dumb to even start using something called dope. He shook his head just thinking about. He'd risked his life before to keep this country free. If something very drastic was not done, the next generation of power people running our government was would be dope heads. If this was to happen then we'd lose our freedom and other countrys would enslave us. This actually was a chance of a lifetime to make enough money to retire on. Yes, by damn, once he had a team put together they'd give the importers hell. This pleased him and he put the mission at rest until another time.

He reached the entrance to his hotel and decide he best go to his room and wait for the phone call.

Sitting around a hotel room was not something Nate wanted to do. However, in working with and for the military he had learned to do so. He tried to take a nap but was unsuccessful. After forty-five minutes, he went to the TV set. Flipping it on, he watched CNN news. Searching around he found a movie that interested him. Kicking back in a recliner, he watched Charles Bronson in Death Wish II. When it ended, he put on his shoes and headed downstairs for a sandwich and a cool beer.

He entered the restaurant and made his way to the counter. A male waiter came and took his order for a ham sandwich and a beer.

The beer came first and was very pleasurable to the pallet. He sipped it slowly as he waited for the sandwich. It soon came and he devoured it with pleasure. It seemed to smooth out the wrinkles in his belly and he felt good again. He ordered another beer and looked around the room. He didn't think he'd see anyone he knew; he just liked to watch people. The lunch hour had been over for some time, but there were a few straglers that either couldn't get to lunch when everyone else did or preferred not to fight the rush.

Most of the patrons at the time were women. He had heard that there were three women for every man in Washington. Many were young interns working for congressional representatives and congressional representatives. They were in town to catch a husband or sleep with one in power.

As he looked around the room, he was aware that several were looking him over. God, what luck? He was stuck in a town of sex-starved females. *His luck was changing,* he thought. They were quite obvious in demeanor that they were on the prowl. If he just walked over and asked anyone of them if he could join them, he knew he could. He signed to have the sandwich and beer charged to his room. Rose from his seat and smiled to the women watching and went to the elevators.

Back in his room, he again snapped on the TV and sat down in the reliner. He sat back and surfed through the channels until he found something of interest. He watches the news, the Price Is Right and other game shows before the phone rang. He was so concentrated on the TV that the ringing of the phone scared him so he actually jumped.

"Hello," he answered.

"Mr. Armstrong?" came a familiar sounding voice.

"Well hello, General, I've been expecting your call. How goes it," Nate answered.

"Quite well actually," replied the general, "we've located two of your people and expect to have found the others by morning. When that happens you will receive an envelope from me with all the information you need to contact them. I think we'll have you out of there by noon tomorrow. You were correct in telling us where we could find them. They are all in the Northwest and shouldn't take long to round them up and head them out. I'll call you in the morning and tell you when to expect the envelope. Airline tickets will be in the envelope for all your people to Hawaii. I'll tell you more tomorrow. A check will be enclosed for the amount of money for each one as you asked. Have fun and goodnight."

Why the old bastard knows I'm playing around on his money, Nate thought. Maybe he's just fating the lamb about to be slaughtered. He didn't really think so but he did chuckle at the comment.

At six PM, a knock came on his door.

Nate got out of the chair and went to the door. He opened the door and there stood the woman, Irene from last night and she was holding a bottle of chanpagne.

"Well, I see you didn't get lost," he said as she whisked by him and into the room.

"Last night was the best of everything and I've found my sexual equal for a change. Here I brought us a bottle and two glasses. It's too early for dinner so let's have a drink," she responded.

He went to her and putting his arms around her gave her a big hug and a sloppy wet kiss. He pressed his body to hers and with one hand on her butt pushed it forward. This made it possible for her to feel his erection. Then he whirled around, taking the bottle and going to the counter. Finding a corkscrew, he proceeded to open it.

Irene came close and set the glasses next to the bottle. She placed her hands on his back, dragging them downwards.

"You naughty boy you. Does that mean you want more and that I was very good for you? She asked.

For some reason women need to know how good they were in bed. If he came back for more one could assume that was true. Women just had to hear it. Some men too.

"Of course, I may be gone tomorrow and it'd be a shame to waste my time on TV. I'll pour us a glass while you undress. Put my long sleeve shirt on. It's just the right length to show you legs and thigh but not anymore. I'll have to look for that myself," he chuckled.

She laughed aloud and headed for the bedroom.

When she next appeared, she had taken her hair down and put on a little suttle perfume. She looked good enough to eat.

He gave her a little kiss and handed her a glass, which she took.

"Come on," he stated and took her hand. He led her to the bedroom where they fluffed up the pillows before sitting down. She lies back on the pillows and watched his every move. After all, she didn't want to miss a thing. He opened the closet door and reaching in, he pulled out a robe. Laying it across the bed, he started to strip. She watched him intently as fewer and fewer clothes remained on his body. When he reached naked, he reached for the robe. Irene grabbed one end and pulled on it.

"Oh, no you don't, I like you just the way you are. Say pretty please and I'll give it to you," she advised.

"Now wait a minute," he said, "You don't want to move too fast do you. After all you can feel around under the robe just to be playful, don't you think?"

"Ok, let's just enjoy our wine. Anything else can come later," she agreed.

They sat for a few minutes sipping wine and talking about nothing in general. Just killing time until they again could make love. After all, making love was one of the most rewarding experiences a man and woman can have together.

He filled their glasses again and sat what was left of the wine on the bedside table. He took a sip, sat his glass down beside it. She sensed a great experience was about to begin and followed suit.

His left hand inched under her shirt and found her titties. He gently played with the nipples and squeezed the breast as he bent to kiss her. She received him graciously as a knight would greet a queen, but not in the same way.

The kiss was a passionate one and she squirmed as sensitive feelings came from her breasts. He pulled her against his body and felt her hand under the robe.

"Honey, you can have anything you find there," he said as she found what she was looking for.

He also was playing with and around her pubic hairs as she moaned with delight. He reached for the top button on the shirt and unbuttoned it. Then he proceeded down to the bottom of the shirt, unbuttoning as he went. When he completed this action, he laid both side of the shirt to each side. She lay very naked as she smiled up at him. She spread her legs to indicate she was ready. His fingers gently stroked the short hairs and his penis grew. Of course, the fact she was playing with it helped.

Soon they were making love as if there was no tomorrow. After they both reached the peek of satisfication, they rested. They would take a sip of the wine and not saying a word. They were speechless and the rest was needed to calm down their breathing. The wine soon gone they again intered into the land of passion.

An hour later, they appeared at the restaurant dressed and freshly showered. Time for dinner and they were starved.

They ate in a quiet sort of way with each lost in their own thoughts. Nate broke into her thoughts as he spoke.

"I'll be leaving tomorrow, I believe but I had a wonderful time and we still have tonight. I want to hold you tight on the dance floor and again upstairs unless you think me too greedy," Nate said.

"Oh, Nate, just as I find a man who can satifiy me and make me feel like a woman again, you leave. I wished we had a week together. Maybe when you come back from wherever you're going, we can see each other again. What do you think?" she said sounding sad.

"Yes of course, I'd like that. It is possible I'll be back in about a year and if you leave me with you name and phone number, I'll call you," he replied.

The food finished they moved to the dance floor and danced until midnight. They had a couple of drinks in between dances but not many. This was a quiet farewell and they just wanted to be close.

At midnight, they took the elevator up to the floor where his room was. As they closed the door behind them in the room, each undressed the other. After all this was a lot of the fun in foreplay.

A phone ringing woke him at seven AM.

"Good morning," spoke the General, "you up yet?"

"Hell no, it's only seven. What's cooking General," he responded.

"By 1000 hours the messinger will be there with your envelope. Be in your room. Your plane leaves for Portland, Oregon at 1210 hours. We've found all your people and it's time to round them up and head you out to Kwajalein in the Marshall Islands for training. A Capt. Simmons will greet you upon arrival. There's fifty thousand dollars for each one of them in the enevlope, plus tickets to Hawaii. At Hickum Field, you'll take a C-130 army plane to Kwaj. Arrange for your crew to meet and fly together aboard that plane. I want you to all arrive together. Capt. Simmons will take you to the trainning area. You will travel back and forth each day. You'll sleep at a military hotel on Kwaj and take your meals at the mess hall. Be sure you stress this is all secret and your people must not speak a word to anyone. Even Simmons has no idea why you're training there and we want to keep it that way. Understand?"

"Shore, my guys won't leak anything. Our lives depended on it in Nam. Don't worry," Nate assured him.

The package arrived at 1000 hours and Nate went through the contents. The money was there. It also contained airline tickets and travel orders for Hawaii and Kwajalein. They were set. He headed for the airport.

Another beer was delivered to Nate as he looked around the room. God what a bunch a cutthroats. It was like looking back to the time of Black Beard the pirate and his cutthroats. How Katrina had survived in this mess was a miracle.

After his second beer, he asked her to call a cab for him and he would return to his boat.

Back at the fishing boats, Nate poured himself a stiff shot of whisky and lit up a Cuban cigar. He then went on deck to smoke and think things over. He took the bottle of whisky with him.

As he smoked his cigar, his mind again drifted back to the past and the search for his men.

The names he'd given the General were Delbert Osborn, Carl Brooks, Dan Hopkins, Brady Jacobs and Edward Chaney.

The first one he contacted was Edward Chaney. Mainly because he was living in Portland. His information was that he worked for a firm called Gunderson's as a welder. This firm made railroad cars. It was located on West Marine drive.

Once Nate had checked into a hotel near the airport, The Sheraton, he rented a car and asked for direction to this plant. The hotel clerk gave him a route that would allow him to avoid most of the traffic.

Fifteen minutes later he arrived and the plant and checked in with security. The security chief directed him into the main office area, to personnel. At personnel, he noticed a short fat woman doing paper work.

"Hi, I wonder if you could help me." Nate asked.

"What can I help you with?" she said without rising for her chair.

"I'm an old friend of Ed Chaney and I wonder if you can tell me what shift he works?" he requested.

"Just a second," she said as she reached for a schedule.

"He's working right now. His shift will be over in twenty minutes. You can wait out by the security shack. That is the gate he will be coming out," she advised and returned to her work.

Nate waited by the security shack and struck up a conversation with the guard. The guard knew Ed and would point him out as the crew came out the gate.

Minutes later a whistle blew and a streaming mass of workers came out of the building and headed for their cars. Nate scanned the group searching for his old friend.

"Hey, Ed, you have company," the guard shouted. He pointed him out to Nate then returned to the shack.

Ed came over and when he saw Nate, his face lighted up at the sight of an old friend.

"How the hell are you Nate," Ed asked as he shook hands with Nate.

"I'm fine and how goes your life, Ed?"

"Ok, I guess not as exciting as our tours in Nam. Actually, it's somewhat boring. I weld here, go home and drink a couple of beers and watch TV. Oh, I know a woman or two but nothing really interesting. They do a good job of taking care of my sex life. That's about it," he answered.

"Well I'm buying dinner at the Sheraton tonight. Why don't you run home and clean up then meet me there. We can talk over old times and I have something to tell you. Will you come?" Nate asked.

"Hell, yes, anytime I can get you to buy, I'm coming. See you there in an hour," he replied.

"Good, I'll be in the bar," Nate explained as they parted company.

Ed had not kept him waiting. He was on time and had kinda of happy go lucky attitude. He was very pleased an old friend had dropped in to see him.

Nate waved at him and they were soon talking about the old days in Nam. They drank and had a delicious dinner of frog legs and all the trimings. Once dinner had settled, the two grew quiet as they lit up a couple cigars.

"Ok, Nate, what's up?" asked Ed.

"What makes you think somethings up?" was the reply.

"Because I know you. It took some doing for you to find me and that means the government is some how involved in your being here. God, I hope you have something exciting in mind. I'm so damn bored I could die. Come on skipper, spill it," Ed demanded.

Nate could still see the look on Ed's face when he found out about the mission. As memory served Nate, Ed was ready to go. He needed no talking into the mission. The fact it was a mission was all he needed to know.

"But Ed there is some risk here and we'll be killing the skum who transport the junk into this country. Does't that bother you?" Nate asked.

"Not a damn bit. There's a war going on and we're losing. If I can be a warrior in this fight, so be it. I've known kids who lost their lives taking the dope and some lost their sanity. Killing is too damn good for this type of trash. Just like Nam, we were fighting so people could live free. Drug just put you in a prison and there you stay. Even without the money I'd go. When do we leave?" came the reply.

Nate pulled an envelope from his pocket and handed it to him.

"Inside are the $50,000.00 and an airline ticket to Hawaii. There we will meet up with our Nam crew and fly out to Kajalein for training. This is top secret and you can tell no one. It's just like Nam except it'll be on the water. Your travel orders out of Hawaii are also in there. We'll all take the same flight out of Hickum Field. Bank the fifty grand and get me an account number so the money we earn can be deposited as soon as we sink a boat or two. It's cash on the barrelhead. In case you're killed, you may want to put a co-signer on the account. Let's have a drink," Nate said.

The two had a couple of drinks and talked over old times as usually happened when old friends meet after a few years. They said so long at ten o'clock. Nate having had a long day and wanted to sleep. Shaking hands, they parted company.

The phone rang, causing Nate to come wide-awake. He picked it up and put it back down. It was room service waking him. He showered and shaved, packed his bag and headed down to the restaurant for breakfast. When finished with his coffee and breakfast he signed off on the hotel bill and asked to have his bag brought down. This was done and he grabbed the next shuttle to the airport. He would soon be in Seattle.

Renting a car in Seattle, Nate headed for the docks. Delbert Osborn was a member of his crew. Delbert worked as a dockworker. After a few minutes of fighting traffic and watching for signs to show him the way, Nate finally pulled up to the longshoremans shack. He went inside.

"I look for Delbert Osborn. Is he working today?" he asked the woman behind the desk.

She looked up smiling.

"Yes, he's over on dock three helping unload a freighter. He can't be disturbed. Can I help you?" she asked.

"No, I need to see Delbert," and with this he laid a twenty dollar bill on the counter. She picked it up and gave instructions on how to get to dock three.

"You must be careful. The docks are a dangerous place. Watch where you step and keep looking up. Sometimes things fall from above. Be careful now," she said as he left the shack.

Nate wandered through the loading and unloading of ships on his way to dock three. Docks were no problem for him. He'd been around and worked on them during the course of his career. As he rounded a warehouse, he came face to face with Delbert. Both stopped abruptly to avoid hitting each other.

"Damn, if it ain't Nate Armstrong," Delbert exclaimed, "how the hell are you?"

"I'm fine," Nate replied, "I come to invite you to dinner tonight if you're available," Nate said.

"Well I have a date but you damn rights I'm available after all these years. The girls can wait. Beside I get a feeling this is not just a social call. Right?" he asked.

"Can't tell you now but will tonight. How's six sound to you at the Sheraton at the airport?" Nate asked.

Nate felt sleepy and he went below to the cabin. His mind would be put to bed and these memories would have to wait. He felt hungry so he walked over to a greasy spoon type of café. He ordered a bowl of soup and a ham sandwich. After eating, he headed back to the boat. He loved the tropics so he took his time walking. Comfortable in a T-shirt with the warmth of the night.

His head hit the pillow yet sleep would not come. He tossed and turned as he went through a plan to sink a boat and exterminate those on board. His mind drifted back again to how he got his men together, did the training and here they were in Colombia. Docked in the harbor of Cartagena, center of the drug trade. Here they would cut your throat for a dollar. For less if they thought you was a fed.

His mind was back to Seattle and Delbert. He could hear the conversation and see him as if it was yesterday.

Nate laid out the mission as the to ate a seafood dinner.

"I have an advancement of $50,000.00 if you're in. You must understand this is a secret mission and once in Columbia, we're on our own, just like Nam. We'll be paid $50,000.00 for each boat we keep from making Cuba. What do you say?" Nate pressed him.

"Damn, I don't know Nate. I'd love to help but I have a good life here and two girlfriends that take care of all my needs in that department. I've even thought of marrying one of them. I'd love to get back into action for something that really counts. This caper does count. God, I just don't know," he answered.

"Well you sleep on it and let me know tomorrow morning. I'll be leaving on a flight to Medford to see Don. I need to know by then. I leave for Boise. From there to Sacramento then off to Hawaii. I have your tickets and the money right here. Lets have a couple drinks for old times and I'll get to bed," Nate said.

"Is the rest of our crew going?" Delbert asked.

"I think so. Ed couldn't wait to say yes. He did so before I even told him what the mission was and the danger," he answered.

"Damn I hate to miss the fun. I'll talk to the girls tonight and see you first thing in the morning. Seven o'clock for breakfast. I'm buying," Delbert said. He got up from the table, shook hands with Nate and hurried out the door.

He'll go, Nate thought to himself. He judged this by the pace, by which Delbert left. He was excited by the challenge. *He'll go.*

Next morning he entered the café and exactly seven AM. He noticed Delbert sitting at a booth in front of a window. Inside he was chuckling that he had been right.

"Good morning, Delbert, how's it going," Nate asked.

"You know damn well how it's going. Last night you knew, before I did that I'd be going with you," he said with a grin.

"Let's have breakfast and talk about it," Nate suggested.

"No need to talk. Just give me the ticket and I'll be on the plane. Both my girls will move into my place and take care of it for the year. I called my boss earlier this morning and he'll have a job for me when or if I return. Hey, waitress, over here," he said and gestered with his hand.

Both had steak and eggs and lots of hot black coffee. They talked about old times, being reacquainted. Nate was glad that Delbert was going. He wanted him to be his second in command. If anything happened to him, he knew Delbert could step right in and get the people out or continue the mission.

After they finished the meal, Nate handed him an envelope containing an airline ticket to Honolulu, travel orders from Hickum Field, plus the fifty thousand. He reminded him he needed an account number in which the General would deposit money for services rendered. This completed they parted company. Nate grabbed the shuttle for the airport after signing and checking out.

His next stop was in Medford, Oregon to see Don Hopkins. He remember Don as a good soldier and dependable. The trip seemed long because they stopped at Portland. However, as always things come to an end and the United Airlines landed at the Medford airport.

Nate rented a car and headed into the heart of town. He knew there was only one Cab Company in town and Hopkins owned that. Nate knew he would be the hardest to convince into taking his offer. He had a going and growing business so why would he want to risk his life on this hairbrained mission.

Not knowing the town, Nate had no idea where the taxi office was so he pulled into a gas station. As he got out of his car, a man approached him.

"I don't need any gas but I'm new in town. Can you tell me how I get to this address," he handed the man a piece of paper with the address on it.

"Yeah, hell yes. You looking for Don?" he asked.

"Yes, we are old buddies and I'm going through and thought I look him up. You know him?" Nate asked.

"Hell yes, we're lodge buddies. Don will be out in a cab right now so park your car over there and I'll call the dispatcher and have him come by," came the reply.

Nate parked the car and waited near the door of the station. Five minutes went by when Nate spotted a cab coming up the street. Don Hopkins recognized Nate before he'd even reached him. He pulled up and Nate jumped out of the car.

"Nate Armstrong, how the hell you are and what brings you to Medford," he asked.

"Need to talk to you privately. Lets go for a ride in you cab and I'll buy lunch," Nate suggested.

"Oh, oh, sounds like the old days coming back to haunt me. Sure lets get moving and we'll go for a drive," Don said in agreement, "We'll run out by the hospital. There's a little Mexican café and we can get a shot of whisky. You still drink don't you Nate."

"Yeah and I could use a drink about now. Let's go," he said.

In five or six minutes, they were passing Rogue Valley hospital. A short distance later they pulled into the Mexican café called Elcazador.

Going inside they sat in a booth way in the back. Again with their backs against the wall. There were only three other patrons in the café and they were at the little bar. This booth would be safe enough for their talk.

They ordered two whiskys each and a couple enchiladas. Good food but not too filling.

"Well it looks like you are doing well Don," Nate began.

"Yeah, I have four cabs which make me a good living and a good woman who loves me. What more could a man ask for?" Don replied.

"I low would like to retire in a year with a million dollars in the bank?" asked Nate.

"I knew it, I knew it. When I first saw you standing at that gas station, I knew you had something in mind," said Don.

"You country need you Don. I'm putting together our old unit and we're going hunting. You are aware of the drug trade and the trouble it's causing our people. I've been asked to take the battle to the cartels. The mission is secret and you must not say a word to anyone. The people in high places have decided to take the war to Colombia. Shall I say more and are you interested?"

"Oh, God, Nate I'm so happy here. I don't know. You are a good friend and a million bucks sounds interesting. I suppose it's dangerous, huh. Oh go ahead I'm listening," he replied.

Nate laid out the whole plan, ending by laying out the envelope containing an airline ticket and fifty thousand dollars.

Don picked it up and looked at the money.

"It would make my life easier and I could hire another driver and not drive myself. I don't know Nate, I just don't know. How soon do you need to know? " He answered.

"Tomorrow morning by nine o'clock. I fly out of here to Boise at ten to see Carl. We need to be in Hawaii later this week. I have two more of our old Nam team to see. I want you all with me on this mission. It's much shorter than Nam and pays a hell-of-a-more," came his answer.

"Well I'd like nothing better than some excitement and working with you was never boring, Nate," Don said, "I'll go home and discuss this with my partner. She also my lover. We've been talking about marriage lately and I just don't know if she'll like this. I know she can run the business alone but a year is a long time."

"Go talk to her," Nate said as he slugged down another whisky, "but remember this is top secret and you can't tell her where you're going or what you'll be doing. Understand. Top secret. Just tell her your government needs and pays good money for our services."

"Can I keep the envelope to show her the fifty thousand," Don asked.

"Sure take it with you. I'll be staying over at the Holiday Inn. Have it back to me by nine o'clock in the morning or sign on," Nate instructed.

"Ok, let me take you back to your car and I'm taking the rest of the day off. I'll see you later tonight," Don exclaimed.

All this Nate remembered as though it was yesterday.

The day went quickly. Nate had never been to Medford so he drove around seeing the sights.

That evening he was sitting in the restaurant at the Holiday Inn, eating his evening meal when he saw Don approaching.

"Sit down Don and let's have a drink," he said. He'd noticed his old friend wasn't carrying the envelope. *A good sign,* he thought. He motioned the server over and the two men ordered drinks. Straight whisky.

Nate finished his meal and when the server returned with the drinks he told her his was finished, she cleared the table and left the two alone.

"Well I discussed your deal with my partner and we decided to take you up on it. The money would be great and we could still keep our fingers in the business but not have to work so hard. I'm with you boss, but only for a year," Don advised. They shook hands and the deal was made.

Someone was shaking him awake.

"Come on Nate the boat we're after today left a few minutes ago. We need to gas up, take on some ice and get going," Delbert said.

"Ok, you take the other boat and I'll dress and follow you," Nate said as he jumped down from the top bunk.

On deck, he started the engine and slowly followed Delberts boat down the line of docks until they came to the floating gas station. Both filled up and Nate paid the attendant in cash. Gas was only twenty-five cents a gallon. From there they pulled around to the ice location. They opened the hold of the ship where the fish would be going and asked the attendant for a ton of ice. A spout swung out over the hold and ice was pumped into the bowels of the ship. When both were full, they were ready to roll and they headed for open water.

The night before Nate had taken down his maps and decided that the dopers would take the shortest route to Cuba. He'd drawn lines on the map and figured their course. He wasn't concerned about catching the boat because the boat they had been given had supercharged engines. They could go three times as fast as the average fishing boat. They just had to hide this secret.

Nate picked up his cell phone and knowing both his and Delberts had a scrambler on it, dialed Delbert's number. The scramblers would keep anyone from listening in. When it was answered, he spoke.

"Delbert, we'll stay close together until we get close. We will then peel off in different directions. You go right and I'll go left for a good mile, and then head north. Once we're ahead of the target we'll move back in and launch our nets. We'll stay with half mile of each other and hopefully they will pass between us. I want you and me to go over the side and sink this one. Ok?" Nate asked.

"Ok, by me boss. When we spot them I'll get the air tank on and have an explosive device on me," came the reply.

"Good. Keep in mind we will have to swim that quarter mile to reach the under side of the boat. I'm hopeing they will slow down when they see us fishing. I'll call you when it's time to go over the side. Remember they have glasses so don't get on deck so they'll spot you. Slip over the side with something blocking their view. Good luck," Nate said. The trap would soon be set.

An hour later Nate gave Delbert a call and told him to move in and lay his nets. Shortly after this was done. Both fishing vessels moved in a circle so as to trap the fish inside the nets. Once the circle was completed, they tighten the nets and began hauling them in. As luck would have it, the sea was teaming with Tilapia and the nets were full. As they were pulling the nets and dumping the fish in the hold, they spotted their target. It was coming straight for them.

"Hurry, men and let's get the nets unloaded before they get here," Nate instructed.

Nate slipped into the cabin and to the lower sleeping area. He hurriedly undressed and slipped into his air tank harness. Next, he applied the shark repellant. He crept to the deck area and peeked around the corner of the cabin to see where the target was.

"Hell, it's coming right at us," he said to himself. He motioned Ed over.

"It looks like the are coming to us, Ed, you handle things up here. Call Delbert and have him move in closer before going over the side. Hurry now, we don't have much time," Nate instructed. With this instruction out, Nate slipped around to the off side of the cabin and slipped over the side. His explosive charge in a little pouch attached to his belt.

He pulled his facemask down just as he went under. Ed had shut down the engine so Nate swam under the boat and waited. Soon the target boat pulled in along side their boat and Nate merely had to swim a few feet to attach his bomb. This done he waited for Delbert. He did not trigger it and would not until Delbert had his in place.

A couple of minutes later Delbert showed up. Nate motioned him to the rear of the boat. Delbert understood and swam to the rear and placed his bomb just feet in front of the propeller. He waited for a signal to pull the igniter. They waited minutes but it seemed like hours. Finally, the engines roared to life on the target so Nate waved to Delbert to ignate the fuse. He pulled his and swam like mad to the far side of his boat. He motioned Delbert to follow.

Nate checked his watch for the fuses would set off the charge in five minutes. He waited to hear the blast. It came right on time.

Nate pulled himself on board and Delbert followed. They were in time to see three men running around looking for life vests. The boat was sinking like a rock. No call went out on the ship to shore radio. In no time the boat was gone and only some sawdust floating on the water. One man floating and waving to them. He could not swim and soon went under. This was the part Nate hated.

"What the hell did they want," Nate asked Ed.

"Fresh fish, boss, that all. We gave them some without charge. It was so nice they brought the boat right to us."

Shark fins cut through the water and it looked like a feast was going on down below.

Nate dressed and picked up the cell phone. He dialed the General.

"Hello, Brown's reality," came a voice from the other end of the line.

"Hello, General. Make a deposit for us. We just sent the first one to the deep," Nate explained.

"Good deal, Armstrong, any problems," he asked.

"No, the explosives were as advertised and there was nothing but a little saw dust float on the water. The sharks are finishing the job as we speak," Nate informed him.

"Good work, my boy, I know how hard it is for you and your men to let others die. Just keep in mind the devestation they are causing and slow deaths in this country. The deposits will be made within the hour," finished the General hung up.

Nate and his boats got the hell out of the area after cleaning up any debris floating in the water, by using their high-speed engines. In minutes, they were twenty miles away. They dropped their nets and went to fishing. The fish finder showed tons of fish in the area. Everyone had a drink and went to work.

A few hours later and with a full load on both boats, Nate and crew headed for home. It was just turning dark when they arrived at the fish cannery. The cannery sent a crew out to help with the unloading process. Once unloaded Nate received a check for his load. It was written in the currency of Colombia but when you translated it to dollars, it amounted to a little over ten thousand U.S. dollars. Not a bad days fishing and if they came under suspicion it would go a long way to show they had done nothing by fish. After all, you don't make a haul like this everyday.

The crew made supper on the boat before deciding what to do for the evening. They felt good and wanted some time on the town.

Nate suggested The El Toro for drink and wild women. They all agreed. Ed went to the pay phone on the dock and called two cabs. Within ten minutes, the cabs arrived and they all headed for town.

As they entered to building, the smoke almost knocked you down. With the door open, it rolled out like a fog. The place was crowded with dirty, sweaty men celebrating the first shipment of "coke" to Cuba. Some looked as though they'd not bathed in months. Nate wondered how Katrina could stand it. She certainly was giving a lot for her country. This is far and beyond the call of duty.

-3-

Katrina saw them coming and motioned them to a table against the back wall. It was the only vacant table and could seat four. She was already taking chairs from another table to seat all six of them.

Just as they reached the table, a filfty, unshave barrel shaped man bumped into Nate.

"By damn this is my table, get out of the way American. A real man is taking the table," he said while leering in Nate face. His breath was foul and he was acheing for a fight.

"No, sir, this is their table," said Katrina nodding towards Nate.

The intriguer reached for a knife he carried in a scabbard on his belt. Nate guessed a fight was the only reason he carried it. It's been for intimidating opponents or fighting. It was too big for any practical purpose.

"Rude bastard, "said Nate as he grabbed the man's wrist, giving it such a twist that he thought he'd broken it. The man went down on his knees in pain. This was a very unexpected move; the man had not counted on. Still holding his wrist Nate drove his fist into his face. Blood spurted and Nate let go as the man fell over.

Nate looked around and noticed his crew had surrounded him, facing the crowd. A preventive measure. The crowd was upset but soon calmed down. Nate doubted this person had many friends, most just wanted to see a fight. Bloodthirsty these Colombias.

The bartender arrived and told a couple of the men to drag out the ugly one. Katrina told him what had happened and he agreed the Americans had the table. Everyone knew the troublemaker had a table down front. The lines had been drawn and Nate knew this was not over, it was just the beginning.

They all ordered whisky with a beer back. Katrina hurried away to fill their order. Upon her return, Nate handed her a twenty and told her to keep all but a five. He did this to get a message if there was one and to conceal from his men that she was the one giving him information. At this point, Delbert was the only one to know.

As she returned, served the drinks and handed him a five-dollar bill. As she bent across the table setting the drinks in front of each one, she bent close to Nate and whispered in his ear.

"This target is a tug boat," she said and pulled away. She, having finished serving the drinks moves on the assist other customers.

Nate's men were having a good time dancing and fooling around with the women. They needed this to relax after todays work. None of these men ever became use to the killing in Nam and this, even though they all understood and agreed this was a war, killing was never easy.

As he watched them, his mind again drifted back to the circumstances that brought them here. Sort of reliving the past few weeks. Leaving Medford, he was on a plane to Boise, Idaho to see Carl Brooks. Carl was an important part of the crew he was putting together. He was and explosive expert, a small wirely man. He was brave to the core. If he liked you, he'd die for you. Nate just had to convince him to go along.

Getting off the plane, he rented a car and headed down the hill to the South end of town. This is where the zoo was located and where Carl worked. Nate couldn't understand it but knew Carl had always loved animals.

Parking in the parking lot Nate walked through the spacious area of the zoo. He saw the deer and elk in their natural invironment. Peacocks roamed the grounds. There were squirrels aplenty. They finally come around to the pens where the bears were kept. Lions and tigers, etc. He looked around for any sign of his old friend and comrade. Finally, down at the far end of the cages he saw a small man coming out of a cage. *That must be him,* thought Nate and he headed that way.

Getting closer he discovered it was in fact Carl. As he approached he hollored at him.

"Hey, Carl, how the hell are you?"

The man turned around and looked at Nate.

"Nate, is that you, you old horse thief," as he waved and headed over to his old friend.

They hugged and looked each other over. It had been a long time.

41

"How about lunch, Carl. I'm buying," Asked Nate.

"Hell yes, lets go. There's a nice little place about half a mile from here. Damn I'm hungry now that I know someone else is buying.

It only took five minutes to get to the place. It was located on the main drag and Nate got the impression Carl ate there quite often. He was right because once inside everyone knew Carl by his first name.

Nate selected a booth in the back corner. They both ordered and while waiting for the food, relived the old days.

"Well, how's the world treating you Carl? Nate asked.

"Fine, I've the best job job in the world. Not getting rich but getting by. I have a girlfriend that takes care of all my physical needs. I live in a nice but modest home. I drive a decent three-year-old car. Life is good. Not the excitement we use to have but it's all right," came the response.

"How would you like to go on a mission with our old crew from Nam? You can make enough to retire on if you wish. At least you could travel some and not have to worry about money," Nate asked.

"What do you have in mind, Nate? Came his reply.

Nate laid out the plan to him and kept his fingers crossed he'd accept.

"If you agree, I have fifty thousand dollars and a plane ticket to Hawaii for you. Every boat we sink will mean a fifty thousand dollars in the bank. The only sticker is we have to stay a year unless we are discovered. Fishing will take care of our overhead with plenty left over," Nate explained.

"How soon do you have to know, Nate?" he asked.

"Now, right now. I'm flying out in about an hour and I need to know. I do need you badly and was hopeing you would go. You like excitement and heres your chance. Might be the last chance in our lives. We'll be doing our country a favor and perhaps save a bunch of lives. The lives of kids who may take the junk," Nate responded.

A quiet time settled over the table as the two-sipped coffee and one was trying to make a decision. After a short period of time, the decision was made.

"Yes, hell yes. Let's get on with it," came Carl's answer.

Nate passed the envelope across the table, dropped a twenty on the table and got up from the booth. Carl followed and they were soon back at the zoo.

Carl got out of the car, walked around to the driver's side and shook hands with Nate.

"See you in Hawaii in a couple days, Carl." Nate said. Carl turned and sprinted back to the cages.

Nate caught the next plane for Sacramento, California. Bradley Jacobs was the last of his team to recruit.

Nate remembered Brad as a very energetic young man who loved excitement. He would always volunteer for the most dangerous job and come through them smiling. Even if he had a narrow escape, he would say to Nate, "Close one that time boss," and laugh about it. He wasn't reckless and he carefully thought out every move he make. He certain was an asset to the team. Nate's information was that he was selling new cars at a downtown dealership. Buicks and Cadillacs mostly. Nate just couldn't see him in that kind of career. He didn't feel there is a problem recruiting him.

That afternoon, Nate arrived at the Sacremento airport. He rented a car and after asking for directions, headed into town.

Several minutes later, he saw a Buick/Cadillac sign about two blocks away on the left side of the street. Signaling to make the left turn, he spotted the driveway. No cars were coming so he wheeled right into the car lot. It looked like a slow day. The sales clerks were lounging around the showroom door. They didn't approach him, which he thought was strange. Halfway from the car to the door, someone behind him spoke.

"Can I help you mister?"

Nate stopped and turned around and found he was looking into Bradley's face.

Bard was a lean mean fighting machine. The thing that threw Nate for a minute was the go-T beard.

"Brad, is that you under all that hair?" Nate asked.

"Well, I'll be damn. Nate, I never thought I'd ever see you again in this life. What the hell you doing here?"

"I came three thousand miles to take you to dinner. Can you get away?" Nate asked.

"Shore, it's quiet. Hang tight I'll go tells the manager."

He returned and found Nate in the driver's seat. He jumped in and Nate fired up the engine.

"Lets go, man we're home free. The boss was glad to let me go. Where do you want to go eat," he asked Nate.

"I see a Hilton down the drag a ways, and I need to check in. Lets eat there. They always have good food," Nate replied.

At the hotel Nate registered and the two went down the hall to the restaurant and bar. Again, a table was where they seated themselves and when a server arrived at the table, they informed her they would order later. Both wanted a cold beer. It was warm outside for this time of year. That's when a beer tastes the best.

The beer arrived and they both took a deep drink of the foamy brew.

"Well Brad, how are things going?" Nate asked.

"Oh, ok, I guess. It's not like the old days Nate. The only exciting thing I have in my life is when I get laid. That's three times a week, but it not the kind of excitement I crave. I guess those days are gone forever. We shore had some great times didn't we," Brad answered.

This was an opening Nate could not pass up so he pressed on.

"Are you married with kids?" Nate smiled as the words dropped from his lips.

"No, hell, no. I'm not and never will be. I'd like to have a woman to live with but I'm not the marrying kind. Why do you ask?" Bradley asked.

Nate cut through the chase and laid out the up coming mission. When he finished he asked if his old friend had any questions. Because he'd been told this was all top secret, he leaned forward so only Nate could hear,

"When do we leave, Nate, you know damn well I'm going?"

"Tomorrow morning I'm out of here for L.A. and to Hawaii. Should be there around 3:00 PM. You have till the day after to get your butt in gear. Then the day after we will all fly to Kwajalein in a One Thirty One military aircraft from Hickam Airbase. I'll be staying at the Holiday Inn at the airport while in Hawaii. Here are your travel orders and $50,000.00. There's an airline ticket also. Now let's eat, I'm hungry," Nate explained.

They waved the server over and ordered a steak dinner, rib eye to be exact. They told her not to hurry it for they wanted more to drink. She took their order and returned shortly with the straight whiskys with a water back. The sat back and relaxed.

God, it seem like a lifetime ago instead weeks, Nate was thinking as his mind returned to the El Toro.

Some of his old crew had paired off with women, except Delbert. He returned to the table after a pit stop and joined Nate.

"Well boss, this is quite a place. Some of the women are whores and others

SEND 'EM TO THE DEEP

are just poor lonely women who live near by who want to have a good time. I think our people know the different. What were you thinking about as I walked up. You seemed serious," he addressed Nate.

"Oh, just recalling some of the old times we had in Nam and what's ahead of us here," came the answer.

About half an hour Nate told Delbert he was heading for the boats.

"Tell the guys we will stay in port tomorrow but I want them home by noon. Ok?" Nate said.

"Sure, I'll tell them and I won't be far behind you. A couple more drinks and I'm out of here. This fishing does make you thirsty."

Nate left a tip for Katrina and left. He went to the pay phone just inside the front door and called a cab. He then stepped outside to wait. Outside he lit up a Cuban cigar. About ten minutes he was climbing into the cab and headed home or a boat that would be his home for some time to come.

Arriving at his distination, he paid the driver and went aboard. He went below deck and found a bottle of whisky and a glass before returning on deck. He seated himself in the bow of the boat in a place where he could see anyone coming on board. A habit of a lifetime. One developed because of his occupation.

He stared at the stars and couldn't help but wonder what was going on back in the states. His thoughts drifted to the General and this covert operation. He missed his TV and the programs he loved to watch. *But what the hell, it's only a year and he'd be back to a normal life,* he thought. He was thinking of finding a nice woman and getting married or just live with her. He didn't want a family at this age and hoped there were women out there who felt the same.

His train of thought was broken when a cab pulled up and Delbert got out. Delbert waved to him and said goodnight and went aboard the other boat.

Nate had divided the men into two groups. One group in each boat. Delbert, his second in command, commanded one boat. His crew was Carl and Don. Nate's crew then was Ed and Bradly. He had a great team.

He dozed off and his mind drifted back to the days on Kwajalein. They had arrived on a Friday and met with their trainer.

As they went through the security check at the Kwajalein, Nate noticed a major waiting in the small crowd. As Nate spotted him, he smiled at Nate and nodded his head.

"Hi, I'm Major Kennedy. You Armstrong?" he asked as he extended his hand.

"Yes, that's me," Nate replied.

"You and your men pick up your luggage and follow me. We're going across the way to the hotel where you'll be staying. After you drop your luggage off in the rooms, we'll head over to the dining hall and eat. I'll bet you're hungry," he said in a friendly manner.

"Starved, "Nate replied then turned to his men.

"Pick up your gear and follow us," he said reaching down to retrieve his duffle bag.

The Kwajalein airfield set at the south end of the island. The island was almost two-thirds airstrip. Coming out of the north end of the terminal it was a short one block across to the military hotel. Anyone traveling to the island such as official visitors, family members, etc stayed here. This island was a restricted military instillation and you had to have special permission to come here. Continential Air Lines stopped here for refueling and some time brought workers with security clearances. As the plane refueled, passengers were allowed off the plane but could not leave the airport terminal building. Security guards were posted at every door to prevent any roaming about.

The island was pretty with all its palm trees, with a huge park like area between the terminal and the main downtown area. Downtown was a two-block strip with local stores like PX's everywhere. You could buy almost anything you wanted including expensive jewely. There was a bowling alley around the corner and laundry. The security office sat across from the bowling alley. The mess hall was behind the stores facing the grassy area.

Long barricks lined the Eastern side of the island. There were two theatres on the island. One was indoors and a large outdoor one. Nate remembers this because he spent many a night there watching a different film every night.

Most people had to sign in at the dining hall. The Major led the way and as they entered, he whispered to the attendent. The attendent handed him some passes. They went thru the line and were soon seated at a table. As they ate, the major talked.

"Here's a badge for each of you. This will get you in without signing in. I've been instructed that you are not to use your names anywhere and that I have *no need to know*. Armstrong is all I know and all I want to know. If you need anything I to get it for you. Right up the street is a nice lounge where you can drink and eat. I've made arrangements for no charge with these same passes. Don't lose them. If you do report it to me at once. No one here knows you or why you're here and we aim to keep it that way. I'm curious but won't ask. After you eat, we'll take a helicopter to another island and show you the training layout. You'll fly back and forth daily to this island with me. I'm sure you've been told I'm a seal. I'm in the army but assigned to the seals. Now dig in," he finished his instructions.

Nate stirred and almost fell from his seat to the deck. He decides it was time to go below and get some sleep.

His dreams brought him back to Kwajalein and experiences there.

The helicopter landed and the men unloaded. It had been a ten-minute flight from Kwajalein. They noticed the Major Retrieved a couple shovels from the chopper. They looked at each other and wondered why. This was to be training in water. Why the shovels? They didn't have to wait long.

"Lets walk inland a ways and I'll show you your equipment," said the Major.

They walked into the jungle for about fifty yards when he stopped them.

"Look at this spot gentlemen. This is what it is to look like everyday before we leave. Now here a couple of you scrape some of this brush away. Right there," he said as he pointed his finger. He held out the shovels.

Nate and Delbert took the shovels and turning them sideways scrapes away the debris. In doing so, they noticed cut ends on some of the brush. This could only mean that someone cut brush to cover this ground. When the brush had been cleared from a twenty-foot area. The Major stopped them.

"Now dig down about four inches and be careful. You'll find equiment buryed, wrapped in plastic. Once you have it out, carry it to the beach. There will be an oxygen tank for each of you. Also fins and facemasks. Unwrap them carefully because you need to re-wrap them when we're done each day," and with this he walked back to the beach.

Rather than dig, Delbert and Nate just scraped the soil away and found the equipment. Soon they were all standing on the beach waiting for instructions.

The Major came by and inspected each tank's air gage before addressing the men.

"Everyone one take a look at the pressure gages on his tank. That much air will last you approximently thirty minutes. This means you should be getting back to your boat or whatever you'll be working from. Ten minutes isn't much time when you running low on air. Remember that. Your lives depend on it."

"Ok, lets try on the tanks. Undress to your shorts. Once the tanks are on your backs, tighten the straps until they feel comfortable. You don't want to be working under water with a shifting air tank. You'll be expected to do this by yourself without help. When you think you have it I'll come by and inspect it for you."

The men mounted the tanks on their backs and did some adjusting. Once they felt comfortable, they said they were ready for inspection. The Major walked down the line and found two; Ed and Carl's were too loose. He tightens them so they got the feel for it.

"Ok, that's not bad. Most of you did pretty good," he opened a sachel he'd brought with him. He tossed each man a bottle before stopping to explain.

"In these waters there are five types of man eating sharks. Those bottles contain shark repelent. Be sure you spray yourself good. I don't want to report to the General a loss to sharks. Spray now, men we're going for a swim. Put you flippers on before going into the water," he instructed. With this, he also stripped to a swimsuit he had on under his pants, sprayed himself, put a tank on and waded out into the water. This done he turned to face them.

"I understand you can all swim but have little experience with the tanks on. We'll start with the basics and work into a swim. The tank feels heavy now but as soon as you're underwater, it will lighten. Walk out until the water is over your head and stop. I want you to get use to breathing underwater. Breath normally and don't panic. If you find that you're not getting oxygen walk back out and I'll check the equipment," advised the Major.

The rest of the afternoon, the team practiced this breathing method. It soon became a second nature to relax and breath normal.

"You men have done very well today and I'm pleased with the results. Tomorrow we will pratice swimming with the tanks on. This will be the crucial and most important part of your trainning. Every one of you must be able to swim a hundred yards. Sometimes conditions will be adverse so you have to be good. I've been given orders to cut you from the team if you cannot perform. So get your rest and eat well. You'll need all the strength you can muster. Now lets get this equipment buried and covered and I'll call in the chopper," were the instructions as they completed the day's work.

Every man pitched in and wrapped the tanks, fins, goggles and shark repellant in the plastic and buried it all where they had found them. They covered the area with the brush after raking it down so there was no sign they'd ever been there. This group was good at this because of their experiences in Viet Nam. In those days, they had to cover their tracks or be prepared to fight and die. The Viet Cong were good at tracking as many Americans found out. Many came home in body bags because of it.

Finished, they walked back to the beach to joined the Major. He was on the radio, calling for the chopper.

Early next morning they were, awaken at 0530 hours by the Major. Dressed they walked across to the mess hall for breakfast. They had a hardy meal before heading for the airport. Each had brought along a pair of swim trunks. A couple had to buy a pair, having forgot to bring a pair, the night before. Everyone was in a good mood, looking forward to the days training. The fresh air, good food and sunshine were good for their morale. This was to be the army combating the drug lords of South America. A small group but very dangerous to those on the other side.

Departing the chopper, the men headed inland to where there equipment was buried. Soon they were in their swimsuits and with air tanks mounted, stood at waters edge.

"Who's the best swimmer here?" asked the Major.

"He is," Nate said pointing to Ed Chaney.

"Ok, I want you to swim out a hundred yards, rest five and swim back. Don't hurry, take your time. If you can do it and the rest gets to where they can, then we'll speed it up," instructed the Major.

Ed walked out into the water until it was up to his waist, and then dove head first into it.

At about sixty yards out, he was slowing down. He seemed to be tiring. He would dog paddle a ways, and then swam as he recovered some strength. At this point, the Major called him back. Ed took his time as he moved slowly to the shore. Breathless he just sat in the water near the beach.

"Now you see what your in for. If he's your best and he's not near good enough. I've got two weeks to make you over into swimming machines. I've never failed on an assignment yet and I won't this time. I won't let you fail. Take your tanks off and swim around till you tire, then we'll take a break," said the Major.

49

He watched while the men swim about. He watched each with the idea of giving each man advice on how to improve his technique. He watched as their muscles pulled at the arms and their feet paddled up and down. He soon noticed what pointers were needed. Most were making the same mistakes. He knew by their eagerness and trying hard that they were strong men. *The kind you need with you in a fight,* he was thinking. If he were in a fight, he'd want these men with him. He was curious about what their mission, but knew better than to ask. They had friends in high places that had arranged this training and that's all he needed to know.

The entire day was taken up with the swimming exercises. The Major would call one in and give instructions on changes each man needed to make. They took many breaks and drank a lot of water. In the tropics a real necessity. Average daytime high was around eighty-five degrees. The humidity was high. Even at night, it remained around seventy-two.

Suntan lotion was supplied to all the crew to protect them from sunburn. By the end of the day, most could swim with the tanks on their backs but nowhere near, where they needed to be. The Major felt they would be in two weeks.

After the call was made for the return of the chopper, the Major made an announcement.

"For the next week we will be trainning at night. You people are making some headway but this sun is a killer. Go to the club tonight and have some fun. You have tomorrow off. I will expect you at the airport a 1800 hours tomorrow night."

All the men nodded the understood and rejoiced a little. They could see a movie or something that night. A little break was reason to be joyful.

After supper, some went their own way. Nate and Ed went to the club while the rest went bowling. After nightfall, Nate and Ed headed for the outdoor threatre. Soon after the movie started, the rest of the gang joined them. The movie was a war movie with John Wayne as the star. It was called "In Harms Way," about World War II. It ended at ten o'clock. The crew walked across the park to the hotel and to bed.

They were up bright and early and hungry. They gathered at the mess hall and took a long leisurely meal. It felt good to just sit around sipping coffee; The Major joined them when they were about halfway through the meal. He had just finished when they saw a full bird colonel approaching the table.

"Stay seated gentlemen," he said as he stopped next to the Major. "The Major treating you men alright?" he said smiling.

"Great," they all spoke at the same time.

"Good, we are quite proud of the Major. He's a great seal for an army person. But as you see, I'm army. We're glad to have you men here and hope all goes well here and wherever else you may travel. Good luck," he patted the Major on the back and walked away.

The men went for a swim in the saltwater pool for bachelors. Dependents had there own pool for swimming. They also had an area fenced off so sharks couldn't get to them. After lunch, some chose to walk around the island. Nate and Delbert went bowling, did a little shopping, and then returned to the hotel. They lie down and took a long nap. Tonight they knew they would need it.

For the next two weeks, they got better and better. The night training did the trick. Without the sun to drain his strength, each man improved much faster. Finally, it was time to learn how to attach the plastic explosives to a ship.

Back on days, they arrived at the island for training to find a couple fishing boats anchored and waiting for them. On shore, they awaited instructions.

"Gentlemen, may I have your attention. Here in this can is the explosive device you will be using when you get into your mission," he held up a can of vegetables. He continued, "Here are some other cans and you will note there are three different sizes. The size dictates the size of the explosive device. You open them with a can opener just like the kind in a supermarket. It's special made for your operation. These you can fit right into your stores of groceries. On the bottom is a little blue star. That tells you it is not what it appears to be. These were created so that if your boats are stopped and search they'll find nothing. The larger cans are labeled coffee and are the largest devices you'll need. Here I'll pass around the cans so you can examine them," finished he passed around three cans. Each of a difference size.

"Oh, I almost forgot. Each can is the same weight as a regular can, so no one should suspect it's a bomb," with this he pulled out a can opener and opened a can.

Turning the can upside down out dropped a cone shaped material wrapped in plastic. The Major pulled off the plastic, exposing the explosive.

"This what they look like. Just remember the larger the can the larger the charge. On this end (pointing to the smaller end) remove this white piece of paper," which he did, "showing the glue that will hold the explosive in place for twenty four hours? The time is not relvent because you will explode this within minutes of putting it in place. Now put on your tank and we'll swim out to the closest boat and I'll demonstrate how you need to attach it," he instructed. Two boats were placed there just for this training.

With minutes, they were at the boat and the Nate's crew formed a circle around their teacher. The device was simple. The glue was sticky and he showed how they could stick them onto the wood bottom. Once he had done this, he motioned for the crew to surface.

"See it is simple. Any questions," after they had their heads above the water. Not all shock the heads, any.

"Good, we'll not spend any more time on this phase. I want three of you to take this boat for a run and the other three take the other boat. On shore, you'll find three cell phones. They are scrambled so no one can read you. I'll have one here on shore and there is one for each boat. Get you engines fired up and run up and down the shore for two ½ miles or so. Get use to how they handle, etc. That will be the only lesson today. Keep doing this until you know your vessel like you know the back of your hand. Men this type of boat you'll be running your mission in. The only difference is the boats you'll have, have engines that are souped up and will be much faster than these. If you can handle these, you can handle the others. Tomorrow we'll go fishing so you'll know how the nets work. Ok men get with it. I'll wait here on shore and have a cold beer. Jump to it," he said in closing.

Nate assigned the men to which boat they would work off of. He knew they would work better if they got use to working together. This was a little different than jungle warfare. They picked up their phones and swam to their assigned boats for a day of "yachting" dubbed one of the men. The Major found a grassy spot, opened a beer and sat down, leaning against a tree.

The day went well and soon came to a close. The chopper was called in and back to Kwaj. They went.

The next day was a piece of cake. The took the fishing boat through a channel into the open sea. They worked the nets till they were blue in the face. They released their catches and practiced again. By noon the Major felt, they had this down pat so they began the last phase.

One boat would go out to sea aways and anchor. While pretending to fish the other boat would come passing by at anywhere from fifty yards to one hundred yards. The men would take turns practicing going over the side, swimming to the underside of the moving boat. They would pretend to attach a bomb, and then swim away. This practice took the rest of the day and they were one tired crew. They made some stupid mistakes but with every try, the got better. Another two days and the Major were satisfied. At the end of that day, the Major used his phone to call the General. Nate was instructed to call him also on his phone.

"We are pleased you have passed the trainning with flying colors, Nate. From Kwaj, day after tomorrow you will be flying into Panama City, Panama. There you will pickup your boats and equipment. The plastic explosives will be on board along with needed supplies. You will have maps and the whole ball of wax, as we use to say. From Panana City, you go to Cartagena, Colombia. You have docks for your boats already waiting for you. The numbers are fourteen and fifteen. Should be easy to find. Once there, you will make contact with our agent at the El Toro bar. It's a dirty little bar in a bad part and a hang out for mostly people working in the drug trade. Contact Katrina, the barmaid. She's the agent Always pay for your drinks with enough money that she will have to give you back at least a five. Written on the five will be a date. That's will be when a target is leaving port with cocane heading for Cuba. Good luck Nate. Keep the phones you have now. Call me after each strike, goodbye," he said in closing.

-4-

A day later, they went fishing. The fish they were after were Tilapia. The waters were teaming with this fish but few people fished for them. The reason was they were mostly working for the cartels and it was much more profitable for them. These Americans fished on days they had no missions, to protect their cover.

They left early in the morning, before sunrise. They had filled with ice the night before and gassed up for an early run.

At four AM, they were leaving the docks. By five, they were a couple miles at sea. Nate was steering the one boat and Delbert the other. They proceeded in the same direction, both watching the fish finders for sign of their game. All at once, Nate's screen lit up as a huge school of fish swam under the boat. They were fifty feet deep and lazely swimming about. He grabbed the phone.

"Delbert, move in close to me. Not so close, we tangle the nets but there is a huge school of fish right under me. Hurry," Nate advised.

Hanging up he told his crew to drop the nets. As the nets were stringing out behind the boat Nate started a wide swing to incircle the fish. Once this was done and the nets have sunk to the depth needed, he ordered the nets be tightened and to start reeling in. The winch howled as this order was carried out. As the nets neared the boat, it was plain to all that this was one hell-of-a-catch. The winch slowed to a low growl and seemed to have trouble with all the weight. The men watched as some of the fish jumped out of the nets to swim free. This was just the overload. Most would be scooped up by Delbert's boat. Delbert was in place and was beganing his circle as nets filled the water behind it. Nate's crew was busy pulling the nets over and pushing the fish into the hold. One member scooped ice over the fish as they poured down around him. It took nearly an hour to clear the nets so they could be cast again upon the waters.

Nate looked over at the other boat and noticed the crew jumping around like the were dancing and singing over the catch. They to had a net full and were pulling it in. Nate swung his boat out to the west a little so they would not get tangled. He began a slow turn to the west and listen to the whirling of the nets as they raced into the water, hungry for fish. Nate glanced at the fish finder and located more just to their left. He turned in that direction and again excitement filled the air with the bountiful harvest. This was how their day ended with a heavy load of fish.

They left the fishing grounds and headed back to their port to unload their prize loads. Reaching the docks, they pulled right up to the fish processing plant and began the unloading process. This took three hours for both to unload. The plant manager handed Nate a check for forty thousand dollars American.

"Senor, I'm very grateful you have come to my country. I was about to close my doors and be like the rest of the crazy people and go to wotk for the Cartels. Few fish anymore and I must feed a family. Now I will take all the fish you can catch and I wish you much luck. Gracias," he said as he passed the check over. He also handed a bottle of Tequila to each boat. A happy man indeed.

The crew was too tired to even fix something to eat. They all took a couple shots of whisky and went to bed. Tomorrow would be a big day. On that day, they were going after bigger fish.

Nate's crew was up at the break of day. Pulling around to the processing plant, they filled up with ice. Down the docks a ways, they stopped at the gas pump and filled their tanks.

Just as the sun was coming up, they noticed a tugboat pulling out, heading northeast. This was the only boat moving and had to be the target. There were piles of sacks piled on the deck, which left little room for its crew to move around. This would help the undercover team when they made for the radio. This would be a more difficult target than a fishing boat. Nate and crew were out ahead of the tug. The race was on to set the trap and hope for the best.

Nate called Delbert on the cell phone.

"As soon as we get out of sight of the tug, we'll open up our engines and get out to sea about thirty miles. I figured their route and we'll set the trap there. Follow me," as he opened the throttle.

An hour later, they were in place and began laying out the nets. They worked slowly, watching for the tug to come into sight. A tug puts out a black diesel smoke and should be easy to see. Delbert had moved his boat a half-mile away, to the East. They waited for the target.

A few minutes later a puff of black smoke showed on the horizon. Nate picked up his phone and dialed.

"Delbert, he's coming. Are your nets out?" he asked.

"Yeah, we just finshed boss," he replied.

"Take the medium sized explosive device and I'll have Ed do the same. You plant one on the bow and he'll plant one near the stern. I'll swim over to and as soon as they go off, I'll board her and get to the radio. You people get back to your boat and I'll follow as soon as I get the radio. Get into your tanks and stay out of sight. They will be looking us over and we don't want to be seemed in swim gear. They're getting closer. It won't be long now," Nate explained.

Before going below Nate ordered the nets be pulled in so the tug could see the work being done making them less suspicious. Of course, they have been making these runs for years so this was going to be one hell-of-a-surprise.

As the tug grew closer, it appeared to be aiming right for them. Brad and Nate had pulled in a few fish, now stopping to the tug. Ed had already put his tank on and was waiting to go over the side. Still the tug appeared to be coming up along side.

"Ed, go over the side now. They will be here soon. They seen me and I'll have to stay on board. You and Delbert will have to take out the radio. Can you do it?" Nate inquired.

"Piece of cake, boss. I always take a pistol with me. Consider it done and he slipped over the side.

Nate called Delbert and asked him to move over closer to save a long swim. He'd caught him just before he went over the side. As he spoke, he saw the other boat turn its nose and head his way.

Minutes later the tug was pulling along side. Nate and Brad ceased pulling on the nets and Nate went over to talk to he tug captain.

"Senor, can we buy some fish from you. I love fresh fish and all we have on board is salted down fish?" asked the captain.

"How many do you want?" Nate asked.

"Maybe a dozen" came the answer, "how much?" and he reached into his pocket for money.

Nate and Brad selected a dozen fish and handed them across to the crew.

"No charge, enjoy."

"Thank you my friend," answered the captain as he waved and the tug slowly moved away.

God, I hope they got the charges set, Nate was thinking.

When the tug was about a hundred yards away it appeared to be lifted up and then gently settled back down upon the water. The bombs had gone off. A minute later five or six pistol shots went off and then all fell quiet, deathly quiet.

Soon after Ed appeared along side the boat.

"Hey, give me a hand," he said.

Nate reached over and pulled him on board. Once on deck, both men looked towards the tug. It was gone.

They started the engines and proceeded in that direction. Sharks were already there and appeared to be in a feeding frenzy. Some sawdust like material floated on the water, but no one was in sight. Everyone had gone down with the boat and disposed of by the sharks.

Nate's phone rang and he answered it.

"Hi boss, I'm back on board and we're pulling in the nets. Where to now?"

"Put her in high gear and head westward about ten miles. I'll follow as soon as our nets are in. By going in that direction we may find someone that sees us in case anything comes of this," Nate replied.

Once they were at the new location, they cruised around looking for fish. An hour or so later they found what they were looking for and dropped the nets and the work began. Nate remembering to call the General dialed his phone.

"Brown Realty," was heard from the other end.

"Hello, general," Nate began, "sir we've just finished sending one to the deep. She was loaded with tons of dope."

"Good work, I'll make a deposit for you and your crew. They must be starting to run a little low on the streets. If not now, soon. Be careful. When this shipment doesn't arrive, they'll be mad as hell. Watch your back, son. Goodbye."

Nate hung up and went back to helping the crew.

The fishing was slow and they fished into the night. A crewmember on each boat cooked as the nets were finally put away.

After the meal they sat on the deck, boats lashed together and had a good old fashion B. S. secession before going to bed.

The following day they slept in till seven o'clock. They began laying out the nets and steering in a circle while breakfast was being cooked. The cooks brought the food on deck so as not to interupt the fishing. All the men ate hardy and fast. Coffee was drank on the run and the day was off to a good start.

Each time they pulled in the nets, they had a light load. Nate decided it was time to look for a bigger school and gave the order. Delbert's crew was to slowly work to the West and Nate would work his boat East and a little South.

Late in the afternoon, Nate's phone rang.

"Hey boss, we've found a good school and are going after them. If you haven't found any you might want to come over this way and give us a hand," Delbert reported.

"On our way. Nothing over here," was Nate's reply. He headed the boat to the Northwest and within half an hour was fishing just a hundred yards from the other boat.

The hold was half-full, so Nate decided to stay out overnight and try to top them off in the morning. He dialed Delbert's number. It was answered on the third ring.

"Pull in your nets and lets call it a day. I want to try again in the morning. Lets head for shore. With our souped up engines I think we could be there in about forty-five minutes. We'll find a nice little cover and have a restful night. Sound good to you?" Nate asked.

"Right behind you boss. We'll be ready in about ten minutes," was the answer.

"Ok, but lets keep an eye out for other boats and airplanes. We don't want anyone to know about these engines. We're about through with bringing our nets aboard. We'll come by close and you wave when you're ready and we'll get the hell out of here," Nate instructed.

Nate had been right; it took just forty minutes to reach Nicaragua. They searched for a cove as dark was falling. Finally, they found a nice little one that was about a hundred yards long and about the same distance wide. It was well protected from the ocean yet the water was deep. Little did they know it but this cove would come in handy later on.

As they pulled into the cove, they noticed brush and huge trees that hung over the edge of cliffs from above. A boat could actually anchor is such a way that it could not be seen from the air.

They anchored near the shore, out of the wind. There was no ocean swells or waves inside the cove so they anchored close together. The men took turns cooking and soon the were eating steak and beans. Of course, while they were waiting, cold beer was passed around. Their moral was high and they seem to thrive on this sort of life.

After the meal was completed and the dishs done, they passed around cigars. Cigars and whisky topped off the meal and after a couple shots, they turned in. Morning would come early with the day starting at five AM.

As the day lighten with the rising sun, the fishing boats left the protective cove and moved into the open sea. They fanned out at a distance of half mile apart, in search for the elusive fish.

An hour went by, and then two before luck was with them. Delbert was the first to spot a mediun sized school and called Nate.

"Hey, boss, we found a nice school over here. If we cast the nets here we can fill both boats and be on our way home in a couple hours," he told Nate.

"Coming over, lets get to work. I'd like to have a woman for tonight wouldn't you," Nate answered. No answer on the other end just loud laughter.

Delbert had been right. Both boats were loaded in two hours and heading back towards their homeport.

It was late afternoon when the boats were unloaded and tied up again at the berths. Nate had received a check for the fish and had gone to the bank to cash it. The men finished cleaning the boats and awaited his return. They had opened an account at the bank in all their names so they would have access in case anything happened to some of them. Nate returned in a cab as the men were waiting patiently for money to get out on the town.

"Here it is," he said as he boarded the boat. He preceded to hand each five hundred dollars. "Remember now you can have a hell've good time on one hundred or less. Don't show your money around and stick together as much as possible," he hesitated, and then went on, "there are people here that will kill you for a lot less. If you get lucky, see if two of you can do the deed together at the same room or house. Hell, you're men I don't need to say anything. Get out of here and have some fun," he finished.

As the men left to boat, Nate stopped Delbert.

"Tell Katrina I'll be by later to see her, I'm going to find a different, higher class place to eat tonight," Nate said, "but send one of those cabs back for me."

They had called a cab and Nate watched as two cabs pulled up and the men headed off into the evening sunset.

About twenty minutes a cab pulled up and beeped his horn. Nate was in the living area of the boat and had just finished changing his clothes. He hurried on deck and waved to the driver that he was coming.

As he got in the cab, he asked the driver if there was a classy restaurant in town.

"Si, senor, very nice place called Loretta's. You want to go there?"

"Yes, I'd like that and I'll give you an extra five if you hurry." said Nate.

"Si, senor," said the cabbie said as he stepped on the gas. Money talks.

A few minutes later Nate arrived downtown at Lorettas's Restaurant & Lounge. Getting out of the cab, he handed the driver a ten and stood looking at the front of the place.

There was a long, tall flashing neon sign mounted on the building. Huge oak doors with carved designs added to the attraction of the outside of the building.

Looks interesting, he said to himself as he opened a door and stepped inside.

The whole interior was quite large. A restaurant you stood facing as you entered. At the far end was the bar area and a dance floor. A huge chandelier was mounted on the ceiling in the center and two smaller ones on each side. The lights were low and gave the place a cool look. Red cloth like wallpaper coverered the walls, running perpendicular. This certainly had the looks of a very nice, rich looking place.

Nate made his way to the bar where there was plenty of room. It was early yet and he wanted a drink. Looking up over the bar, he saw a huge painting of a beautiful naked woman. It was very tasteful yet exposed the whole front of her body.

"God, I'd like to meet that woman sometime," he said as he ordered his drink. The bartender was American.

"If you hang around another hour, you will," come the reply, "she owns this place and she likes to greet all new comers to her place."

"You mean that woman. She's beautiful. I wouldn't think that a woman owning the same place would hang a picture like that. She must get hit on all the time," Nate announced as if talking to the air.

"Nope, everyone treats her like a lady because if they try anything we have our orders. You can look but not touch," replyed the bartender.

"Ok, thanks for the tip; I'd never touch without permission anyway. However I'd like to."

Nate had two whiskys at the bar, sipping them slowly, killing time waiting for the woman to appear. Finished with the drinks he decided to eat. At some time tonight, he had to be at the El Toro to see Katrina. He told the bartender he'd be at a table and would he send over a server. The bartender nodded in agreement.

Nate picked a table in his favorite place, next to the wall and waited for service. Soon a server came to his table. Being around fish all the time he decided on a roast beef dinner. He was quite surprised that such an American dish would be on the menu. For the tourist he guessed. He ordered another whisky also.

The whisky was brought to him right away. He sipped it and watched for the owner to appear. The place was starting to fill up. Quite a few people but not yet crowded.

All at once, he noticed her walking slowly down the bar. She was patting people on the backs and shaking hands as she came. *God,* he thought, *she is just as beautiful in real life as in that picture.* She stopped to say something to the bartender who nodded toward Nate, she turned to look.

She smiled and whispered to the bartender, who immediately poured two brandy glasses. She picked up the glasses and headed straight for Nate.

Nate felt a little uncomfortable. He felt like he was about to meet a queen and he wasn't sure what to say.

She reached the table. Nate stood up and waited for her to speak.

"Try this brandy," she said in perfect English, "it beats whisky anyday."

He took the glass and toasted her then setting the glass on the table. He moved around, pulling a chair out and seated her.

"You are very kind," she said. "I hear you are the gringo fisherman that is the talk of the town."

"Yes, that's me," he admitted, "and thanks for the brandy. What kind is it?" he asked.

"Napoleon," she answered, "do you like it?"

"Yes, it's very nice and you are right it does go down smoother than whisky. I must say you are the prettiest woman I've seen here. That's a beautiful picture. Do you have one I can take with me? " He asked.

She laughed and said it was too big for a small fishing boat, but he could come by anytime to see it. He said he would.

Just as they finished their brandy, the music started. Loretta looked across the table at Nate.

"Would you dance with me?" she asked.

He almost choked on his last swallow.

"Yes, that would be nice," he finally got out.

They rose from the table and walked to the dance floor. He held her in his arms and across the floor the moved. She was light as a feather, following his every move. She held him tight, which bothered him a little. He glanced over at the bartender and found he was waiting on other customers and not paying attention to them. He figures it must be all right so he pulled her tight. Her perfume was a very gentle smelling type that seemed to linger in the air after you've moved on. Very suttle, very nice.

The tune was over and Nate let go of his partner until she spoke.

"Oh, lets do another, it's been so long that I've danced with someone that can keep up. You are a smooth dancer," she stated and just then the music started again and it was also a slow one. Apparently, the band knew her taste in music, for dancing.

"You've not been a fisherman all your life, have you?" she inquired.

Nate kind of stiffened at the question, wondering what she was up to. She felt his stiffing and asked about it.

"I'm not getting noseing, just interested," she said.

"No, you're right; I'm a career man in firearms. Just down here for a few months to get some sun, salt sprey and excerise. My crew and I always wanted to do this and so we took a year off and here we are," he answered.

"The story I've heard is you had some trouble in the U.S. and you're down here till things cool off," she said.

"Boy, people gossip down here too, huh," he stated.

"Yes, it's the same the world over," she said.

His mind was spining. He had to be convincing and maintain his cover even if it mean't this woman losing interest so he had to agree with her.

"Yeah, you're right. It's not the very bad kind of trouble, but I had to get away for awhile," he told her.

The music stopped and he walked her back to the table. Once seated, she raised her hand and soon two more glasses of brandy appeared on the tray of a server. She places one in front of both of them and moved away.

"Before this goes any further let me introduce myself. I'm Loretta Rodriquez"

"I'm Nate Armstrong," he said.

They talked another half hour before she got up saying she had to circulate. But before going, she spoke to him.

"Fish for Tilapia," she asked.

"Yes we do," He replied.

"Every time you come in, bring me thirty pounds. I like to serve only fresh fish to my customers. My uncle speaks highly of you." she announced.

"I'd don't believe I know your uncle," he replied.

"He's the one you've saved from bankruptcy. He runs the fish packing plant. Have a good evening and do hurry back," she said and walked away to greet other customers. Nate watching her go noticed she looked back and smiled. A normal red-blooded man could not help but wonder how she'd be in bed. Someday he hoped to find out.

He looked at his watch and found it was eleven o'clock. He had to get to the El Toro and see Katrina. He paid his bill and asked if they would call him a cab. He stepped outside to wait. It arrived in five minutes and whisked Nate away to the El Toro.

Entering the place he found it fairly well crowded. He spotted his crew at the far end, close to the dance floor. A couple of them were dancing and the others sitting at the table. Those at the table saw him coming and taking a chair from another table made room for him.

Walking through the crowd, he saw Katrina. She smiled an acknowledgement and followed him to the table to take his order.

Just several feet from the table, an ugly one-stepped out of nowhere with knife in hand.

"Now, gringo dog, I kill you," he said as he lunged for Nate. Nate sidestepped and hit him along side of the head as he went by. This floored him and Nate jumped on top of him. He grabbed the knife and in the struggle that followed the knife slipped and cut off the end of the ugly one's nose. Blood squirted. The knife dropped to the floor as the ugly one grabbed his nose and screamed in pain.

"Boys should not play with knifes, they might get hurt," Nate said as he looked down at the mass of human flesh. At the same time he noticed his men were on their feet, looking around there were several Columbians pushing his way.

Katrina spoke to them in Spanish and they stopped. The bartender arrived and asked what had happened. Katrina explained the Americans were just good customers and the ugly one had started the fight.

The bartender gave orders to a couple of men and they proceeded to drag the bleeding man out of the area. One stopped to pick up the piece of nose lying on the floor.

Nate pulled out a fifty-dollar bill and handed it to the bartender.

"This should take care of any damages," he said.

The bartender took the money and agreed it would, then walked back to the bar. The music started and people went back to dancing.

As he reached the table, he spoke to Katrina and thanked her for her help. She nodded and smiled.

"Drinks all around," he told her as he seated himself, "hi guys how's it going?" Directing his attention to the men.

"Fine boss, how was your evening? You come here for exercise or to relax with a woman." one said and they all laughed.

"Watch that one," referring to the ugly one, "boss he'll not quit till he's dead. When you come here you best have at least one of us with you," Ed making an observation.

"That goes for the rest of you too. He knows we are together and may try to pick us off one by one.

Katrina arrived with the drinks. As she leaned over Nate to set drinks across from him, he looked closely at her. Under all that makeup, she looked to be a pretty woman. Much different than he first thought. When she finshed, he handed her a twenty. She handed him back the change, which included a five. The rest of the change he gave to her.

"Thanks," she timidly said and went back to work. As he straightens out the five, he noticed an ink mark. Looking closer he noticed tomorrow's date and the time of five AM. On the other, side an inked in one. This was new and he must ask her what it meant.

The men all had selected a woman to dance with and went back to this action with gusto. Nate sat alone. He caught Katrina looking at him. He wagged his finger in a motion that was asking her to come over.

She arrived and bent down to listen to him. This would not look suspious because the music was loud.

"What are the number one mean and the back of the five," he asked in a low voice.

"Fishing boat. A tug will be a number two and a three a different type and bigger. I thought you would like to know. How's it going," she asked.

"Both to the bottom of the sea. No problems but by tomorrow the first one doesn't show in Cuba, then the second one, all hell will be to pay. Be careful. I case of an emergency we'll get you out. Do you have my phone number," was his response.

"Yes, I must get back to work. I'll pretend you ordered a whisky and bring you one. This bunch will never know the difference.

The whisky arrived and he paid for it. The music had stopped and the men returned to the table.

"Fun's over boys, we sail at five in the morning. It's now midnight so lets get out of here and get some sleep." he informed the crew.

Going pass the bar, Nate asked if he'd call a couple cabs for them.

"Si," he nodded his head and they walked outside to wait for the cabs.

They were up, had finished eating when five o'clock rolled around. They started their boats and moved them over to load ice. Then to the gas pumps. A fishing boat filled up right behind them. This had to be the target boat. Nate pointed the boats out to sea in a northwestern direction. Same as the other boat should on it's way to Cuba.

They crused along at a normal pace. At five miles out to sea, they began looking for fish but kept their heading towards Cuba. No wanting to get too far out in case the target turned and chose another route. At a distance of ten miles from land, they spotted a school of fish that would be worth taking. At a hundred yards apart the two boats worked in their circles and pulling in the fish. One man on each boat kept watch for the target boat. This was a nerve-wracking time for they never knew, but what the other boat might pass them by hiding in swells. This was a fairly quiet day on the water.

Their hold, about a quarter full Nate picks up the phone.

"Delbert, pick up your nets and cruse to the east a couple miles. We'll ease out to the west. Damn, I hope we didn't miss them."

"Ok, boss, I agree we may have missed them. Ok, I'll let you know," was Delbert reply.

All nets were retrieved and the search was begun. Forty-five minutes later, Nate's phone rang.

"Hey, boss we've spotted them. They are about two miles ahead of us at my location. If you turn on the engines and go about five miles northeast and circle this way would be about the same. You'll be in front of them. I'll swing east about the same distance and meet up with you. Lets go hunting," Delbert's enthusiasm showing.

"Roger, see you soon," was Nate's reply as he reved up the motors and headed for the hunt. The success of this mission was getting every damn boat carrying the junk to Cuba.

Minutes later Nate scanned the horizon, locating their target. He called Delbert and told him they were in place. He got an acknowledgement and judged about where the boat would pass by. He reeled out the nets and began circling to fill them with fish. This time he didn't give a damn about fish. His concentration was on the object of the mission. *Davey Jones get ready to receive another to your locker* ran through his mind.

Again, he guessed right. Delbert was in place and had his nets out. The target boat was only a half mile away. Nate went below and doned his tanks. He had instructed Delbert to do the same. A quarter mile closer and Nate slipped over the side. He went under the boat, and then swam around to the front of the boat. He surfaced here and peeked around the stern. The target was coming along in a path where he'd only have to swim about fifty yards. He felt his pouch to make sure his explosive charge was there. It was. He pushed off and swam directly in front of the path of the on-coming boat and waited. He didn't have to wait long. He saw Delbert coming up to join him.

Nate pointed Delbert to the bow and he'd take the stern. They removed the charges from the pouches, tore off the white plastic across the glued end and were ready.

The boat was over them and Nate reached out while swimming along. Finally, he reached out and attached the bomb to the bottom of the boat. Finished he turned to look toward Delbert. Delbert waved and they both pulled the underwater fuses and swam out from the boat. A few yards out Nate tredded water waiting for the devices to do their work. He saw the boat rise up and set back down. He felt some concussion and swam forward.

As he pulled himself up on the side of the boat, he saw a man in the cabin. The man had just picked up the radio. Leaping onto the deck, Nate ran to the cabin door. He fired point blank into the man's body. The man slumped to the floor and his life escaped him.

By now, the water was a foot deep on the deck and the boat was going down. Just as Nate reached the side of the boat, a man came running around the cabin. He raised a pistol and fired at Nate.

Seeing it coming Nate, dived into the water and swam away. He saw bullets racing into the water around him. Then all was quiet. He came to the surface and looked around. The boat they'd planted charges on was gone. A couple bodies floated near where it had been. They were bleeding and soon the sharks would clean up the mess. He turned and saw his boat coming for him. Ed reached over, helping pull Nate on deck. He was soon aboard.

"Pull away some distance," he instructed. As the boat turned away from the grizzly sight, Nate looked across and saw Delbert was following suit. About a half mile away, they dropped anchor and just sat waiting for the sharks to clean up the mess, before checking the scene.

Nate picked up the phone and dialed. It rang on the other end.

"Brown's Realty," came a voice, which could only be the General's.

"One sent to the deep, sir," Nate spoke to inform his commander of their success.

"Great, Nate your deposits will be made today. Be careful. The Cubans are sending out gunboats looking for the one that hasn't arrived yet. Your first target. When the tug doesn't arrive, you may have several out looking for what's happening. We picked this up by monitoring their radios. Good work, talk to you later," was the General's reply.

Nate moved into take a look at the damage after an hour had gone by. On their approach, he saw nothing floating on the surface except one life preserver. Apparently, one of the crewmembers had gotten to one but was unable to get into it and died with the others. Picking it out of the water, they were ready to go.

"Haul ass, Delbert," Nate said over the phone. "Lets get back closer to Columbia so open those engines and follow me."

At full throttle for thirty minutes, they covered a lot of water. Nate got a fix on their location and found they were east of their port and approximately ten miles out. *This is good,* he was thinking, *we're at least thirty miles from the sinking.*

Back to normal speed they cruised back and forth searching for schools of fish. After an hour, they found a nice sized one. Both boats moved in and strung out their nets. They were working close together when a Columbian gun ship came by. They hailed the fishing boats that they were coming aboard. Both vessels ceased and waited for the military to board.

"What the hell do they want?" asked Brad.

"Not sure," answered Nate, "probably just a routine check for boat and fishing license. Play it cool and I'll do all the talking.

Delbert had pulled in close and anchored as had Nate. They waited anxiously as the gunboat pulled alongside.

A smartly dressed Lt. boarded, as did two other soldiers. Nate greeted them was a smile and relaxed composure.

"Good afternoon, Lt., what can I do for you," he said.

"We're searching all boats for contraband. If you have any onboard it's best you say so and show me where it is," he spoke in perfect English.

"No sir, we have only my men and fish. Help yourself and search," Nate replied.

The Lt. motioned the two soldiers to go below. He stood with his feet apart and his hand on the butt of his pistol. He looked like he expected trouble. Five or six minutes ticked away before the two emerged from below deck. When they did the Lt. Spoke to them in Spanish. Their answer seems to put him at ease. He directed them the hold. They pulled the hatch cover off and looked in. They took a long pole and poked around through the fish. Nate thought this was kind of foolish, but said nothing. He and all the crew held their breath and hoping it didn't strike one of the air tanks hidden under the ice. They were smart to bury them under the ice along the side of the hold. Anyone looking for something would poke around the center of the pile, not along the edges. Nate had been smart in doing this. A trick he'd learned in Nam, but still they held their breaths. Apparently, they didn't think anything of a rifle on each boat nor a couple pistols lying in plain sight. Nate had long known that anglers carried rifles to shoot sharks caught in their nets. This alone would not raise any suspicion. At last, they finished and the crew started breathing again. *I've got to think of a way to have the tanks on board,* Nate was thinking.

"Sorry for the inconvenience. Now we go the the other one." said the Lt.

He directed his men to get back on board and once done, they pulled over along side Delbert's boat. They went through the same routine search and soon the soldiers departed and the Lt. waved at Nate as they pulled away.

The nets were reeled in and the catch unloaded. They iced them down before taking a break. They anchored and had a couple of drinks, basking in the late day sun. Nate spoke.

"I'm glad this happened. We now have the Lt. as a witness of where we were at this time of day. We're not in the direct line to Cuba and therefore above suspicion. Be ready for more of this in the days to come. Keep the cans with the explosives in them behind the other cans. Once they find out that ships sailing from here to Cuba are coming up missing, we can expect this on a daily basics."

They all agreed and were thankful the oxygen tanks were not discovered covered with ice. There were those minutes when the soldiers were poking in the ice with the pole that caused the hair to rise on the back their necks.

After the soldiers were out of sight, Nate motioned Delbert over so he could address the men.

"From now on we keep the rifles on deck and I'll have the General to secure us four more and ammunition. When we're on the boats and not sleeping, they'll be kept on deck. We need them in reach in case they find something and try to arrest us. Put them in places where they might not be spotted and yet easy to reach. Understand?" Nate ordered.

They all nodded and said, "Yes." The war against drugs just took a turn for the worst. From now on, they must operate with care and perhaps further out to sea. Nate knew Katrina must be warned to be extra careful. It would be best to let a boat go that take a chance of getting discovered. He picked up the phone and dialed.

"Brown's Realty," came an answer to the ringing phone.

"Sorry to disturb you General but I need a favor," he began and went on to lay out the story to him and the request for the rifles.

"What type do you need, Nate?" questioned the General.

"Thirty thirty carbines and several boxes of shells. We don't dare get caught with automatics. It would bring suspicion on why we have them. If they think their ships are being taken by rivels, they could jump to the opinion we were that group. How soon can we get them General?" Nate asked.

"I'll have them out on a special flight today. They'll go to Panama City to our airbase there. You'll contact Colonel Kennedy. Call him by phone and he'll deliver right to the to docks. They be packed in boxes that look like can foods. This way they'll not raise suspicions if anyone is watching. He'll be in plain clothes and will arrive at the docks the same time you do. Give me half and hour to reach him, then call his number and make the arraignments. Pull in and receive the supplies then go back to sea. Don't hang around the port," came the General's reply.

"Ok and thanks General," Nate answered and hung up after receiving the number.

Half hour later Nate called the number.

"Colonel Kennedy," came the answer.

"Hi, Colonel, Armstrong here. Did you hear from the General yet," Nate asked.

"Yes, your requested equipment will arrive by tomorrow evening. When will you come for it?"

"Not until the following morning around seven ARE. Does that meet you with schedule?"

"Yes, that will be fine," replied the Colonel.

"Ok, see you then," Nate said and hung up.

-5-

Nate was sitting on the deck at Nine o'clock that evening, smoking a Cuban cigar and drinking a glass of whisky. He was deep in thought about how they should take the next few boats. Getting to the radios before anyone could send out information about what was happening was still the key. Things could get sticky if the Columbians sent out aircraft to help guide the drug ladden boats. They wouldn't be able to go out too far into international waters, but they might. Perhaps if the boats were sent out at night the odds would be better. Dark nights would be great. Running without lights would not only keep them from view of ships and aircraft, but would allow them to get closer to their targets, unobserved. He needed to mention this to Katrina. In her position, she may be able to plant an idea in the drug runner's minds that it would be safer. *God, that would be great,* he thought. Yep, he had to go and see Katrina.

He flipped his cigar into the water, picked up his phone and called a cab.

Minutes later, he was at the El Toro. Inside was the usual crowd. He had been here often enough to recognize some of the patrons. A bloodthirsty lot if he'd even seen one.

He worked his way through the crowd to an empty table against the wall and near the dance floor. Just a few feet from it, a one eyed, dirty looking man stepped in front of him.

"That's my table, gringo, pick another one," he growled.

Nate recognized him as being with the ugly one on earlier days.

"You fight for the ugly one now. I knew he was a coward and you are dumb. Get out of my way before I turn you over my knee and spank you. Go play with yourself," Nate pushed to make him mad. A person makes bad decisions when mad, this gave Nate the advantage.

The intruder pulled a knife and lunged at Nate. Nate quickly stepped aside, grabbing his wrist and twisting. This stopped the man cold and he screamed in pain. Now down on the floor on his knees, the opponent tried to pull loose. Nate twisted his wrist some more, opening the handhold the knife and took it away from him.

"I doubt this blade is even sharp," Nate announced, "lets find out."

With one swift movement and a swing of the knife, he removed a finger from the right hand of the attacher who again yelled out in pain. Nate threw the knife into the floor. He released the wrist and and grabbed the man by his collar, pulling him to his feet.

"You tell the ugly one he's not finished with me yet," Nate said as the crowd urged him to kill the attacker. A bloodthirsty lot to be sure. They cared not if it was one of their own or a stranger. They just wanted blood. The scum of humanity.

"Get out of here before I kill you and please the crowd," Nate spoke in no uncertain terms. He pushes the man into the crowd and sat down. The table was his, at least for now.

Katrina came over and took his order. The bartender sent a man over with a mop to clean the blood off the floor. The joint was back to normal in no time.

Katrina was back and Nate handed her a twenty. She handed him change and started to move on when Nate spoke up.

"Meet me in the ladies bathroom in ten minutes. You go in first and make sure we sure, it's safe to talk. I need to tell you something tonight."

"No, it's not safe. The walls are thin and people will listen in. Go to my house around two AM and I'll let you in. We can talk there," she suggested.

"Where do you live?" Nate asked.

"Come up three blocks from the docks, on the main street leading there and I live in the little blue house on the corner. Don't be seen. Come to the back door. There are enough bushes you can sneak there unnoticed," she said.

"I'm going to kiss you now and you slap me. If I'm seen going to your place they will just think I'm trying to get into your panties," with this he grabbed her and pulled her down to where he could kiss her. To his surprise, she returned it, moved away and slapped him. She dropped his change on the table and walked away.

Picking up the bill, he noticed ink marks on the five. Another message had gotten through. He drank his drink and headed for the door. At the bar, he dropped a ten spot in front of the bartender.

"Thank you, amigo," he said as Nate passed by.

SEND 'EM TO THE DEEP

Returning to the boat, Nate had about three hours to wait till he was to meet Katrina. He had spotted her house on the ride back in the taxicab. It was within an easy walk from where his boats were docked.

He lit a Cuban cigar and poured a drink upon getting home. He seated himself on deck where he could watch what went on at night along the docks. He gazed at the stars and wondered at the brightness of the moon. Not being too far off the equator the moon and stars looked larger. He concluted it was because there was little on no polutition along the docks. Further downtown there was some but not like Portland or Washington D.C. He had long ago arrived at the conclusion that man destroyed everything he touches. Pollution confirms this thought.

He enjoyed the warmth of the weather and knew he'd regret going home to cold winters and hot summers. He toyed with the idea of staying after the mission was completed.

The clock ticked slowly away. Time was dragging and he was getting sleepy. He dosed off a couple of times but soon jerked back to reality. The docks were quiet. He'd spotted no one since his return to the boat.

Finally, his watch told him it was time. He tossed the remainder of his cigar into the ocean and put the whisky away. He stretched and slowly went ashore. He was nonchalant with his movements in case he was being watched. He walked down the dock and out onto the street. He kept in the shadows as much as he could. There was brush along the way but he had to be careful not to look suspicious. Up ahead was Katrina's house. He could see it was dark and wondered if she was home. He found a break in the brushes and stepped through it. It was dark as sin and he carefully picked his way. Soon he was at the back door. No light shown from anywhere in the house. God, he hoped she was home.

He gently knocked and the door opened. She had been waiting just inside. A candle was burning in the living area giving out a little light. He slipped through the open door. She closed it behind him.

"Would you like a drink?" she asked.

"Yes, that would be nice," he answered her.

"Whisky ok?"

"Yes."

She poured and handed him a glass. They clicked glasses and downed the jigger of raw whisky.

73

"What's so urgent that you need to talk to me?"

"Well, you must be very careful. By now, the cartels know that two of their drugs boats have disappeared. The military searched our boat today. They found nothing. We do know they protect the drug lords. Be very careful they don't suspect you. I want to plant a rumor that another gang has raised their heads and are possibly hijacking the shipments. If we can spread this story as just a rumor it would help keep suspicious off us. They're bound to suspect us for a while because we're new here. Besides none of this happened until we arrived on the scene. We must throw suspicion off if we're to complete our mission," he related to her.

She poured another drink and hand him his glass. A thought flashed through his head that she was trying to get up courage for something. He waited before going on. They drank the liquor without saying a word.

"You should also know that we will rescue you if you get into trouble. I'll give you my phone number before I leave. It's fixed so no one can intercept any conversation," Nate told her.

"Well, that's it. Oh, one more thing before I go. We need to know what type of vessel they will be using with each shipment and what time they leave port. I think they will start trying to hide this information. So please be careful. I don't want to lose you," he announced, remembering the kiss.

He turned to leave and she grabbed him by the arm.

"You're not going anywhere buster until you make things right," she said a little loud, considering the circumstances.

"What the hell are you talking about?" he said in total shock at her attitude.

"That kiss you gave me opened up a lot of passion and desire that you need to take care of. I've been too long without a man and you are it," she announced.

With this, she put her arms around her neck, pulling his mouth close to hers. Even in this light, Nate could see she was a very pretty woman. She had removed the makeup and looked fresh and pure. Their mouths collided is a passionate French kiss. They both shuddered at the passion that flowed between them.

She was unbuttoning his shirt as he pulled her blouse from her skirt. She slipped the shirt off his arms and her blouse soon followed. He unzipped her skirt and dropped it to the floor. She stepped out of it and returned the favor. His trousers hit the floor along with her panties and his shorts.

"Where's the bedroom," he asked as he picked her up. She pointed the direction and kissed his neck all the way to the bed. He gently placed her on the bed, the springs squeaking under their weight.

"Here let me," she said as she rolled over and on top of him. Connecting the passion that ran rampant through their bodies. They were now in there own world and nothing mattered except pleasure through the passion.

An hour later, they lie side by side resting. No words were spoken for sometime. Finally Nate spoke.

"I've got to go, it's getting late. You get some sleep and I'll stop by tomorrow night.

As he dressed in the dark, she spoke up.

"Be careful of the ugly one and his friends. Always bring someone with you to the El Toro. Tonight I will sleep better than I have since I got here," she announced, "thanks to you."

Dressed, he kissed her then let himself out the back door. She locked it behind him, still naked and walked back to bed. As she closed her eyes, a smile came across her face and off to dreamland she drifted. She felt a peace inside that she'd not felt for years.

Next morning Nate was on deck, shortly after breakfast, when he noticed a group of men coming down the street to the docks. They were soldiers and they coming straight for the boat.

"Senor, Armstrong, I am Lt. Garcia of the Colombian Army. I have been sent to check your papers and search both boats. You understand I don't need a warrant, Si," he exclaimed.

"Si, go right ahead and search," Nate said, and then looked away. Looking towards the other boat, he saw Carl just coming out of the cabin area. He ducked quickly back inside. Nate assumed it was to make sure everything was out of sight.

The Lt. issued orders and two soldiers came aboard and two went to Delbert's boat. Delbert came on deck as did Carl and Don. They stood aside as the search was made both on deck and in the cabin below. Minutes passed and tensions began to mount. Nate notice the men had moved closer to the guns they had stashed on deck. At the first sign of anything wrong, all hell would be to pay. Nate decided to get into a conversation with this young Lt.

"Maybe you can tell me about scuba diving around here. I'd kind of like to

KEITH R. KIRKWOOD

get a couple air tanks, fins and equipment so that when fishing is poor we can
go diving. What can you tell me?" he asked of the Lt.

"Si, scuba diving is good. Underwater is beautiful. If you do go you need
to take a camera and take pictures," the Lt. Answered.

"Do we need a permit for this," Nate asked.

"No, senor, no permit. If anyone says anything just tells them you talked to
me," came the answer.

"Thank you, have a cigar," Nate offered him a Cuban.

"Si, thank you," he accepted the cigar and Nate struck a match and lit it for
him. Just then, the men came up from below deck and said something to the
Lt. in Spanish.

"Thank your for your patiences, we are finished," said the Lt. They both
looked across to the other boat and the soldiers were coming off it onto the
dock. They repeated what the other soldiers had told their commander.

As they turned to leave, Nate spoke up.

"Do you know where we could buy the scuba gear and camera to do a little
diving?" Nate asked.

"Si, go over one street and up two blocks and there is a shop that sells both,
He said pointing his finger in the direction he mean't.

Nate's crew gathered around and passed out coffee cups. This would
make it seems like a morning gathering to anyone who was watching.

"What are you up to boss?" Ed asked, "Are going fishing or scuba diving.
I don't understand what that was all about."

"It's a get out of jail card. The Lt. can vouch that we had no diving
equipment, etc. He'll say we asked him about diving and he thought it was a
good idea. We'll even bring him back a couple pictures. This covers us for
having air tanks on board. As long as they don't find the explosives, we're safe.
Now lets get to work and wash down these tubs and make them look halfway
decent. You can all go to town but no one man should go to the El Toro alone.
I'll be going to Loretta's tonight. We leave early in the morning so come home
early. Another mission," Nate explained.

Nate arrived at Loretta's at seven PM. The place was only about half full.
It was a weeknight and people did work, so as in America, people partied on
weekends.

He seated himself at the bar and was greeted by the same bartender as before.

"Good evening sir, you made quite a hit with the boss. She wants me to ring her if you come in. Can I get you something while you wait," he said.

"Yes, give me a beer and thanks for the info," replied Nate.

A beer was sat in front of Nate and the bartender stepped to the house phone. In a couple minutes, he returned.

"You're invited to come upstairs to her apartment. Take the stairs on the left of the front door. At the top push, the doorbell and she will buzz you in. The beer is on the house," he told Nate.

Nate dropped a five on the bar and headed for the stairs. At the top, he pushed the doorbell and was immediately buzzed in. As he opened the door, he saw her standing just a few feet inside. Again her beauty dazzled him.

She was dressed in a pink, sheer dress that showed off all her curves. It was almost a see through but not quite. *She didn't know I was coming and look how she's dressed. Wow,* ran through his mind, *I wonder how she'd dressed if she knew I'd be here.* He coal black hair highlights her looks. She was smiling as she turned towards him. She'd been talking to an employee and excused her at the sight of Nate.

"My friend, I'm so glad to see you again. I just ordered dinner for us. I hope you like seafood. It's Talapia with a baked potato and stir-fry vegetables and a fine white wine. I hope you like stirfry," she spoke as she reached him.

Standing on her toes, she kissed him lightly on the mouth as a hello. *Keep that up babe and we'll be going to bed before this night is over,* was his thoughts.

"Sounds delicious," he answered.

She stepped to the little portable bar and asked," Can I get you something?"

"Yes, a whisky please," he said

"Please have a seat," she said pointing to the sofa.

As he walked the few steps to it, he looked around the room. It was done all in a Spanish décor, bright colors and was beautiful. The carpets must have been imported from the Asia. They were about two inches deep and were the most beautiful he ever seen. A small chandelier of fine Crystal hung over the living space of the huge apartment. Two lamps with red shades and bulbs sat on each side of the bar. From the living room, he could look into the dining room. An Old Spanish table, hand carved with six matching chairs. The chairs were typical Spanish, probably from Old Mexico and were a hundred years old. A red, yellow and orange cloth lay down the center of the table. Two huge candelabrums sat about two and a half feet in from the end, of each end. The candles were all diferent colors. Drapes behind it were solid red with yellow borders. He was sure the drapes were made of satin. They were hung with a huge circle at the top and draped down the walls at each end. Sheer curtains hung over the large window.

Nate seated himself on the sofa and Loretta hand him a glass of whisky. She then sat on the other end of the sofa. Nate could smell her perfume. It was nice and not strong. It kinda of lingered in the air when she walked by.

"Do you treat all you new patrons like this," Nate asked.

"No, of course not. You kind of strike me as a man who can be trusted and if you were someone's friend, you would do anything to preserve that friendship. We all need friends. Good friends and a lover. I want to get to know this fisherman that has arrived in our city and creating quite a stir," she said.

"I wasn't aware that I was creating a stir. My crew and I just came down here for a year to fish, get back into shape and wait till things cool down at home. Don't misunderstand we did nothing real bad but need a vacation," he grinned at her.

"Well the drug trade's curious and so am I. The old man at the packing plant is my uncle. You have saved him from bankrupty. You made a friend of him and I want to be your friend," she spoke is soft tones.

"What is your name? I can not dine with a man whose name I do not know?" she asked and stated at the same time.

"Armstrong, Nate Armstrong," he answered.

"Pleased to meet you, Nate," she said.

"Let's have a glass of wine," she said as she rose to get it. At the bar, she poured a pink wine into two glasses. She returned to the sofa and handed him one.

He took a sip and found it to be a very nice wine. Sweet but not too sweet. *Just right for wine he thought.*

They sat there over half an hour, getting acquainted before the food arrived. The food arrived with two waiters and a server carrying it.

They placed it on the table along with the silverware. Nate notice one plate was placed on the end and the other just to the right of the first. *Well at least we're both sitting at one end of the table,* he thought.

Loretta got up and offered Nate a hand.

"Come on, lets eat," she said maintaining a good grip on his hand.

The sat and had a very good dinner and the wine she had mentioned earlier was superb. They talked a little but not enough to spoil a calm of the night. A sort of magic was taking them over. They looked at each other, smiling and each grateful they were together. Once the meal was completed, she rang for the server and had the dishes cleared away. In Spanish, she told them she did not wish to be disturbed the rest of the evening.

"Si," said the server smiling like the cat that had caught the canary. She left and Loretta poured them a brandy. She turned the lights off in the dining room and had Nate join her at the window.

"See what a view I have of the city. Sitting on this little hill and living on the second floor, I can see a great deal of it. I love this view and it's even nicer when you have someone look at it with you," saying this as she moved closer to Nate and taking his hand.

Nate had to admit it was a great view. You could see the harbor in the distance. He sipped the brandy and waited for whatever surprise came next. He knew she had something on her mind and he hoped it was only seduction. He was ready.

Stepping away from the window, she led him back into the living room. She went to a stereo player and put on a country tune. Slipping off her shoes, she asked him to dance. He agreed and kicked off his shoes so his stocking feet would move over the rug. It was not the ideal dance floor but who was complaining.

Her hair smelled fresh and clean as she pressed her body next to Nate's. He took advantage of her closeness and placed a hand on her butt. He then moved her closer with that hand. She said not a word as they danced. It was almost like she expected it. An erection was beginning because of this closeness. She placed her head next to his chin and snuggled there. After a few tunes, he just had to do something about this budge.

"Which way to the bedroom, "he whispered in her ear. She just pointed and allowed him to lead her in that direction.

The music just stopped as they entered the bedroom. He noticed not how it had furnished. There were other things on his mind.

They stopped and he leaned down and kissed her passionately on the lips. She put both her arms around his neck and returned his kisses.

He gently unzipped her dress down the back. He pulled the dress forward as she pull her arms out of the fabric and it dropped to the floor.

Her breast were rising and falling faster than usual and her breathing increased. He looked down at her breasts and with one hand; he lifted the bra over them. He then played with the now bare breasts, which brought her to say.

"Oh, Nate, you do make me feel like a woman. Take it off," she said regarding the bra. He obeyed unsnapping it and throwing it on the floor. She was naked except for her panties.

She was unbuttoning his shirt so he concentrated on the pants; He undid the top button and unzipped them. She had finished with the shirt and as he slipped out of it, she pulled down his pants. He stepped out of them and removed his shorts. He then knelt and slipped her panties off and kissed her bare belly. Several kisses later, he rose and laid her on the bed. Two hours later, they came to their senses, remembering only that passion had taken them to far distance planets. She had several orgasims and he had three. A night to remember.

Next morning, Nate was back at the dock, ready to go after another target. The time was three AM. He woke his crew and in short order they were headed out to sea. Nate had a policy to gas up, fill with ice every night they came to port. This way they were always ready to move out in a hurry. He knew full well that in their business, they could be discovered at any time and may have to run for it.

At twenty miles, they began to circle and look for fish. This went on for a couple of hours before they spotted a school worth going after.

"Hey, Delbert, swing ups ahead a couple hundred yards. I've found a pretty good school and they're swimming your way. I'll start circling around them and you can scoop in what I miss," Nate said over the phone.

"Roger, boss, we'll get right on it," came the reply.

It was early afternoon before they sighted a sail from a pleasure boat. It was cutting through the waves at a good clip. They wind had picked up and pushed them along. Nate watched the craft as it veered off to their right. This had to be the target boat. Nate plotted its course by the direction it was taking. It it maintained its present course it would be going directly to Cuba.

It veering off could only mean they were suspicious of everyone on the sea. He had to come up with a way to get closer or pull up the nets and head north.

That would only raise suspicion. By now, they knew what they looked like and would know something was up. He looked at Delbert's boat and noticed their nets were out of the water. He quickly ran his phone.

"Delbert don't put your nets back in yet. Cruse over next to us. I'm going to try to get that boat over closer," he said.

"On my way. Be there in five," Delbert responded.

Hanging up, Nate went into the cabin, picked up the mike to the ship-to-shore radio. He triggered the mike.

"Hello schooner, this is the fishing boats lay off to your left. We have need for your help, over," went across the airwaves.

A minute then two minutes went by before a response.

"Schooner to fishing boats, whats the trouble, over," said a gruff voice.

"One of my boats has run out of oil. The dumb skipper forgot to load extra supplies and we can't move it until we get oil. Do you have any you can spare? Just enough to get it back to port, over," Nate asked.

"Yeah, we could let you have a gallon for a hundred American dollars. My orders are to stay away from other boats, but I could use the money, over," came the answer.

"I have the hundred dollars and I'll put it in a bottle an throw it to you. You just put something around the can so it will float and drop it in the water. Thirty yards is as close as you need to come, over," Nate said.

"Ok, get it ready so we don't have to stop, over," was the answer.

Nate knew this vessel had two radios, one by the steering wheel and one down in the cabin. He had to hurry with a plan to get to these and quickly. He dialed Delbert's boat.

"Brad and Don can do this one and plant the charges and I'll come from this side a take out the radios. Get your tanks on and get in the water. Stay out of sight. We don't want to spook them," at this, Nate shut off the phone.

"Ed, come here," Nate said, "here's a hundred dollar bill. Grab a bottle quick from the kitchen. When they get close, toss it to them. They'll drop a can of oil for us but forget about that. Just throw them the money."

With this, he went below and stripped down to his birthday suit. He jumped into a swin suit and slipped into the harness of the tank. He then hurried to the deck and slipped over the side. He swam to the port side and waited by treading water.

Looking back towards where the schooner was coming he soon saw the bow cutting through the water. Looking across to the other fishing boat, he could just make out two forms. It had to be his crew and they were ready.

As the schooner came close to the fishing, it had slowed down. This Nate had hoped for and they played right into his hands. He pushed off and met Brad and Don already underneath the water. He helped them place the charges then pulled himself up on to a small ledge and the rear of the vessel. Here he hung on for dear life.

All at once, the boat seemed to lift up and then settle. He heard a dull thud. This told him the explosives had gone off. He pulled himself up to where he could see what was happening on the boat. He saw four men running around wondering what was happening. He saw one of these run for the cabin. This one, he knew was going for the radio.

He jumped aboard and rushed after him. He heard a pistol firing and looked to his left. A man stood there firing at him. Still running, Nate fired at the man midruff and saw him fall just a he reached the cabin. The man inside turned to look at him. Nate fired point blank into his body. He dropped to the floor, releasing the mike an it swung back and forth below the radio. Nate fired into the radio and seeing the lower area was filling up with water and hearing no noise from there knew no one had reached the lower radio. He turned to see what was going on behind him.

Bags of the drugs were floating on the deck. Nate knew he had to get off and swim away to avoid getting sucked under with the boat. A man next to the railing turned to fire at him. Nate shot him while in a dead run, with his last round and the man fell overboard.

Where the other two had fallen, the water was turning red with their blood. Nate ran to the side nearest his boat a jumped overboard. He was about halfway to his boat when he noticed a shark starting to circle. They must have been close by and with blood in the water, they were already there.

Damn, Nate said to him, *I forgot my shark repelent. Hell of a time to remember that.*

He yelled to Ed who was standing near the edge of the boat, on deck.

"Ed, get the rifle, I forgot my shark repelent and this one is after me," with this he swam as fast as he could, hoping for safety. As he was nearing the boat, he heard the rifle being fired. Ed had gotten to it.

Reaching the boat Brad and Ed leaned over the edge of the boat and grabbed his arms, hoisting him on board.

"That one damn near got you, boss and he's a big bastard," Ed informed him.

Nate looked back and saw the shark floating. Ed was a good shot. One of the men from the schooner was struggling with a shark and went under in seconds.

"A couple of the bags were floating away. Lets get them and get the hell out of here," Nate ordered. The pickup of floating debris was quick and was soon done.

Nate motioned to Delbert to follow him and opened up the engines. With in minutes they were several miles away.

Nate dialed and waited for the General to answer.

"Brown's Realty, how may I help you?" Nate recognized the General's voice.

"Nate, here, General. We just sent another to the deep. How's everything on your end."

"Cocaine is disappearing from the streets and the price has gone out of sight. All this is causing a minor crime wave but the cops are handling it ok. Nate you must be careful. Cuba has sent out gunboats in a twenty-mile area, around the island. They suspect something is happening to the Colombian boats. I wouldn't be surprised if they sent escorts down there, to escort boats back to Cuba. They have to be careful though. They don't want us to know why. This would tie them to the drug trade and the whole world would know. I believe the Colombian military will start playing a part also. Just be damn careful, Nate. Anytime you want to pull out just does it? My group will understand," said the General with great concern.

"Hell, it's just getting interesting, general. Beside my crew and I don't withdraw just because of a little trouble. Hell if we have to, we'll blow the bastards up right in the harbor. If they think they're hurting now, just wait another month. By then their entire product will be gone and they'll have to wait till more is manufactured and made into dope. That could take at least a month. With you permission and a generous fee, we'll go inland and take out their factory. I think we can pinpoint it and by going through the jungle take it out. If we do this though I'd want to have Katrina onboard and then we'd run for it. Think about it and see what your group thinks. We might as well do as much damage as we can while down here. Bye, General," Nate hung up.

-6-

Knowing they had to keep up the act of being fisherermen, Nate prepared for fishing the next day. He would first take one of the men with him to the El Toro and see if Katrina had any new information. They were starting to hurt the cartels and must keep up the pressure. Nate called a meeting of his men to give them instructions on security matters. Once they were all onboard, Nate passed around a bottle and handed out cigars. Once they all had a snort and had their cigars going, he began.

"From now on no one man goes to the El Toro alone. That goes for me too. It's starting to get dangerous and I know that's when you people do your best work. From right now one-man will stay on board at all times. I leave it up to you how you handle that. Draw straws or something. There are six of us and I'll do a turn each week we are docked. Stash a pistol and a rifle on deck but out of sight. Hide them close to where you will be sitting, so they'll be in easy reach. I have a gut feeling the army will become more active and harass us from time to time. We are not ready to pull out of here just yet. Our work is not done but we must be careful. At guard duty, you must stay on deck to where you can see both boats. We don't want anyone sneaking onboard either boat. When the army comes around feed them whiskey and cigars. Make sure the C-4 is at the back and behind the real groceries. When you take one out, move the cans around to conceal the rest. Are we clear on this?" he asked them.

"Right boss," some of them said and the rest nodded their heads in a yes fashion.

"Oh, one more thing. I asked the General what they would pay for a little jungle warfare," he said and noticed the frowns on their faces.

"We have all been in a jungle fight before and I said we'd go inland and destroy their packing center and any location we could find that was processing the poison. Are you with me on this?" he asked.

"Damn rights we are," coming from Ed, "this is what made us the team we are today."

"Well now, I want you to all sleep on this and let me know when we're on the high seas. This jungle fight will be easy going in, but hell coming out. Some of us may die," Nate reminded them. He finished up by saying he was going to the El Toro and asked who would accompany him. Bradly volunteered.

The rest of the men talked among themselves about who would stand guard that night.

Nate and Bradly was off for the El Toro at seven o'clock civilian time. Past experiences had shone that this was early enough to get a good table but not so early they bringing attention to themselves. Bradly had mentioned he was interested in a certain young woman and was looking forward to a night of dancing.

Entering the bar, they heard the music coming from the dancing area. There were several people already there and they had to find their way through those, on their way to a table near the dance floor, but with a wall behind them. They saw their usual table was available and they headed for it.

They seated themselves and waited for service. A server came by and took their order. Katrina was nowhere to be seen. This worried Nate and he hoped nothing had happened to her.

They had just finished their first drink when the ugly one came straight for them. As he neared them, they could see where his nose had been stitched back on and really looked like hell. The scar left by stitches was quite predominant and gave him a weird look. It made an ugly bastard even uglier. He had blood in his eye. Nate knew this time this man would kill him. He would have to take him out quickly or there would be one hell've a fight.

Nate sat calmly as the ugly one approached. Just then, he caught a glimpse of Katrina talking to the bartender and pointing their way. Help would soon be on its way, but not soon enough.

Nate slipped out his knife and held it under the table. No one had noticed so he had an advantage.

"Get up American dog. Tonight I kill you, get up or I'll shoot you where you sit," he was saying as his hand slowly pulled the gun out of the holster.

Nate knew he was dead if he didn't move now. He sprung from his seat catching the ugly one by surprise. He hit him with a head butt in the chest, with such force, knocking him over backwards. As his body hit the floor, Nate had him pinned by sitting on top of him. His arms were pined so he could not move them.

"You ugly bastard, I think you need some more cosmetic surgery. No fee, this one is on the house," Nate said aloud so everyone could hear.

With his knife at his throat Nate, quickly move the knife and sliced off an ear.

The ugly one yelled with pain and tried to free himself from Nate. Nate jumped to his feet as blood poured from the man head. The ear lie on the floor and as its owner reached for it, Nate kicked it into the crowd.

"Stay away from me you bastard or next time I will kill you," Nate said.

"Take this man to a doctor," said the bartender to a group of men standing around watching the fracas. He motioned in the air and the band started playing and the crowd dispersed with everyone going their own way. Dancing began.

"That one is asking to be killed," said the bartender, "I'm surprised someone hasn't already done it."

"I'll pay for any damages," Nate informed the bartender.

"No, keep your money. I'm buying the next two drinks for your table. Everyone here was waiting for a fight tonight and they have had their bloody desires satisfied. They will now eat and drink and I will make money," said the bartender. He turned to Katrnia and told her to jump to it and bring their drinks. He then walked back to the bar and went back to work.

An hour later Nate was paying for the drinks. When change was brought back to him, there was no ink numbers on the bills. Katrina leaned close as she moped the table with a rag and whispered to him.

"Nothing for the next three days," finished, she quickly moved to serve other customers.

Nate informed Brad that he was going to Loretta Restaurant and Lounge.

"I'll stay a little longer if you need the time to get your girl friend to leave with you. I won't leave you alone in this place," Nate told him.

"Oh, I'll be ok boss. You nailed the only son-of-a-bitch that would give us trouble. Go ahead, I'll be fine," Brad responded.

"No, I won't go and leave you here. That bastard is a part of the cartels and has friends here. They may be waiting to get one of us alone so they can get even for their pal. You ask her to go with you or you go to her place, if you trust her not to be one of them," Nate advised.

"Ok, one more drink and a dance and I'll ask her," Brad said. Nate nodded ok and settled back into his chair. He thought of using his cell phone but didn't want to chance someone over hearing the conversation. He sipped his drink and thought of the beautiful woman waiting for him.

Brad was having so much fun on the dance floor that he hated to break it up but it was necessary to. An idea struck him and he waved Brad and friend over to the table.

"If you folks want to stay Brad, take my cell phone outside and call Delbert and see if one of the men would like to come play. Would she be able to have a woman for anyone who came?" Anyway, go make the call," Nate handed him the phone.

Brad and the woman with him went outside and were back in about five minutes.

"Delbert will be here as soon as he can get a cab," Brad told him.

"Ok, I'll leave as soon as he gets here. You all have fun now, but stay sober and watch your backs," Nate remarked. Brad nodded in agreement, as he escorted the woman back to the dance floor.

Nate thought, *it was nice seeing Brad have a good time.*

Thirty minutes later Nate arrived at Loretta's place. He walked up to the bar and spoke to the bartender, the same one who was always there.

"Damn, do you work all the time?" Nate said.

Looking up from his job of dunking glasses into hot water, he smiled at Nate. "What will it be?" he asked.

"A black haired beauty and whisky," was the reply.

"Here's the whisky and I'll buzz the lady," advised the bartender.

"Ask her to join me. I feel like dancing tonight," Nate said as he walked over to a table close to the dance floor. The music was good old country and western.

Several minutes he motioned to a server for another whisky. Once this was done, he looked at his watch and wondered what was taking the woman so long. He did realize she was a woman and had to primp before coming down. He knew she was worth it and didn't really mind the wait. After all before the night was over he would have her naked and in her bed with her. This was worth more than the wait, so he sat and sipped the whisky. He felt at ease in this place. That was different for him because the Viet Nam War had trained him to be on guard everyday and every minute. His life depended on it for years and the habit was hard to break. This woman and her place had a very soothing effect on him. He hoped he wasn't just being foolish. *Oh, well right or wrong, it was exciting for him,* he thought.

As his second glass was going dry, Nate saw Loretta coming down the bar. She looked up and smiled. She greeted several people before heading to Nate's table.

"Hey, I know you," he said as she reached the table. "Can I offer you a drink and a seat?"

She laughed at his foolishness but loved it. This man was having an impact on her life and got her to thinking of love and the good things in life. She was impressed with his independence and confidence. Few men these days had these to qualities. She liked this person. At the same time, she knew that he might be just fooling with her and she might get hurt. She didn't care. She would try not to fall in love but wanted the experiences he was putting her through. Since their last time together, she had found herself waking up all hot and wanting his body. She would dream of how great it was to make love to him. *God.* She thought, *I'm acting like a pupil. I can't help it. I want to kiss him right now.*

"Why yes, you can" she said restrained herself.

He rose to his feet and came around the table to seat her.

"Don't touch me," she whispered, "I'm afraid if you do I'll have to kiss you very passionately.

He pulled out her chair before returning to his chair. She saw a big smile on his face and this warmed her. She wished they were alone.

"By patience, my lady. I want to hold you and much more. It can wait so we can dance. I'll still be holding you and it will be good for both of us. Other things will happen so lets enjoy us. The night is long and just beginning. What can I get you to drink?" he asked as he waved at a server.

"The waitress will know. I'll have my usual," she replied.

Nate ordered a beer and for the server to bring her usual to Loretta.

"Yes, senor," she said and moved away to bring the drinks.

The drinks arrived and Nate paid the bill under the protests of Loretta. She wanted to take care of it but he'd have nothing to do with it.

"What would a lady think of a man if he couldn't afford to buy a drink," Nate said in a way of dismissing the subject.

Both took a sip and the music began.

"Dance, my dear," Nate asked and rose out of his chair. She nodded and rose to take his extended hand as he led her to the dance floor. She moved into his arms and her pulled close. It was a slow dance and they danced without saying a word. It was as if they didn't want to spoil a perfect moment. They were lost in their own thoughts. Unknown to each other, they were both thinking the same thing. They wanted to be like this, together. Her perfume was a faint but a wonderful smell. Her head lie on his chest and he bent slightly, so she understood he was proud to have her in his arms.

The tune ended yet they stood motionless on the floor. The band noticed this and quickly started playing again. Another slow one and their feet began to move as around the floor the moved. Their bodies press close to each other. Warm feelings course through their bodies making it an even more pleasant time. The music stopped and Nate led her back to the table.

"Thank you, my dear," he said, "your dancing is enchanting."

"Why, thank you sir," she replied, "you're not bad yourself. Do you always hold your women so close to you?"

"Only the beautiful ones," he smiled as the words rolled off his tongue.

"Well, Nate, if you keep me so close and rub your body against mine like you do, I won't be responsible for my actions. God it feels good to feel like a woman and to be with a real man," she expressed her feelings.

Neither man nor woman could remember when they had such a good time. The two just hit it off and was very comfortable with each other. They drank, danced and had food but they were not intoxicated. It was like a dream and yet it was not. Their bodies touched as they danced but it was not an act to excite anyone and yet it did. Loretta was coming back to a place she had not been in since she was married. Yet this seemed different. It was kind of, like she was a young girl about to have an affair. She was excited and shakie inside. She wanted to go upstairs and feel the thunder of making love. She had been almost in a trance since the night she slept with this American.

Nate was having the same type of feelings and was a little confused by it. He had no intentions of staying here after the mission was completed. Yet this woman had a grip on him that he could not explain. The sex was great and he wanted it very much. He was having second doubts about going further with this woman. He didn't want to hurt her, but he didn't want to stop either. He knew deep in his heart he had to tell her, but damn he didn't want to spoil such a good time. Not only was the time with her good but also fulfilling. This was different. With other women, he could take what they offered and walk away without looking back. He was starting to feel like to do that would be difficult this time. It might even be impossible. He didn't want to get hung up on a woman. In his line of work, it wasn't fair to the woman. *God,* he thought, *I just don't know what to do. He was confused and that was far different than with the other beautiful women in his life.*

After a couple hours, Nate asked her if she had any of that good wine upstairs. Like the kind, he had tasted there before.

"Yes, I do. Would you like to come up and have a glass," she said smiling. She didn't want to tell him she was having a hard time staying in the bar. She so wanted to go unstairs with this man and experience everything he had to offer.

They rose from the table, Nate threw a fifty-dollar bill on the table to pay for what they had consumed. He took her hand and she led him to the stairs.

Once upstairs, Nate kicked off his shoes and sat down on the love seat. Loretta poured a couple glasses of wine and sat down beside him.

Leaning over she kissed him lightly on the lips before speaking.

"I didn't think I'd ever get you up here tonight. I really thought you'd dance, drink and perhaps run. But then I remembered the last time you were here and knew you wouldn't," she said.

He placed his glass on the coffee table, reached for hers. She gave it up willingly and he placed it beside his. He leaned forward and took her in his arms and kissed her. It was not a little kiss but one of passion. She gladly returned it as they again drifted away to their own special world. A couple kisses she rose from her seat, taking his hand and led him into the bedroom.

"Nate, take my clothes off and kiss me after each article. Kiss my body and make love to me," she was almost begging him.

"How could I pass up such an offer, he thought, and proceeded with this lovely way of starting out to make love. Her beautiful body was soon naked and she helped him out of his clothes. The bed seemed to reach out to these two lovers and they did not resist.

Morning came early or so it seemed for Nate and Loretta. They woke in each other's arms just as they had slept. He kissed her and that was all it took to begin the lovemaking all over again.

At eight AM, they showered together and Loretta called down stairs, ordering breakfast once they were dressed.

Turning from the phone, she noticed Nate standing at the window. She walked over to him and stood by his side. Feeling her presence, he put his arm around her while gazing out the window.

"You have a wonderful view of the city from here. Even the docks can be seen. Next time we have a meal, let's have it out on the veranda," he stated.

"Ok, let's have breakfast out there. I'll have the food placed there when it arrives," with this, she opened to doors to the veranda. "I often eat out here and sit alone at night watching the lights of the city. The city is beautiful with all the different colored lights. I would often think of the future and wonder what it holds for me. As a silly woman. I would fantasize of a prince on a white horse coming to rescue me. We would marry and live happily ever after. Silly, no?" she asked.

"Not at all, it's perfectly normal to have such dreams. Most are daydreams but some come true. We all wonder about the future while some worry about the past," Nate replied.

"You seem far away this morning, Nate, is something wrong or are you now day dreaming. If so I hope, it's a beautiful dream. You deserve happiness. I can feel you have had happiness before but now you are lonely. I feel this when you take me in your arms and make love to me. I don't mean to be unkind but why you are not married?" she asked.

"Oh, I don't know. I guess I've not found the right woman yet. I was at one time, no kids. When it ended, I just concentrated on working. I got into the habit of taking my women wherever I found them and left them where I found them. Kind of cold, huh," he said.

"I want to talk to you about that," Nate started, "you are different and I like you very much. With you it is not all sex, then run away. I don't know but I'm having strange feelings about you and I'm not sure that is a good thing. You are special and I don't want to hurt you. I think you could get serious about a poor angler and you deserve more. Do you really think we can keep seeing each other and not get serious?" he asked.

Just then, the door opened and her staff was carting in food and hot coffee. She turned away to advise them where to set them up for breakfast. In a matter of just minutes, the table was set and fresh flowers adorned the table. It was a very inviting setting. The two employees finished and left.

Nate pulled out a chair for her and seated her. He sat next to her around the corner of the table. She poured him coffee and filled her cup. He wasn't sure whether to continue the conversation they were having before the interuption or not.

"Eat, Nate, we'll talk later," she said as she handed him a plate of eggs.

The breakfast was a nice and quiet time. There was little talking. When the did talk it was about the gentle breezes that blew gently over and around them. She asked him if he was glad to be in Colombia and was he having a successful season fishing. He told her he was glad to be here and that she was part of the reason. He very much enjoyed being on the water and filled her in on the skin diving and picture taking underwater. She was glad to be here it and asked him for a favor.

"Take a very nice picture and have it enlarged so I could hang it in the bar or perhaps in the apartment. I love the sea, but get little chance to get out on it. Maybe some day you'll take me fishing and teach me how to fish with a pole. If you will, I'll fix a very nice lunch and bring a couple bottles of champagne. Please, would you," she asked with that pleasant smile on her face.

She leaned forward which he took to be she wanted to be kissed. He leaned over and gave her a very gentle, sweet kiss. *God, I love kissing her,* he was thinking.

"It would be a pleasure," he replied, "how about tomorrow. We're not going out till day after tomorrow so that would be perfect. The early morning is the best time. Can you get up early and come to the boat. We could be underway by six."

"Yes, of course I can get up early and if you would spend the night with me, I'm sure you would see to it," was her response.

"You sure you won't get tired of me?" he asked.

She smiled shyly and rose from the table.

"I'll have the table cleared and have the kitchen fix us a lunch for tomorrow and to chill the champagne."

Returning to the table, she pours coffee and sat down. It was a quiet time as they both drifted off in their own thoughts. When they had finshed the coffee, Nate looked at his watch.

"Well, I must go. I have to re-stock the boats with supplies and water. I'd love to spend tonight with you. I have a call to make around nine, and then I'll come by. Is that ok?" he asked.

"Yes, that will be fine. I'll have a dinner ready for you and we'll have a chance to chat," she answered.

She walked him to the door. When reaching the door, Nate turned and took her in his arms. They kissed long and passionately before he turned to leave.

Downstairs he calls a cab and was whisked away with thoughts of love and passion on his mind.

Returning to the boats, he called his crew together and told them of his plans for tomorrow. As he finished Delbert spoke up.

"The army was here again and searched the boats. They wouldn't tell us why but if you were concerned you could come by that Lt's office and talk about it."

"No I'm not going to fall into that trap. If I go to him, he will guess or at least think we are hiding something. I won't do that. I think they are testing us and want a response. To hell with them. Just make sure everything that might cause suspicion is well hidden. They are trying their damnest to figure out what's going on with their boats. They will soon figure it out but we need to keep them guessing as long as possible. Don't fight with them and let them be. If we resist they will have reason to seize the boats. If they do and their boats start getting through, they know it's us. We cannot let that happen. If they get too close for comfort, we'll blow their damn boats up right here in the harbor," Nate said in addressing the crew.

"Day after tomorrow we go out again, fishing," he smiled when he said it. You men travel in pairs when you go into town or anywhere. We must be careful. Just being Americans makes us suspects even if they don't know what's going on. We'd better have two men on guard duty, day and night, to be on the safe side. You see to it, Delbert. Ed you and Carl come with me and we'll get supplies for the boats. Don't let me forget water. When I get back tomorrow we'll ice and gas up for the following day."

Nate, Carl and Ed walked to the pay phone on the dock and called a cab. Several blocks up the street was a supermarket and that was where they were headed.

They entered the store and each grabbed a cart and started down the isles to make their selections. Each was assigned items to purchase. Going into the store Nate had made arrangements to ring up the supplies and stack them by the door until they were done. He also advised the store manager he'd be paying in cash with American dollars.

The shopping took a good hour and all were glad when they were through.

Nate paid for the supplies and asked the manager to call for a couple cabs to take them back to the boat.

"Si, senors and please come again. If I know when you are coming I will have my cousin deliver the supplies for no charge," the manager said to Nate.

"Thank you, we will be back next month and I'll call ahead," he told the manager.

The cabs arrived and they were soon unloading their purchases onto the boats. They had just started when up drove a truck loaded with army troops.

What the hell now, Nate thought as he stepped off the boat to greet the Lt.

"Sorry, but I must search your boat again," said the Lt. As he motioned the troopers to began.

"What are you looking for now?" Nate asked in sort of a sarcastic voice.

"Ships are disappearing on the high seas and my government is concerned. Have you seen anything suspicious on your fishing trips," inquired the Lt.

"No, I don't think so. When we are fishing, we're working our butts off and have not time for nonsense. Fishing is damn hard work and I kind of resent these searches. We've done nothing wrong. Our papers are in order and we deliver fish to the plant every time we go out. Some days we have a heavy load and others not so good. That's life. We don't understand all this. What the hell is these missing boats carrying that someone would want to hijack them?" Nate inquired.

"Just merchandise for Cuba. That country is a good trading partner with us and that is our concern, senor," came the reply.

"Ok, you have a job to do and I understand that. Have a cigar and drink with me?" Nate asked.

The Lt. looked around, smiled and said, "Si that would be good." Do you have Cuban cigar.

"Hell, yes, best cigar in the world," Nate replied as he reached for a cigar in his shirt pocket. Nate reached around and pulled a bottle of whisky from under a tarp. He stepped over to a container and removed two shot glasses. He filled the glasses and handed one to the Lt. They made a friendly gesture towards each other and downed the whisky in one gulp.

Nate fired up his lighter and lit both cigars and filled the glasses again.

After the second drink, the soldiers were through searching and came topside and reported no findings. This was done in Spanish and Nate didn't understand it all, but got the just of it.

Handing back the glass to Nate, he ordered the men off the boats and started to leave.

"Is there someone I can complain to about all this?" Nate asked.

"Si, Col. Pedro Valdez, is my commanding officer. His office is across town. Just ask any cab driver and he will take you. Please report that I was through, but not abusive. Some of the men are abusive to those they search thinking everyone are criminals.

Nate noticed this time they went down the line and searched every boat. *They are getting concerned,* Nate thought, *this means our mission is causing great pain and hundreds of millions of dollars is losses.* He smiled knowing thousands of American kids may not become addicted because of the disruption in the drug supply. If they knew, all of America would celebrate.

The supplies put away and nighttime had fallen, made the men anxious for a trip to town. So was Nate. He could hardly wait to get to Loretta's place. He needed to get The El Toro and see Katrina first.

"Ok, gang, I'm going to The El Toro for a couple hours. I will then be staying over night at Loretta's. A couple drinks with some of you fellows would be good. Who wants to go with me?" Nate questioned.

"Hell, let's all go," Carl piped up, "you never know how many of those drug dealing bastards will be there. Lets go," as he turned and started towards the dock.

"Yeah, lets all go," coming from Delbert.

Enough said and they all left the boats for the dock. Ed went to the pay phone and called for a couple cabs.

"Wait a minute," Nate said, at least one of you have to stay here until relived.

Brad volunteered and Carl said he'd be back around eleven PM. Brad could then go for the night. Carl knew that Brad had a girlfriend at the bar and he didn't.

That was one of the things Nate loved about this crew, they always considered each other.

The cabs arrived and the five were off to raise hell. Little did they know what waited for them?

-7-

As they entered The El Toro, Nate's crew sensed something was wrong. They worked their way through the crowd to a table of their choice. As they worked through the crowd, they noticed people turned to look at them. Some even moved away for them. Reaching the table, they sat down and motioned for a server.

"Somethings wrong, guys," Nate said.

"Yeah, you can cut the tension with a knife," Ed said.

Katrina came to the table for orders.

"Beers all around," Carl said, "I'm buying."

"No, I will," Nate, stated, "our fishing is paying off good and that's our mad money."

Nate laid a twenty on the table so Katrina could take it and return with any message. She returned in five minutes and leaned over Nate as she placed a frosty mug in front of each.

"Be careful, the ugly one is back and he's going to try and get even tonight. There's a tug boat going out the day after tomorrow," she said as she handed him his change. The five, he noticed was marked.

Nate nodded and picked up his mug.

"On your toes guys, the ugly one is back and wants to get even. That means he'll have help. Get ready the fun is about to begin," Nate said. He had spotted the ugly bastard near the bar.

The bartender was argueing with him, but the ugly one just pushed him away and started towards their table. As he walked, he motioned to areas of the crowd and other men began moving their way. Nate counted seven in all. Five to seven seemed like fair odds. Nate and his men stood up, planted their feet like prizefighters and waited. They had fanned out to get room to fight. The crowd now aware of the impending fight, scrambles to get out of the way.

Panic sat in with some of them and people were being knocked aside and walked over. The area was clear is seconds.

"Hey, American dogs get out of here. This is a Colombia bar for Columbians only. Go home, fishermen," the ugly one said. His nose stood out like a red light. The scar where the stiches were taken out was very noticeable. A piece of ear missing was not very flattering either. *What an ugly bastard,"* Nate was thinking.

"Go to hell, Ugly, we are thirsty and have not intentions of going anywhere. I may kill you this time so get out of my face," Nate exclaimed.

"I have men with me so you won't cheat this time. We intend to kill you unless you run for it. Then we chase you halfway to your country. You will not screw our women nor steal our fish. We are the welcoming committee and you are not welcome. I think you steal our ships and our drugs and now you pay," this coming from the ugly one as he lunged forward.

Stupid bastard, Nate thought, *this person makes the same mistake he always does. Tipical barroom fighter style and hell he's not even good at that.*

Nate stepped to one side, grabbed a chair and brought it down hard on his head. This put the ugly one out. Nate quickly whirled around to confront the next attacker. A fat man was bearing down on him with a huge knife. Same type of fighter as old ugly. Out of the corner of his eye, Nate saw his men fighting others. He wasn't worried, he knew his men.

Nate met the charge by doing a little side step grabbed the man's arm by the wrist. With the man's speed and weight, Nate snapped backwards on it as hard as he could. He heard the bone snap and the man was falling. Just as he hit the floor, the blade turned upward. It plunged into the man's stomach. Blood spilled out and onto the floor. Nate saw the man's face turn white and he let go his grip. The color was gone in seconds and Nate knew he was dead. He turned to see if any other combants were still standing. There were none.

The bartender rushed in to stop a fight that was already over. He stopped and put both hands to his head.

"My, God what a mess. What have I done to deserve this," he said.

The crowd moved in to view the carnage on the floor. Broken arms, crushed noses and beautiful black eyes were everywhere. Some of the men stirred and the bartender said something in Spanish. At this, some in the crowd assisted in helping the men up and some were shouting for water and soap.

"This one is dead," Nate said to the bartender.

"The cartel won't like this but I saw it all. You only defended yourselves. I will tell them that," he said to anyone who would listen.

Nate couldn't resist one more move to make sure the word got out that the Americans were no ones to fool with. Seeing a knife on the floor, reaching down and picking it up, he bent over the ugly one. With swift movement of the knife, he removes a four-inch patch of his hair. This he stuffed in a back pocket of the dead man.

"What are you going to do with him," Nate asked of the dead man.

"The men will be right back to load him they will dump him in the ocean a few miles from here. You senor owes me five hundred dollars for the burial fee. Sit down I'll buy the drinks," said the bartender. He motioned for the band to start playing. The broken chairs were replaced and the floor now clean, erased all signs of a fight. The men came for the body and all was well again.

Katrina came by with drinks for the table. As she was bent over setting the glasses of beer in front of each man, Nate pulled her head over and kissed her. While in this position, he whispered in her ear.

"It's getting too dangerous coming here. From now on when you have information for me, put a candle in your window. I'll check every night and if you do, I'll sneak around to the back and knock. Now slap me hard and move away."

She did as instructed then went back to tending tables. Nate hoped the slapping would take away any suspision of her involvement of them. Most men would just think he was fresh and maybe drunk. He knew he had to protect her at any cost. Besides her place was much nicer than this stinking old bar.

"Well guys, this joint is getting too dangerous for us to come here," Nate said in a lowered voice. "I'll call Brad and tell him not to come here tonight. One of you dances with his girlfriend and tell her to meet him at Loretta's. Give her a twenty for cab fare. I'm going there myself tonight and will be staying all night. Loretta and myself are going boating in the morning. You're all invited to come down to her place tonight, but not boating in the morning. I'm leaving now. The rest of you get out in the next half hour or so. Let's not take any more chances."

Nate paid the bartender the five hundred and left. Out into the darkness of night he went. It was a warm night, with no moon. He lit a cigar and waited for a cab he'd called for. In seven or eight minutes, it arrived and he got in.

"Loretta's Bar and Restaurant," he told the driver.

Minutes later, he arrived and Loretta's paid the driver and went inside. He walked up to the bar to speak to the bartender. The same one he'd come to know when seeing the owner. A friendly chap that seened to approved of his affair with his boss.

"Nate, it's good to see you again. Shall I call her and tell he you're here. I think she's getting ready for you in her apartment. You are good for her, you know," a statement not a question.

"Yeah, call her but tell her my crew will be here shortly and will be joining me for a little R&R. She need not hurry. Do you have a table big enough for five or six next to a wall?" Nate asked.

"Sure do," and with this he raised his hand and snapped his fingers. A server appeared and the bartender spoke to her.

"This man needs table number six. Four or five more people'll join him. Take good care of them. They are friends of Loretta."

"Si," she said and asked Nate to follow her. She took him down to the dance floor making a left turn and arrived at a table close to the dancing. There was no table behind them, just the wall. There were chairs on the backside barring anyone from getting behind them. Nate thanked her and asks for a draft beer and she left to get it.

He had called Brad and filled him in of the El Toro and advised him to come to Loretta's when he was relieved of his duty. He said the woman he wanted to see would be here, as would the rest of the crew.

"Ok boss, I've never been there. Is it a nice place? I'd like to get my woman friend out of the neighborhood of The El Toro. She's too nice to go to that joint. She's poor and can't see how to get away. Thanks boss, see you later" Bard had responded.

"It's a very nice place and a better clientele. You will like it. I'll introduce you to the owner and you'll be treated royally," Nate had told him.

About thirty minutes, Nate saw his crew entering to club. He waved at them. They saw him and headed over to the table.

"Nice place, boss," some of the men said.

"I'll not miss that other joint when I can come here," Ed piped up.

The place was about half-full of people. The server saw the men enter and came over to take their order. Nate told her he was buying and to start a tab.

"Si, senor, I'll have to ask the bartender if I can do this," she said.

"Ok," Nate said. He knew the bartender would start a tab for him.

The men looked over the crowd for women that were alone. Soon they had spotted enough to go around and they headed in their direction. The music had already started and soon they were all dancing.

After half and hour Nate saw Loretta talking to the bartender, who pointed his way. This told him she had asked for him. He smiled and waved at her. As she approached the table, he reached over to another table and pulled over a chair and seated her. She was smiling widely as if very pleased to be there. Nate introduced her to the men as they returned to the table. They would glance at the picture of her on the wall, then at her. They would slap Nate on the back, while grinning like a Chester cat. The men were starting to drift away to other tables where single women sat. Nate had told them just to put their drinks on his tab.

Brad had showed up and was with the woman he wanted to be with. Nate hoped he wasn't getting serious, but figured he was a big boy. He certainly knew what he wanted. She was a pretty little thing and the men all seemed to like her. He stayed at the table with her. They danced a lot and this left Nate and Loretta time to talk.

"Would you like to dance?" he asked her.

"Of course, I love dancing with you," she said.

On the dance floor, the two danced a couple of slow ones and were silent. They were enjoying each other's company and found they didn't need words. In fact, words might spoil the moment. She was cuddled in his arms as they moved across the floor. When a fast dance started, they headed back to the table.

"You are a good dancer. I've always had a problem-finding women that I could dance with. I learned the two-step in junior high school, in gym class. Since then I've put a little step or two into it and that's what I do. I can fast dance if you feel the urge to do one," Nate advised her.

"No, lets save our strength and just enjoy the evening. I've ordered dinner for us and it will be here shortly. I hope you don't mind," she replied.

"What are we having?" he asked.

"Swordfish, with a horseradish cream sauce. I hope you'll like it," she said. He leaned over and kissed her.

"I like everything about you," he replied, "that's what scares me.

"Don't be scared, I promise I won't hurt you," she said as she laughed at the idea. He also laughed. Both felt good around each other and it was time they both had laughter in their lives.

In a few minutes, the meal arrived and looked so good that Brad and his woman ordered the same thing.

Nate picked up his fork as Loretta looked on. He cut a piece and put it in his mouth. Biting down on it, he found it very tastey. Loretta was waiting for a response from him.

"Damn it's good," he finally said.

This pleased her very much and she dug into to the meal herself. Both were hungry and finished about the same time.

"Now, you rinse your mouth with water to clean the palet. I'll order a fine wine. She ordered the wine and the server brought two bottles. One for Brad and his friend and one for Nate and herself.

When eleven o'clock rolled around, Nate and Loretta said goodnight. Nate reminded Brad that he would be taking Loretta on a boat ride tomorrow. He asked that Ed be told and to be up early. They would be leaving early for a little excursion and picnic on the high seas.

"No problem boss, I'll see to it," Brad confirmed and was off to the dancing again.

Loretta and Nate walked to the bar and as Nate settled his tab, Loretta excused herself. She told Nate she was going to the kitchen to have a picnic basket filled with food for the morning.

Nate tipped the bartender and left another twenty for any drinks the men had after he left.

"Gee, thanks. You and Loretta are getting along good. I'm glad to see it. She needs a good man. I'm happy for both of you," mentioned the bartender.

"Hey, we're just good friends," Nate protested.

"Sure you are. I see the way you look at each other and I think there's something cooking that you don't realize. Have a nice night," excusing himself and moving down the bar to wait on other customers.

Loretta came back and took his arm.

"We're all set for tomorrow. Great food and wine to wash it down. If if we get lost at sea, we could eat a week on what we'll have. Now get me upstairs so I can get out of these shoes," she said. It was more of a comment than instructions.

Upstairs Nate took his shoes off and Loretta excused herself and went into the bedroom. In a matter of just minutes, she was back with a robe on. She was holding another one. This one was a man's robe. It was a pretty blue, his favorite color.

"Here's a gift for you. I went shopping this morning. Jump out of those clothes and into the robe, I want to see how it looks on you," she said.

He went into the bedroom and stripped to the skin. He slipped into the robe. He looked into the mirror and liked what he saw.

Returning to the living room, Loretta was standing waiting for him.

"You look wonderful," she said.

"Look no clothes," he said as he flashed his robe open, exposing his naked body to her.

"I can do that," she said and opened her roble wide.

He looked her over and she just stood there letting him get his eyes full. He moved closer to her without saying a word. Now next to her he kissed her without putting his arms around her. His hands were busy elsewhere on her body. She just stood there like a statute. His hands felt good and showed promise of better things to come this night.

He bent his head and kissed each nipple of her breasts. He gently massaged each breast. They were so wonderful to touch. They were just the right size for her body. He then sucked on each nipple and gently bit at them. Passion was rising within her body with each nibble. He dropped one hand to the short hairy place between her legs. He worked his fingers until he felt the warmth and moist part and that is where she lost it. She let go the robe and put her arms around him.

"If you don't get me to that bed right now, I'll die. Hurry Nate, I want you now," she said with hot desire in her voice.

Next morning they were at the boat at six AM. Nate carried the picnc basket aboard. He took it below and set it where it would not fall. He was pleased the crew was nowhere in sight.

Returning to the deck, he fired up the motor and they were soon heading out to sea. It was a great mornig to be alive. The sun was up and there was a promise of a good day. There was not a cloud in the sky and a light wind was blowing. As he guided the boat out of the dock area, Loretta stood beside him. Her arm around his waist, but not tight enough to hinder his movements to operate the craft.

"Oh, Nate, it's such a grand moring for this. I want to thank you for bringing me. I haven't been out on a boat for years. I'd forgotten how quiet it could be. Only a sea gull flying overhead and the chug, chug of the engine to disturb out thoughts. Oh, such a grand day," She went on.

Nate smiled.

"I came all the way down here from the U.S. just to take you on a cruise," he said.

"You did not," she said poking him, "you came here to fish."

"Well, maybe so but look at the prize I've caught," he returned in answer.

"I can't argue that," she said, "you do have my utmost attention. If only you weren't such and interesting man and good lover.

When they were about five miles out, he dropped anchor and brought out to fishing rods. They were full equipped and ready to go. He drug out a cooler with live bait in it.

"If I came to fish then we'll fish. Feel up to it?" he asked.

"Certainly, I was hoping we could, it's a long time till lunch and we need something to do," this she said with a twinkle in he eyes and a broad smile.

"Shall I bait it for you or can you?" he said.

"I sir, can do my own but if I catch anything you can take it off the hook," was her comeback.

"That's my job," he answered.

With hooks baited and the poles placed in the holders, they sat back to enjoy the wait. This time was spent with small talk and enjoying the sunny day. Nothing serious was said until Nate brought it up.

"I don't want to spoil a perfect day but we need to talk. I greatly admire you and really enjoy our relationship. I must tell you though that one-day I'll be returning to the states. I don't want marriage. It just doesn't work for me. I don't want to hurt you and we can call off our seeing each other if you want. I think we both are feeling the same and if we're not careful, we'll soon be in love. What do you think and how do you feel?" he asked almost afraid of the answer.

She waited a long minute before answering. She stood up and walked around in front of him. She was close against him, put her arms around his neck and pulled his head down a little. She kissed him hard and long with feeling. He returned her kisses, but wondered what she was doing. It was at least a minute before she pulled away.

"That's what I think. We are falling in love and I'm just as afraid as you. I'm not giving up this relationship for anything. We've found something very special and I'm hanging on. We can have our cake and eat it too, as you Americans say. Neither of us need marriage and yet hand onto what we have. An old saying you Americans have is *that it is better to love and lost than to never have loved at all.* I'm willing to risk it. They're little happiness in the world and I want as much as I can get. We have maybe eight to nine months before you'll be going back if I understand what you've said. Lets hang on and enjoy the ride. If you do go back to the U.S., I believe you'll always come back on vacations, etc. I'll give you good reason to return," she said.

She had never let go of him and tightened her arms and kissed him again with much passion. *God what a woman,* he was thinking.

"Now that's our talk so lets get back to fishing," was her answer.

She jumped up beside him as they waited for a bite. She was just barely seated when his pole's line started zinging out.

"Fish on," she said and jumped for the pole. She didn't realize it was his pole. She began reeling in what she yelled was a monster. Nate just sat watching and enjoying the sight. She was excited and was enjoyable to watch. In minutes, she had landed a twenty-one inch Tilapia.

When it hit the deck, Nate jumped down and grabbed the fish. He removed the fish and placed it in a container with ice. He slammed the lid tight to calm the flopping.

"I've caught the first fish, oh mighty fisherman," she smiled looking at Nate.

"Sorry lady, that's my pole and so it's my fish. Thanks for catching it for me. Now hurry and catch your own," he said laughing out loud.

"Damn, I believe you're right," she said, but the day is not over yet. With this, she rebaited the hook and cast it out into the water.

By lunchtime they were both hungry. The sea was calm and so Nate brought out on deck, the card table and sat it up. He drug out two chairs from below and they were ready to spread out the food. He stood back and watched as this lovely woman put out a wonderful spread, complete with wine glasses. He watched her as she moved around in her slacks and tank top. Both were tight and showed off her body. He smiled and thought of having her naked in his arms, just a few hours earlier. Apparently, she felt he was looking at her and turned to face him.

"Like what you see?" she said waiting for a reply.

"Yes as a matter of fact I do. The chicken looks great. Hand me a piece would you?" he said laughing out loud.

"I'll give you a piece of chicken, alright," with this she flung a chicken drum stick at him. He ducked and it went overboard. They both heard the splash.

She walked over and kissed him.

"Come on lets eat," she said.

They chatted as they ate and drank their wine. When finished they tossed scraps into the ocean.

"That's one thing about boating and fishing. No garbage except maybe paper and foil. No food scraps. We leave that to the fishes?" Nate replied.

With everything put away, Nate cleaned the fish they'd caught, washed his hands and ask if she minded if he smoked a cigar.

"Not at all, I like the smell of a good cigar," she gave her permission.

"This is a good cigar, Cuban," he explained.

Evening was falling fast and the couple headed for homeport. Later he put her in a cab, kissed her and thanked her for a great day.

"When do I see you again?" she asked.

"Couple or three days. We're going out early in the morning and I want to get good nights sleep. You do the same," he suggested as he raised her chin and kissed her goodbye. The cab pulled away and he waved at her until the cab went around a corner and out of sight.

"Nice day huh, boss?" someone behind him said.

He turned and saw Delbert standing there.

"Yes, a great day. Now this evening I'll go to Katrina's place and get what information I can on the next shipments. We have to be careful. The General told me the other day that Cuba is sending warships, down this way. They'll give the dopers an escort for the last few miles. He'll warn us if they decide to send them all the way down here and escort them all the way. They've lost billions and are getting desperate. Things are getting tight and dangerous. Now the fun begins, Delbert. I'm going to take a nap. Wake me at midnight. Good night," with this he went below and flopped on his rack.

Nate was aware of someone shaking him as he awoke with a start. He had been in a deep sleep an instinct told him something was wrong. Words came through the fog of sleep.

"Time to go boss," a far away voice was saying. He quickly sat up and saw Delbert peering down on him. In his hands was a cup of coffee. He could see the steam rising from the cup.

"Thanks, Delbert, is everything else ok?" Nate asked.

"Yeah, everything is ok but we are being watched. In the shadow of building number, four is a nosey person. He's been there for around three hours now," Delbert said.

"Military or a doper, do we know?" was the reply.

"Not sure but he is a smoker. If you peek out the door, to the left, you'll see a red glow. A stupid person or he wouldn't be smoking. That's one of the things that got our people killed in Nam. This one thinks he's clever. He apparently walks back out of sight to light up, and then returns to smoke. Dumb, really dumb. You're going to need to be careful slipping away to see Katrina. My guess someone wants to make sure we're what we seem to be or not. Losing those ships must really be getting to them." Delbert advised.

"Here get me another cup while I clear my head and think," Nate asked as he handed over the cup.

Delbert took a couple steps to the little range and filled the cup, then returned it to Nate.

A couple minutes later, Nate spoke.

"I'll wear swim trunks and swim down about a block, then come ashore and run across the street. I'll be far enough down he won't be able to see me from his position. Katrina doesn't live far and I'll work my way through backyards and around buildings. I think I can do it without being seen. This will take some time to do so don't worry about me. I'll crawl onto the deck and slip into the water. Why don't you go on deck just after I'm in the water? Take a cigar and smoke it. Also a whisky bottle. The spy will think you can't sleep and came on deck to have a smoke. This will divert his attention. He'll be watching you. Ok?" Nate asked.

"Sure boss," was the reply.

Nate put his swimsuit on and crawled onto the deck. At the same time, Delbert walked out onto the deck and seated himself along the rail on the side where the person hiding in the shadows could have a good view.

In the water, Nate swam quietly until he reached a spot where he was sure he couldn't be see by their unwelcome guest. Climbing up the dock, he peered over and looked back to where he was hiding. His judgment was good. The building that was providing the shadow for the person was now blocking his view of anyone at his location. He pulled himself up and ran across the street. He reached a building and stopped to listen. He heard not a sound. He waited three or four minutes just to be sure and started working his way away from the docks.

Nate stayed in the darkness at ever occasion and worked his way up the street to Katrina's place. He stopped often and listened. This was a little like the jungle warfare he'd gotten use to. At last, he was at Katrina's back door.

He knocked two quick but light knocks. He knew Katrina would be waiting. She was.

The door opened and he slipped inside.

Katrina was dressed in a sheer nighty. It was dark and he could not see this but he had brushed against her and felt the material as it pasted over his skin.

She lit a candle and turned to look at him. She started laughing.

"What the hell's so funny?" he asked.

"The way you dress coming to see a lady."

"Well, we're being watched at the boats and I had to swim to get out of there unnoticed. Beside this is a business meeting not a girl boy thing" he replied.

"Oh, I don't know about that. Last time you were here, it was both. That's the way I want it tonight. You've turned me into a woman and I have certain needs and because it's your fault, it is the least you could do is contiue." she said with a devilish smile and glistening eyes.

"Ok, but lets get business out of the way first," he said as he wet his lips.

"A sailing vessel is going out tonight, just after dark. A schooner type vessel fully loaded with cocaine. Several tons if I heard right. Apparently, we are making a difference. Cuba is running short. The Cuban Navy is sending a couple gunboats down to escort this one. You must be very carefull. Rather that sailing a direct course they will be setting course towards Belize until the get aways above Jamaica. They think it could be Jamaican pirates stealing their boats and killing their crews. They deem this as a take over of some sort and soon will try to sell the drugs on the open market. They're not sure but it seems like they said once before they had trouble with these pirates, several years back. You must be very careful. The boats will be more heavily guarded than before. You may need to change your tactics. But that I'll leave up to you," she reported.

Nate digested the information for a couple of minutes. Finally, he put his arms around her and pulled her close.

"Good job, Katrina. I'm worried about you. This thing could get real hot and someone might catch on that you're passing information along," he expressed his concern.

"Someday they might, but it will be awhile. Remember these dopers are fooling around with the whores and cheap women. When they get drunk, they talk a lot. Any woman in the place could be giving information out to rival gangs. If they do start looking at me, I'll let you know. If I can't reach you, I'll call the General. I have his number at Amax Realty, in Miami," she told him.

He was taken aback a little because the General had not told him this.

"You do, that surprises me a little," he said.

"Yeah, he has a swat type team standing by in Panama just to get me out. I'm to try to get to you first, but if I can't, I'm to call him," she advised.

"That's good to know," Nate said, "because if we get in a pinch we can draw on that force. I'm glad you told me." he repeated.

"You also have his number don't you?" she asked.

"Yes at Brown Realty in Maimi," he told her.

"Let's exchange numbers," Nate suggested, "just in case."

She told him the number and Nate replied.

"Hell that's the number I have for him and he always answers Brown's Realty. "Really, I wonder how he knows it's me and not you," he scratched his head.

"Must have his phone fixed so it comes in on another line, I guess, maybe number I.D." was her response.

She smelled of a light perfume and a clean smell as if she had just showered. Remembering the last time he was here, he pulled her close and kissed her. She returned it with passion. Soon they were French kissing as their passion soared. He brought one hand around to the front of her body and squeezed a breast. It was full and warm to the touch. Not huge but very firm and just right for the size of her body. As he ran his hand across the breasts, the nipples harden and he could feel her body responding to his touch. He continued with a movement across them and heard her breath increase. She would squirm about just a little, but not enough to interfere with his actions.

They both worked on removing her clothing, which were very little and she helped him discard his swimsuit. It was tight and took a moment or two. It soon dropped to the floor.

She dropped to the bed and pushed back so she was in the middle. She spread her legs and waited for him. He soon moved in between those lovely legs and the night was lost in their movements.

An hour later Nate was working his way back to the docks. Once he reached the area where he had pulled himself out of the ocean earlier, he stopped. He looked up and down the street to see if their spy had changed his location. He saw no one but still he waited. The boats looked normal and he saw no one on them. Most were asleep he figured and diverted his attention back to the area where prying eyes could be watching. A couple minutes went by when he saw a wisp of smoke floating from behind a building. The man had not changed his location.

Nate rushed acrossed the street and slipped down to the lower dock. From here, he eased himself into to ocean. He swam to where his boats were docked and pulled himself out, holding the boat between himself and those prying eyes. From there he crawled along the deck and down the steps to the quarters below. Ed moved in his bunk but didn't wake. Nate dried and slipped out of the swimsuit. He eased into his bunk and fell asleep.

-8-

The gas pumps and the cannery ice loader opened at six Am. Nate and crew were pulling in just as they opened for business. They filled up with both and were soon on their way to sea. Nate figured they would spend more time at sea to maintain their cover. Once they were, three miles out Nate slowed down and motioned Delbert to pull his boat along side.

"We'll turn West and fish over closer to Panama. We'll pull into the port there for a lunch. It's important we are seen around. We'll have to depend on our faster motors to get us around. We need to appear to be miles from where we sink these bastards. Things could get hot and we must be ready for it. We'll be inventive. Cuba is sending gunboats down to escort the drugs. They'll lie off shore at about five or six miles so that people won't see them. I'm going to put together a plan to blow one of these boats right in the harbor. If we do this, we'll need a witness. I'm thinking that Lt. would be ideal. It'll take me awhile but I'll get there. For the time we fish. Tonight, shortly after dark, a scooner is leaving our port. They think the darkness will cover their departure. It will help us but not them," Nate told him.

"Sounds exciting, boss, the men are looking forward to it," Delbert replyed, "with our souped up engines we can almost be in two places at one time."

They turned their boats west towards Panama. When out of sight of land, they opened up the engines and in an hour were many miles away. Coming within twenty miles of Panama, they decided to fish. They positioned themselves about a half mile apart and began the search for schools of fish. By crisscrossing the ocean, a large area could be checked. They relied solely on their fish finders. Two hours went by when the spotted a small school of fish. Delbert called Nate and told him he had some spotted and would began lowering the nets.

"You go ahead and scoop them up. I'll continue our pattern and see if a bigger school can be found. Look off towards the west. A boat is coming our way. It not a fishing vessel. Looks like a military boat of some kind," Nate told him. He had just spotted it when Delbert called.

Its good luck to be spoted. Now they would have witnesses to where they were fishing and make a nice alibi, Nate thought. He watched the boat coming straight at them. It was close enough now the see the Panamian flag being flown from it.

As it closed on them, an officer hails him through a horn.

"Ahoy the fishing craft, prepare to be boarded by the Panamian Navy. Heave to and stop your engines," came the order.

Nate shut down the engines and swung the boat around so the other one could come along side without turning. In a couple minutes, the navy vessel through them a rope. Brad caught the rope and secured it. No sooner done than a young Lt. Came aboard.

"I'm Lt. Flores, Antonio Flores of the Panamian Navy. May I see your papers," he said to Nate as they shook hands.

"Sure, just a minute," Nate advised and stepped into the cabin. He drew the papers out of a drawer and handed them to the Lt. He examined them for a couple minutes before handing them back.

"They are in order. Now we must search for contraband," he said. With this, he signaled a couple of his men to come aboard. They landed on deck and began searching under everything. They found a 30-30 rifle and handed them to the Lt. before going below to search the quarters.

"What is this for?" asked the Lt. Holding up the rifle.

"Sharks," came the answer.

"Good, is that the only weapon you have on board?" he asked.

"No, we have a couple pistols for protection and a spear gun. We skin dive and take pictures when the fishing is poor. The spear gun also is for sharks," Nate told him.

The Lt. yelled to the men in the cabin and asked if they had found weapons. The answer from below was of two pistols and a spear gun.

"Leave them, I know about them and hurry up, we must search the other one," he finished and the two men came up on deck and returned to their boat.

"That your boat over their fishing," asked the Lt.

"Yeah, hey what the hell is going on? We are outside the three-mile limit in international waters. Our papers are in order. What are you looking for," Nate demanded.

"Please excuse the search but in these water we sometime find criminals bringing in guns and running dope through our ports. We prefer to stop them before they reach land. Once they land, they disappear like rats. We search every boat we find. It is true you are in international waters and you may file a complaint. Our intention is good and saves Panama much trouble. Thank you for your understanding," he said as he returned to his boat. The rope was untied and his boat moved away. It headed straight for the other fishing trawler. Nate grabbed for the phone.

"Delbert, Panamain military coming your way. They will search your boat. Don't resist. They're looking for drug dealers. We want them on our side if we ever have to make a run for it," Nate spoke into it when Delbert answered.

"Sure, boss, I've been watching them go over your boat. Don't worry, I'd never resist unless you told me to," came Delbert's reply.

A few minutes later to the searches were over and the anglers went back to fishing. Fishing was decent and they had a quarter of their holds filled. It was a little pass noon and Nate told them the would head into a port in Panama. They reved up their engines and headed west.

An hour later, they were crusing along Panama. They found a small town and a small dock. They pulled in and tied up their boats. Leaving the boats and going onto the dock and old man approached them.

"Senors, the fee for tieing up here. How long will you be here?" he said to the group.

"An hour or more. We are hungry and wish to get food and a drink. Can we do this here?" Nate explained surprised at the fact the man spoke perfect English.

"Si, that will be three American dollars," the old man said holding out his hand.

Nate dropped three silver dollars into the man's hand. The man dropped the coins into his pocket and pointed to a white building about a hundred yards away.

"The saloon is there. The food is good and the drinks strong," he said. He then turned and walked away, entering an old shack off to their left.

They walked the distance and entered the saloon. It was an old, but clean establishment. The tables were made of driftwood. The bar was a long plank that had to belong to a ship back in the days of wooden ships. There were three men seated towards the rear playing cards. They looked up at the strangers then went back to their card game. A big fat man stood behind the bar. They took a table near the bar and the fat man walked over and asked for their order.

They ordered cold beer and each an order of chili beans. He nodded and walks around the end of the bar and through a door. He came back out of the kitchen and went to a beer spicket and began fill huge beer mugs. They were foamy and icey, just right for drinking.

He placed the mugs on the table in front of each man before going back to the bar.

Each man picked up the beers and drank until the mugs were empty. They waved at the bartender for more and soon had a fresh supply. Five minutes later a fat woman came our of the kitchen carrying food. She placed a pot of chili in the center of the table. She tossed a loaf of bread and a bowl of crackers on the table. She waddled back to the kitchen and returned with a stack of bowls and spoons. This she sat on the table next to the pot of chili before returning to the kitchen.

Hungry, the men dug in and were soon feeling better. It seemed a long time since they had eaten and the chili tasted oh so good. It was hot, filled with onions and peppers.

An hour later, they left the bar and walked back to their boats. Once on board Nate told them his plan to go out twenty-five miles and at dark the nets would be pulled in and they would eat their evening meal and wait for the sailing schooner. It would be well lit and they should have not trouble finding it. Lighted, as it would be, it would be seen at a distance of five miles if the sea were calm.

The fishing was slow and no one really had much interest in the quest for fish. They were on the hunt for much bigger game and were getting edging. The waiting was a killer and no fighting man liked the waiting. It had long been said in the military that it was a hurry up and wait game. Who ever first coined this phrase knew what he was saying. They were montoring the radio for chatter from boats in the area. All the men were huddled around the radio as the sun sat. Darkness fell quickly as it does in the tropics.

Finally, about two hours after dark they picked up chatter from a couple of new voices and call signs.

Nate looked at Ed and Brad and smiled.

"That's them. If I understand what they're saying, they are headed for the part of the Tucatan Peninsula that's closest to Cuba. They'll stay close to shore, but not too close. They seem to be saying that Jamaican Pirates could be the raiders. So they are staying as far away from Jamaica as possible. That's good for us," he said.

More chatter coming and he listened intently. Finally, he spoke to the other two.

"They say they'll be staying exactly twenty miles out to sea along the coast of Belize. Once they reach the peak of the Pennisula, they'll make a run straight across to Cuba. They'll be running in radio silence from now on until it's time to cut and run for Cuba," Nate was pleased with this new information. He reached for the phone and called Delbert.

This was going to be easy getting close to their target. They will just anchor and wait for the right time. Nate tried to determine the approximate time they would in range. His best guess was two hours. They sat back and had a drink. They talked about home and the job they were doing. They were all a little home sick but proud of the job they were doing on the cartels. The time dragged and it seems forever before Nate's phone rang. Delbert was on the other end.

"Look south boss and you'll see a light. As it rises and falls it, seem to be lit up like a Christmas tree. It's got to be it. I'm getting into my gear. In just a few minutes it will be in range," he reported to Nate.

Nate checked it out with his glasses and recognized what Delbert had told him. Damn he was right. Time for action.

"Delbert, make sure no one lights a cigarette and keeps quiet. Sound travels some distance across water. No engine sounds. I'll be going with you and so will Brad. We need three charges for this baby to go down quickly. Bring Carl with you. He'll have to go on board and disable their radio if he can. If he's spoted tell him to throw a charge into the wheelhouse and get the hell off," Nate ordered.

Not wanting to take any chances at letting this one get away, he slipped into the water and swam in the direction the schooner was heading. This would be an endurence challenge for him and the others. A long swim would be tiring with little left when the target was in place. By leaving now, he hoped to get a couple minutes rest before having to dive under the boat and placing charges. On this type of vessel, there were no handholds. It was a slick bottom schooner.

They would have to hurry and set the charges while it was moving. *Oh, well,* he thought, *this is what they were trained for.*

Twenty minutes later, he was in place. It was so dark he couldn't see if Delbert and Carl were nearing the spot. Of course, they were a little closer on the East side of the craft and their swim would not be quite as long. If they had swam straight across from their boat to where the schooner was heading, they may already be setting their charges and Carl posied to go aboard and do the radio. Nate knew Carl could handle it. He was small and wirely, able to move across the deck in record time if he had to. This was one of those times when he had to. The schooner was coming on and Nate saw that the crew was using spotlights on the water. They weren't taking any chances of being boarded that were for sure.

Nate dove deep under the ship and bumped into Delbert. God it was dark. It causes both men to smile as they went to work. Nate was in place and mounted his charge. Once done, he swam out from under the ship in time to see Carl go over the side and onto the deck. He said a little prayer for the man.

Carl, seeing his chance to board the vessel took it. A rope dangled over the side, just barely in reach. He grabbed it and pulled himself up onto the ship. He looked over the side to see if anyone was on the deck in his area. Seeing none, most were up front working the lights; he slipped onto the deck and raced for the wheelhouse. As he was in front of the door, which was open, he saw the man steering the boat. He was gripping the wheel and looking straight ahead.

Carl coughed to get the man's attention. When the man turned, he realized the danger and reached for a pistol in his belt.

With one shot to the forehead, Carl shot him dead. He then fired five shots into the radio, and then turned to run. At this moment, he feared for his life. Just coming around the wheelhouse, was a man carrying a rifle. He had seen Carl first and had the rifle at his shoulder. Carl saw the flame leap from the barrel and fired his pistol, except it was empty. The hammer went click as a burning pain shot through his side.

Carl knew he had to get into the water and off the ship. He made it to the edge of the deck and as the ship rolled gently downward on this side. He slid into the ocean and was out of sight. The men on deck were running about and yelling. There was mass confusion. Carl had felt the jolt of the explosions before he was able to escape. He hit the water and fought to stay on the surface. In his struggle, he failed to see Nate come up behind him.

Nate grabbed Carl by his air tank.

"Calm down, Carl, I have you. Delbert will be here shortly and our boats are coming we'll have you in you sack in no time. How's the bleeding, can you tell?" Nate asked.

Not too bad, but it hurts like hell. I could use a drink of whisky right now," both men laughed and the smart remark.

Delbert arrived to help and soon the fishing boats were along side. Everyone had forgot about the schooner because of his wounded companion.

By the time they were all on board the schooner was gone. Three men were in the water and swimming towards them. Ed was the first to spot them and yelled at Nate.

"What do we do with the ones in the water, Nate?" he asked.

Nate turned his attention to this new problem.

"You take care of Carl. Delbert you and your crew get back to your boat and get the hell out of here. We'll be right behind you and we'll keep Carl with us," Nate said then turning to Ed.

"Fire a few shot in the water in front of them, then get us out of here. We'll head for the Penninsula but we can't go until we do something about those in the water."

No sooner were the words out of his mouth than he saw the sharks. There must have been twenty of them. Nate thought he saw a great white in the group. The problem was out of their hands. The sharks were taking care of the problem. Nate's crew could not have saved them anyway. The sharks were much faster and soon there were no one to be seen in the water. There was nothing to show except a bloody froth on the surface where the men had been.

"Hit it Ed, let's go. Nothing more we can do here. Open it up for a few miles. We need to put space between us and this place," as he finished he felt the boat set down in the water as it speeded up.

They put on fifteen miles, when Nate changed his mind. He picked up the phone and dialed Delbert.

"Set your course for Jamaica, Delbert at high speed. We'll put up there for a couple days. We'll go ashore and be seen. All hell will be to pay now. Cuba will send gun ships to escort the drug dealers from Colombia to Cuba. We'll rest and try to form a plan that we can work off of. See you in Jamaica. Let me know how bad Carl's been hit. We may get him some medical care when we reach Jamaica," Nate instructed.

"A ready know about Carl. We cleaned the wound and the bullet just barely hit him. It passed through his body at the right edge and was only about two inches in. It was a little bloody be we've stopped that and plugged the hole. No vitals were hit and he's sitting up. He'll be fine in a few days. A little stiff in his movements, that's all," Delbert told Nate.

"Ok, we'll lay off the coast and get some sleep at about five miles out. Ok," Nate said.

"Check," came the answer and that completed the call.

Nate dialed again.

"Brown's Realty, how can I help you?" said the General.

"Hello, General. I'm checking to tell you we've sent another to the deep and about six men with her. This is getting a little tricky but so far so good. We're cutting down on the people in the cartels. Of course, that's not a problem. There must be hundreds waiting for a job with them. Anything new on your end, sir?" asked Nate.

"Yeah, all hell's loose on the streets. Not only has the price for a fix gone out of sight, but also seems to not be any for sale. You people are doing great. God, I wish I could be there with you. I'm damn tired of desk duty and would like to be back in the action. Be careful Nate. When that ship doesn't reach Cuba, we have good information that Cuba is sending gun ships as escorts. Maybe it's time we brought you home," responded the General.

"No, hell no, if we can just get another month and have the luck with us, their supply will be gone. I'll bet they have the farmers and workers processing the junk working overtime. They can't have a hell of a lot left in storage, so lets try for it all?" Nate said.

"Well it's up to you and it's your neck, but don't wait too long. How do your men feel about it?" he was asked.

"Hell, they're just getting interested. They wouldn't want to quit now. We're too close to making a real difference. Just imagine the lives we may be saving by staying. I'll let you know when we're ready," Nate replied.

"Ok, I'll bank your money. Good luck and pass my thanks to your men," the General's last words as he hung up.

A little before sunrise, they anchored off the Jamaica and crashed. It had been a long night and they needed to sleep.

The anglers began to stir, just before noon by the driven force of hunger. Ed was the first up and made the coffee. He yelled across to Delbert's boat to get the men there started for the day.

Once everyone was up, it was decided that they'd have breakfast on shore.

The sailed into the Jamaician port and tied up. They all piled onto the docks and started for town. A man in some sort of military uniform approached them.

He spoke to them in English.

"Americans, you must pay to tie up here, ten American dollars a day for each boat," he said and held out his hand.

Nate dug into his pocket and pulled out a twenty. He passed it to the man, and then asked a question.

"Is there a good place to eat near by? We're starved. We slept just off shore last night and could use a couple days ashore."

"Si, just one block up that street is a nice little place, good food and cheap," came the reply. With this, the man turned away and started walking along the docks. It was a small area with only four places for boats to tie up in this sleepy little village.

The crew walked to the restaurant and entered. The door squeaked telling everyone who entered here that it was getting old and not oiled often. There were three booths along the windows and a counter that would accommodate ten people. You could smell food cooking in the rear as you entered. Just the smell of food made their bellies growl, wanting to be fed.

A tidy woman in her forties was working behind the counter. She was neat and clean and her hair was well kept. It was piled on top of her head with a long stick through it. She had on a clean apron indicating the food would be good and worth a try. It was far from a greasey spoon.

"Good morning," she addressed them as they walked in and to the booths. "Would you like coffee?" she asked them without coming out from behind the counter. She spoke perfect English, which was always a surprise in this part of the world. The globe was getting smaller every day.

"Yes, and lots of it," a couple of the men replied.

She turned around and picked up a tray on which she put six coffee cups. She then placed a coffee pot on it and came to the booths. In front of each man, she placed a cup and when completed with this little chore, she filled each with coffee. The men were spread out into two of the booths, so she placed the coffee pot on the table of one and hurried back behind the counter. She quickly returned with another pot, placing it at the second booth.

The men had found the menus and were anxious to order. She took each order and returned behind the counter. She went through a door into the kitchen. She came right back and put on another pot of coffee. Finished with ths she took napkins and tableware to the booths.

"Just set them on the table and we'll pass them around," Nate said referring to the silverware and napkins.

She did as he directed and she returned to the counter. There were two men sitting there and she refilled their coffee cups before disappearing into the kitchen.

The breakfast was served family style with eggs on one platter and steaks on another. The server returned to the kitchen and brought back two more platters. One was pile with hash brown potatos and the other held steaks. This often was the way food was served in this part of the world.

The men dug in as though they hadn't eaten for weeks. Soon the food had disappeared and they all leaned back and sipped coffee. Each pulled out a Cuban cigar and began puffing away.

An hour later, they got up and slowly walked for the door. Nate stopped at the counter and asks for the bill. It came to twelve dollars and ninety-five cents. Nate handed her a twenty and told her to keep the change.

"Thank you senor, please come again," she called after him.

They entered the street and walked towards the center of town. It was a small town with a few old cars running about and one cantina. The building were dilapidated and run down. Even the houses looked very old and tired. They showed damage from the winds that come with storms and violent rains. In places, patches showed in the roofs where they once leaked. Poverty showed everywhere. The main street was three blocks long. The street was in need of repair but this was a town without money. Just to make a living must have been a chore. They heard music coming from the cantina and now they were full, a drink sounded good.

Nate was considering what they could do to bring attention to themselves and maybe get arrested. They need to leave this place with everyone in town knowing they were there. If done right they would not be suspects in the boat disappearances.

They entered the cantina and stepped up to the bar. It was a bar like the old west had in old saloons in movies. They felt right at home. With one foot and the railing, they ordered whisky. All six through the firey liquid down their throats and sat the glasses back on the bar, the cantina bartender refilled the glasses and left the bottle. This bartender was a big man with coal black hair and a fat stomach. He appeared to be about fifty. He had on jeans, a white shirt and a black vest. He looked like he could handle any problem that came up.

They drank for a couple hours, but were careful with their talk. No mention was made about their mission. The talk was about the old days in the U.S. and fishing. As men usually do, the conversation turned to women.

The bartender, hearing this talk came over to the table with a fresh bottle of whisky.

"You men like to have a woman?" he asked.

The men looked at each other, all thinking the same thing. *The only women we've seen, we sure don't want one of them. They're all fat and not very good looking. Older looking made that way by their hard life.*

"That would be nice," said Brad, "but not the old broads we've seen so far."

"Oh, no senior, beautiful women that needs the money to live. For a five each, I can put you in touch with some. I think I can find six that would keep you men company till morning. You have rooms?" he ploughed on.

"No, we sleep on the boats. Do you have a hotel in this town?" Carl piped up.

"These women are women of class, but have fallen on hard times. They share a big house together. Interested?" he advised.

"What would be the cost for their company?" Delbert asked. It was quite apparent the men wanted some action.

"For the night, $25.00 each." came the answer.

The men looked at each other. Some with a puzzled look and some with an eager, excited look. They were quiet for a while. The bartender stood at the table waiting for an answer.

"Yeah, why not," said Ed, "we need something to make life more interesting. If they are our cup of tea, then we can always come back on other trips."

"You guys go ahead, I'll stay here and stay with the boats. It's my turn. Besides I've got more women than I can handle now," Nate said, "tomorrow we fish. Soon we will be back in Colombia. I'll wait till then."

"Ok, make the arrangements," Delbert said. He dug into his pocket and pulled out some cash. He handed the bartender a twenty and a ten. He told him to keep the five in change.

The bartender went to the ancient telephone on the back wall and cranked the handle. He spoke in low tones for two or three minutes before hanging up. He returned to the table.

"Go up this street to the end. There you will find a huge two-story house. The women will be waiting. They ask that you bring a couple bottles of whisky or rum. If you put up another fifteen dollars, they will cook for you. Both the evening meal and breakfast. I can sell you the booze. You can pay when you are ready," he finished.

After a whisky and some lighthearted talk, the people got up to leave. They told the bartender to put out a couple of bottles of whisky and a couple of rum. They all dug down and came up with the money. They paid and bid Nate so long. However, he spoke up.

"Don't forget to be at the boats by six AM. We go out to fill our boats with fish. I'll be at the place where we ate breakfast at five AM. Don't be late," he reminded them.

Nate sat on deck under a wonderful Jamaican night. The moon was full and it was 72 degrees. Not a cloud in the sky and he was very comfortable in his thoughts. He could only imagine what was taking place in the big house up the street. He didn't care either. His thoughts were somewhat mixed. He was confused with his feelings about Loretta. Katrina was nice and great in bed as was Loretta. He felt like a teenager when with Loretta. His feelings fought the idea of getting serious over her. He loved being single and his life style, but she could and does make him feel complete. Plus he just couldn't get her off her mind. She was always there.

About an hour later, he was near to dozing off when he felt someone coming. He jerk awake and grabbed his pistol. Looking forward he saw a petite woman was coming onboard. As she got close, he called to her.

"I'm back here. Who are you and what do you want?" he challenged.

She kept coming his way, a little uneasy on feet. He could tell she had never been on a boat before. He looked her over now that she was near. She was an attractive woman of about thirty years of age. Coal black hair and dark skin. He assumed she was Jamaican.

"Mr. Nate, is that you," she said in answer to his question. She continued, "I've come to talk and keep you company for a while. I'm one of the women from the house where your crew are visiting tonight. No man came to see me, so I came down to you. I'm just here to talk and not for sex unless you want to."

"No, I don't want sex," he said, "but you can stay and talk for awhile if you wish," he lowered his pistol and relaxed.

For an hour, they sat and talked. He provided the whisky and he learned she had been married in Kingston, but was abused. She divorced him and moved out to this quiet little town. She told of being bored and was thinking of going back if she could find a job. He was a good listener and did enjoy her company. She finally excused herself and said "goodnight" and left the boat. She disappeared into the darkness. Nate felt sorry for her. Here was a lovely, lonely woman wasting her time in this place. It was an escape to nowhere for a woman.

About then he heard laughter coming down the gravel road. He assumed it was his crew coming home. Seconds later, they came into view. They were joking and pushing each other around. Apparent all had a good time and were coming home to roast. Nate flipped his cigar overboard and greeted them.

"Well, it looks like your little trip to town paid off. Your in good spirits and ready for a work out tomorrow. Get some sleep. We'll be on the water by six AM." he said laughing as he went below. In ten minutes, it was quiet except for some snoring.

As usual, the sun came up just as the crew was heading out to sea. This time they were looking for fish and really, need to catch more so as to convince anyone who came nosing around, that they had been fishing.

Just as they were spreading their nets around a school, the phone rang. Nate was quick to answer it.

"Nate, is that you," the voice of the General coming across the line.

"Yeah, it me, General, what's up," Nate answered.

"Where are you right now," the General asked.

"About thirty miles southwest of Jamaica. Why do you ask?"

"Cuban gun boats are searching the area where your last target went down. They've found some floating debris and know something happened to the vessel you sank. They and the Colombians are mad as hell. We've been montoring radio transmissions and it looks like the fats in the fire. They're out for blood. I hope to hell you have an albi other that just fishing. They may not buy that anymore. They're stopping every boat in the area. I don't think they'll come that far, but you never know. Get out anytime you want. We've hurt the bastards and hurt them bad. The east coast and Florida are damn near dry. If they catch you my boy, they surely will kill you and it won't be pretty. Remember Nate a wise man knows when to run. Just let me know when and we'll get you out. Don't forget Katrina," he finished saying.

"Don't worry we won't and thank for the tip. I'll be seeing you one of theses days. Just stay close to the phone. We're going to start blowing the bastards up right in the harbor," he chuckled as he hung up. He knew this would bother the General, who was becoming like a mother hen over a brood of chicks.

The nets showed signs of filling up and were being pulled up. The school of fish they gotten was a big one and with luck both boats would have a full load in a couple of hours.

They worked hard and fast and Nate had informed them of the General's conversation. These were men who enjoyed danger and for the three years they'd spent in Viet Nam, they became accustomed to it. The word that the Cubans were now into the action, they became even more eager to to destroy the drug trade. They began singing as they worked.

The nets had provided them with a nice catch. Their holds were full and Nate decided that was enough and they headed for Colombia at high speed and what ever awaits them there. Either way, they were in high spirits.

-9-

It was after dark when they pulled up to the packing plant. Loretta's uncle was just closing up. He saw Nate coming in and opened up. He ran up to stop a couple of his men to help unload. They got out the buckets, hooked them onto the cables and began unloading fish.

As this was being done, he went ashore and stopped to talk to the old man. The old man was grinning from ear to ear over the amount of fish. Nate offered him a Cuban cigar, which was gladly received.

"Well, old man, this will keep you busy a couple days. Say do me a favor and sent a batch to Loretta's place for me. No charge. Ok.

The old man just grinned and answered "Si."

Nate lit up and just started puffing when a jeep came around the corner, of the street. Four soldiers jumped out and the Lt. with them ordered the boats be searched.

"What's going on Lt," Nate asked.

"My superiors ordered me to do this senor. There's been some trouble up north and every ship, boat and barge are to be inspected, coming or going," he explained.

"No problem, Lt., relax and have a cigar," Nate said and handed him a Cuban.

Several minutes later, the search was over and the soldiers left, having found nothing. The Lt. waved as he left and was shaking his head. Nate took the head shaking as he was thinking how ridiculous it was to continue searching the same boats over and over again.

At one o'clock in the morning, Nate was knocking at the Katrina's door. The door opened just a crack, then wider as she saw who it was.

"Hi," Nate said as he entered the house. The door closed behind him as he seated himself on the couch.

Katrina was dressed in her nightgown and appeared about ready to turn in for the night.

"Hi," she said as if she was a little surprised. "This a business visit or for pleasure," she jokingly said.

"Business and I need to tell you something," he replied. The General advises that Cubans are sending gun ships down here to escort the drug vessels all the way to Cuba. You've got to be careful. If they ever find out you have been giving us the information to destroy these bastards, you're dead. Be careful how you get the information. We're being searched every time we come into port. So far so good and I hope to keep it that way. You should know that we are going to blow up at least one right here in the harbor."

"I was going to warn you about the gunships. I heard some of the dealers talking tonight about it. They will be here in three days. They'll anchor off shore, beyond the three-mile limit and wait for the ships to come out. This way the Colombians won't know about it. Some people in government would like to clean out the drug mess, so this must be kept secret from them.

"Do you know what kind of ships they'll have hauling the stuff this time?" he asked her.

"Yeah, they have a tug boat and two fishing boats like yours. They are going to pile on all the drugs they can get on because they have little in storage. After this trip, they have to wait until more can be prepared for shipments. I understand they have the farmers working overtime to process the junk. It may be a month before they'll have enough for another shipment. Getting this group is urgent. They will be armed to the teeth and so Nate, my friend, you had better be careful. Now tell me why blow up one in the harbor. I don't understand that at all.

"Well the way I figure this is if we can do that, then it will convince that a rival gang is trying to move in on them. They are already suspicious of Jamaican pirates stealing their ships. Maybe they will keep that suspicion. Anyway, it will be a challenge and will never suspect it's us. Not only will we blow up a ship, we'll dive down and cut open the bags so no one can retrieve them. It may kill a few fish with that much dope in the water but it'll serve its purpose," Nate told her.

"Ok, that's your decision. I hope it doesn't backfire on you. Don't worry about me. The bartender/owner protects me. He thinks someday I'll be so grateful he'll get into my pants. I got news for him. I hope we can get this job done so we can get the hell out of here soon," she replied.

"I think you need to start taking a walk down along the docks. Do it daily and say it's for excerise. Do it during the day, everyday so everyone sees you. That way if we need to get the hell out fast, we will try to get you during your walks. Give me an idea when you will and stick to the time. I would suggest around one PM. Don't stop at our boat, just walk on by. Someone maybe watching and we must assume so. Sound alright to you?" he questioned.

"I can do that. I'm up by then and the fresh air will do me good. Sure, I'll do that. I'll have more information after you get this next three. God, I hope you can do it. If they are the last three we ever get it'll be good and our work will have a success," she stated.

He took her in his arms and kissed her hard. This was returned with interest.

"I don't have time to fool around tonight. I've got to get back," he said in a whisper.

She pulled away before she spoke.

"I couldn't anyway, it's the wrong time of the month. But next time should be good to go," she said.

He smiled and slipped out the back door. She quickly closed it behind him and went to bed.

Nate decided to stay in town the next day. The three boats posed a problem even without the gunboats. It would take every man and all their strength to pull this one off. His thoughts drifted back to the idea of sinking a boat in the harbor. They would have to pay attention to what boats were being loaded. They would all be docked together, he was willing to bet. Should be easy to spot. The loads will be coming out of the jungle, so the trucks would have mud on them. That alone would give them away. He'd tell the men to be watchful. The single man we have watching the boats could do this for them. He was sure the men would want to go to town. Their little experience in Jamaica would whet their appetite. *You couldn't blame them,* he thought, *they work hard and may die before this mission was over so why not live a little.*

It was about four o'clock the following afternoon that Nate calls all his crew together for an announcement.

"I'm going to Loretta's tonight and suggest we all go together. We'll get a table in the back, close to the dancing area and decide what we can do to about the fortilla of boats leaving in two more days. Be thinking about ideas and we will compare notes tonight. Does everyone have enough money in there or do we need to go past the bank and make a withdrawal?" he asked.

All agreed they should go to the bank and get some money. They all washed and combed their hair, put on clean clothes and were ready by four thirty. They knew the bank closed at five.

Cabs were called and they went to the bank where they had opened an account after their first catch. Nate and Delbert went inside to make a withdrawal of funds.

They walked up to the teller window and Nate presented a slip for $5000.00. The teller looked at him and excuses herself. She took the slip back to the bank manager. He looked at the slip, then at the two men.

The teller came back and asked them to see the manager, a Mr. Garcia.

"Hello," Nate said and shook hands with the man. Garcia was a halfbreed. Part Colombian and half-American of the white persuasion. He spoke good English and required all his employees' do the same, except when dealing with those who spoke only Spanish.

"May I ask why you need this much money?" asked Garcia.

"What's the problem," Nate asked, "we have a lot more than this in the account. I don't understand why you need to know this."

"We are going out on the town tonight and want to be sure we have enough money. Also, this will get us by for the next month for pleasure, shear pleasure. You may come with us if you wish," Nate told him.

"Oh, no senior, I don't want to go with you. You must excuse me for asking but the military has frozen all accounts. Withdraws may be made but not large ones. If you ask me, they are getting paranoid about missing boats these past few months. Let me mark this, as operating cost for your fishing boats, then no questions will be asked. I must report this amount to them. You understand, sir," Garcia stated.

"That will be fine," Nate agreed.

Garcia motioned the teller back over and told her to get the money from the vault. She obeyed and soon came back with the cash. Garcia swallowed hard at the idea these men were going to spend that kind of money for a night on the town. Nate thanked him and they left the office.

Once outside, Nate gave each man a thousand dollars and advised them the balance from their fishing days was $210,000.00. Garcia was watching out the window with keen interest. As a bank manager, his entire salary was not as much as these anglers had withdrawn. He went back to his desk and thought what he could do with that kind of money. *American dollars go a long ways down here*, he was thinking.

A cab ride and they were at Loretta's club. Nate led the way in and to a table back in the corner, yet fairly close to the dance floor. On their way back, Nate waved at the bartender. The greeting was returned.

Soon a server appeared and took their drink orders. Nate asked if she would also bring a menu, as they would be eating later on. The drinks were served and menus deposited on the table. All the men had ordered beer to start with. The glasses were frosty and the beer foamy.

It was quiet in the place. It was early yet. The crowds would come in, in an hour or so. This being a weekday it wouldn't be crowded. It was the same as back home in America. People just don't go out as much on workdays as the did on weekends.

"Ok. People I need your input and ideas on how we can take out two boats when Cubans was escorting them gun ships. They are sending two down to escort the drug boats. Castro is just as greedy as the cartels, so he's decided to get involved. It's going to get exciting boys. Anyone wants to cut out and go home may do so. I'm staying and doing my best to destroy the cartels.

"Hey, we're not going anywhere without you boss. We're a team and we'll stay that way. Right boys?" Ed questioned the crew.

"Damn rights," piped up Carl, "we're staying until we all leave together."

Everyone else agreed and asked what Nate might have in mind.

"Well, first we're going to blow up one the son-of-bitches, right out of the water right at the docks. I figured this would make them think that another gang is out to get them. This might take their attention away from the sea. We'll take four of our explosion devices and make one. I know how and we'll plant it under the boat. The boat will blow with such force that they'll think someone planted one on board. Hopefully the suspicion changes to someone on land," he said.

"God damn, this is going to be fun," sighed Delbert.

"At last some real action," stated Brad.

"Now tell me how we get to the other two out on the sea, with two Cuban gun ships escorting them?" asked Nate.

"Same way we did in Nam. Set up a diversion. Divide and conquer. Remember, it worked every time. One of us would fire a few rounds off to one side, and then some of the gooks would come to see what was going on. We then jumped the remainer and killed them. They never caught on. Why not use the same method," Carl finishing his remarks.

Ed slapped him on the back then spoke.

"Damn that's it, it will work. Carl you're a genius. The sticky part is getting in close enough to plant the charges. Any ideas on that point," he asked.

"If we can get one of the guns boats away for just a few minutes, it could be done. Another way would be to rig a timing device and plant the charges in port and set the timers for a couple hours. They go off to sea and suddenly disappear right before the eyes of the Cubans," Nate surmised. He continued, "Trouble with that is we don't have the time to run over to Panama and get the devices from the Col. the General would see to it if only we had time. We don't, so what else."

Silence fell over the table like a curtain being drawn to shut out the light. The server had returned for their re-order.

"Beer all around again," Ed said to her.

The men were quiet until the beer arrived and they were again alone. People were starting to come in, but none chose to sit near them.

"I think I know how we can do it. My mention of the General brought something to mind. We'll do the diversion and hope we have enough time. Hopefully they won't be too suspicious of fishing boats. The main problem is finding them. We'll do the after dark thing and hope it works. I'll call the General and have him get us some satelite time. The satelite zooms in on them and we follow to a point where we have the advantage. That's what we'll do. Now lets all relax and have fun. Tomorrow we go to sea after we blow the one at the docks. Hopefully it will be loaded by morning. Don should know after we get back. Guarding the boats, he should see what goes on at the docks. You boys ask him when you get back, I'm spending the night and here she comes now," Nate finshed just in time to stand up and greet Loretta to the table.

He introduced her around and pulled out a chair for her. She sat down next to Nate and waited for the conversation began. The wait was not long and it seemed all five jumped in at once to ask her about the picture of her on the wall. She explained it just as she had told Nate when he first saw it. The server came over and placed a drink in front of her.

"Drinks all around for the table, on the house," she said.

"Yes, miss," the server said and took the orders from the men. Two continued on beer and the rest switched to whisky.

The place was starting to fill up. The men looked around in an attempt to locate single women. The search didn't take long. Carl and Delbert excused themselves and went off to find company. Two lovely women were sitting alone and they moved in. They started a conversation and soon they were invited to sit down. Nate smiled at them and their approach. He knew they would be on the dance floor when the music started. But it was early yet and they hadn't eaten.

"We're about to have dinner. Would you like to join us?" Nate asked Loretta.

"That would be nice," she said, "yes, I would. Let me order for you. I'll order the fish you had uncle send over. It will be done in a very special way with a cream sauce, with a hint of garlic and horseradish. You'll love it."

Ed, Brad, and Nate agreed to let her order. She raised her arm and caught the bartender's attention. He nodded and sent the server right over.

"Tell the chef we'll have the fish with the cream sauce and all the trimmings as I discussed with him today. For dessert, we'll have the cake with ice cream with the brandy syrup over it.

"Si," replied the server replied and move away to fill the order.

Twenty minutes later the four was digging into the fish, boiled carrots, with the little onions and sugar peas. There were hot rolls with butter. A green salad was also served. The server had to make three trips to the kitchen to carry the food out to them.

All were hungry and there was little talking except to comment on the delicious food. The men had two servings of the fish. The meal was followed with hot coffee, spiked with brandy.

Finally, after the ice cream, they pushed back their plates and polished off the coffee.

"That was delicious," Nate, said, "I'll have to eat here more often," he smilingly said as he winked at Loretta.

The music had started and the crew had drifted off to dance with the women.

Nate stood up at the start of a slow song, bowed at the waist and spoke to his woman.

"Would you care to dance my dear?" extending his hand.

"Why yes, how could I say no to such a galant young man and cute invitation," she said as she took his hand and rose up from the chair.

He led them to the dance floor and taking a firm grip around her waist guided them across the floor. They said not a word and seemed oblivious to the other dancers.

The dance ended far too soon for this couple. They stayed frozen to the floor until the next one started. It to was a slow piece. The band had noticed their boss dancing and how she preferred the slow dances. They also saw the way she danced with this stranger and felt obligated to please. This angler seemed to have gotten her interest and this was new for her.

A few minutes later, they were back at the table. One of the men had returned and was sipping a whisky. Brad greeted them and stood as the woman was seated.

"You two make a handsome couple. You dance well together. I'm still looking for one who can dodge my feet," Brad said.

All three laughed at his comment. Loretta waved a server over and ordered a round of drinks.

"This round is on the house," she told her. The woman smiled and moved away to fill the order.

Ed came over and told Nate he and Carl were with a couple women and would find their way home by themselves. Nate nodded in agreement.

The music started again and Brad off to find a woman. It was a fast country rock piece. The first woman Brad asked nodded yes and followed him onto the floor. Nate watched as the couple did their thing. They were both enjoying each other and Nate knew he was now on his own. That suited him just fine because before long he knew he'd be upstairs. He and Loretta danced a few more before he whispered in her ear.

"Let's get out of here and have a drink upstairs," he said.

"You must be reading my mind," she said and lead the way off the dance floor. He stopped at the bar and handed the bartender a hundred dollar bill. This is for my bill. Split the change between you and the server. The service was great.

Hand in hand, the two made their way to the apartment at the top of the stairs. Stepping through and closing the door behind them, they took each other into their arms. The kisses were passionate and lasting. Foreplay was not necessary. He picked her up in his arms and carried her into the bedroom. He tossed her on the bed, stopping to take off his shoes. Once this was done, he removed her shoes. She had started unbuttoning her blouse.

"No, don't do that. Half the fun is in undressing you. Let me do it," he said.

"Ok, I'm at your mercy and loving it," came her reply.

He gently removed her blouse, partly exposeing her breasts. He hesitated to kiss her and to plant one between her breasts.

"Ok, stand up so they come off easier," he mentioned.

With her standing, he again kissed her passionately. He unfastened her bra and released the beauties. They stood straight out and delighted to be free again. He threw the garment on the floor. Reaching up her gently rubbed his hands across the nipples and felt her quiver. He kissed each one and moved on. Her slid her dress down to the floor. She stepped out of it and waited. He kissed her bare belly as he pulled her panties off. She now stood naked before him.

He leaned back and looked at this beauty, standing before him. *"How did I ever get this lucky,"* he was thinking.

"You'd better hurry before I change my mind," she said laughingly. She moved around behind him a spread her body out on the bed.

He stood up and undressed laying down beside her. His hands felt all over her body as he kissed her passionately. She returned them with eager enthusiasm. Her hands examined his body with pleasure welling up inside her. She could wait no longer and told him to hurry.

Of course, his goal was to make love to the gorgeous woman and soon they were enjoying this very act.

Half and hour later, they rested and gave him time to recharge. They propped themselves up on the pillows and rested. Minutes later, she got up and went into the living room and returned with a glass of wine. She offered him one, which he took. The lay there side by side, talking and drinking the wine. By now, they both knew they were falling in love. Both were a little afraid to admit it, but it was always on their mind. They were aware of the impossible situation they were in. One was going back to his life in the U.S. and she was staying here. She would never consider moving to the states. Life was good except for the covert operation he was involved in. They were taking life as it came and were grateful for the time they had together.

Morning came and found the couple wrapped in each other's arms. They'd barely moved all night. Nate stirred first, being use to waking early. He eased out of bed and easing into a robe, went to the intercom to the kitchen. He ordered fresh fruit, fresh bread, hot coffee, before returning to the bedroom. He waited for the food delivery and assisted the workers in bring in the food cart. He unloaded the cart onto the table and sent the workers back downstairs.

He walked back to the bed where Loretta lay sleeping. He felt her stir, leaned over and kissed he on the cheek.

"Good morning, little one. Breakfast is on the table. If you don't hurry, I'll go ahead without you," he said with a big smile on his face.

She rolled over to look at him.

"You'd better not. If you do, I'll punish you by being hard to get. Ha Ha, that's fix you," she laughed and rose to sit up. Her bare breast seems to glisten. They raised and fell with her breathing. *What a beautiful sight,* Nate thought.

He leaned over and kissed each, then helps her from the bed, handing her a robe.

Nate arrived back at the boats around noon. All the crew was onboard. They were cleaning the decks and the living quarters. This was one of the advantages of having this crew. They did what was needed with out any squable over who does what. They worked as a team on everything. He was grateful he'd been blessed with them.

"Delbert, you take one of those underwater pictures up the street to the photo pace and have it blown up to a three foot by three foot. Have it framed and bring it back here. I need a rush job. I'm making out a list of supplies. If anyone wants anything special, write it down so I don't forget. I want to get all this done before late afternoon. We need to be out to sea by five PM," Nate addressed the crew. They jumped to it and within minutes, Nate had a completed list for supplies. Delbert had left on his errand. His was going to be the hard one to complete.

Nate called a cab and headed to the grocery store. Don accompanied him.

Delbert returned with the picture. It was of three fish, one red, one blue and a gold fish. The gold fish was the largest and was in the foreground. Some corral in one corner set it off as a beauty. The corral was white and some was black. Black corral is a rare verity in the oceans of the world.

"Great picture, Delbert. Give me the receipt. The army Lt. will love it. "I'm going there now. You gas up the boats and fill them with ice. I'll be back soon," Nate said then called for a cab. The rest of the crew pitched in and stored the supplies.

The cab arrived and Nate jumped aboard.

"Army headquaters," Nate told the cabbie as it speeded away.

About ten minutes later, they were at the destination. Nate left the cab, paid the cabbie and asked him to come back in twenty minutes. The cab driver agreed and said if he couldn't he'd send a different cab.

Inside the front door, a guard stopped him and spoke to him in English.

"Who do you wish to see, senor?" he was asked.

"I don't remember his name but he's the one searching boats for firearms," Nate replied and described the Lt. to him.

"Oh, si, I know him. Down the hall to the end. His office is the last door on the left," he told Nate glancing at the photo.

Nate walked down the hall to the office and entered. A fat older woman sat at a desk and looked up.

"I'm here to see the Lt.," Nate said.

"Si," she said, "wait here." Again, he was amazed with the number of people who spoke English. They must teach it in school.

The woman reappeared, with the Lt. Right behind her.

"Senor Armstrong, you came to confess," he said with a grin. Nate wasn't quite sure if this was a joke or if he was serious. He invited Nate in and closed the door behind them.

"Here, the picture I promised you. It was taken off the shore of Jamaica. It is beautiful and would look great on the walls of this office," Nate said.

The Lt. stiffened. His face turned red and his right hand dropped to his revolver.

"Sir, if this is a bribe, I could have you arrested. I cannot take gifts. It is not proper in our army. I don't know what you, in America, have heard but we don't accept bribes," he finished. His voice had risen and sounded with anger.

"No," Nate fired back, "you guided us to take under sea photos and you asked for one. No bribe because we have done nothing. You have searched us as have the Panama's Navy. We are poor humble anglers. That's all. If you don't want it, I'll take it back. I'm just honoring a promise. You can tell everyone I was from the photo shop. Here is the receipt. You can show it and prove you paid for it. It was for your office. No problem. Your senior officials should understand that."

The Lt. took the receipt and examined it. He examined the picture as through he thought a concealed mike may have been planted to easedrop on him. Finally, he smiled.

"Yes, now I remember I requested a nice picture. Thank you. Help me put it on the wall. Over here on this wall," he asked Nate. Nate breathed with relief. The picture was not a bribe but was a way to get on his good side. Perhaps making them above reproach. That was the hope for these poor anglers.

The wall had two nails driven into the wall. They were just about right for this picture. Nate took one end and the Lt. the other. They lifted the picture into place and stepped back.

They viewed the picture from across the room.

"Ah, it is beautiful," he stated and turned to Nate. "Thank you senor, I accept the picture in the manner it was intended. Honoring a promise."

"Good," Nate said, "come down to the boats for a ride sometime."

"Si, I may do that," came the reply.

With this, Nate left and found the cab waiting. He was taken back to the boats. Once back, he had everyone over to his boat. He passed around cigars and whisky so that it appeared they were having a party.

"Don, has informed me that those three boats down at the end of the dock has been loaded and are our targets for tonight. We are going to blow one out of the water right here in port. Keep your voices down and I'll explain. It's getting hot for us, even though they don't yet know whose doing what to the missing boats. There are two Cuban gunboats waiting outside the three-mile limit, in international waters. They will be escorting those three to Cuba. We'll be attacking those tonight. I figure if we get one in port, people will think it's a local gang trying to take over the drug trade. Don you have first crack at blowing that last one down there all to hell. Lets do it in the next thirty minutes. You want to do it Don? " Nate asked.

"Yeah, hell yes. Lets do it. Tell me how it should be done, boss," he said.

"Simple, take two charges of the c4 and blend it together. When you stick it to the boat, just place it in a blob. I'd place it where the engine's propellers come out of the boat. There's a little room there and it'll set off the fuel at the same time. Make sure you set the timer for, oh, thirty minutes. That should be enough time for you to get back here and to our party. You have to hurry back. The army will be here very soon after it blows. You must be here, dryed and dressed. Your tanks will also be dryed off. You can bet they'll search us. Sink the cans that the explosives come out of. They are just vegetable cans and if found should not raise suspicion," Nate explained.

"Got you boss," Don replied, "I'll get the tanks on, you fix the bomb."

"Ok, get ready. I'll get the c4," Nate said.

Both men went below, while the rest waited. All were excited and anxious to get the show on the road. Minutes later Nate reappeared with the glob of plastic explosives. Don came to the top of the steps and waited till the coast was clear. The men line up block the view from land. There were no ships at sea near by. Nate handed Don the bomb and told him to go. He was advised to swim under the docks as much as possible. Over the side, he went and disappeared from sight.

Don understood that by swimming under the dock, he would not be detected. If per chance he tried swimming out where the boats were tied up, some one might spot him. The water was so clear that someone shore or on a boat could easily see him. As he made his way over and under bridging for the pier, he could see many schools of fish of all colors.

When he came to a cross member that helped support the docks he would dive under and sometimes over them, if room permitted. He was glad to be on this mission. So far, his help had been minimal and he wished to do more.

Finally, he came to the boats and he saw the bottom of the first boat. By the looks of this, he knew it was a fishing trawler. Several feet beyond, he saw boat number two. It was a tug. He swam on to the boat number three tied up at the end of the pier.

Excitement was building inside him as he turned and swam under it, making his way to the rear where the shaft running the propellers was located. Reaching this goal he felt around where the shaft came out of the boat on which the propellers. He reached in far enough to feel the rubber flap that sealed it opening from the sea. He pulled out the explosive and began working it into this crack. He was able to compact it all the way again and some through the rubber flap. It was compacted so tight that he knew it would make a big bang when it went off.

He pulled out a thirty-minute fuse and rammed it into the explosive. He looked around to make sure the coast was clear before he pulled the fuse. That takes care of the rest.

Turning he swam like hell to get out of there. He swam under the two-moored next to the target. In his haste he'd was swimming west and not back under the docks. He changed directions and in a couple of seconds, he was back under and out of sight of prying eyes. He breathed easier, but not slowing down. He had to be back on the boat before it blew. He was sure he had plenty of time, but was still eager to get out of the water. *A good shot of whisky would taste good right now*, he thought, *and maybe a cigar.*

The men sat around smoking the cigars. Occasionally they sipped whisky but mostly for show. No one wants to be drunk because of the work they had to do tonight.

Nate picked up the phone and dialed the Brown's Realty number.

"Hello," came across the wire.

"General, I need a favor. I need you to get time on a satellite and track four boats tonight for me. You need to stay close to the phone. Our targets are going out tonight with tons of "coke" and we'll never find them without your help. They are running low on "coke" and this is a desperate attempt to get some through. Tonight, if we can pull it off, we'll put them out of business for a month or so. I'm sure the have the farmers working overtime to harvest and make more. This will take them some time. Can you do it? I need to know," Nate was talking fast. He wanted this call over before Don returned and the target exploded.

"Damn, Nate, that's damn short notice. I think I can. One of the men you met in Washington has some influence in this area. I'll call him and get to where we can observe the course of the boats. How soon do you need to know?" answered the General.

"In the next hour, if possible. We'll be going out to sea shortly and I'd like to know before dark," Nate said.

"Ok, I'll get back to you," he said and hung up.

Don was dressed and on deck just as she blew. The explosion was deafening. Everyone on the docks looked down towards the eastern end of the dock. Wood was flying everywhere. Then the fuel exploded and finished off the craft. From where they stood, it looked like thirty feet of the dock was also blown away.

"Maybe we used too much C4 boss. There's nothing left but small pieces of wood and some life jackets floating in the bay," Don exclaimed.

"No, we did not," Nate, said, "we used the right amount. Now you take a couple quick drinks. The army will be here soon. We must all smell like we had a party before going out to sea. If you're asked, Delbert, we're heading over towards Panama then up to Belize. Depends on the fishing. We'll be gone four or five days unless we get lucky with the fishing. Got it," Nate said.

"Yes, sir," came the reply.

About ten minutes later army jeeps rolled onto the docks. The anglers could see the Lt. Standing up in the first jeep, which was headed to the blast sight. Other army personel spread out, blocking off the entire dock area. They had rifles and looked as if they meant business. They took up positions and waited for the Lt.'s orders. They didn't have to wait long. He came back from the blast sight and ordered every boat be searched and everyone. If there was someone on the docks without business, they were to be arrested. Nate understood that much Spanish.

All the anglers were seated on the railing or equipment when the Lt. stopped in front of their boat. He dismounted and came aboard. When he was close enough, Nate spoke up.

"What the hell happened, Lt.," Nate asked as he forced himself not to smile.

"Some damn fool blew up the boat at the end of the dock. It was to be out of here tonight along with those other two," The Lt answered, pointing toward the explosion site.

"Son-of-a-bitch, it's getting deadly around here. Maybe we'd better move our operations to Panama. Might be safer," Nate seems concerned by smiling inside.

"No, senior I see no need for that. You seem trustworthly. I'll tell you what it is if you don't tell anyone. That goes for your crew too," the Lt. leaned forward and told them that it was because of the drug trade. It appeared to him a rival cartel was trying to take over a local operation. As long as they were fishing and not hauling drugs, they were told they were in no harm. He also informed them that the army was taking over the port and it would be closely guarded.

"Good, good," Nate said, "go ahead and search our boat if you wish. We are about ready to head over towards Panama and see how the fishing is there. If it's not good, then I intended to head up the shoreline to Belize and fish there a few days. Would that be advisable, Lt.," Nate asked.

"Si that would be fine. I'll just walk through your boat and pretend to search. Come below with me," he instructed.

Just as soon as they reached the point where Nate could look inside the cabin, his heart nearly stopped and his blood ran cold. In the space between the bunks was a flipper Don had used. It was wet. Nate put his hand on a knife that lies on the little table. He may have to kill the Lt. And make run for it.

As the officer reached it, he kicked it aside and said something about gringos being sloppy. Nate relaxed the grip on the knife and began breathing again.

"That's all," the officer who turned around and started up the steps. Nate followed.

On deck, the officer turned and shook Nate's hand.

"Good luck fishing. You may cast off anytime you wish. I am glad you were here when this happened. It now proves to me that we must look in our own country for the gangsters. Poor fish. The bags of cocaine were blown to pieces and that may kill many. But the tide will be in soon and carry the poison out to sea.

"Thanks, Lt.," Nate said, "we'll be casting off shortly."

No sooner had they started their engines, untied and started moving towards the open water, than the phone rang.

"Hello," Nate answered. He knew it had be the General.

"Ok, Nate, I have the satellite time. You call me and I'll have it positioned over your area and relay the information to you," he said.

"Oh, General, before you go I'd like to have you makes another deposit for us. He just blew one to hell right at the pier. Took out some of the pier. Guess we used a little too much power. Anyway, the army came and cleared us so we've just pulled away from the pier and headed north. I think we'll swing a little west. I have a hunch they still want to take a longer route, thinking it's a safer route. Will they be surprised," Nate informed him.

Nate could hear the sucking of air as the General received the news.

"Damn it Nate, you've declared war on Cuba. Now I want you to leave the Cuban ships alone. If you can't sink the other two drug vessels without attacking the Cubans, let them go, understand," said the general.

"We'll see," Nate replied, now ready to hang up.

"Don't go yet, Nate, I have more information for you. Under the bottom bunks on each boat, I've had weapons stored just for this sort of occasion. Actually, it was to help you in a getaway if you needed to run for it. Take the screws out of the front panels and be careful when the last one is lossened. Under there, on each you will find, a ground-to-ground missile launchers, some AK assualt weapons, hand grenades, lots of ammunition for all the weapons you find. God speed, Nate and I'll make the deposit," said the General as he was indicating he was going to hang up.

"How the hell could you have packed everything in so tight? I've knocked on those areas of the boats and they sounded solid. Even the army was fooled. How in the hell did you do it?" Nate asked.

"You'll find out when you take off the panels. Good hunting and goodbye," he said and was gone. Nate stood there almost dazed at what he had heard.

Could this crafty old General had planed or knew they would take on more than anyone figured on, he thought.

They had swung a little to the west so as to miss seeing the Cuban gunboats. They didn't want them to see the fishing boats leaving dock this late in the day. Nate knew they would meet the drug vessels as soon as they hit the three-mile limit. He was sure they would travel in a northwestern direction towards Belize.

It was dark in half an hour and time to call the General to get the position of the target boats. He dialed and hearing the response of "Brown's Realty," spoke into the set.

"Has the boats left the harbor yet, General. I need a reading on their course if you can give me one," Nate relayed to his superior.

"Yes, I can give that to you. They are traveling in a northwest direction. It appears they maybe headed towards the tip of the Tucatan Penninsula. The Cuban boats have just joined up with your targets and are proceeding in that direction. The Cuban boats are escorting them in military fashion. There is one on each side of the drug boats. I had the satellite zoom in on each boat. Nate each boat is carrying five men. That's a lot. Twenty against six doesn't seem fair. Are you sure you want to do this?" asked the General.

"Hell, yes, it's just starting to get interesting. All the men are pumped and so am I. I'll start easing our boats over to the east. Let me know if I'm moving in the right direction. Call me as soon as you have us on camera," was Nate's response. He laid the phone within reach and gave orders to Ed. Delbert's boat was right close and followed suit.

Minutes later the phone rang. It was the General.

"Go ahead, General," Nate said.

"You are about twenty miles west of the others. If you adjust your course five degrees, you'll be within three miles in an hour. Do you have a plan of action yet?"

"Yes, but it's on a need to know and you don't need to know. Just keep the satellite in position. Its dark here now and we'll be running without lights.

Contact me if you see us getting close to other boats. We'll be watching but you have a better view," Nate chuckled and hung up.

Damn him, thought the General. *I do need to know. Damn it.*

"Nate comes here," Brad yelled up from below.

Brad had taken off the panel over which the lower bunks were mounted. Nate arrived just as Brad drug out a wooden box. It was about four feet long.

"Here how it was packed so you'd never suspect by rapping on the space that the space was hollow. These boxes were placed in the space so tight that it didn't seem hollow. God, that took some doing," he concluded.

"Lets open this one and see what's inside," Nate told Brad.

With a crowbar, the box was opened.

"Holy cow," Nate said, "that's a hand held missile. It's just what we need to take out those Cuban ships. Quick find the ammunition, Brad. I'll call Delbert." He returned topside and grabbed the phone.

Delbert answered as soon at the phone rang once.

"Delbert, have you removed the panel under the lower bunks," Nate asked.

"Yes, we just did, have you?" Delbert questioned.

"Yeah, we shore the hell did. Did you find a handheld missile launcher?" Nate asked.

"Yeah, there's enough stuff here to start a war, boss." came the answer.

"Good, that's what we need to take out the Cuban boats. When we get in range, I want you to ask the General to direct you to the east side of the group. I'll have him direct me to the west side. You and I will do the swimming and leave the others to fire on them. I have him sneak us within a hundred yards. From there we will swim to the drug boats and set the charges. Well give the people twenty minutes from the time we leave before they are two shoot their missiles. Have them aim about two-thirds from the bow. That should hit right close to the fuel tanks. Should be one hell of an explosion. Hopefully we'll have the charges set to fire about the same time. We have to get this right, Delbert. We have no way to communicate underwater so lets go like hell once in the water. Ok," Nate instructed.

"How about the Cubans having radar, boss. Won't they see us coming?" Delbert asked.

"No, Castro has never put radar on these small ships. We'll have them dead to rights before they ever know we're here. Our motors have been insulated so we'll make almost no noise getting in close. Say a prayer, just in case," Nate said as he hung up. They both knew this was going to be a long night.

They soon spotted the boats by their lights.

The General had done his part, guiding them within a hundred yards of the four targets. Brad and Don had been selected to fire the missiles. Ed and Carl would handle the boats.

Everyone had their instruction and Delbert and Nate slipped over the side. They were in place and so far, all had gone well.

The swim was on as Nate and Delbert put everything in to it they could. One advantage they had was the boats were moving slowly because the crews were eating the evening meal.

Nate saw the bottom of the boats as he swam under, selected his target and placed the charges. As he turned to swim away, he saw Delbert doing the same. They didn't go far because they still had to get back to them as soon as they blew to insure no one sent a message. They surfaced and quietly thought this over. It would be difficult because of the burning oil and gas that soon would be on the water. They heard and felt the thump as their charges went off. Both dove under the water and swam back.

In the meantime, the rockets had just been fired and the Cuban boats went up like a ball of fire. These explosions shook the swimmers as they rolled with the concussion. They just then reached the boats.

As Nate came out of the water, old ugly face, from the El Toro was leaning over the side of the boat, looking into the water. Luckily, Nate had his knife in his teeth. He grabbed it and as ugly face, started to move, he grabbed him by the hair and held his throat up. By now, his upper torso was hanging out over the water.

"I told you, I'd send you to hell someday," as he rammed the blade deep in his lower throat. He ripped it sideways, and then pulled it out. Blood spirted everywhere and ended as Nate pulled his body overboard. He released him and he started floating away.

Quickly he jumped on board and looked toward the pilothouse. He saw a man on the radio, his back to him. No one had seen him so he threw the knife, hitting the man between the shoulder blades. Hitting his mark caused the man to slump forward.

Nate quickly jumped into the water and swam back in the direction they had come. Soon he was next to one of his boats and hands pulled him on board. It was Brad. He could hear the phone ringing from where it rested.

He reached it and hit the on button. Before he could speak, he recognized the General's voice.

"What the hell have you done, all the ships have disappeared except your two. Damn it, I told you to leave the Cubans alone," he was yelling. Nate hung up and decided he'd talk to him after he cooled off. He knew that the General didn't give a damn about the Cubans. He just wanted to show who was boss of this operation.

Nate called Delbert and when he answered gave him instructions.

"Turn on your lights and open your engines wide open. Follow me. We'll head over to Belize and find a nice cove to hang out in. In a day or two, we'll see if we can't fill our holds with fish and head back to port. Also, fix up the area under the bed. Pack everything back and remove all traces that space hid weapons."

"Right on boss," Delbert replied.

Brad and Ed had heard the instruction and Brad hurried below to do the same.

-10-

As daylight flooded earth, the two fishing vessels were anchored off Belize. Some of the men took naps. Nate just wanted to be out of sight for a while. He knew the radioman he'd killed had gotten off a message. He didn't believe he been able to identify anyone or a boat. You can bet that boats from Cuba and Colombia were on their way to the scene. His crew had not had anytime to clean up the mess they'd left. Pieces of the gunboats were scattered all over the ocean. Cuba might even send out planes. He'd feel better if they were undercover.

He pulled up anchor and proceeded South with the other boat following. They not went two miles when Nate spotted what looked like a cove. He steered over to have a better look. Getting close he saw twigs and leaves hanging from vines that almost closed the entrance. He stopped and measured the depth of the water. It was forty feet and plenty enough to float his boats. He woke his crew as did Delbert and they began cutting away some of the growth. This had to be done so the could pass into the cove he could see through the branches.

In an hour, the chore was completed and Nate guided his boat between the rocks and into a small cove. Delbert watched as Nate moved through and he followed as soon as he knew it was ok.

Once inside they found a nice quiet place to sort of hide out in. They anchored along side the seaward side of the cove. The entire wall of the cove was cut from solid rock. One of those wonderful creations of nature. Where they chose to anchor put them in the shade for most of the day and yet the climate was warm.

"This will do boys," Nate exclaimed, "lets fix a meal and have a shot and a cigar."

The men needed no encouragement to have a drink and a smoke. After a couple of shots, Nate called the General.

"Hi, general," he said, "and how are we doing this morning."

"Well I'll tell you," came the reply, "I'd be having a hell of a lot more fun if I was down there with you. Cuba has sent out planes to look for anything suspicious. I hope you're somewhere safe. Right now, I see two aircraft that has lifted off and three gunboats. They're all headed your way. Oh, by the way, just where are you. I can't find you even with the satellite."

"We're hid out in a little cove and will stay here a couple of days. We're in Costa Rica. When we pull out of here, we'll ease South and fish off the shore of Panama. We'll do some eating and drinking there so we'll be seen. Kind of as an albi. With our high speed motors no one will ever guess it was us who sank those boats."

"Don't forget the deposits and what do we get for Cuban boats," Nate chuckled imagining the look on his superiors face.

"Not a damn dime," came the answer and the clicking of the phone as it was hung up. Nate just grinned.

The cove was a nice charming place with vines hanging down the walls. It was picture perfect as if it was in the movies or a painting. The men had little to do so the fished with rod and reel. This gave them a verity of fish for eating. They did understand that if anyone found this cove and sailed into it, they would be trapped.

They rose early on the third morning and after breakfast of bacon and eggs, they moved into the open sea. They went out about a mile and found the fish they wanted. They strung their nets repeatedly and still their hold was not full at the end of the day.

They headed south in the darkness of night and did not stop until the were off the coast of Panama. They anchored close to shore for the rest of the night and slept. The weather was calm and they decide they'd go into town for breakfast. The pulled the anchor and headed south. They found a town with a many docks and moved in and tied up. From the sea, this looked like a major city. They went ashore. They spotted a sign telling them the name of the town. It was called Colon and close to the canal.

They spotted a sign that said Harbor Master and walked over to it. An American was on duty and for a fee allowed them to dock where they were for the day and night. He directed them up the street to several cafes. He told them the city was a big one of 70,000 people. They thanked him and headed into town. They had decided to walk for the excerise.

They soon entered the business district and entered the first café they came to. These men were hungry.

A short, fat woman in her sixties waddled over and handed each a menu. She returned to the counter and poured glasses of water from a pitcher. These she placed on a tray and returned to the table. Placing a glass in front of each one of the men, she asked if they were ready to order.

Each man ordered something from the menu that they'd not had since being in the region. Biscuits and gravy, with eggs and sausages to be washed down with black coffee.

She spoke in English and seemed pleased to see them. Nate could see and older man through the window to the kitchen. He'd bet they were man and wife. This was a mom and pop business.

There were a dozen or so people in the café talking about local problems, etc. Nate noticed that quite a few of them spoke English. Some would switch from Spanish then back to English. The resturant was clean and tidy. Everyone seemed friendly. Of course, this had a lot to do with the money Americans were pouring into the canal area.

The old woman returned with coffee and the men turned over the cups in front of them so she could pour. Instead, she placed the pot on a rack in the center of the table. This was a do it yourself kind of service. Ed filled his cup and asked to pour for the rest. They passed their cups around and received hot black coffee in return.

As the sipped there coffee, waiting for food; two soldiers entered. They looked around the room and seeing Nate and crew, headed their way.

They walked up to the table and spoke.

"Good morning, men, are you the fishermen that just docked a short time ago," asked the Sgt.

"Yes, we are," Nate, answered, "would you like to see our papers?"

"No, senor, this is just and inquiry. How long have you been at sea?"

"Three days but caught just a few fish so we thought we'd try off Panama and perhaps change our luck," again from Nate.

"While at sea did you see anything suspicious? We were asking to inquire by the Colombians. Apparently, there was some trouble further up north and ships were sunk. We are looking for terrorists who blew up two Cuban gunboats and sunk a couple of their boats carrying produce to Cuba. I can't understand why anyone would want to sink these kind of boats, but it's a crazy world out there," coming from the Sgt.

"Wish we could help you, but we were fishing off the coast of Costa Rica. How far north did this happen?" Nate inquired.

"Some where off the Tucatan Penninsula. This would be much further north of where you were. Please excuse the inquiry. Enjoy you stay in Panama," said the Sgt. as he turned to leave.

"Just a minute Sgt., we'll be fishing off your coast about ten miles. Is there any danger for us? If so we'll return to Colombia right away," Nate inquired.

"No, I don't think so. If you stay inside the three-mile limit, we can protect you but that far out, you're on your own. It's safe. I haven't seen any Cuban vessels near here," and he walked away smiling. Apparently, he didn't care for Cubans.

The meal was great and the men were in no hurry to move out. They smoked cigars, drank coffee and joked with each other. When Nate was sure, their appearance here had been noticed and people would remember. He paid the bill and tipped the server a ten spot. He also brought a box of Cuban cigars and they all returned to the boat.

Again at sea, the nets were laid out and fishing began in earnest. They had spotted a school of fish and were hauling in partically filled nets. They fished all day and into the next while making they're way slowly toward Colombia.

On the second day and with the cargo hold about three quarters full they headed for home. They were running low on ice and had to get the fish back before they started spoiling.

It was just getting dark when they pulled into the unloading area of the fisheries. They worked hard and fast to unload and most were hoping on heading to town and women. After what they'd been through, they need some fun and relaxation.

Unloaded they pulled over to their docks and tied up. All the men were below when they heard someone entering on deck.

This was on Delbert's boat and he hurred up to see what was going on. As he left the cabin, he ran face to face with the army Lt. They'd given the picture too.

"Oh, forgive me, I thought this was Senor Armstrong's boat. How was the fishing? I notice you unloaded some, so the trip was profitable for you," spoke the Lt.

"Yes, we had several tons but not a full load. Armstrong's boat is right there. Here I'll get him for you," answered Delbert. "Oh, Nate you have company," he yelled at the top of his lungs.

Nate came on deck and looked over that way.

"Hello, Lt.," he spoke, "come on over I need to talk to you.

The Lt. left and walked the few feet to Nate docking spot and went aboard.

"Good evening, Lt. how goes the battle," he said as a matter of factually and a way to open a conversation.

Nate handed him a cigar and lit it for him. He poured him a glass of whisky and he leaned back to also enjoy a cigar and a shot of whisky.

"What the hell's going on, Lt. we talked to a Sgt. in Panama yesterday morning and he said there was some trouble up north. Something about Cuban boats being blown up. Is this true?" he asked the Lt.

"Yes, senor, it is true. You witnessed the explosion at the dock before you left to fish. Now this other trouble up north. I don't know what is happening," he relaxed as he spoke. The whisky tasted good and he asked for another glass. Nate poured and refilled his own.

"Were the Cubans hauling drugs from Colombia?" Nate asked.

"Oh, no, senor, but I think the two boats with them could have been. They were also sunk. I think you may be right, senor, when you said that a local gang is trying to take over the drug trade from the cartels. Soon we will get a break and then we catch these criminals. You can be sure of that," expressed the Lt. But without much confidence in his voice.

"Damn it, Lt. It only a matter of time before someone attacks us. They are sinking fishing boats and tugs. It's only a matter of time before they hit us. Can you protect us or not. We may just go home to the U.S. We're not going to die for fish." Nate expressed concern.

The Lt. stiffens at Nate's words and his hand fell to his pistol as he spoke.

"How did you know they boats sank were a fishing boat and a tugboat?" he said with a very hard look on his face. From the lights of the docks, Nate saw his face-harden and he felt he'd made a mistake.

"I said how did you know?" the Lt. again asked.

"The Sgt. I spoke with in Panama told us. He offered us protection if we'd stayed inside the three mile limit," Nate said. He went on to tell of the encouter in Panama and described the café and the Sgt. and told him to check it out if he wished.

With this, the Lt's face relaxed. He believed Nate and knew they had informed the officials in Panama.

"Damn but you're jumpy," Nate said, "don't start accusing friends. My God man, get a hold of yourself.

"Si, I am jumpy because if we can't stop this disappearing of boats, I may be made to disappear. My superior is not forgiving and will blame me. He knows we have nothing to go on but still he demands action. He is a colonel and a cruel man. I have a plan that might work, but I need your help," said the Lt.

"Oh, is it something I can hear or is it top secret?" Nate asked him.

"Si, it is top secret, but you must know because you are a part of it," came the reply.

"Oh, no, I'm a coward and I'm not poking my nose into that kind of a mess. I'm just a hard working angler and that all I'm doing. I like you Lt. but even you could not talk me into doing something crazy like helping against the Cartels. If some other gang is out to take over from them, it could get bloody. My blood is staying right where it's at, in me. Don't ask?" Nate finished.

"Senor, I'm not here to ask you anything. I'm here because the colornel has demanded it. You and your men will help us with this problem or you'll have to leave Coloumbia. You have no choice," said the Lt.

"Well, tell me what you want done but I'm not saying I'll do it," Nate said.

"Senor Armstrong, all you have to do is come along on a trip to Cuba. The cartels are putting every bit of "Coke" they have left for a run to Cuba. To make it look right, it's going by fishing vessel. Your boats will merely go along so it looks like this other boat has joined you in fishing. We will head north as soon as I get the word. We will fish and have a good time all the way there. My government will supply you with all the gas and supplies you need. Cigars and whisky to," voice the Lt.

"No, that's insane. If they, who ever behind all this, think we are carrying dope they will blow our boats. Will your government buy me new ones and replace the men I might lose. Huh," Nate said.

"I did not want to tell you this but now I must. This morning the colonel froze your bank account here. It contained a little over three hundred thousand dollars. You will forfet this money if you don't help. You could run away and return to the U.S. but the money stays. Understand?" the Lt. was deadly serious. His eyes told you so.

"I don't know. I need to talk to the bank first. I'll do that first thing in the morning. If I change my mind, when would we leave for Cuba," asked Nate.

"One week. They have the farmers working round the clock to make as much "Coke" as they can. They must then bring it out of the jungle to be loaded. They will tell me and then I'll tell you. Do not discuss this with anyone, not even your men. You can do that once we're out to sea. I'm going along with six troopers. We'll get this next load through," he said.

"Damn, I would never have guessed that your government would be working with the cartels," Nate expressing concern.

"It means billions of dollars for my country. We need the money. Some, like the colonel, take bribes to allow the drug trade to flourish. If he did not then the cartels would kill him and replace him with one of their own. That's how it works. I must go now. Tomorrow you will call me, yes, and you are not to go to sea, even to fish without my permission. Understand?" finished the Lt.

"Yes, hell yes," Nate said. With this the Lt. Left the boat, got into the jeep and drove off.

Nate felt the need for female company and advised the crew. They were also getting ready to go to town. Apparently, they all had the same need. They all had been told that they wouldn't be going out tomorrow. A drink, women and some dancing would help take their minds off the mission. These men were not killers except during time of war. They all believed in what they were doing because they knew of the hell drugs were doing to the young people in the U.S. Programs to educate the takers of drugs, seem to do little good so there was no choice but to go after the cartels. The U.S. public just didn't seem to get it. Every purchase is supporting organized crime and drugs kill. Therefore, they felt it was a preventive measure and had to be done.

Nate went on ahead of the men and arrived at Loretta's place. He passed the bartender he'd become aquainted with and stopped for a minute at the bar to say hello.

"Want me to call the boss and tell her you're here?" he asked Nate.

"No, the guys are joining me in a few minutes and she'll be down before long. Let's surprise her," was Nate response.

"Ok, what'll you have? Whisky?"

"Yeah, whisky and have it brought it over to our table. I see it's vacant. Looks like a quiet night, huh," Nate observed and left the bar and seating himself at the table.

The server arrived with the whisky and was asked to start a tab.

"Si, senor," she responded and made her rounds from table to table. *A cute woman,* he thought but he wasn't interested. He had found something he had been looking for most of his life.

Nate had just started on his second whisky when his crew came in. He waved at them and they came over. They moved another table against the one Nate sat at before sitting. The server saw them come in and was right behind them. Nate told her to put their drinks on his tab and advised her they all would be having dinner.

She nodded and left, heading for the bar. She picked up some menus and returned with silverware.

"Are you ready to order now or wait awhile," she addressed Nate.

"Lets wait a while and have our drinks. Another round, please," Nate ordered.

The music started before Nate realized it was getting later than he thought. He waved the server back and they all ordered dinner. Just as she left, Nate noticed Loretta talking to the bartender. He waved at her and she came right over.

"Good evening, gentlemen," she spoke, with her eyes on Nate.

"Have a seat, honey," he said, "we were about to have dinner. Would you join us?"

"No, I've eaten, but I'll be back. I'll greet my customers and save a dance for me," she said smiling.

"I'll save them all for you, my dear,"Nate told her. Nate watched her go. He little butts had a slight swing and he felt it was for him. He'd swear she knew he was watching her every move through the room speaking to each customer and having a short chat with them.

Dinner was served and the men were hungry. There was no talking, just sounds of men chomping on food and slugging down water or drink. They would slow close to the end of the meal. A sure sign they were getting full.

Soon, they lit cigars and pushed back their plates. A couple of young boys came from the kitchen and cleared the table. They ordered whisky and settled back. The music was playing some slow country and western style music. The men looked around the room and each spotted a woman that struck their fancy and they were off for a conquest. Nate often thought it funny that as alike these men were, each desired a different sort of woman. Of course, like all men the wanted them pretty. They didn't need to be beautiful, just pretty. Each man was very respectfull of woman and didn't push a woman to do anything they might not want to do. However, they were men and that meant they would make their desires known after a while. From there on it was up to the women.

Nate saw Lorette heading his way and waved at the bartender to send the server.

She walked up to Nate and kissed him. This took him by surprise. This was the kind of woman who did not believe in showing that kind of affection in public.

"Hi, Nate, I'm glad to see you. May I sit down," she asked as he came out of his shock.

"Ah, ah, of course you can," he finally said. She was giggling at his surprise.

"You Americans are not the only ones who like to make a good joke," she said.

"Damn, I really didn't really expect that kiss. You know a kiss is always good if it's from you, but why now?" he questioned.

"Everyone that comes here knows we are seeing each other. You know how tongues will wag; besides everyone has noticed a change in me. They all are happy for us both. When I go from table to table, everyone one hints about us being lovers. I don't mind, do you?"

"No, not at all. You a very beautiful woman and yes I think I'm falling in love. I know you are and if I wasn't, I should say so before you get hurt. I can't, I just can't. I think about you all the time and I love it. You make me feel like a teenager again. There are times I just want to come here and to hell with fishing, but I must talk to you. There's something about me you don't know and you should," he stopped to see her reaction.

"Oh, I already know you may go back to America, but I don't think you will. You may have to go on business but not to stay, but we talk about it later. You are staying the night, aren't you?" she said.

"If I had a invitation, I sure would. Do you think the lovely lady who lives here will invite me?" he said, as a very pretty smile crossed her face.

"Sir, I would guarantee it. She is a very generous woman," she leaned forward as she spoke, "but you already know that," she whispered.

They both broke out laughing at the silly game they were playing. But that's what love is all about. When bitten by the bug it removes years from you and you do silly things.

She ordered a fine wine for them. Once it arrived, they toasted each other. This done the glasses was placed on the table.

"Come dance with me I can't stand, for another minute, not having my arms around you," he stated. He stood up and handed her his hand. She took it and they walked to the dance floor.

Once there she floated into his arms and he pressed her close. No words were said or needed. They just enjoyed the moment. Her suttle perfume scent caught his nose and made the moment ever more rewarding. Each was in their own thoughts. He couldn't believe he'd been so lucky to have this woman thinking about him the way she was. He knew he was in love with her and that he must disclose to her his mission for being in Colombia. He hoped and prayed it would not make a difference. That she'd understand this war he was fighting.

Her thoughts were along the same line, yet different. She was praying he'd not go back to the U.S. but stay here with her. She would not demand a ring, just him. Her feelings were so wonderful around him. The first time they made love, she knew she could be happy with this man. She was too much of a woman to beg him to stay. She was quite confident he wanted to stay and be with her. She however did not even suspect what he was about to tell her and his mission.

These two danced through the night, rarely noticing what went on around them. When they did, they realized it was close to closing time. Only three couples were on the floor besides them. The band had kept playing only because the boss was on the floor.

When Nate and Loretta noticed, they looked at each other and smiled.

"Well, I guess we'd better call it a night and go to your apartment and let these other people go home," Nate said.

"Yes, I'll be right back," she responded.

She walked to the band and told them the shut down. Next, she went to the bar and told the same to the bartender. She then returned to Nate and hand in hand, they adjourned to her living quarters.

"Whiskey, wine or me," she said when they were safely locked into her quarters.

He looked into her glistening eyes before responding.

"Would you hold it against me if I said YOU," and with this he grabbed her up into her arms and carried her to the bedroom.

They both awoke in each other's arms stark naked. She was the first to stir and slipped out of bed for a pit stop. She then got on the phone and ordered breakfast from downstairs. This done she went back to the bedroom and eased under the covers.

With one hand, she reached and gently touched his belly. The touch was so light that it caused the hair to rise up from static electrical impulses. This tickles more than anything and brought him to.

"Waking a man right in the middle of a delicious dream is a crime and now you must pay the price," Nate told her. At this, he began to tickle her as she rolled with laughter. When he stopped, she had a question for him.

"Tell me about your dream and was it about me. If so, you can re-enact it right now but you must hurry. Breakfast will be here in about fifteen to twenty minutes. You must eat to keep up your strength," she laughingly said.

He kissed her and moved over on top. All the talking he'd planned was forgotten. He didn't even think about it all night long.

They finished the lovemaking just as the food arrived. Both jumped out of bed and hurriedly put on robes. Loretta hurried out to greet the employees bringing in the food. She thanked them as Nate came out of the bedroom. The two employees smiled great big smiles and started to leave. Loretta advised them she rings if they were needed and they went away chuckling.

Nate and his lover settled into a very nice breakfast. Croissants and fresh fruit, scrambled eggs with orange topped the menu. Hot black coffee seemed unusually good this morning.

Once the meal was completed, Loretta poured both a brandy. Handing it to him, he accepted it, then spoke.

"Honey, lets go out onto the balcony and talk. I really need to have this conversation. I just hope it won't ruin what we have. Come on babe," he said as he extended his hand.

"Oh, this sounds like it could be serious," she said as she took his hand and followed him onto the veranda. They sat close and for a moment enjoyed the beautiful day beginning. The brandy gave him courage as he began.

"You are right, Loretta, I do love you. I need you to understand what I'm about to tell you. You see I'm not quite, what I seem to be. What I'm about to tell you must be a secret. If anyone found out it could mean my life and those of my men and you must promise to keep it that way. Promise?"

"Yes, of course. I love you also and have been thinking of being with you. Nothing you could tell me would every change that. Please go on," she encouraged him.

He told her of his time in Viet Nam and stories of his past life. He slowed a little when he came to currents events. She must know, so he moved on.

"My men and I are down here on a secret mission to disrupt and destroy as much of the drug trade as we can. You've heard of missing boats and men. That is what we are doing. We've sunk several and are about to do another one. It's a war, honey and one we must win. The drugs flowing into my country is destroying the minds of our youth. Our governments do not have the guts to fight it as we do. A small group has arranged for this mission. It will soon be over and then we can talk of the future. Please understand. In a couple of days, we have been ordered by your army to accompany a ship to Cuba. The ship is loaded with cocaine and we must sink it. Problem is the army is sending three troops with us. We must sink this one, as it will take the cartels perhaps three months to get enough dope to even try to get it to Cuba. I guess I'm telling you I have blood on my hands and I have killed. Yet you know me as a sensitive man and very much in love. I don't believe I've put you in danger but it is possible. People know we've having a relationship and when this whole thing explodes, the bad ones might come after you. They don't know who we are yet, but after this trip, they might. Believe me I'd cut off an arm before I'd hurt you. These things you should know. If you want me to stay away and not see you again, I will. It would be damn hard, but I would," he related to her.

She was quiet for what seemed a lifetime. Actually, it was only about two minutes. Then looking into his eyes, she spoke.

"I'm in love with you and I know that the whole world is fighting the drug cartels. I've seemed the damage it's done even in my country. It's misery is everywhere and it causes deaths. I'm proud you are in this fight. I support you. Just be careful and don't get caught by our authorities. I wouldn't want you to be kicked out of the country. I wish you to live here and help my run this business. You must tell me right now if you will do that. Will you stay when your mission is competed?" she asked.

"Yes, I will. I will have to go back to America to close my place, sell property and close my bank accounts. On second thought, I will leave the money and we'll draw on it, as we need it. In our country, the money is protected unlike in Colombia. Yes darling, we'll marry when the mission is over. This must be a secret until we are through. I don't want to draw you into it. Lets just keep seeing each other and I'll try to end the mission as soon as I can. Come here," he said.

He pulled her close and the kiss was passionate as usual. Her heart was pounding so loud she feared he could hear it. It might burst with happiness. The silence was broken by two words.

"Oh, Nate."

A couple hours later, he was back at the boat. Some of the people had not yet returned from their night out. Don had been the sentry for the night and Nate relived him. He went below and fell into his rack. He'd barely hit the bed when he was asleep.

During the morning hours, the rest of the crew came back. Nate looked them over and could tell they all had a good night. Tonight would be Don's night to howl.

When they were all on board, rested and getting bored, Nate called them all together. He felt it was time to let them in on what was going on. Kinda of a warning as to what was to come in the near future. He cast a weary eye along the docks for anyone lounging about. What he had to say to the crew has to be kept quiet. Their lives would depend on their actions in the next four or five days. They had a right to know.

"Men, it's time to tell you that the army Lt. has recruited us to go along with the last two boats, filled with cocaine, to Cuba. Now the way I see it we have a couple of options on how we handle this imposed journey. We have no choice but to go or be forced out of Colombia. These last two shipments are important and there won't be any more for perhaps three months. I see this as an opportunity. It's like putting the fox in the hen house and locking the door. There will be no Cuban gunboats this time just three fishing boats, fishing their way to the land of enchantment, Cuba. We will be spending ten days on the water just fishing around. The drug-laden boat won't fish, but from a distance, we will look like a group of hard working anglers. Anytime during this trip, we need to sink the bastard and get the hell out. The only problem is that the Lt. and a couple of his men will be going along. Probably one on each boat. That's no real problem but the problem is we may not be able to return to Colombia. We are going to sink this boat. I don't want to kill a soldier. This Lt. seems to be a nice person and is only following orders. Same as we would in his shoes. If we take them prisoner, we'd not be able to go back to the docks. We could find a cove to the east where we could anchor. I don't like it but if I can't change it, we'll do it. We'll take them prisoners and maybe find a place to store them until we're ready to leave. Hey, maybe that cove we stayed in a few days ago. Also, I believe it's time you knew where I've been getting our information from. Delbert knows but because this is getting dangerous, you need to know. Katrina, the server at the El Toro is an agent. If anything goes wrong, you must promise me you'll get her out. When we run for it, she goes too. I've promised the General and intend to keep my word. You all promise me?" he asked.

They all nodded their heads yes, and the matter was closed. Nate knew they would keep their word even if it met their deaths.

"Good, then I'll call the Lt. and get permission to go fishing. We must keep up our front no matter what. A day or two on the sea will do us good," he finished and made the call. Delbert's crew went back to their boat to make ready to go to sea.

Hanging up, Nate announced they could go out for a couple days. He was told not to try to run and to report in when they returned.

The fishing boats loaded their ice and gassed up. Within an hour, they were heading out to sea. They didn't go too far out and began searching for schools of fish. The two boats worked a quarter mile apart. They kept their eye on their fish finders. This kept on for over three hours when they spotted a pretty good school. They began their turns and the nets went out.

A couple of hours later they had scooped up most of the fish in the school. As soon as all the fish was on ice, they stopped and anchored. They had lunchmeat sandwiches and cold beer. The two boats were anchored close together so the men could talk back and forth from boat to boat.

After each man downed a couple of sandwiches, the questions began coming.

"Do you have a plan on how we could take this boat and get away alive?" questioned Carl.

"I'm working on one. I just have to work out the details. I don't want to kill the guards, but it might be impossible to accomplish without it. I'm still thinking," was Nate's response.

"Could we just tie them up, dump the cargo and put the boat a drift? We could then hurry back, pickup Katrina and head for the U.S. If we advised the General he could arrange to have us picked up," Don's two cents worth.

"No, I don't want to do that. It could happen that no one would find them before the died. I'm planing on coming back to Colombia and don't want a warrant for my arrest to be waiting. On the other hand, they might be discovered in a matter of hours and they get to us before we get picked up. It's too risky. Just let me think on it awhile. I'll go see Katrina tonight and see if she might have a idea we could use," Nate explained.

"Ok, that's good enough for me, lets get back to fishing and return to port. We can go into town and have some fun. We don't know when we have to go with the boat to Cuba," Delbert said.

"Let's do that," Brad said. He got up and took the wheel. "Ok to start up boss."

"Yes, lets go, I'll have a plan by tomorrow and will fill you all in. Push off and let's head east. If we find another school about the size as the last one, we'll scoop them up and head for town," said Nate.

The motors roared to life and the search began.

They hadn't gone far when Nate spotted a fair size school. They appeared to be about the size of the fish they were after. Nate called Delbert and the nets went into the water.

Scoops of fish were taken in until a problem presented itself. As they were pulling in the nets and filling the holds with fish, Delbert turned his head a second when disaster struck. He failed to notice a shark was caught in the net. Seeing Delbert's arm, it struck. Lunging it grabbed the arm. Delbert screamed with pain. Don was the closest and came to give assistance. He used a clubbed and hit the shark several times before the shark let go. Teeth marks showed through the shirt and blood was running down the arm and into the hand. Carl came to help after calling Nate.

When the shark let go, his teeth slid down the arm a ways causing streaks down the arm from the teeth marks. At least the arm was in tact.

Carl grabbed the first aid kit when he came over. He took Delbert's shirt and torn it into a couple long strips. He then wrapped it around the arm, above the wounds. He cinched it tight enough to stop the bleeding. He gave Delbert a pain pill as he noticed Delbert going into shock.

This helped and kept Delbert from passing out. Carl poured alcohol over the wounds and then gently sopping up the blood.

Nate arrived and jumbed aboard. He looked at the arm and approved what Carl was doing.

"You were lucky that you didn't lose the arm. I think you'll be ok. We will pull up and head for port. We'll use the high speed for a ways. We just can't do it too close in, as this has to stay a secret. Hold on Delbert. I'll get you some whisky," Nate told him.

No sooner had he mentioned this than Ed spoke.

"Here's a bottle," he said handing it across to Nate. Nate handed it to Delbert and told him to take a good swallow. He did.

Soon after the wounds were dressed and the boats were in high speed towards port. When they were about two miles out, they slowed the boats and ran the engines at the regular speed. They glided into port just as the cab Nate had called arrived.

Nate helped Delbert ashore and into the cab. He told the others to unload the fish and get paid for them. He'd stay with Delbert and call them as to his condition.

The cab driver, seeing the problem rushed towards the closest hospital. In seven or eight minutes, they drove up to the emergency room. A doctor and a nurse came out and took Delbert by the good arm and helped him inside. They put him in a wheel chair. The doors closed behind them as they entered another room.

Nate went into the waiting room and waited. Nearly an hour later, a doctor came out and talked to Nate.

"He's going to be fine. We've stitched the bites after cleaning it out. I'm putting him antibiotics to keep him getting infected. I want you to see to it that he leaves this bandage on for two days. Then change the bandage everyday for a week. Then he can leave it unwraped and open to the air. He must not work at physical work for about three weeks. He needs to avoid getting seawater on the wounds. The bite went to the bone but the groves did not. He was lucky. You can take him back to the boat in a few minutes. He will have scars. You can come back tomorrow and pay the bill," the doctor advised Nate.

Twenty minutes later, Delbert came walking out with a nurse. He looked like hell, but much better than when he came in. He was naked to the waist and his arm was bandaged to full length, from the shoulder down. He forced a weak smile.

"Hi, boss, how do I look," his try at a sense of humor.

"Like hell, but you'll do. I talked to the doctor and you are going to be ok.

It will take a little time and you'll have scars, he told me. No work for you for at least three weeks. Come on, lets go home," Nate returned comments.

A cab was called and they were soon back at the boat. The crew welcomed Delbert and teased him about trying to wrestle with a shark.

"You're too damn old to wrestle a shark, so lets knock it off," came from Brad and the rest seem to voice the same or similar coments. Delbert took it well and returned fire.

"Guess what, fellows I can't work for three weeks and guess who's going to do my share. No more fish nets for me for a while," he said turning to Nate. "I feel bad about not being able to help on the next mission, Nate. I really wanted to get in on this one."

"Never mind, we'll get through it and you can steer a boat. That is something someone has to do. That'll be your part," was the reply.

"That reminds me, I've got to call the Lt.," and went below to make the call.

-11-

Nate was put through to the Lt.

"Hello, Lt. this is Armstrong and how you are today. I'm just checking in. We had a man hurt today. A shark wanted him for lunch but he'll be all right. He can't work for three weeks so I thought you should know. We can still run our boat and fish along the way, as you explained we would do. Perhaps one of your troops could fill in for him. We could use some help in clearing the nets of fish and putting them in the hold," Nate spoke to him.

"I'm sorry to hear that. Yes, I'll bring an extra soldier. The time is not yet set for our little trip," said the Lt. with a grin, "but you are to be ready to set sail as soon as I get the word. Gas up your boats and get extra cans so we can go as far as possible. The other boat will also carry fuel. Fill up on ice so everyone thinks we are just going fishing. We must be careful and not give away our goal. You must be close to your phone at all times. When I call, you will have thirty minutes to cast off in. Make sure you have supplies enough to make the trip. Once we return here, you'll be paid for your services. We have known for some time that someone has been giving out information to those who are doing all this business. When we get back maybe, we will arrest her. That is confidential and must not be told to anyone. Understand " he voiced in a hard, cold voice."

"Yes, sir," Nate agreed but questions were forming in his mind. He knew he dared not ask for the identity of the informer. He had a cold feeling about this. Could they have caught on to Katrina? If so do they know, it was his crew and himself doing the damage. He didn't think so. If he thought that, he'd never take them as an escort to Cuba. Maybe they did and this trip was just a way to get them to Cuba and kill them. They would then make sure they were never found. What if they suspected Katrina? *I'll get word to her tonight,* he thought and has her get ready to run for it. No way would he leave her behind.

The conversation was over and Nate went topside.

He got the men together for an update.

"Men, you must go out in groups, when going to town. We have been put on notice by that pissy little Lt. that we and on call and must be ready to sail in thirty minutes. I need you to do this so I can call you, once I get the call. Delbert can do without the phone unless he goes into town. Who ever stays here need not worry. We'll know where he is. We may have a serious problem on our hands. The Lt. tells

Me they know that someone is feeding information to the gang that is causing all the trouble. They may make an arrest when we return from Cuba. He could mean it is Katrina and I'll warn her tonight. First, I'll go to Loretta's place for supper and a couple drinks. Then around one o'clock, I'll come back and sneak up to her place and hope no one is following me. I don't think the danger is eminent, but it is a problem. I'll call the General a little later and fill him in. Goodby boys, I'm heading for town."

Dropped by a cab, Nate went inside and up the stairs. He waved at the bartender, just as he entered the staircase so he'd know he was there. Reaching the top, he pushed the buzzer. Half a minute later, the door opened and Nate rushed in. He grabbed her, picked her up in his arms and carried he to the bed. She was holding onto him for dear life. This was totally unexpected. He'd never done this before.

He tossed her lightly on the bed, and then fell along side her. She rolled over and kissed him hard and passionately. He returned the kiss and they came up for air.

"What in the world has gotten into you, Nate," she exclaimed.

"Just needed to be with you tonight, for a while. We may be going to sea at anytime and I needed a kiss. Surprised," he stated.

"But you'll be coming right back, won't you?" she asked, yet afraid of the answer.

"Yes, we'll be back and I'll tell you all about it then. It's going to be a little bit dangerous, but exciting. I'm going downstairs and order the biggest steak you have and eat it. You may, of course, join me," Nate explained.

"I'll join you shortly, darling, have them fix me the shrimp I like. I'll be there in about fifteen minutes. Order the wine I like, too," she said.

"Hell, I didn't pay attention when you ordered wine so I don't recall the name," he responded.

"Just tell them the white wine. They'll know the difference. Jerry the bartender pays attention and knows. Now go, I need to fix myself up a little," she said.

He got off the bed and through her a kiss, as he headed for the door.

Reaching the bar, he motioned Jerry over.

"Good to see you again, Nate, what can I do for you?" he asked.

"I'm having dinner so I'd like the biggest, tenderest steak you have. Make it medium rare, baked potato, soup and some sort of bread. Loretta's joining me in fifteen minutes. She wants the shrimp she likes and a bottle of white wine. She said you'd know which one. Send me over a shot of whisky now and kind of stall the steak until she gets here. Start me a tab, would you?" Nate told him.

"Done," Jerry said.

Nate moved away to his favorite table. The whisky arrived and he threw the shot down in one forward motion and ordered a couple more.

It was a fairly busy night and before long Nate's crew arrived. They spotted Nate and walked over.

"Can we join you boss or is this going to be a private party?" Ed asked.

"No, you all can sit down. Thinking of what we're going to be going through pretty soon, I just felt like getting out for a while. Loretta is going to join me, but I'm not staying the night," he looked around before going on. "I'm going to see Katrina and form a plan to get her out if all hell breaks loose when we get back from the coming trip.

"You can bet it will. Don't anyone breathe a word to Loretta. Clear?"

"Clear boss, you know we'd never disclose a mission," came from Carl.

"Yeh, I know," Nate replied, "I don't know why I even said it. Delbert's staying at the boats, huh."

"Yeah, he's not going to feel like going anywhere for a while. Damn, he was lucky," Ed, said.

The server arrived and took their orders. They all wanted whisky. The drinks came and everyone settled in for a night on the town. The music was playing and the men looked around for women to dance with.

"Hey, there the one I danced with last time. I think she likes me. I'm going dancing so I'll see you all later," Brad informed them.

"Remember you can't go anyplace where I can't see you. We might get the call and have to get out of here. I can't run all over town looking for you," Nate reminded everyone.

"Not to worry, boss, I'll be right over there," he said pointing at a table where sat two women. Attractive women at that. Nate smiled and nodded.

Soon the other men found interests at other tables and one by one slipped away.

Nate looked in the direction of the bartender, who pointed over towards the entrance. He turned his head to see what was up and saw Loretta starting to work her way through the tables and chatting with everyone. Nate watched her as she came his way. How light on her feet and with the respect of everyone she meets. Of course, he couldn't help but notice she was moving a little faster than usual. Her petite body was a pleasure to watch. At times, he was sure she was dreaming about him, this woman, when she arrived and kissing him hello.

"Hi, God you look like an angel walking around and greeting everyone. Are you sure we're not dreaming and this will soon go, poof and all disappear," his greeting to her.

She just laughed before she said a thing. Finally she spoke.

"You must love me or you'd never have those kind of thoughts. Yes, my dear, this is real. It's hard for me to believe it sometimes, but it is good and real. Did you order food?" she inquired.

"Yes, and as soon as Jerry saw you coming, he told the chief to start it. I'm buying tonight. Your favorite wine should be coming any minute also."

They sat quietly and talked, and ate the meal and both enjoyed the wine.

As soon as they finished, the server returned and cleared the table. They had all got to know him and the tips he always left. Even more important they knew Loretta liked him and they all could see how happy she had become. All because he had come into her life.

They danced several dances, many without saying a word. They were lost in their thoughts and each other. He knew he had to tell her he would be gone for more than a week possibly, but hated to break the mood. Finally he did.

They were seated at the table, watching the people dance when he turned to her.

"Honey, we're going to sea and may be gone a week or more. When I return, we're start-making plans for us. I'll get this nasty business settled and then it's just us. Sounds nice, huh," he said.

"I understand," she said, "be careful Nate and come back to me

At 1 AM, Nate rounded up his men, kissed her so long for now and departed.

Upon returning to the boat, Nate told his crew he had to go out and see Katrina. He was taking the phone with him in case the call came, while he was gone. The crew went to bed as Nate put on his fins and tanks. He goes as he'd done the last, just in case someone was watching. He slipped over the side and swam down to the location he'd arrived at before. He was quite sure he could go this way undetected. He had to risk it.

Reaching the place, he pulled himself up to where he could see what was on the docks. He paused about five minutes as he looked around. Seeing the way was clear, he hung his tanks on a nail, and then sprinted across the docks to the shadow of the warehouse. He peeked out to see if anyone or anything was moving. He saw nothing so he turned and worked his way to Katrina's house.

He knocked at the back door, just once and it opened. Katrina stood there and whispered for him to come in. A candle burned in the living room. That was the only light on in the house. She didn't want anyone dropping by, that she didn't want to see.

"Hi, Nate, I'm glad you came. I was wondering what was going on and almost called you," she said and seemed pleased to see him.

"We've been out fishing and got back in this evening. I need to tell you a few things. Things are moving fast and soon they will be going much faster. We may have to make a dash for Panama soon," he advised.

"Why," she asked, "Did you overplay your hand. I heard about the boat exploding at the dock. Some say a couple Cuban gunboats were blown up. I wondered if you did this and why be so bold."

"Yeah, that was us. So far, not a boat got through and the General is pleased. Well, he's not too please about the destruction of the Cuban boats. He's prepared to help us get out when I say. You'll be going with us. That's what I need to talk to you about. There's an army Lt. who has pressed us into assisting the last boat for a while, getting to Cuba. Kinda like locking a fox in the hen house," he smiled as he said it. He liked this turn of events and liked how it played right into his hands.

"God, I'll be so glad to get out of that damn saloon. The patrons are really slimey. You need to know that there is less talk about drugs and shipments. Do

165

they know someone if giving information? I hope they don't suspect me," she shared with him.

"I don't think they know about you but it is always possible. This Lt. knows someone is and he mentioned an arrest would be made when we return. He's going with us to Cuba as are a couple of his men. We are to fish out way to Cuba and hope that the gang that is trying to take over doesn't get wise. Ha Ha Ha. You see the problem. We have to kill or take on the guards and this person. I hate to kill anyone of them. They are not involved except to following orders. He did admit to me that his command officer is taking bribes to let the drug trade flourish. I wouldn't mind kill him," he answered.

"I hope you have a good plan to get us out of here. I hear you preformed miracles in Nam. I hope you still have the touch. Go ahead, I don't mean to interupt," she said.

"We have to play it by ear for a while. The General had loaded us down with more firepower than we knew we had earlier. We discovered a hidden cove on the coast of Costa Rica. I thought we would get up that way, overpower the troops and drop them off in that cove with food for a week. We should be done and on our way out of here within a day or two. I need you to call in sick a couple days after we leave here. I'll let you know the day we leave, by phone. You wait a day or maybe two, and then call in sick. Yeah, make it three days. If we don't get back in that time, call in again. I don't think you have to because with our engines are really souped up. All depends on how long it takes us to get to Costa Rica. Change all that. I'll call you when to call in sick. That will be the best. If something happens and we're on the run, I'll call you to get out quick. If you do, get to the docks and hide out. Watch for us and we'll pick you up. If we can get away and out to sea, maybe the General will have us picked up by a ship or chopper. Anyway, that's the plan. Don't worry; I'll get you out. We're not going home without you. If something happens to me, all the men know about you and will come for you. If you don't make it home, we'll come to the El Toro and take you out. Understand?" he asked.

"Yes, I'll be ready. I'm not taking anything so I can be gone in seconds. One change of clothes and I'm ready. Anything else," she asked.

"No, that's it, just be on your toes and don't try to listen in on conversations of drugs. That time is over. I want you to quit doing it. I don't think the Lt. has any idea you're passing information on. Just serve drinks and all will go right. I can get you out of The El Toro much easier than out of jail." he said with confidence.

She smiled and moved closer to him.

"Yes, sir," as she stretched to kiss him. He took hold of her shoulders, stopping her.

"Katrina, the time we had sex was great, but it can't happen again. I've found someone. I'm getting serious about her and will remain true to her," he said.

"I understand, but you started something good last time you were here and I want that feeling of being a woman again. Just once more Nate. She doesn't need to know and I won't say anything. It can be the last time, I swear," she pleaded with him.

"No, I just came from her and have had enough, shall we say, excitement for one day. No offense, that's just the way it is. Now I must get back. The call may come at anytime. Remember if I can't make it when we need to get you out one of my men will. You've seen them all so there should be no problem. Ok, got to go," he said and left by the back door.

Retracing his tracks, he returned to the docks. As he peeked out from behind the warehouse, he saw a couple of soldiers walking guard post. There was one about twenty-five yards from when he was and another down the docks about fifty yards. There was a boat down that way that seemed to have something going on around it. It was a fishing vessel and Nate was willing to bet it was his target. He smiled. He always got a happy feeling when he thought he had been chosen to escort this boat.

Crips, I returned in time. If that boat is the one to be escorted, it will be loaded by daybreak, he thought.

"Damn good thing I got back when I did," he said aloud and to himself.

He watched the guards until he got their routine down pat. There was only one time when he could sneak to the water. He noticed that when the guards came together at a few yards down from his boat, they sometime would look out to sea and chat for about five minutes. They would light a cigarette each and smoke them. Once they did this, they would not be looking in his direction. That would be his opening. He waited.

Ten minutes went by and he was starting to worry. He had to get to his boat before that boat was loaded. All sorts of thoughts went through his mind. What if the Lt. didn't call and just arrived and went straight to his boat. He just had to get back and soon.

No more had these thoughts passed through his mind than the two guards, stopped to talk. They took turns lighting each other's cigarette and turned to look out to sea. This was his chance.

He ran as fast as he could to the edge of the dock. He hesitated just a second, then turned and climbed down to the water. He took his tanks down from where he'd hung and swung them over his back. He hooked the strap in front. Then came the googles and he was in the water. Five or six minutes he was at the boat. He reached up at the stern and pulled himself up on board. He kept low and slipped down the steps to the living quarters. Quickly his tanks came off and stored. He slipped under the covers of his bunk.

Within minutes, Nate's name was called out in a loud booming voice.

God, it's the Lt., he thought and leaped from his bunk.

"Coming," he answered the call. The men in their bunks leaned forward from a seated position in their beds.

"What up, boss," Ed said.

"The Lt. is here. I think it's time we go. I'll be right back," he said and started to go up the steps. Looking up he saw the Lt. looking down at him. The Lt. proceeded down the steps until he reached the bottom.

"Well, quaint quarters. But they will have to do," said the army officer.

He was looking at the men sitting up in there beds. It was obvious they had been sleeping. His smile froze and a frown replaced it.

"Armstrong, your hair is wet and the floor has water on it. You been swimming?" he asked.

A cold chill went through Nate's body. He was thinking fast, and then spoke.

"I just took a shower. I couldn't sleep so I got up. Are you here to tell us we are going on the mission," he said, trying to change the subject. His heart felt cold for he knew if the Lt. checked their mini shower stall, he'd not find it wet, exposing him as a lier. He moved on.

"Get your clothes on men, I think we're going to sea. If you give us a couple minutes, we'll be dressed and ready to go.

The frown was still there, but Nate noticed a softening. He hoped the subject was changed.

"Of course. Hurry we must get some of my supplies on board and be ready to go in thirty minutes," orders thrown out by the Lt. He turned around and hurried back to his troops. The men hurriedly dressed and went on deck. Nate saw soldiers loading several boxes. They appeared heavy. The Lt. directed them to be placed on the deck and lashed down. As they began stacking them across the back of the boat.

"Wait, you can't put them there. They will interfer with the nets. You need to spread them out along the railings. Come Lt. I'll show you,"Nate said.

He walked along the railing, the Lt. Following.

"You stack them here and here on both sides. How many do you have?" Nate asked.

"Twenty for each boat," was the reply.

"Wait a damn minute," Nate started, "that can't be food. Are you loading drugs on our boats?" Nate exploded.

"Yes, this is the last trip to Cuba for maybe three months. Those who are behind this need every gram they can get. You will take it for them. Neither you nor I have a choice. Understand?" questioned the Lt.

"Yes, I understand, but I don't like it. You've drug me into a drug war and some of my people might get hurt. I don't like it at all," Nate finished saying.

Nate yelled over to the other boat. Don was on deck watching every move of the soldiers.

"Yeah, boss, what do you need," Don asked.

"Have them stack the boxes along the railing in the areas they are on this boat. Make sure they tie them down tight. If we get into some rough weather, we don't want them going overboard," Nate instructed.

"Ok, will do," came the reply.

Nate turned back to the Lt.

"Make sure your men tie everything down tight. I'll inspect them before we push off," he instructed the Lt.

"Yes, we will. I have a feeling that if we lost even one of the boxes, we all would lose our lives. We must protect them beyond all costs," was the answer.

"You know that these fishing boats are not built for loading cargo. Unless we put the boxes below, anyone seeing us on the open water, will know we are not just fishing. Hell from two miles, was strong glasses, they will know we have something else in mind. The price of that stuff means anyone would kill us all for just one of those boxes," Nate informed the other man.

"We have no choice, my bosses have instructed and we are doing it. I don't want to put it below because we all need a place to sleep and prepare food. They stay on deck. I suggest we take turns sleeping. It will take a while to complete this trip," the Lt. said in disgust. Nate could have sworn it was in disgust with his bosses and not of him.

They set sail in the morning light. At a distance of ten miles the Lt. ordered Nate to lower the nets and begin fishing.

"Hell, you don't know much about fishing do you. First, we find the fish on our fish finders, and then we lower the nets. If you are trying to make this look like a fishing trip, this is how it's done. Does your boat have a fish finder on it?" Nate asked.

"How would I know," came the reply, "I am a soldier not a damn fisherman."

"Get on the radio and contact them and find out. If they do have them stand by for instructions?" Nate said while becoming a little irritated. It was apparent that he did not want on this trip to Cuba, but was being told to go. At least he was a good soldier and was following orders. *This person and I could become friends with if he would just relax. Maybe a cigar and a couple shots of whisky would help*, Nate thought.

Soon they had the other ship on the radio and the Lt. was waving to Nate to come into the cabin. Ed was at the wheel, smiled and nodded to Nate.

"I have them on the radio, they have a fishfinder but it is broke. They have always been used to run the drugs and not fish. What do you want them to do?" asked the Lt.

"Well they have to act the same as the rest of us. Tell them we will fan out, a quarter mile apart. He will be in the middle. We will zigzag back and forth across the ocean. When we spot fish, we'll call them and advise. When they see us drop our nets, they will do the same. Have them watch how we do it and copy our movements. That should fool anyone watching. They don't even have to catch any fish, by keeping them in the middle; it will look like they are fishing. That's good enough," Nate finished and the Lt. gave the instructions to the other ship.

"Copy that," Delbert's voice came over the radio. "Should we start the zigzag now boss."

"Yeah, pull off to the East and I'll pull a little to the West. Let the other ship in between and be careful. They don't know the first damn thing about what we do and we don't want to slam into them. Keep that quarter mile apart and we should be ok," Nate now in control of the radio.

The next couple of hours the zigzagging continued. The Lt.'s patiences were wearing thin. Nate brought up a bottle of whisky and a couple cigars. As he passed Ed, he shugged his shoulders and smiled. Ed nodded in return.

"Here, Lt. has a cigar and a shot of whisky," Nate said and handed him a shot glass. He took it and responded.

"Ok, the whiskey might help. So this is what you call fishing. Damn if I could do it. This trip is going to be the death of me yet," he said and held his glass out so Nate could fill it.

Nate had to smile because the Lt. might be closer to knowing he may be right. He knew he would regret doing it but the mission had to come first. The Lt. seemed a decent person, maybe in the wrong profession.

"Salute," Nate said as he threw down the whisky. The raw fluid ran down his throat causing a warm feeling. The Lt. followed suit. He wasn't as used to drinking as Nate and the liquid brought tears to his eyes.

Nate popped a ciger in his mouth and offered the army officer one. He took it and Nate provided a light. They sat and looked out over the ocean and chatted about the weather and such.

Finally, a call from Ed brought Nate to his feet.

"Hey, boss, there's a large school of fish under us now at about forty feet," Ed said.

"Ok, I'll call Delbert's boat. You and Brad start dropping the nets," Nate ordered, then turned to the Lt. "You better get inside the cabin, Lt., there you'll be in the way."

He picked up the mike on the ship to shore radio and called Delbert.

"Large school of fish over here, move in a little closer but leave room for the other boat between us, over," he announced. "Lt. gets on the radio and informs your boat what we're doing. They can move up a little and they are to stay between us if they can. We will be going in a circle to net the fish so he'll have to do the best he can."

They started their circle and strung out their nets. Thirty minutes later, they were pulling in full nets. Nate looked across at Delbert's boat and saw they were doing the same. He drew attention to this fact with the Lt.

"Now we are really fishing. Lt. There are tens of thousands of dollars in those nets. This is a hell-of-a-big school of fish. We'll fill our hold here alone. The other boat is doing the same. From here on out we'll have to pretend to fish. We'll take the nets off and lower the arms and pretend to fish. I think we can work our way to Cuba faster. This is a lucky break for us. I know you're not interested in our catching fish, but now we can all concentate on watching for boats. Our catch will hold till Cuba. Do you suppose we can sell them there?" Nate finished.

The Lt. nodded and watched the wiggling fish flopping on deck as the crew shoveled them into the belly of the ship.

They continued circling the school of fish and pulling them in. Soon the radio came to life. It was Delbert.

"Hey, boss, we're so damn full we could hold another fish if we tried. We're pulling in our nets and quitting. How are you coming with your load?"

"Soon as we have the nets empty this time, we're loaded. Anchor and take a lunch break," Nate told him.

"Aye, aye skipper. Will do," was the answer.

Nate picked up the bottle and offered the Lt. another drink.

"Here have another drink. I think we'll anchor here and have something to eat. I'm starved, aren't you?" he asked.

"Yes, I'll call our boat and advise them to do the same," said the Lt.

First, he took his drink and threw it down before going to the radio. He called the Colombia boat and had a conversation in Spanish.

Nate noticed the other boat had stopped. His crew finished scooping the fish into the hold. They dropped anchor and set back for a rest. The whisky was passed around and they all lit cigars. They sipped the whisky and enjoyed the cigars. After a few minutes Ed spoke.

"I'll cook and we'll have steak, mashed potatos, gravy and canned peas. I'll let you know when it's ready," as he went below.

"How do you want your steak, Lt. we take ours medium rare?" Nate asked.

"I'll take mine the same. Can I have another drink?" he asked.

"Sure," he replied holding the bottle out. The Lt. took it and poured himself another shot.

"I'm getting tired of calling you Lt. Why don't you tell us you given name? We are on the boat quite a while and it's just friendly that way. This way we feel we are under arrest or something. Can you do that?" Nate asked.

"Yes, I can do that but it's a western name and you might think it funny for a Colombia. My first name is Dennis. My mother wanted to go to America when I was born and so she named me. All her life she wanted to go but my father refused. I to would like to go the America someday. It would be what mother wanted. Sigh, maybe some day," was his comeback.

Nate noticed the whisky was taking effect. Dennis was talking too much and that's a good sign.

A few minutes later Ed stuck his head out and said here comes the food. He carried two plates. He handed one to the Lt. and one to Nate.

172

"I'll be right back," he said and went to get the other two plates. Back on deck, he gave one to Brad and they all sat down on the deck and ate their steaks.

When finished, Brad gathered the plates after they were scraped into the ocean.

"I'll clean up, Ed, damn good grub," he said.

Ed pulled out another bottle and passed it around. They all took a shot and enjoyed a few minutes of quiet time.

The radio blared out.

"Hey boss, there's a fast boat coming at us from the north. Could be Jamaican gangsters. Tell your Lt. we are going to arm ourselves. I don't want this soldier to shoot me if I reach for a gun," Delbert informed Nate.

Dennis heard the message and jumped for the radio. He spoke into the mike for a minute and turned to Nate.

"I've told them not to be concerned with you people, but to get ready for the oncoming boat. We fight side by side. The other boat has more fire power than we have and they will be ready."

"Great, lets get our rifles and make ready," Nate, ordered. He started the engines and was sure Delbert had done the same.

"Why the engines?" asked Dennis.

"If we can't out fight them we'll be ready to run for it. These boats are not fast but there are three of us and only one boat coming. Everyone start scaning the horizon for any other boats. We don't want one sneaking up while we're watching this one," came Nate's order.

Nate put his glasses on the oncoming vessel and watched its approach.

As it neared, Nate thought he knew the colors it flew. It was close enough to see men on deck.

"It's Jamaican alright. Everyone on your toes. This could be it," He related to all aboard. He was doing quite a job of play-acting and had the Lt. fooled.

Nate looked at his crew. They had taken cover behind anything they could. They had all gone below and grabbed a rifle. The Lt. provided his own and they were ready, as ready as could be.

The boat drew closer and sure enough, it was Jamaican. It looked like an old PT boat the Americans had in the Pacific during World War 2.

The flag was Jamaican and as it approached, it appeared to be up to no good. It was getting close and was not slowing down. Nate thought it would ram them. He waited till it was fifty yards away and ordered his men to open fire. The weapons exploded with noise and bullets pentrated the shell of the on coming boat. Nate grabbed the wheel, shoved the engines into reverse and opened the throttle. The boat veered backwards so fast it came close to knocking everyone off their feet. The on coming boat passed within twenty feet of them. Everyone fired into it as it passed by. For some reason it kept right on going for a distance of a quarter of a mile. It then turned around and headed back towards them at a slower pace.

Delbert saw what was going on and swung into action. He opened the throttle and headed to the rescue of Nate's crew. He reached it before the attacking boat was on them. He pulled in behind Nate and waited. The men on the other boat saw this movement and decided to leave well enough alone. One hundred yards away they made a quick turn to the east and went around the fishing vessels, staying a comfortable distance. They were soon out of sight.

-12-

The excitement over, Nate approached Dennis.

"I suggest we head west a little and maybe get in close to Costa Rica. The fishing is good there, even though we couldn't use any more. It would take us away from the island of Jamaica and their kind. They may be laying in wait for us closer to home. If we can get up close to the Tucatan Penninsula, you can call Cuba and get us an escort. The drug dealers I've read about from Jamaica and killers. We must be careful. From here on out we must be on our toes. We can go ahead and fake fishing, but we won't fool them. What do you say Lt., I mean Dennis, shall we. It's your decision. What do you want to do?" Nate posed the question to him.

"Yes, that sounds right. Anything you say. If we don't get this boat through, we're all dead anyway. You do what you think is best," came the answer.

Nate relayed the message to Delbert and the Lt. informed the other drug ship. The were under way and grouped close together for safety. Then Nate's phone rang. Everyone froze. His crew knew not to use the phones on this trip. Nate's mind was in high gear. Was it Lorette, Katrina or the General? He knew he had to answer it, but the Lt. was standing right there.

"Excuse me, must be a girlfriend," Nate excuse himself and headed below deck.

"Hello," he said into the device.

"Brown's Realty calling Mr. Armstrong," said the voice on the other end.

A cold shiver went through Nate's body as he wondered what the old man wanted.

"A nice touch, don't you think? Me sending that old PT boat out there to help you to be beyond suspicion. Did it work?" said the General.

"What the hell do you mean calling me. Yes, it worked but you could have gotten those you sent killed. We fired on them you silly bastard," was Nate quick response.

"Well that's thanks I get for helping. We have you on satellite again. Are you about to sink that damn boat and come home or what?" came an angry voice from the General.

"You go to screw everything up if you don't wait till I need you. I can't sink her now. I'm waiting for the right time and I need to go back to get Katrina. Remember," Nate said in a disgusted tone.

"Ok, alright, I'll leave you alone," was the reply. The phone went click as his superior hung up.

All this time, Nate had his back to the steps leading up to the deck. He turned to join the men on deck and saw Dennis standing there.

"How long have you been standing there," Nate asked.

"Long enough to hear you're going to sink something. The drug boat perhaps. You are the ones who have been stealing drugs from the cartels. I thought so at one time but then you blew that boat at the dock and fooled me. I thought we were becoming friends," he said with disappointment in his voice.

Nate notices a pistol lying on a bunk next to him. He grabbed it and pointed it at the Lt. who was just pulling his weapon out of its hoster.

"Don't be a fool and you'll be alright. I don't want to kill you but I will if you interfere with our mission," Nate said in a loud voice.

Ed heard him and appeared at the top of the stairs.

"Everythings ok, if he drops his gun. Come down behind him and take it from him. Don't kill him unless you have to," Nate instructed.

Ed moved and took the pistol from the Lt.'s hand.

"Tie him up for now. Don't harm him. Break out the heavy artillary. I'll call Delbert and have them do the same," Nate said dialing the phone.

"Yes, boss," Delbert's voice came over the air.

"Delbert, get somewhere safe to talk. Don't let the guard hear what I'm about to tell you. I'll wait," Nate said.

"Ok, let me move up front. Our army friend is having a shot of whisky. Hold a minute," he advises.

A couple of minutes went by before he again came on the phone.

"Ok, Nate goes ahead," Delbert, said.

"We've had to take the Lt. Prisoner. He overheard my conversation with the General. You'll have to take your guard prisoner. If he's drinking whisky, keep pouring it down him. Don't give him enough so he gets sick. Just enough so he'll be easy to handle. Do it below deck so the drug boat's crew doesn't see you. Tie him up and keep an eye on him. Break out the firepower under the bunks. The time has come to show these assholes just who they are dealing with. Let me know when you have the guard taken care of." Nate instructed.

"It's as good as done. Give me twenty minutes. I'll pretend to drink with him and make it easier. I'll tell him we always do this after a good catch. That'll suck him in," he said and hung up.

As Delbert hung up the phone, the guard came walking towards him. He was carrying the bottle and glass with him.

"Senor, this is very good whisky. Would you join me in a drink?"

"Shore, we always celebrate a big catch. Hand me that bottle," he said.

He poured himself a shot and threw it down. He refilled the glass and looked at the guard.

"Here, your glass is empty," with this he reached out and took the guard's glass. He filled it up and handed it back.

"Oh, no senor. I should not. The Lt. might find out. I want no trouble from him."

"Here take it. I just talked to the other boat and they are doing the same. It is our custom," Delbert explained.

"Let's go below and sit where it is comfortable," Delbert said and started hobbling down the deck to the stairs going down to the living quarters. He heard the guard behind him. *This is damn near too easy,* he said to himself with a smile.

Reaching the living area, Delbert parked himself on a bunk. He poured the guard another shot, as soon as he was seated across from him. He watched as the guard threw it down. He bumped the bottle against his glass while the guard was looking elsewhere. This was to fool the guard into thinking he'd just poured himself one.

"Here, have another and we'll quit for a bit. We'll be moving out before long. Lets just sit here and talk," Delbert said.

The guard held out his glass and it was filled. He sipped it this time. He felt warm all over. The whisky made him feel good.

Delbert was looking for signs the booze was having it effect on the guard. He noticed his words were coming out more in Spanish rather than his poor English. He was beganing to slur his words and he was starting to sweat. It was time to take him.

"I must call one of the crew to see if he's had any word on when we move out. Ok with you?" he questioned.

"Si, si, does it," announced the guard.

"Don would you come down here," he yelled. The guard's rifle had been left on deck. *This should be a piece of cake,* he was thinking.

Don stuck his head in, at the top of the stairs.

"You call me, Delbert?" he asked.

"Yes, come here, I have a chore for you," he replied.

Don took the three steps and walked up to where the two men were sitting.

"Yeah, what's up?" came a question.

"I just talked to Nate and he said it's time to take back our boats. Take this guy prisoner right now," Delbert ordered.

Don took one-step backwards and drew his pistol. Pointed it at the guard and issued an order.

"Hands up or I shoot," Don ordered.

The guard, totally confused with this action, did as he was told. Don stepped up and disarmed him by removing his pistol. He did a quick pat down search.

"He's clean. What now?" Don asked.

"Tie and gag him. Then tie him to a bed. We need to keep him quiet. Nate's got the Lt. Prisoner. It's time for action. The Lt. overhead Nate talking to the General so the fats in the fire. God, I wish my leg were well so I could do more. I'll meet you on deck. Hurry up, you won't want to miss what comes next I'll bet. Also, break out the firepower under the bunks. Looks like we'll use it," Delbert Responded.

Delbert hobbled up the three steps and from the cabin, onto the deck. He called Nate.

"Problem solved, he's tied up and tied to a bed. Don's doing it now. Does this mean we won't wait to blow that boat out of the water," Nate was asked.

"Settle down, now, all in good time. What I think we'll do is work our way over close to Costa Rica and sinks her there. I don't want to kill the prisoners and have the Colombia army after us. I'm coming back here to live and I don't want to have to hide from the law. No future in that. I don't think anyone will think of looking over there. I've got to talk the Lt. into talking to the target and convince them to come with us. I'll get back to you," Nate said and hung up.

Nate went below to see the Lt. Dennis.

"Well now you know it's been us doing all the damage to the cartels. Their drugs are killing thousands of our people and it's time we stopped it. Now I need your help. You are in no danger as long as you do as I say. I need you to call the boat on the radio and tell them we're going in close to Costa Rica to avoid other Jamaica thieves. If you help me, we will not have to kill those on board. Understand," Nate finished talking.

"Si, I understand. I don't trust you. How do I know you will keep your word," was the response from the Lt.

"I'll show you something," he said and yelled for Brad.

"Lets open the space under the bunks and get all the stuff out where we can use it. I'll help," Nate said.

Off came the front portion of the lower bunks. The two men started pulling out the weapons. The Lt. looked on in awe at what he saw. Nate picked up the tube that fired the ground-to-ground missiles.

"Do you know what this is, Lt.," he asked.

"Looks like a tube that fires something. Is it a missile that's fired or what?" he asked.

"It's a missile launcher. A shoulder held one that we can use to sink that boat. If I choose to use it, it means everyone on the boat will be killed. I'll have no choice now that you know who we are. So think it over for a few minutes. I'm going to have a whisky and a cigar. You want the same?" Nate asked him.

"Yes," he replied.

Nate got a bottle and some cigars. Ed and Brad both joined them. The boat was just drifting on the current. No big deal. The hands of the guest were untied so he could handle a glass and cigar. They all set around talking and watching the Lt. They were certain he thought he was going to be executed any minute. His face showed it and he was sweating a little. All at once, the radio blasted with a Spanish voice.

"Times up Lt. If we don't answer that they will run for it. We can hit it from here. The other boat has the same type of equipment. I'll tell you also that we have souped up engines and can run circles around them. Be there is a problem. If we don't hurry and answer, they will send a radio message back and tell everyone who we are. I can't let that happen. So lets go," Nate ordered.

Up the steps to the cabin he forced the Lt. to go, they stopped at the radio just as the man on the other end shouted into his mike.

"Answer it, damn it, and be careful. I know just enough Spanish to know what you're saying. Answer and tell them we're going to be turning towards Costa Rica to avoid the Jamaicans. Do it or so help me I'll kill you right now," Nate instructed. He pulled his pistol and placed it on the Lt.'s head.

The Lt. spoke into the mike after triggering it to open up. He spoke a few words in Spanish, and then placed the mike back into its cradle.

"There it is done. You've made me a traitor to my country. I'll never be able to return. Please take the gun away," he requested.

Nate uncocked the pistol and put in back into it holster.

"We've not made you a traitor, we've freed you from the gangsters running drugs. If you don't want to go home we can take you to America with us," said Nate.

"I can't go, I have a family," he hestated for a minute then went on. "Could you get my wife and daughter out if I help you?"

"I don't see why not," Nate said. Secretly he wanted to help this person. They had put him in a terrible position. His supervisor's probably shoot him if he returned. If not, the drug cartels surely would.

They turned to boat towards the west. All the nets were onboard and would stay in there current position. No more faking fishing. Nate hoped the drug boat would not catch on to what was happening. He noticed it fell in behind their boat and Delbert fell in behind it. They had to be careful not to travel faster than this type of boat would go. This would surely tip their hand and he'd have to sink the boat sooner than he wanted to.

"Well Lt. we are on our way. Sometime late tomorrow we will sink that boat. I'm sure that by morning, they will get curious of our actions and I will expect you to control them. I don't want them to suspect a thing. Will you do it for me? If you do and continue to help, we'll take you home with us. I can arrange to get the family out before they will expect you home. Ok?" Nate was asking.

"I hate to do this but you are right the drugs are bad and have destroyed many lives here. I don't know if I can trust you. Do you give your word?" asked the Lt.

"Yes, Dennis, you have my word. I'll shake on it," Nate said and extended his hand.

The Lt. took it. The two men shook hands and both felt that a bond had been formed between them.

"We will be watching you and if you give us cause to doubt you, you are dead. I trust you but must make sure we are safe with you aboard. Any act that indicates you trying to damage this boat or warn the drug boat it all over," Nate told him and made a motion of dragging a knife across his neck.

"I give you my word. I can't go back and I can make my mother's dream come true by going to America. What do you want me to do," he asked.

"Nothing. Lets all have another drink and cigar. Brad saw this coming and had go below. He now returned with the whisky and four cigars.

The night was quiet on the ocean. The water was calm. It was a beautiful night. The moon was full and bright. A good night for romance if they were elsewhere. Still it was a night to enjoy.

Nate and the Lt. stayed up late. Brad and Ed had turned in early. They would relieve him later and one would guard their prisoner. The two men talked of home and friends, family and such. It was a time of getting aquainted. For some reason, Nate trusted this man. A sixth sense told him he could. The Lt. chose to sleep on deck. He was given a blanket and pillow. He curled up and was asleep in no time.

This was gratifying to Nate as it showed the man was comfortable with his captors. If the man were planning anything, he would not be so anxious to sleep with these men.

All this is a good sign and Nate relaxed as he gazed at the stars. His thoughts were of Lorette and the future. He knew when he married her his life would be different. His only worry is that the drug lords found out about him. If so, his life would not be worth a plug nickle. So far so good. His mind was spinning on a plan to so disrupt the drug cartel, they would only be thinking of surviving. Their business was everything to them and their life.

If a man could break their backs so it would take a year to get back in business, they would not even try to find out whose responsible, he thought. The plan was forming and he was smiling. He knew the people would go for it. They loved the danger and if he could get the General to come up with a few bucks, they'd cripple the drug trade for a while. Time would tell.

Nate awoke to the blareing of the radio. Spanish words were being spoken. It sounded like a request to speak to the Lt. Ed stuck his head through the door.

"Hey, boss, the drug boat is calling," he said,

"I'll be right there. Get the Lt. on deck quick," Nate replied.

"He's up here now, should I put him on."

"No, not till I get there. You don't understand Spanish. I'm coming," Nate told him.

Nate rushed on deck in his undershorts and T-shirt. The Lt. was waiting at the cabin to answer the call.

"Ok," Nate said, "go ahead but remember our deal."

"Si, I know, I'll be careful," as he picked up the mike.

After a minute on the radio," he terminated the call and turned to Nate.

"They were checking to see if all was right and why we were not pretending to be fishing as was the plan. I told them we were just going to do that but breakfast came first. I told them not to bother me with stupid questions, just follow us," he related to Nate as Brad and Ed listened in.

"Ok, good answer. I caught some of it but not the rest. Sounds like you're playing ball. Brad you keep your eyes on that boat and if it turns away, let me knows. We'll blow it out of the water if it does. Now lets get that breakfast." Nate ordered. This was a hint for Ed, who was doing the cooking, to go below and fix it.

Ed did just that. The rest just lounged around the deck waiting. Nate did start the engines and began their course to Costa Rica.

Minutes later, Ed came up and told them to go get it. He carried his own plate.

"You first Lt.," Nate said and followed him down the three steps and into the living quarters. One by one, they served themselves slices of ham, scrambled eggs and warm biscuits, then returning to the deck to eat. They all carried cups for their coffee. Brad returned to get the pot.

Breakfast, soon over, they rinsed the plates in the ocean. Ed did the rest down in the little kitchen area.

About an hour later they started zigzagging, pretending to look for fish, yet coming closer to Costa Rica. A couple hours went by when Nate had the nets taken off the apparatus that held and to drop the machinery down so it looked like they were fishing. This being done, they circled as they inched their way forward. Just before dark, Nate estimated they were twenty miles of the coast. Time to despose of the drug boat.

"Lt. Come here a minute. We're going to sink the boat now. Are there any men of yours that are worth saving," Nate posed the question.

"No, senor, not a one. They are all mean and in the drug trade or taking payoff. No one worth saving."

"Ok. Ed, do you want to be the one to do it? They can all go to hell together. One of you goes below and gets the missle launcher. I'll call Delbert and have him fire one also. We can't afford to miss," Nate stated. Ed went below.

He called Delbert and told him the same. He would coordinate the firing while on the phone. He said he would stand by until both men were ready.

Roughly, six to seven minutes later they were all ready for the fireworks.

"Alright, everyone is loaded. Both of you fire on my signal. Ok, take aim, fire," came the order.

Both crews watched the curl of the smoke that came off the tail of the missiles. Both appeared on course from where Nate stood. He was watching through. The men on board spotted them just a second before both missiles hit. There was one hell of and explosion and pieces of wood, supplies and miscellaneous junk went a hundred feet in the air. Dust, fire and smoke were thrown skyward, then quietly settling back to the sea. Nate scaned the water for survivors. There were none.

"Good shot," Nate said. "If we're out of missles throw the tubes over the side. If we have missiles, we may need them later on. I have a plan but first lets find that little cove and hang out there for a day or two. I'll tell you my plan. First, I must call the General and have him make a deposit. He must approve my plan because I need him to do things for me. Full speed ahead to the shoreline."

The General was sitting in his easy chair when his special phone rang. He had just received a report on the blowing up of the boat. It was good news and has proved the drug cartels can only get by with what we want them to. The battle must be taken to the field, as Nate and crew have done. He too has recognized the fact that there will always be drugs coming into the country. By attacking them where they live, so to speak, they can find it difficult to opperate. If we had teams operating around the globe, many lives could be saved. The price would go out of sight and reach of the average person. Only the rich could afford it. More dealers would be knocking off competition and stealing their inventory. In the Carribean, Castrol's Cuba's economy would be in shambles. All that really supported it now was the billions in drug money.

The congress may never go for it, but it could be and answer. It would give countrys like Colombia a reason to teach farmers to grow different crops. This would take them out of the cocaine trade. If it were here, he'd go in and bomb the hell out of the locations known to have been used to produce cocaine from the cocoa plant. If the citizens could not make a living growing it and were getting killed with the bombing, most would stop. The cartels would then have to force laborers to work for them. This would call for a revolution against the government. The politicians to pass tough laws and enforce them. The U.S. could help and the world would be a better place. This was the frame of mind he was in when Nate called.

He answered it with the usual, 'Brown's Real Estate, whose calling please."

"Armstrong, General, and how are you tonight. I'm calling to tell you we've sent another to the deep. I also have a matter to discuss with you. Do you have time and can you talk," Nate started out.

"Yes, I'm at home and sipping a good brandy. I'm alone so shoot Armstrong. Oh by the way, good work. I saw it on satellite feed."

"I've been thinking there is more we can do now that we know it'll be three months for enough cocaine can be manufactured for shipment. Without some thing besides fishing, my crew will want to come home. I would join them, but there's more to do. I want you to give the ok for us to attack the few places we know of where drugs are made and packaged. You would have to worry about us attacking Cuban ships, etc. I haven't talked to my people yet but I'm sure they'd be for it.

"What in the hell are you taking about? That would be fighting on another country's soil. They could deem that as and attack on them.

Beside you only, have five men beside yourself. You just don't have enough to do it with," the General said, somewhat surprised.

"That's where you come in. I need ten rangers like the ones in Nam and their supplies. This plans means jungle warfare and I don't have time to train anyone. Once we get started, I'd have a place for you the send a couple choppers in to pick us up. I'd have Katrine with us except in the jungle. She can watch the boats and keep them safe for our get out on time escape," Nate answered.

"God, you don't want much do you. If I ever get caught of putting this mission together, they could send me to prison. You want rangers and choppers. That also means you'll need a ship several miles off shore to set the choppers on. What kind of damage can you do to the cartels? Tell me again," spoke the General.

"Well, sir, I believe we can so disrupt their supply chain of drugs. This would be by raiding the villages raising the crop and even more important, the making and packaging of the poison. During the raids we perhaps, if lucky, could kill the leaders. This would terrorize those involved. They would have to reorganize, purchase new boats and recruit new people to help. I'm sure this would set them back a year. Just think General. This would greatly cut the number of new people starting on drugs and many that will find they can live without them. The price would go through the roof and only the rich could afford the junk. I think it's worth it regardless of the cost. What do you say, sir?" Nate finished with a question.

"Damn it Nate, don't you understand you're declaring war on a neighbor. The government may not see it the way you do. There is new leadership there. Maybe. Ok let me bring this up to the same group of people you met with and get their feelings on it. Maybe the Pentagon knows a General down there that could either get approval from the President of Colombia. You understand it would have to be a covert operation. If you get in real trouble, you will not be able to count on the military to come storming in and save your hides. However, to sneak in, attack and get the hell out quickly could work. How many days do you think it would take?" him finished.

"With the rangers, three days. We'd go in like lighting, strike and run back to the ocean and our boats. You have a carrier or some ship laying twenty or thirty miles out to sea. The choppers can come and pluck us off the fishing boats, which we can sink. This would leave no trace that Americans had anything to do with the mess. What do you think General?" Nate said needling him.

"It might work if your crew is willing. This may take three or four days, maybe longer, to put together. Stay out of sight for a while. Plan it well and I'll get back to you. Go to Panama or somewhere to hide. I'll call for your exact plan if I get the approval. If I don't get the approval, grab Katrina and get the hell out of there. Ok, Armstrong."

"Yeah, we'll put in to a little cove we know for a day or so, then go to Jamaica and a little place we know. The boys might like to walk up that hill to the house on top again. They enjoyed it before," Nate replied.

"God, is that place still there. I was there twenty years ago. I know right where it is you're going. Those women really know how to please a man. I'm sure they are all new and younger, but they had good teachers. Good thinking and have fun. I get back to you," and he hung up.

About four hours they sailed into their private cove and anchored. They all went to their bonks to sleep, except the Lt. and Nate. Nate had volunteered to watch both prisoners. The one from Delbert's boat was transferred to his boat. In four hours, Carl would relieve him. All would get the sleep they needed. The guard from Delbert's boat was very quiet and Nate didn't trust him. He always seemed to be thinking. He watched the men and their movements very closely. This was what Nate would do if he were thinking escape.

-13-

For the next two days, they loafed around, eating and sleeping. The men had found some fresh fruit and had managed to bring it back to the ship. This occurred while they swam. Delbert's wounds seemed to be healing quickly. This because he was swimming in salt water. It would hurt like hell, he'd say getting into the water, but in a minute or so, the pain was gone. Nate checked the wounds and they looked good. They quit bandaging them leaving them to the air. It seemed to work.

Nate worked out a plan of attack; as good as, he could, not knowing some facts. He decided he'd call Katrina and ask for a favor.

He waited until after one AM, then dialed. The phone rang three times before it was answered. He began to worry. Finally, her sweet voice spoke to him.

"Hello," she said and waited.

"Hi, Katrina, it's Nate. Can you talk, he asked.

"No, I can't talk, I have a dozen men with me. Of course I can talk," she stated.

"I need to ask a favor of you. If you can't please say so. If you can, it would be a great help," he said.

With this, he laid out his plan for attacking the location they knew about in the jungle. She listened intently.

"What I need to know is when will the big fish will be there. It may take the General three or four days to get permission for the attack. If you can it would be a big help. I want them there so the can't walk away when we destroy their operation," he said.

"Well, before you started sinking their boats, they would visit the camp on Wednesdays. I'm not sure now. Yes, I think I can find out that information. I'll do it even if I have to bring one of the pigs home with me," she expressed herself.

"No, don't do that," he shot back at her.

"Nate, I was only kidding. When are you coming for me?" was a question he could not answer.

"I don't know honey, but we'll be there. Once we're thirty minutes out, I'll call you and you head for the docks as fast as you dare. If you're not there when we are, we'll head for El Toro. I really don't want to do that because it could get bloody. Understand," he emphasized.

"Yes, of course, quit treating me like a child. I'll get the information. Bye, Nate," she signed off in the sexiest voice she could manage.

He sat in the dark thinking. He was smoking a cigar and trying to work the kinks out of his plan. Finally, his memory brought back something Loretta had said. She had mentioned that her uncle, now the fish merchant, once worked at the camp. *It had to be the same one,* he thought to himself. *I wonder.*

He dialed Lorette's number. It rang several times before she answered.

"Hello, darling," he spoke into the phone.

"Oh, Nate, what's wrong?" she questioned.

"Nothing honeys. I just need a big favor," he reported.

"Wait a minute till I sit up and turn on a light. Ok, go ahead. Do you realize what time it is?"

"Yes, but I needed to talk to you. You once said your uncle worked for the cartels at the camp where they packaged their poison. Correct?" Nate asked.

"Yes, that's right. This was before he brought the fisheries. Why?" she asked.

"Do you think he could draw a map of its location and how to get there?"

"Sure, but why?" she asked.

"I can't tell you right now but if he can, have him do it for me. I'll return for the favor. I'll arrange for him to get and keep the two fishing boats we've been using. He'll really be independent then and never have to worry about going out of business. Please tell him that for me. If he will, have him draw it and keep it with him. As we come close to the port, I'll call you and you have him be ready to hand it to me. We won't be docking, but I'll pull into his place. We'll grab the map and be out of there. Keep this a secret. If anyone finds out he did this, they would kill him. I'll call you later today to see if he will," Nate explained.

"Oh, Nate, I'm worried for you. Please be safe," She said.

"I will, darling, for we are going to marry as soon as I attend to some last minute business. Love you. Bye," he said and hung up.

The days were boring and the men started asking if they could go to Jamaica.

"Ok," Nate finally gave in. "Fire up the engines and lets go," was the order of the day. The men all gave a cheer and rushed to comply. In minutes, they cleared the cove and opened the engines wide open. They skimmed across the water as if they were PT boats on an attack. A few hours later, they had arrived at the destination. It was late but the old man was still on the dock. The engines had awakened him and he came to meet them and collect the fee. Nate paid him and asked if the restaurant up the street was still open.

"Yes, if you hurry," he replied and went back to his shack.

This crew fast walked up the street and found it to be open. It was plain the owners were cleaning up with the intent to close.

"Could we get something to eat," Nate asked, "we'll pay extra?"

"Si, we have plenty of meatloaf left, with all the trimmings," said the old man.

"That will be fine. Six plates and some cold beer. Ok?" Nate said for all the crew.

Half-hour later the men were full, having two beers each and topped it off with apple pie, with ice cream.

Nate paid the bill and added a twenty as they left the restaurant

"Good night gentlemen," Nate said as he started to the boats. The rest of the crew headed up the hill towards the big house and the women. Nate went to bed.

They were still docked in Jamica, when the General called.

"Armstrong, you've got more guts than sense, but we'll back you. Your scheme is crazy and it's sheer sucide. The rangers will be in Panama tonight. They'll wait for you to call and your call sign is major. I've got you in the military at last," he laughed.

"Why a major? A Sgt. would have been good enough," Nate announced.

"Hell, boy there's a captain with this group. You'd be taking orders from him had I not done it. Don't worry. He'll never know you're a cilivian. He'd never live it down. They have all the equipment you'll need, with what you have on the boats. You do have some weapons and ammunition doesn't you?" snarled the General.

"You get up on the wrong side of the bed this morning, sir. You sound a little grumpy. It just won't do for you to have an attitude. Remember what you tell your men. Just do it," Nate followed up.

"God, Nate," said the General said, "I hope you don't get caught and I would love to be there with you. Remember this is top secret. Only you and I and those men you met here are involved. The rangers have been informed you're in charge and the mission is to wipe out terrorists. It's off the books and they understand it. Just bring them all back safely, Nate."

"I will General. I've arranged for Katrina to meet us at the docks when we get back. A Lt. From the Colombian Army has agreed to help us if we will get him and his wife and daughter out with us. Can do, yes," Nate fired back.

"Do you trust him? If he helps you and is sincere, yes we can. He has my word on it," was the response.

"Here, you tell him. He's standing right with me."

Nate handed the phone to Dennis and told him it was a General on the phone.

The Lt. spoke into the phone and listened a couple of minutes. He started grinning after a minute or so. He nodded his head a couple times and spoke only one word several times *"Si."*

The phone was passed back to Nate.

"What's the name of this Captain?" Nate asked.

"Jim Adams, for your ears only. That's the only name you get. The captain will handle his men. Remember, this exercise never happen. If you or one your men get caught, we will disown you and your crew. You know, the same as in Nam only more so. One thing in your favor is that the President of Colombia has agreed to not persue. He wishes you well but can't help you either. He's new in office and it wouldn't go well with his people, if he allowed American troops to invade his country. This isn't an invasion but the newspapers will make it seem like one. We need this person in power. He's going to start his own methods of routing out the drug cartels. We may even send support in the form of equipment and a few rangers. He's going to locate the farms, spray the plants with Agent Orange to kill them. We've told him about the civilian deaths if he uses this chemicial. He doesn't seem to care. His view is that if the farmers are killed, so is it. They shouldn't be growing the stuff. Well enough of that. How do you want the rangers delivered to form up with your group?" asked the General.

"Have them delivered to Panama, have the Colonel that we dealt with before handle it. I want to meet them and spend a day or so with them. In jungle warfare, you need to know each other, etc. From there they can be flown in or better yet have a sub deliver them. A sub can't be seen and a plane can. I'll tell the captain. I think I'll have a map to share with them. I'll also make sure we are anchored, in the cove, when they arrive. They're a lot of heavy jungle between Cartagena and this location. There's a little stream that runs down for the mountains to the sea. The camp we're after is set up on that creek. All we have to do is follow the stream and we'll find the camp. I have an informant who used to work there. He's drawing a map for us. I'm hoping he marks where the land mines, alarms etc are. This would make it a lot easier for us to surprise them. Three days from now, we'll be anchored in this cove. Have the sub come in around midnight. They'll have to row the last two hundred yards. Don't land them until they know we're there. I still have to pickup Katrina and get the map. We've got to sail into the dock area. In and out quick. I'll have Delbert go ahead and anchor there. That's about it general. Any questions?" Nate asked.

"No, good luck. The rangers will be there," he said and hung up.

He passed the word on to the men. All seemed pleased they would have rangers to support them.

Nate dialed another number.

"Hello," Loretta's voice came over the line.

"Hi, honey. Did you talk to your uncle and will he do the map?" Nate asked.

"Yes," he's willing to help. He hates drug dealers with a passion. He'll do it with out payment of the boats in case you have to sink them. The map should be ready now. If I know him, he sat down and did it right after I left him. I didn't take a chance on the phone and went by car. A friend took me so there's no record at the cab company. Oh, Nate, I'm scared. Please be careful. I want you to come back to me," she stated.

"Don't worry, I'll be careful. I'm coming back to you and never to do another mission. I'll help at the club and enjoy a beautiful woman for life. We'll go sailing, quiet dinners and good wine as we grow old. I'll be back as soon as I can, honey. Take care. Got to go. Tomorrow we'll swing in and pick up the map about dark. Please tell your uncle. Bye honey," Nate said.

The two hung up and Nate turned his attention to more pressing things.

Everyone but Carl was at the boats. Carl had stayed at the big house on the hill. Apparently, he had found someone he could relate to or something else.

"Carl's not back yet so I'm gong after him. Delbert you get the boats gassed up and fill the extra cans. We'll need all we can get before this next run is completed. Then meet me at the restaurant. We'll eat before we leave. Snap to it, " were Nate's instructions.

Nate walked up the hill towards the house of ill repute. He didn't have anything against these types of women. His feelings were that they preformed a service and made a living at it. It is the oldest profession in the world and a needed one. Even here in a poor country, they fill a need. Nate's feelings were to live and let live. He soon arrived at the door. He rang the bell.

A nice looking blonde-haired person opened the door, smiling at him

"Well come in handsome, what can I do for you?" she said in a joyful sort of way.

"I'm looking for one of my men. His name is Carl. We're about to shove off. Could you get him for me, please?" Nate asked.

"Sure, but isn't there something I can do for you." she enticed.

"Not now, honey. Hurry up please."

"Well, you don't have to be so bossy. He's in the room at the top of the stairs with Rita. Go get him yourself. You should knock before you enter. They're involved." was her reply.

Nate assended the stairs on the red carpet. The old house was in good shape for its age. Nate wondered how many times it had been remodeled. A crystal chandlier hung over the main lobby area, just inside the door. The bulbs clear in color. This made the whole room bright. The carpet was a beautiful red, the same as on the stairs. The walls had brightly colored wallpaper with many designs. Nate had never seen anything like it. He liked what he saw. Reaching the top of the stairs, he stepped up to he door and hesitated. Should he just walk in? These rooms had no locks on them. It would be interesting to see Carl in a sexual embrace.

Nate's mind went to Nam and a scene such as this. It was late at night and he had to get back to the camp. Carl and Don had been with him earlier. He'd found Don and they were looking for Carl. Finally, they found a joint where he had been seen earlier. It was a bad part of town. A place where the Viet Cong killed Americans. At least one fourth of the people in this area were supporting the Cong. Here they would steal from the Americans. The girls would take them into back rooms and screw them. Getting them drunk first, then a friend would come along and hit them over the head. An hour or two later the would wake up in an alley, stripped of their money, weapon and boots. The Cong were always short on shoes.

Nate had entered this dive and offered a twenty to an old woman sitting near a bar. Nate explained as best he could what he was looking for. The old girl held up three fingers and pointed down a dimly lit hallway. He took that to mean the third door and gave her the twenty. Walking down the hall, her reached door number three. He had left Don out front, in case there was trouble.

He pushed the door open just in time to see a man raise a club over Don's head. A naked woman sat a few feet away. Carl was drunk and looked up as Nate entered. The other man didn't. His mistake. Nate pulled his pistol and shot him dead. The woman reacted in horror at this sight. Nate turns and struck her across the face with the forty-five. A deep gouge appeared and blood ran down her face. *She's not so pretty now and may have a hard time of getting another G.I. alone,* Nate thought.

He picked Carl up and walked him to the front entrance. Don saw him coming and gave a hand. They made it to their jeep just as two people came running out of the joint.

"Hang onto Carl, Don and duck down. Those guys have guns," Nate yelled as he floor boarded the jeep. Gunfire sounded behind them and they could hear the buzz of bullets whistling by them. They made it out unharmed.

That was a long time ago, but the thought brought a smile to his lips.

This of course was a different sort of caper, but what the hell. Nate pushed the door open and stepped inside.

The two on the bed grabbed for covers. Both naked and were surprised at the interuption. Nate sat down on the foot of the bed, looking at the two.

"Hi, Carl, everything ok," Nate asked.

"Yes, hell yes, what do you want?" Carl sounded a little upset.

"We're pulling out and thought you might want to go along. Was I wrong?" Nate said as he smiled at them.

"Right now?" Carl asked.

"We're going to have a meal at the restaurant down the street then we're gone. You come."

Carl planted a little kiss on the woman's lips and jumped out of bed. He dashed to the bathroom. Nate heard the water come on and knew he was in the shower. He stood up, starting for the door.

"Sorry, honey, but we have to go," Nate said as he turned and looked at her. She was a pretty little thing and he didn't blame Carl for wanting to stay. Business before pleasure in their line of work.

Nate stopped on the front porch and waited. Within ten minutes, Carl appeared and the two of them walked to the restaurant. The other men had already ordered and were waiting for them. Seating themselves, they ordered steaks and all the trimmings. Coffee was passed around. The men were quiet all in his own thoughts. They knew the mission was turning dangerous. They all looked forward to it but as always, they were quiet before jumping into battle. This wouldn't last long. As soon as the idea of danger passed, they would get boisterous. They would joke with each other, push each other around. This was a way of keeping busy and freed their minds of what was to come.

"Are we gassed and ready to go," Nate asked.

Delbert nodded his head as he slurped the coffee. The meal came and they all dove in. They were hungry and all knew this might be the last of a good home cooked meal for a week or two. From the time they reached the jungle, till they returned, it would be k-rations.

Even though they were all anxious to get started, they were looking forward to getting back to the states. Once there they could pick up their lives and enjoy life.

Back at the boats, they prepared to cast off. Nate knew they would have to run with their engines wide oped to make it back to Cartagena. He hoped the motors would stand it. They moved out into the open water and once out a mile, they opened up and were on their way. Nate took the lead and Delbert brought his boat up behind. They made quite a sight. Just to see a couple fishing boats speeding like P.T. boats would have caused anyone to scratch their heads.

Ten miles off the coast of Colombia, they stopped. It was a little early for the run into the port. Pickup Katrina and the map. It should be an easy chore but you never know. The Lt. had taken off his uniform and replaced them with regular work clothes. Some of the men gave him a couple changes and he seemed content in them.

They swung into port, right on time. They waited a few minutes for Katrina. She was not there. Something was wrong. Nate had a bad feeling about this and moved his boat to the gas pumps.

Loretta's uncle saw them and came running to Nate. He handed him the map and told him news of Katrina.

"Were you to pickup Katrina over at your area?" he asked.

"Yes, we were. Do you know what has happened to her?" Nate asked as he took hold of his shoulders.

"Si, she is under arrest at her home. An army Sgt. Padro Rodriquez, a mean bastard, is her guard. Do you know where she lives?" He asked Nate.

"Yes, can we tie up at your place while we go get her?" Nate asked.

"Yes, we will take our time and load your boats with ice. Move over as soon as you have the gas," he said and hurried back to his business.

The men heard about Katrina and were all ready to march up to the house and rescue her.

"Let me go boss." Ed asked, "I'll take Brad with me and get her back."

"Ok, let me tell you how to find her house. Go in the back. Don't knock, just break the door down and be quick," Nate said. He gave Ed directions to the house and wished them luck.

Armed with the directions, he and Brad took off up the dock area, to the road and up towards Katrina's place. Both had armed themselves with 357 Mags. For the trip.

They moved the boats and proceeded with the ice loading.

"Delbert, you listen for shooting up where Ed and Brad have gone. If you hear any, sing out. We'll go after them. In the meantime the rest of you make sure all the firepower we have on board is out from under the bunks. Make sure the light arms are loaded. If we have to shoot our way out, by damn we will. Shake a leg boys, it's time for action," Nate ordered them.

Like a well-oiled machine, they went into action. Everyone knew how the others worked and the did their task without interfering with each other.

Up the street a ways, Ed spotted the house. The color was a dead giveaway. There was no other house that color for many blocks. The two men went around to the back and approached the door. Ed listened for a minute and thought he heard a faint whimper. He nodded to Brad they were going in. He stepped back a step, raised his boot and slamed it hard against the door latch. The door went flying open and both rushed in.

Katrina was lying on the bed, her clothes torn completely off. She had a few cut and bruses. She had been struck across the face and a faint trickle of blood ran down the corner of her mouth. The Sgt. was just crawling on top of her when they rushed.

"What the hell," he said.

Ed rushed forward and knocked him off the bed. As he hit the bed, he shot him three times. All movement stopped. Three holes were oozing out his life's blood. Ed had little patience for rapist. Brad grabbed Katrina and pulled her to her feet.

"Grab a change of clothes and put some on. Be quick. Those shots will bring someone we don't want to see," Brad advised.

Katrina ran into the little bedroom. In a couple minutes, she was dressed and back. She worn jeans and a shirt. She had a small bag.

The three left by the back and ran a block before slowing down. A couple of the neighbors had seen them, but no one seemed excited. None interfered.

They did a fast walk and were soon entering the dock area. They looked to the east and saw their boats. They ran in that direction.

Nate saw them coming and yelled at the men.

"Lets get the hell out of here?" he said. He ran inside to speak to the old man.

"Twenty miles up the coast, where the stream runs into the sea is where I'll leave the boats for you. Thanks friend. Tell Loretta thanks and I'll be back just as soon as I complete some business. Don't go for the boats until I call Loretta and tell her we are out of there. Ok?" more of a question than an agreement.

"Si," smiled the old man. "Give them hell, Armstrong," he yelled after Nate.

"Everyone on board?" Nate asked as he jumped on board and cast off one line.

"Yes, sir," replied Ed, "we're good to go."

Nate looked over at Delbert's boat and got thumbs up.

"Put the pedal to the metal and lets roar," he yelled as if he was on a racetrack.

In just a couple of minutes, they were out of sight. They were heading for Panama. The plan was to make anyone watching think they were out of there. Nate hoped the drug lords would think them on their way back to the states and out of their hair. To make a bee line for the cove would have telegraphed the wrong message to them and sure as hell sent them looking for them. With engines wide open, they cut through the water with ease.

Nate wanted to see the rangers with his men, so they would recognize each other in the small war to come. In the jungle, you need to know how each man moves, smells and looks. Life and death depends on it. A remimder was flashbacks to Nam. He was sure this was occurring with his men. Those years were tough and here they were throwing themselves right back into a similar to one of the missions of their own free will. *We must be crazy,* Nate was thinking. However, this fight was not to free a nation-fighting communism. This was a fight to free people from the drug habit and to keep others from falling into this velvet trap.

He often thanked God for getting them in and out alive. This time it would be two to three days up the creek to the drug camp and maybe two days out. He hoped they could get out in two days. Beyond that, the chance of capture was great.

Nate remembered he had a number for the Colonel who he met earlier. He called the number and waited through four rings before it was answered. Finally, a voice answered.

"Colonel, this is Armstrong. I need your help."

"Wait a minute, this is Lt. Brooks, and I'll see if the colonel will speak to you." He was put on hold.

A minute later, the colonel came on the line.

"Armstrong, where are you? I've been told you'd be calling. What can I help you with," he said.

"We're about to land in Panama, same place as last time. We want to meet with the rangers and get some food. Once we tie up, I thought we'd take a cab out to the base if you'll clear the way for us. I fact it will take several cabs. To hell with it. Could you send a truck? Once your people arrive, pretend to take us as if we were under arrest. Have the rangers waiting in a far corner of the mess hall and we'll eat together. I want my people to get to know them a little, without names. Are you ok with this, sir?" Nate finished talking.

"Hey, I've been told by a general that I'm to cooperate with you fully. What ever you say. Consider it done. You'll be tieing up in ten minutes or so. The M.P.'s will be there a minute or two later. See you soon. Anything else?" he asked.

"No, not for now. Thanks, Colonel," Nate said and hung up.

No sooner had they docked but a group of six M.P.'s walked up to the boats, the leader was a Sgt. who was the only one to speak.

"You and your party are to come with us," he said in a gruff tone.

"Ok, but what's the problem," Nate asked because he noticed several people looking on.

"You'll find out later. Come on snap to it," was the order.

The eight, single filed it up the ramp and into the waiting truck. They took a seat as four of the six M.P.'s climbed in behind them. They sat at the tail in case anyone was looking. This was all done for the benefit of those looking on. Nate heard one person speak of it.

"More damn drug dealers. They should be shot," said and old angler mending his nets.

Nate didn't mind this at all. It was good cover for who they really were. If anyone came snooping around they would come to the conclusion they were drug smugglers.

The ride took fifteen minutes, so Nate figured the base was about ten to twelve miles from the docks.

The truck pulled up in front of the messhall and everyone piled out. The colonel was waiting on the steps for them. Nate walked up to him and shook his hand.

"Thanks, Colonel, good show. It's good to see you again," Nate announced.

"Same here Major, congrats on your promotion," he said with a smirkly grin. He knew Nate was not in the military. "Come on in the food will be on in minutes. Have some coffee. You have the whole place to yourselves. That far corner over there is best for quiet conversations. Do you want me to stay?"

"No, that not necessary. As soon as I finish here, I would like to sit down with you for a few minutes and discuss our delivery and escape plan," Nate said.

"Sure, I'll be down the street two buildings. My office is on the second floor. I'll be waiting for you. I will now leave you to your business," he said.

"Grab some coffee, guys, and we'll sit over there," Nate pointing at the far back corner of the dining hall. They all took coffee as they passed by where the serving line would be.

No more were they seated, than ten men came through the door. They to took coffee and walked to Nate's table and seated themselves after pushing some tables together. The last one over was the one Nate took to be the Capt. He was right.

The man approached Nate to within arms length. He stopped and extended his hand.

"Capt. Adams, at your service, sir," he said addressing Nate.

"Glad to have you Capt. I think you'll get a kick out of what we are about to do. Lying around training and training and training can get boring. I'm going to give you rangers some real action. I just wanted to meet you and have my people be able to recognize yours after they put on their war paint," Nate took a breath then went on.

"You been briefed Capt.?" he asked.

"No, sir, the General said you would do that and I was to do as you said. I do understand it is a dangerous mission and my people are ready. You were right when you said it gets boring, just training and not getting any real action. The general says you're crazy as hell but smart. My rangers are ready for any task sir. I've hand picked them and would trust my life to any of them," he proudly bragged.

"That fine Capt. But now I have to be sure I can trust the lives of my people to them. Our mission will be a hit and run one. No doubt there, will be killing. Some of them might not make it back. If they listen and follow orders, we'll all come back safely. I believe in some famous words by General Patton, during World War 11. I don't expect you to die for your country, but rather make the other side die for theirs. The bastards we're going after are fighting for money not country. That's what makes us winners," Nate paused to look over these rangers.

Most were in their thirties, that mean't the were career soldiers. That's a good sign. Those who went for a career, believed in what they were doing. It's also a second nature to them to follow orders.

"Ok, gather round men, pull your chairs up close and I'll give you the plan before the food gets here. If you have any questions, hold them for now. The Capt. and I will answer them later," Nate asked.

The men moved their chairs in a huddle around Nate.

"I have a map here of our target and directions on how to get there. A man who once worked for the Cartels gave it to me. Yes, cartels. We are going after the drug lords. We are going to strike a blow that will put them out of business for a while. We're to kill anyone who resists our actions. This goes for the farmers who grow the plants. We are mainly after the facility where they turn the product into cocaine. Anyone has a problem with this?" he asked.

No one moved or said a word so Nate went on.

"This is top secret and must never be told. Don't discuss it unless you know you cannot be heard. You never know who works for the cartels or has a friend or relative working for them. It's a matter of life and death. Understand?"

They all nodded their heads so Nate went ahead and laid out his plan. He told them he would have the colonel make copies of the map and they would be handed one when they landed at the jumping off site. He told of trip mines and all sorts of bobby traps once they neared the camp. He told them their best guide was the stream. If anyone became separated from the others, they were to follow the stream back to the ocean, etc.

"One more thing. We cannot leave a trace that we are Americans. If a man is killed, we carry him back with us. Is that clear?" Nate said rathered loudly. Everyone nodded.

The food was being brought out of the kitchen and everyone was told that was the briefing. More would come as they started inland.

"Lets eat," he announced.

Everyone put there chairs back at tables and went to the serving line.

With trays of food, they returned to the tables to eat. Nate spoke to the Captain.

"Lets set over there," he said, "and let the men get aquainted."

"Sure, whatever you say," was the reply.

They sat down at a small table and began eating. After a few bites and swallows of coffee, Nate began the conversation.

"How well do you know these men?" came the first queston.

"Quite well, we became a team about three years ago. Since then it's been in training, year after year. We did help in kidnapping Noreaga when that happened. I know what your next question will be and the answer is no. We have not seen action in jungles, but eighty percent of our training has been in jungles. We've run the gaulant many times with all the benefits of a training officer who had. The General told me to tell you his name, as it would help in our crediablity. It seems you know him. Chris Taylor was his name. Did several tours in Viet Nam, I understand," answered the Captain.

"Not little old Chris Taylor. About five foot six, one hundred sixty pounds. Coal black hair and all muscle. In his forties, maybe fifty. A real women man.

But on duty, his was like a bulldog. He never lets up even when he knows you know. That Chris Taylor?" Nate asked.

"That sounds like him. Apparently, you do know him. I'm to tell you that he personally picked us for this mission," the Captain said proudly.

"Well if Chris picked your group, he must really have confidence in you. Hell, yes I know him. We did things in Nam together. He was military and I was a C.I. A. contractor. God, it's good to hear he's ok," Nate explained.

Both men sat in silence as they ate. Nate thinking back to those things he and Chris had done in Nam. Some were not pretty but all done to advance the war to victroy.

Both men finished about the same time and pushed their trays away. Refilling their coffee cups and returned to the table.

"Well if you have such faith in your men and Chris trained you, you're proably the best team I could get. I hope none of them are squeamish this could get messy and they must perform at their best," Nate was saying as he looked over at the men and Katrina at the other table.

They were talking and seem to be getting the idea. The idea that each one is dependent on the other to survive.

"I didn't know the was a woman on this mission?" said the Captain. "What job does she do?"

"She not goes inland with us. She was an undercover operative whose job is done. We're getting her out with us. For the time being, she will guard the boats while we're in the jungle. You never know when they might come in handy. If for some reason, like fog, and the choppers can't get to us, we'll make the run in the boats. Their engines have been souped up and they can move. If that happens we'll be out to sea and the navy can pick us up there. Why, you don't have a problem with it do you?" Nate finshed his explanation.

"No, not at all. Just wondering," said the Captain.

"I have to go to see the colonel and discuss our pickup plan. When, where and that sort of thing. We can keep the submarine as a backup. I'll know in a few minutes. You and the men get aquainted and I'll be back in half and hour, I think."

Nate reached the Colonel's office, opened the door and went in. A Sgt. was sitting at a desk in the outer office.

"I'm here to see the Colonel," he told the Sgt.

"Yes, sir, he's expecting you. You may go right in," said the Sgt.

Nate opened the door and stepped into the Colonel's office. The Colonel was sitting behind a huge desk. He was taking a sip from a whiskey jigger. In his left hand, he held a cigar. Cuban of course. It seems to Nate, everyone down here smoked the same kind of cigar.

"Sit down Major. Would you like a drink and maybe a cigar?" asked the Colonel.

"Don't mind if I do. Sure, both please," Nate, replied.

The Colonel reached inside his desk drawer and pulled out another glass an cigar. In another drawer, he pulled out a bottle of whisky and fills the glass. This he handed across the desk to Nate. He filled his glass again and raised it high.

"Here are to you Major and the success of your mission, what ever it is," he said as he downed the whisky.

Nate followed suit and both sat their glasses on the desk.

The Colonel leaned forward and waited for Nate to speak.

Nate pulled the map from his shirt pocket and handed it across to the Colonel.

"Would you have the Sgt. Out their make a dozen copies of that and one for yourself? On second thought, make two for you. What I need you to do with your copies is to give one to the submarine Capt. and one to the flight leader of the choppers that will be picking us up," Nate asked.

"Sure, can do," he said and raised his voice and hollered at the Sgt. to come in," the Sgt. came in and was asked to make the copies.

"Yes sir," he replied and walked out of the room.

Nate looked around and just had to comment on the nice office and furniture the Colonel surrounds himself with.

"You seem to have it made here Colonel. Good whisky, cigars and the food were excellent. You're going to miss this when you go back stateside."

"I know so I'm taking advantage of this wonderful country. You need to stay over a couple days and nights and meet some of the women," he said and rasied his fingers to his lips and kissed them. This was his way of saying they were beyond in their beauty. He continued.

"The women are beautiful and they love Americans. The married ones don't fool around. These people have strong family values, but the single ones are great. Not cheap women either. It takes a while to get one in bed, but when you do, God knows the wait was worth it," he expressed.

"Sorry I can't spare the time. Besides when the mission is completed, I'm going back to Colombia. I've met the woman of my dreams and she loves me. That's another reason we don't use names, etc. I don't want anything hanging over me when I get back," Nate said.

"She sounds great. Where does she live in Colombia?" asked the Colonel.

"Cartagena, she runs her own business. A first class bar and nightclub. She's great and she waits for me," Nate said.

"What's this ladys name? I know some people in that town. Maybe I know her," explained the Colonel.

"Loretta. I'll keep this on a first name only conversation," Nate answered.

The Colonel leaned across the desk as he spoke.

"Is this Loretta the one who has her portrait painted on the walls of her club?" he asked.

"Yes, have you been there?" Nate asked.

"Yes, many times and as I understand it she is above reproach and not interested in men. She's still in love with her dead husband. God what a beautiful woman and she are waiting for you. I'm jealous. Good for you. Invite me to the wedding, will you? I can't believe anyone is able to get close to her. Man you are one lucky son-of-a-gun," finished the Colonel.

A knock came on the door and the Colonel answered with a "Come in."

The Sgt. was back with the copies. He handed them to the Colonel and left the room.

"Here you go Major, I take my two and lock them up. I'll use them as you say and when you need them. The sub should be in after dark tonight. The Capt. is a good man and he will put the ranger's right where you want them and always on time," he said.

"Good, that's what I'll need. I assume they also know that this is top secret, now and forever? Ok, now let me show you where I need the sub to drop the men. We'll be close by and pick them up for the last few yards. I don't know how deep the water is there so I'll just have to leave it up to the Capt., as to how close he can come to the shore," Nate," said.

"Oh, yes, the General speaks in very certain terms. If you don't comply, he'll have your head. Everyone connected with this have his or her instructions. Another drink before you goes?" he asked.

"Sure, why not," was the answer and Nate pushed his glass back across the desk. It was promply filled and handed back. The two men talked for a while and Nate departed.

Nate returned to the men who were playing foortball with the rangers. They had divided into two small teams and were enjoying the game.

Nate whistled at the group. As he did so, he saw Katrina in the game. She stuck her head up in response to the whistle or he'd never identified her as a woman. Kind of a tomboy, she was.

The men all gathered round him, waiting for instructions.

"Ok, gang, we shove off a little after dark. You have the rest of the day off. I suggest you go to the P.X. and get whatever smokes you need. Get some tape for you rangers to tape your dogtags together. We want no jingle, jangle in the jungle. You rangers show my men how to blacken their faces and give them the product to do it with. Anything else you can think of Capt.," Nate was looking at the Rangers commanding officer.

"No, if I think of anything, I'll get to it. No problems here, sir," he said with a smile.

"Ok, then, I'll buy drinks starting at four PM at the N.C.O club. Take your bars off Capt. We'll sneak you in," Nate said with a small chuckle. His men broke out in laughter. He continued, "We eat together at the mess hall and Part Company for a couple days. We will see each other again very soon. Now get the hell out of here," he stomped his feet as he would to kids. It worked, they scattered with laughter and he went for a stroll. The laughter was the best way to reduce stress. He knew every man there was thinking about the mission and who may not come back. He also knew they would never say a word to each other about it. That's just the way it is.

-14-

Just at the end of twlight, the two fishing boats were on their way out of port. As darkness was falling they passed by a sub, just surfacing an everyone felt better. They knew that soon the rangers would be joining them. The sub was a guarantee. Nate and his crew were on they way to an experience they would never forget.

Katrina and Carl were leaning over the side and talking in low tones. They were starting to get acquainted. These two were thrown together on this mission and there seemed to be an attraction for both. Nate had noticed but said nothing. He felt good about these two. They both needed someone in their lives. They were good people looking towards the future. It confirmed Nate's suspicion when Katrina wanted to ride in Delbert's boat. Nate silently wished them well. He prayed he could bring them back safely.

In the open sea, Nate opened up us boat to maxium speed. Delbert did the same. The two ran side by side for hours. They had two days to get to the cove, but Nate wanted to get there a little early. He was always that way and because of it he had came home from Nam in one piece. Had he not been early a couple times, he and others would have walked into a trap. A wicked crossfire. This causes it to become second nature for him. *Besides the early bird gets the worm,* he was thinking.

Ed, Brad and Nate opened a fresh bottle of whisky and passed it around. Nate went below and got cigars for each of them. For the next two hours, they talked of women, sex and other manly items, such as fishing and hunting.

That night they took four-hour turns at the wheel while the others slept. The trip was without incident except for the dolphins swimming in their wake. This was of interest during daylight hours. In the late afternoon of the second day, they pulled into the cove and anchored. Nate called a meeting. The boats were anchored side by side so the crew on the other boat only had to move over to the side where Nate stood. They didn't have to leave their boat.

"If anyone comes by, we will tell them we have a mechanical problem. No help needed. We have it under control. I'm going ashore with a couple volunteers and pick some fruit. That alone will make people think we are having a problem with the boats. Who wants to go along and help with the fruit?" he said.

Don and Brad spoke up, "we will."

"Ok, lets go. The rest of you get some sleep or fix food. We'll spend the night on the boats. At first light, we enter the jungle and the fun begins. Remember after dark the rangers will join us so clean the decks of junk so they will have room to sleep. We won't be gone long," Nate, advise.

The three entered the jungle on the hunt for fresh fruit. Nate was also looking for signs of people being there. He wanted to know if they might have company after entering the jungle tomorrow. While Don and Brad picked some bananas, cocoanuts and assorted fruit Nate went into the jungle. He walked upstream for three hundred yards or so. He kept his eyes scaning the underbrush, but also the water in the stream. If anyone upstream stepped in the water, it would muddy it for a short distance. He left the stream from time to time looking for a path in the jungle. He looked for broken twigs, scuffed markings in the soil, etc. He would kneel down for a closer look. Had anyone watched it would have been like watching a bloodhound looking for a scent?

He returned to where Dan and Brad were waiting. They had more fruit than the three could carry, so they made two trips.

Hot food had been prepared and they ate and had just finished when darkness fell. Some were still munching on the fresh fruit. They passed the whisky bottle around and cigars for those who wanted one.

Nate took a slug out of the bottle and moved to the bow of the boat. He fired up a cigar and stared out to the sea. A few minutes later Katrina joined him.

"I understand you are in love and are planning on coming back to Colombia. Is that right?" she asked.

Nate hated this type of conversation because he was afraid she was going to be hurt. He didn't want a scene and just because he had sex with her, didn't mean he was serious. Of course, she had been without for a long time and she may have taken it as serious. Well he had to face and answer he question.

"Yes, that's correct. Does it bother you?" his answer.

"No, I was kind of hoping we might get together, but not for serious stuff. I'm glad for you Nate, I believe you need a wife. That's proablely all that will make you give up and quit these types of missions. Can I ask you a question?" she asked.

"Sure, what's up," he responded.

"Well, this guy Carl seems to be a quiet man. I judge him to be a good man and perhaps needs what I do. He's told me all about his life and I may be interested in him. Is there anything I need to know about him, before I spend more time with him? I'm interested, but I don't want to get hurt. I know he's your friend and he was with you in Nam. But please be truthful with me. I know the types of friendships that can be formed under the dangers of war. Please Nate be truthful," she encouraged.

"There's nothing about him that would be adversely affected by your relationship. He's a good honest, hard worker. His word is good and that's to everyone, a not just friend. I have a feeling any woman who is lucky to have him. I have a feeling he's very tender and loving. Go for it, he deserves someone like you," he answered.

"Thanks, Nate, I think I'll go over and start a conversation with him," she said.

"Go for it kid, go for it," Nate added.

She gave him a quick little kiss and moved back along the deck where Carl was leaning over the rail, staring out to sea.

As Katrina walked up to him, Nate saw the smile that lit up his face. Inside he was glad for them.

About an hour later, Nate saw a blinking light at sea. It was a good quarter mile away. Nate took the flashlight he had come with and flashed it toward the light. The night was dark and no moon. He strained his eyes to see the conning tower on the sub. He couldn't, it was too dark. *A good night for covert operations, "* Nate thought.

The light stopped blinking. He knew the rangers had arrived. Nate looked around at his crew.

"Hey, everyone, the rangers are here. Get ready to bring them aboard," Nate ordered.

Minutes later ten men scrambled aboard the two fishing boats. Whisky was passed around a couple times, and then put away. No one needed to get drunk.

They would have to be at their best tomorrow. Before they turned in for the night, Nate met with the Captain. He told of going ashore and snooping around.

"I found nothing to indicate men had passed this way. There is no trail leading up the creek. We will have to pick our way through the jungle. We need to be careful and not leave any signs we had been here. These people must have scouts out looking for anyone that might try to sneak up on them. After the damage, we've done to them, they will be jumpy. They'll likely fire at any thing that moves. There will be times when we will have to crawl for long distances, on our bellies. You and I will tell them when. Come morning we will divide our forces and go up both sides of the stream. We need to stay about fifty yards out from the stream. We must inch our way to our target without being spotted. Fewer will die that way. You brief your men at first light. Mine has already been briefed. Captain, my men who will be with you, you need to listen to them. They were in Nam with me and know this kind of war. So pay attention and lets forget about the rank. We're all the same here, except I give the orders. Is that clear?" Nate asked.

"Yes, sir, it's clear," replied the Captain.

"Ok, we'll sleep up here. The woman will use my bunk. Your men will sleep on deck. Grab a sheet from below if you need one and lets get some sleep."

Nate knew from years of duty, most fighting men could not sleep the night before an attack. He knew he would not. All sorts of things came to mind when you think you may not come back. Dumb things, silly things, etc. It couldn't be helped, it just happens.

There is an old saying that "today is the first day of my life." Well to fighters it reads, "Today may be the last day of my life." A normal response for a men going into war.

Nate was right. He did not sleep a minute. His mind kept going over things that should be done, what hasn't done, etc. Deep down he knew there was no way to prepare for what might happen. It was a trial and error methods were common. The problem being, they could make no mistakes. He didn't really know these men, but he did the trainer. If he were still the man he once was, these men would be ok.

After leaving Nam, he had pledged to never be responsible for the lives of men again. Yet here he was, doing just that. Once this job was done, he was set financially and would never have to do the dangerous jobs he once did. This mission had to go right. Well it was too late to turn back and with the General scanning the area with a satellite, it should go well.

The men were all awake at four am, to a meal of hash browns, eggs, sausage and toast two large pots of coffee waited their waking. Katrina had been up an hour before the men. She worked around them to cook in the crowded space. Most of them were awake, just resting and waiting for the food. She had no more finished than; they piled out of bed with shorts and t-shirts on. They helped carry the coffee and food on deck. It was still dark, but they had no problem finding the plates which the filled with food and sat down on the decks to eat. This was taking place on both boats. The men helped by passing platters of food to the other boat. They had there own plates. Delbert had also put on coffee.

The meal took thirty minutes and the dishes were stacked and the men put their unmarked clothes on. The last item they put on was their back packs in which were packed K-rations and rounds for their pistols. Each man carried a knife as well. Weapons were checked and loaded. In no time, they were ready for the jungle.

Nate pulled Delbert and Katrina to one side for a talk.

"You're not going Delbert because of your arm. Katrina is also staying. I'm depending on you two to protect the boats. Remember, if anyone gets curious, you're broke down. One of us has gone to town for parts and the rest of the crew is in the jungle looking for fruit. Stick to that story. This should satify most everyone. I don't think the cartel has anyone right close. They proably have a short cut into town a couple miles in. You call it as you see it. If you think you are in danger of being found out, kill anyone in your road. If this happens, take the body or bodies out to sea. Half a mile should do and dump them. Get right back. I don't know how long we'll be gone. It's going to be slow going and we have about ten miles to go. Some of this will be searching for mines, boobie traps or alarms. We're not going to hurry. I want our little visit to be a secret, until we attack. You two alright with this?" he finished.

"Well I sure I speak for Katrina when I say we'd like to be going with you. Yes, we are ok with our duty. You won't have to worry about the boats. We'll be right here when you return," Delbert answered.

"Good," Nate said, "on our return, I'll have the General get the choppers in fast and we'll be on our way home. They will pick us up right here on the beach," Nate said and shook hands with both of them. He turned and went ashore and waited for the men to group for final instructions. He had a couple of minutes, so he brought the phone and dialed the General.

"Brown's Realty, how may I help you," answered the General.

"Good morning General, we are at the cove and ready to mount our assault into the jungle. Get the satilite in place and scan the area from the ocean to the camp. Let me know if you see anything suspious. If you find something you don't understand, relay it to me and we'll check it out. Our lives may be in your hands. When you find out how long we have the satilite on us. When it goes out of sight, tell me. To those controlling the device, have them give you times when we are on our own. They should have a good idea. I know we can't have it on us all the time. We will wait when we are nearing the camp, to have it checked out. We'll need to know how well its guarded. You know, any information will help make us successful," Nate informed him.

"You must remember you're talking to a General, Mr. Armstrong," came the reply.

"Yeah, I know, but you see I'm not in the service. I'm a civilian. I'm not getting smart, just covering all bases. You've been behind a desk so long you may have forgotten what is needed," Nate came back at him.

"I have the answer to your satilite question. Write this down and hurry, this long distance call is costing me a fortune," chuckled the General.

"Hold a second," Nate said, "I'll get a pencil."

The information was passed along and Nate thanked him and hung up when the General wished him luck.

The group formed on the beach for final instructions.

"Captain you take the left side of the creek and I'll take the right side. I want as little chatter as possible on the radios. In fact give me that radio," he ordered a young man.

The radio was passed over and Nate carried it to Delbert's boat. Delbert saw him coming and walked to the bow of the boat.

"Here Delbert, you take the radio and I'll take your phone. This will make it much quieter for the trip. You can still get in touch with us if needed. Now don't call us unless it's a real emergency," Nate mentioned.

"Yes, boss, to bad we didn't have phones in Nam. I agree and good luck," he said and passed the phone over. In return, he received the radio.

Returning to the beach, Nate passed the phone to the Captain.

"We'll use this instead of a radio. Have your other operator keep his on in case there's trouble here at the boats. Delbert will let us know if he gets into trouble. Ok, lets go," he said

The men disappeared like ghosts into the jungle. It was just light enough for their trek up the creek. They fanned out as Nate had instructed. The heat was already causing the sweat pour out of the men. Each felt the weight of their packs, but would soon get use to them. The men moved at a distance of five to six yards apart.

They were soon into thick jungle. Their instructions were not to use their knives to cut their way through the underbrush. This would make the trip a very slow process. The two groups would use the phones every thirty minutes for a while to pace them. They needed to stay about even so all would arrive at the camp at the same time. It would be dangerous to wait in close to camp. The last half-mile would be crucial.

The jungle heated up fast. Nate had almost forgotten how like a pressure cooker it could be. It had been a few years since Nam.

A mile in he checked with the Captain.

"How's it going Capt., are you troops holding up in this heat?" Nate asked.

"Yeah, there are doing fine. The heat is kind of nasty. I'm glad we're taking it slow. The men are trained and know how to conserve their water. What's going on over there?" he asked.

"The same as with you. Have you spotted any signs of people? Any footprints or branches broken?" Nate inquired.

"No, not yet but we're looking. If I spot any, we will stop and call you at once. Any idea when you think we'll start finding booby traps, etc."

"I can only surmise that the closer we get to the camp, the more likely we'll find some. After another mile, we need to concretrate on looking more carefully. Sounds carry in the jungle and if we set one off, they can hear it for three or four miles. Watch for a trail. If you find one, don't walk on it. Have a couple of your men go each side of it. That's where they are likely to find some. They set them across the trails. A close examinination in the brush will disclose where they are. If you do find some, disarm them but don't make any signs that would disclose that. We maybe coming back in a hurry and have to use the trails. We want them safe. If you find one you don't know how to defuse or can't clear a trip wire, call; I have a man who can. In fact, you have him with you. Carl is our demo expert. Let him do what needs to be done on any traps you find. We'll do the same over here. Lets take a half hour break. Lets set our watches so we know we have the same time. Mine shows eight thirty on the nose," Nate said.

"I'll have to move mine up a couple minutes." A hestation then, "Ok we're right on," came from the Captain.

Thirty minutes they shoved off and tackled the jungle. Their advancement was slow and treacherous. They discovered many snakes along the way. Some very dangerous and some not. Seeing some hanging from tree limbs made the journey kind of spooky. Rather than kill the snakes they encountered, they changes course a little, going around they.

Places in the underbrush were wet and soggy. They usually didn't see these spots coming until they stepped into them. It was difficult to keep the men quiet. When they spoke, they spoke in low tones so the sound did not carry far.

Nate would stop from time to time and listen. He hoped he heard nothing coming from across the creek. Ever so often, he would work his way over to the water and examine it for signs of discoloration that might disclose some one had crossed it up ahead. He found none to this point and always breathed a sigh of relief. He would then work his way back to where his team waited. Again, the progress was slow. Most of the men felt like turtles just barely making a mile or two in half a day.

Lunchtime was taken after Nate called Captain Jim and advised him.

"Jim, it's time for lunch. Pull out the K-rations and lets eat. We'll take an hour and let the men rest. We make better time tomorrow. The jungle thins out in several places from here on to the camp. From now on, you'll call me Nate and I'll call you Jim. In case anyone might hear us talking, we don't want anyone thinking the U.S. is behind this raid. Ok by you?"

"Fine, good idea. I'll call you in an hour when we're through with lunch and ready to move out," was the reply.

Nate gathered his men for the lunch period.

"Pull out your K-rations and let's eat. You can talk but in low tones. No smoking. The smoke from a cigar or a cigarette travels for several yards. We sure don't want to warn them we're coming," he instructed and picked a fallen tree to sit on while eating.

The cardboard cartons that lunch came in are waxed and made little noise when opened.

Nate was satisfied with the progress. They were a couple miles in from the ocean. At this rate, he figured they'd reach the camp on the third day. Going back would be one hell've lot faster. There would be no need to be quiet then. The quicker they got out the better their chances of survival. These thoughts ran throught his head. He would do his best to bring all the men back safely.

One hour on the button, Nate's phone rang.

"We're ready to move out if you are, Nate," said Jim.

"Give me a couple minutes to call the General. I'll get back to you," Nate answered then dialed the other number.

"Brown's Realty," came an answer.

"General," Nate here, "tell me what the satellite is seeing up ahead. We and about two miles in from the ocean. We're going up both side of the creek. Can you spot us?"

"Just a minute. I'm sitting right in front of the screen. Oh, ok I have your group. I see them on both sides of the creek. Up ahead is a trail that crosses the creek about two miles up stream. The jungle thins out some and your going will improve. Looks like a small shack about where the path crosses over. No one moving around the shack. I'll keep my eyes on it as long as possible. The shack might be a good place for you to sleep tonight. How are the men I sent doing," he said

"So far, they are doing fine. I just hope they can handle the fireworks later on. I make it to be another day and a half before we get to the camp. I'll keep in touch and you keep the choppers warmed up. See you General," Nate said signing off.

Nate called Jim and repeated what he had heard.

"You will come to the path before we will. Don't travel on it but disconnect all the booby traps you can fine. We'll move slowly and I could come across helping. We want to stay close together. Call and give me a progress report every thirty minutes. Ok?"

"Ok, be talking to you soon," Jim said and hung up.

It was a couple hours before he heard from Jim again.

"We just found the trail. It looks so harmless. It would save us some time if we could use it. We won't," he hurried to say.

"Remember Carl knows what he is doing. Have him disarm any traps and listen when he speaks. Your lives maybe in his hands, let me know how it goes."

As Nate and his men were closing in on the cabin, his phone rang.

"We found one, Nate, Carl's working on it now. Keep your fingers crossed. Call you when he's done," said Jim.

"Why a booby traps this far from camp, Nate was thinking, *I wonder if there's something important about that shack.* They would soon know.

"Ok, thanks. I think the shack up ahead is of some importance. Be careful the closer you get to it, the more traps you may find. We'll sit tight until you're done," Nate replied. The conversation over, Nate put his squad on alert. They were spaced out and sat on the jungle floor, all eyes looking and ears listening. Weapons at the ready, just in case.

Minutes went by and they heard nothing from Captain Jim Adams. Nate was getting nervous. Carl was good at his job and should have been done before now. Of course, he'd not had any practice for several years. He still had faith in Carl. He knew as soon as he got involved again, his training came back to him.

Nate jumped at the ringing of the phone. Even though it was turned down low, it startled him. This showed how up tight he was.

"Yes," he spoke into the mouthpiece.

"Jim, here. Carl has disarmed the trap and we are starting forward again. This man of your's is something. He's fearless. He works slow, but God does he have nerves of steel."

"Yeah, he's good but that one took him too long. He's getting rusty. Tell him I said that and watch him perk right up," Nate said jokingly before going on, "We'll be a few yards behind you. I'm going to touch base with the General and see what he can tell us. The satellite is do to go out of range any time now. Let me know when you're in sight of the shack. Stay a good fifty yards away until we can all merge on it from different directions"

He dialed the General and waited. It rang several times before his voice was heard.

"Where the hell were you, General. I need to know if the satellite has picked up anything yet," Nate spoke to him.

"Mr. Armstrong, must I remind you that I'm a General and you a civilian. Even us Generals must go pee from time to time. Besides, I have news for you. About fifty yards from the shack, on your side of the creek it appears to be a camp of about six men. They are armed with rifles and possiblely handguns. That's all. There doesn't seem to be a reason for them to be there unless they are protecting the shack from a distance. I think you're right. That shack plays a role in this game. Be damn careful, boy. In two hours, I'll have the satellite back and will call you if there is anything new. Good luck," he finished up. The clicking of the phone mean't he'd hung up. Nate put the phone away and waved one of the rangers in close to him.

"Go to every man on our squad and tell them of a camp about fifty yards from an old shack up ahead. There are six men with rifles and handguns there. They seem to be watching or protecting the shack. Tell them to be on their toes and check very close for bobby traps as we inch our way forward. Understand?" Nate asked.

"Yes, sir," he said with eagerness and he moved slowly off into the jungle. Nate called Adams and informed him of what he had been told.

This could be an outpost to give the main camp plenty of warning of trouble. It could also be a plan to get any attacking party to rush up the paths, thereby blowing most of them up. It would be a cunning plan, Nate was thinking.

-15-

Back at the boat, Delbert was talking to Katrina.

"Do you think we should get rid of some of this firepower we have? We really shouldn't need it when they get back. I'm concerned some military boat might come by and decide to search us. What do you say we pack, what we don't think we'll need, into the jungle?" he asked her.

"You might be right. The military is on the side of the cartels and they may patrol this area. Ok, lets do it. We don't need to pack it too far, maybe fifty yards and hide it. Any partol will only check the boats, not the shore. Yeah, I'll take the heavy stuff, you are careful of the arm," she answered.

For two hours, they packed automatic weapons and the two firing tubes for missiles. They made two caches, one on each side of the creek. They covered them with underbrush. After they were done, they erased all signs of the activity.

After they were through, they concealed the two automatic weapons for their use and ammo. A box of grenades was pushed under the bunks.

"Good job," Delbert said, "that should do it. We still have enough to defend ourselves if need be. Lets have a shot of whisky and I'll have a cigar."

"Right, it's time for a break. This heat would be a killer if we weren't use to it. I feel for the rangers. They maybe use to Florida heat for training but its hotter here," she replied.

A bottle of whisky was brought our and passed around. Delbert fired up a Cuban and puffed on it. Minutes passed and Katrina was getting a little bored. She went into the wheelhouse and picked up the fishing pole.

"I'm going fishing," she announced, this waiting is killing me.

"You might as well get use to it, this caper may take up to three days. They might make it in two if they don't meet much opposition. It's slow going because of the traps these types set. Tonight they will sleep in the jungle, if you can call that sleeping. You always have one eye open even if you have guards out," he finished.

Katrina got out a couple pieces of bacon and baited the hook. She walked to the bow of the boat and cast her line. It had barely hit the water, when a fish hit it. The pole jerked downward and Katrina pulled back hard. In a couple of minutes, she was landing a two-foot long fish. Delbert got her some ice for the hold to pack it in.

This excited her and she soon baited up again and made a cast. This time it took about ten minutes to get a bite. It was the same type of fish, but about four inches shorter.

"What kind of fish are these," she asked Delbert.

"Damn if I know, don't you?" he fired right back.

"Well, I fix them for dinner. Fresh fish sounds good, don't you think?" she asked him.

"Yeah, sounds alright," he stated.

They sat around for another hour before she went below to prepare their evening meal. At least they didn't have k-rations. Both were thankful for that. During this hour, they both had a couple more shot of whisky. Delbert finished the cigar and had sat down where he could just look out to sea.

Twlight was falling as they finished the meal. Darkness would soon be upon them.

"That was great fish. You are a good cook and can cook for me anytime. Do you know what you going to be doing when you get back to the U.S.?" he asked her.

"No, not yet, I guess I'd better start thinking about it. The General has promised me a desk job when I get back, but I don't know if I'd like a sitting job. My butt will get big and I'll be bored to death. I just don't know," she replied.

"Noticed you and Carl are becoming friends. He's great man. When we were overseas during Nam, most of us went into town looking for women. Not Carl, he would come with us and have a few drinks. He never got drunk and was our driver. We never worried about not getting back to base. Carl took care of it. We owe him a lot. He's brave, which he won't admit to. He saved our asses several times. He lives in Boise, Idaho. It's a beautiful area. You just minutes from mountains or from high desert. The weather never goes to the extreme. He works with animals at the zoo. He loves animals and it shows. On these missions, he will kill if he has to, but would rather avoid it if he could. Yes, he is short but we see him as a tall man. If he calls you friend, it's for life," Delbert told her.

"Why are you telling me all this. I have just met you people and really don't want to get serious. He is a nice man and I enjoy his company, but that may be a far as I go," she said.

"Well, I just thought you'd like to know a little more about him. It helps to build friendships. That's all," he said.

Later they sat in the moonlight with their own thoughts. Hardly a word was spoken. Each was thinking of the future and what life might bring. These were thoughts of service members coming home after a war.

Delbert sucked on a cigar and had a couple whiskys. Katrina was wondering what the General had in store for her. Her thoughts drifted to Carl. She admitted she liked him. He seemed sensitive and good. She could relate to him and he would not laugh at some of her comments, when she was mean't to be serious. Other men would laugh and think her silly. He didn't. That's a good quality in a man. She started wondering how good he was in bed. It didn't really matter, but most people were curious.

Back in the jungle, Nate and his men were waiting for another trap to be sprung. Finally, the all clear came over the phone.

"Good, I'd like to take that shack just before dark. Your path crosses just below it. Looks like it goes right to the camp where the men are waiting. Jim, you work into a range of fifty yards from your side and I'll do the same on this side. Then we look over the situation before we take these people out. I'd rather not kill them, but may have to. Are your guys good at taking out the enemy silently?" Nate said.

"Yes, they are. Usually they have been trained to kill with their blades and not take prisoners. You do know that if we take prisoners that will cut our force down in size. You might want to re-think it, Nate," he answered.

"We'll decide when we're in position. How long do you think it'll take you to get to the creek, just below the shack?" Nate asked.

"An hour at our pace. Of course it depends on how many traps we find between here and there, " he answered.

"Well, there shouldn't be many more. I don't believe there will be any close to the shack. Once you're in place, have Carl belly crawl forward and verify.

Call when you're in place. We should have the satellite back any minute, if this schedule is accurate. I'll call and get an update," and he hung up.

"Hi, General, do you have the satellite back yet? We'll be in place in an hour. We need an update to make sure there have been no changes. We're going to strike just before dark. We'll use their camp site for the night," Nate asked.

"No, not yet. About ten minutes and I'll call you. Take care and be careful," responded the General.

Nate waived his squad forward. They walked very slowly through the brush. It was tough going and Nate knew the men were cussing to themselves, with every step. Nate smiled because he too was thinking some choice words.

Ten minutes went by and at twelve minutes, his phone rang.

Nate answered it and listened to what the General was saying.

"No changes Nate. Still six men and it looks like they just finished supper. They are drinking now and should be easy to take. How do you intend to do take them?" the General asked.

"Not sure yet. The Captain thinks we should kill them. If we don't, we'll have to leave a man to guard them. Also, they will be able to identify us as Americans. That would be bad news. I'm leaning to agree with the Captain. They are animals that sell death and disaster everywhere. The world would be better off without them. Does it make a difference to you, sir," he asked the General.

"Damn rights it does. This is a covert operation and we cannot afford to let anything point a finger to us. I say kill them. You'll need every man you have to take and destroy the main camp. In fact, I order you to kill them. Don't go soft on me now, Armstrong," the General has spoken.

"Ok, you've got it, sir. It'll be done just before it's dark down here. I'll call you when it's done and we are in control of this shack. We'll all know how it fits in the ballgame. Bye General," Nate hung up.

Sometime later, the phone rang.

"We're in place, Nate, what next," said the Captain's voice.

"The General advise that everything is the same. The four have eaten and are now drinking. They should be easy to take. His orders are to kill them. No prisoners this trip. Your men wouldn't shy away from this will they? To kill a man the first time is a very unpleasant experience. I need to know if they can do it. Talk to me," he said.

"Hell, yes, they can do it. Lets get on with the show. We'll creep in from this direction and you from that one. We will stay down and behind brush until we get a chance to get them from behind. As I understand it, you will do the same. We'll be close enough to see each other and when you give a signal, we all move in fast. If we do this right, no one will get hurt," he replied.

"Right, start moving in. This will be all over within five minutes or less," Nate ordered. He turned to the Colombia Lt. and told him to pass the word to the squad to move in closer to each other and to move forward. They were to wait for his signal to attack. This was to be done quietly. No guns unless absolutely necessary.

As soon as he reaches the little clearing where to drug runners had their camp, Nate stuck his head up to view the scene. One of the men had gone into the jungle a little to their right. Nate signal to a ranger to get that man. The ranger moved off in that direction. Couple minutes Nate heard a little rustleing in that direction. Soon the ranger raised his head and gave thumbs up to Nate.

Good, that's one man down, Nate said to himself. Five to go. Jim's squad was within ten feet of another one. The other two had their attention on the whisky they were drinking. Nate gave the Captain thumbs up and pointed to that man. He made a motion across his throat. The ranger didn't hestate. He rose off the jungle floor and walked right up to the man. There was the flash of a blade, as the man was grabbed around the mouth. Nate saw the blade enter in the kidney area. This was a place where the victum could not make a sound. It was the place you could kill a man and he'd not make a sound. The deed was done and as Nate watched the other, the Captain moved out of the clearing and into the jungle. They disappeared like ghosts. The other two had no idea what was taking place.

Now it was time to rush the four and finish the job. Nate was twenty yards from them and so were the others. This would be a hard run. It had to be quick. Once the men woke to the fact they were being attacked, they would pull their pistols. They must not be allowed to use them.

Nate raised his arm, moved it in a circle and started the rush. Rangers from both sides of the clearing arrived ahead of Nate. The four victims, alert to what was going on jumped to their feet. That was the last thing they did in this life. The rangers were very good at their jobs. They were right on top of them and it was over in a minute.

"Good work men, now look around and see if we can find a hole or a ditch to bury them in. Jim and I are going to the shack to see what's inside. A couple of you come along and be ready for anything. For some reason this place is important to the cartels," Nate said.

The four men approached the shack. Nate and Jim in the center and the two other men, one on each side as a cover. Nate slowly pushed the door open. It was dark inside with only the light from the open door to see by. Nate and Jim rushed in.

The Captain had a flashlight, which he now turned on. Horror and shock took them by surprise as they looked upon the scene before them.

Tied to bunk beds were three naked women. It didn't take a brain to tell they had been repeated raped. The fear in their eyes was the worst Nate had seen since Nam.

"Get them loose and lets find out what's going on. Get them some clothes to wear. Some of our shirts will do. On second thought, the shirts off the dead if they are not bloody. Hurry down and strip them of their shirts and boots," Nate ordered a ranger.

They got the three women to sit up by telling them they were safe now. The men were dead and they were now free. The Americans gave them water and asked if they were hungry.

"Yes," said one it, "very hungry. They only fed us once a day. We have been here for three days."

"But why," asked Nate, "what the hell for."

"It was the only way they could make our family work for them. We were to be returned in a couple of weeks. I think we would have been dead by then. They are bad. It is good they are dead. Thank you so much," the tallest one said.

Just then, the door opened and in came the ranger with the clothes and shoes. At first, they did not want to wear the clothes of the evil men, but finally gave in. They said they would wash the clothes in the stream after all men were asleep.

Nate ordered K-rations be given to the women and for all of the men to leave. In turning to leave, Nate noticed a pile of sacks over in the corner. He walked over and with the use of the flashlight checked them out. The bags were filled with something. He took his blade and cut a slit in the side of one bag. A white powder spilled out.

"You want to bet on what that is Jim?" Nate asked.

"I'd bet a years salary it's "coke," he answered.

"Yeah," Nate agreed after tasting it. "Lets get out of here and let the women dress. We'll make some coffee from the supplies of those we killed."

The rangers had started a fire and put the pot on when Nate and Jim came out of the shack. It was a smokeless fire and small. Their workday done, they all opened K-rations and chomped down on them. Several minutes later, the women came out of the shack. They were giggling at the way they looked in men's shirts. They approached the Americans very cautiously. The taller of the three and proablely the oldest, spoke to them. They spoke good English.

"What do you intend to do with us. We thank you for freeing us but are we free to go. Our parents are very worried because these men usually would kill us. What do you intend to do? Please will you tell us?" she said.

"What is your name?" Nate asked.

"Rita," she answered proudly.

"We do not intend to hurt you, but there is a small problem. We are on our way to the main camp to destroy it. We can't let you go until our work is completed. That may take two days. We just can't risk anyone warning the camp. You understand, don't you?" he asked.

"Si, we understand. You can't think we would after what those bastards did to us. We are so ashamed. No, American, we would never do that. Can we be of help to you? If you cannot let us go, can we go with you? We've been to the camp and know where it is and where everything is located," Rita suggested.

"Are you sure about this?" Nate asked.

"Yes, ask them. We all are. It will give us a chance to repay these drug people for the sins they have forced upon us. Please, sir, please," she peaded with him.

Nate turned to Jim and Dennis, the Colombian Lt. and asked what they thought of allowing this.

"Well, they seem sincere and with them knowing the layout of the camp, could be a big help," Jim replied. Dennis agreed they needed all the help they could get. They still did not know how many people might be at the camp.

"Can any of you fire a gun?" Nate asked.

"Si, two of us. We will be no trouble and would like to see this camp and those people destroyed.

"Please, sir, please," she again asked.

"Let me think about it. Get some coffee and have as much food you want. All we could bring is K-rations but they will fill your bellies. I'll let you know at first light. You women sleep in the shack and we'll sleep here and outside the shack for your protection. Does anyone ever come to this place at night?" he finished.

"No, never," she answered.

"Ok, no lights and everyone hit the hay. Put out the fire," Nate ordered. A ranger took care of it and the darkness settled in.

"Post guards over there and over there," Nate pointed to the positions he wanted, "just in case."

A fog had settled in overnight. The camp of the Americans stirred. The rangers were the first to roll out and prepared for the morning meal. A small fire was started and the coffee put on. Once this was done, they went through the camp and woke everyone. Nate awoke with a jerk when a ranger shook his shoulder.

"Time to get up," the ranger said.

Nate was a little embarrassed because of his action. He had been in a deep sleep and to be awakening in this manner could have been dangerous. Everyone was up tight when in enemy territory. That is Nate's men were. The rangers seemed cool, calm and collected. Nate walked to the creek and washed his face. The cool water helped. He picked up and handful and dumped it on his head. Running his fingers through his hair, he felt he could now go on.

He went to the fire and a ranger handed him a cup of coffee.

"Thanks, I need this," Nate said, taking a big swallow of the black liquid. He took a K-ration and ripped it open to begin breakfast. He noticed everyone was talking in whispers. *These rangers are well trained,* was his thinking.

The guards came in from their posts, having been relieved by others. Nate motioned to Jim and Dennis to one side for a mini conference.

"We'll proceed as we did yesterday, Jim your team go up the other side of the creek. Be even more careful that yesterday. The closer we get to the camp, the more booby traps we will fine. Dennis you stay with me and keep the women quiet and together. Tell them we must not make any noise. They must not take any steps out of where our people are walking because of these booby traps. Remind them if they goof, we could all be killed. I think we should leave one person behind to guard this shack. Someone may stop by and discover the women gone and alert the others. We'll plant explosions and detonate it on the way back. You have your men take care of that, Jim. Tell them to hurry. We'll move on ahead. Ok, lets move out," he finished.

He approached Don to issue an order.

"Don, you stay here and guard this shack. Someone may come by to check on the women. If they do, you need to kill them. They can't be allowed to send an alarm. The rangers are planting explosions now and we'll blow the hell out of it on our way back. Ok?" Nate asked.

"Yeah, I'd would rather be with you on the raid, but I'm a team player. What ever you need, boss," he answered.

Nate dialed the General and waited through four rings. He became worried, but his concern was short lived.

"Hello, Armstrong, I'll just bet you want to know what the satellite is seeing today. I just had a report before the thing went out of range. Your target is just coming awake, it looks like. They have a fire going and appear to be preparing breakfast. I count the same number of men. Their setup is the same. They have no idea you're on the way. They are careless and you should hear them a mile before you get there. Be careful. They're too comfortable which means they have booby traps around. Everything ok with you?" spoke the General.

"Yeah, but we've picked up three people. Three women were being held prisoners in the shack. I couldn't leave them behind. They say they wish to help. I buy their story. They've been raped repeatedly and they want to get even. They've been to the camp and can guide us with how it is set up. I'll get back to you around noon our time. Keep me apprised of any changes. Signing off," Nate said as he hung up.

Nate joined his patrol and began the slow task of creeping through the jungle. If all went well he hoped they would be in striking distance by the next morning.

They had made about two miles, when Ed held up his hand and motioned Nate to come forward. Nate joined him.

"Look right there," Ed said.

Nate looked to where he was pointing. A thin, almost invisible wire stretched between clumps of bushes across to a small tree.

"We need to disarm this one carefully. It looks like it's a land mine. One of the gut busters that come up waist high then spins around in a circle. It will cut several men into if the damn thing goes off. Get Carl up here," he explained to Nate.

Nate move back a ways and found Carl who was on his patrol this day.

"Go up to Ed, he has a little chore for you. A mine he thinks, a nasty mine. I'll call Jim and tell him what we found," Nate said as Carl moved ahead.

When the connection was made, the conversation began.

"Better hold it up. Jim. We've found a belly buster mine. These babies are nasty. It's wired to a small tree with a trip wire. It's not on a trail, just in the brush. Be damn careful," Nate explained

"Roger that. I've seen what they can do to a group of men. Thanks for the heads up. We'll be more careful. Let me know when it's done," Jim responded.

"Will do," was Nate's reply.

Nate next dialed the General.

"Satellite back yet?" Nate asked.

"Just coming over the horizon. What do you need?" asked the General.

"Have it take a look at us and the camp and give me the distance from where we are to it. The booby traps are getting thick. I would like to know. We won't attack till morning. Also, I need to know how many people they have on site. It would be helpful if I knew where their men were stationed. Call me when you get it. Thanks General," Nate signed off.

-16-

Back at the boat, Delbert and Katrina were trying to keep from getting too bored. They tried their hand at fishing and it was going fine. They were catching too many so entered into a catch and release program. They would bet each other on who could catch the most and the biggest fish. This was the morning of the second day. They tired of this after half a day. Katrina prepared lunch, which consisted of hamburgers and coffee. They did have cold beer and would dip into it once in a while.

Delbert had opened the hatch that lead down to the engines. He left it this way in case anyone came by and questioned why they were anchored here. They had agreed to a story of having engine trouble with both boats. Perhaps some bad gas or oil. They had sent a man to town via way of the beach. He would get parts and rent a boat to come back for repairs. They thought it would also help if they said two or three men were in the jungle searching for food. This would discourage pirates if they came by. Perhaps the fact that someone was coming back to the boats would discourage anyone from causing trouble. As long as the drug cartels believed, it was all that was necessary.

After lunch, they laid down for a nap. Both were on deck with a mattress pad and no covers. They slept in their clothes so they would be ready for anything. The heavy arms had been stored in the jungle, but they kept a pistol and a thirty thirty for protection. They also had hidden some small arms around the boats, just in case they were needed.

An hour or so later, both were jarred awake by the sound of a motor from a boat that was coming along side. Delbert was the first to respond. He jumped to his feet and looked at boat and it's occupants. There were four men in the boat. To Delbert, they did not look like anglers. They were dirty and sweatly. A motly looking crew to say the least.

Delbert knew the next five minutes would decide if they were in trouble or left alone. He decided the best form of action was to get with the flow until it was decided it was the wrong course to take. He raised his hand in greeting as the boat scraped along side and the men jumped to the boat. Landing on their feet, they stared at the two. Katrina was just up and was rubbing the sleep from her eyes. Her skin felt a crawling sensation. She knew these were bad people. She leaned against the side of the boat, with one hand behind her. In that hand, she held a Smith & Wesson, 38, relvolver. Slowly she cocked the hammer and slipped her finger into the trigger guard. She was ready to fire.

The leader of this boarding party was a man in his fifties. He wore a wide brimmed hat. His clothes were wrinkled and soaked with sweat. He was unshaven and when he smiled, showed a missing tooth. His grin was more of a smirck than a grin. Delbert knew this was a dangerous man.

"Well isn't this a pleasant scene. A man alone with a beautiful woman and yet they sleep alone. Ha Ha Ha. A foolish man indeed," he said with that crooked smile. All at once, it went sober and his voice had a hard sound to it.

"We are having motor trouble with both boats. We have sent a man to town, by walking the shore. He should return with help and parts we need. Who are you, fishermen?" Delbert asked.

The leader had a hard time taking his eyes off Katrina. The expression on his face told what was on his mind. Katrina had seen the look a thousand times. She gripped the pistol tighter.

"Fishermen, ha ha ha ha," he said looking around at his men, "he thinks we are fishermen," voiced the man's disproval.

"Well, we are gentle people, waiting for repairs. What can we do for you, senor?" Delbert remarked along with the question.

"You can do nothing for us. We are here for you. What are you doing in these waters?" the stranger asked.

"I told you we are waiting for repairs. That's all. What the hell is it to you anyway?" Delbert said with an angry tone in his voice.

The leader backed up with this tone and for a second, Delbert would have sworn he saw fear in those eyes. This might be a plus for them.

"We are patroling these waters for a large corporation. We make sure no one trespasses on its property. Understand?" he questioned.

"Our men went into the jungle to pick fruit and to get some fresh water from that creek. That's all. As soon as the parts get here, we'll be gone. You need not worry about us. If that is all, I'll ask you to leave this boat. Understand?" Delbert responded again in an angry voice.

He was looking at the man's eyes and saw the fear flash through them, for just a second. No doubt, this man was a coward and was in fear of Delbert. He wasn't alone. A lot of people were afraid of Delbert.

"No senor," said the man as he pulled a pistol and pointed at Delbert. "We will wait for those on shore return to make sure you steal nothing. Sit down right there on the deck," he ordered Delbert, and then turned to Katrina.

"You also," he said, "sit on the deck and are quiet."

She slowly slid to the deck and the invader's attention turned to Delbert.

"It is very suspicious that both boats broke down at the same time, Senor," stated the man with the pistol.

"I understand that there are cocane dealers in the area. Is that true?" Delbert attempted to keep the conversation going.

"Si, I hear that also. That is why we must be very careful. We do not want anyone stealing our drugs. Other groups are trying to take over our trade. We don't like that, so we patrol. Perhaps we have caught one now, huh," the man said with a crooked grin.

The other two went back to their boat, but stood or sat where they could see Delbert and Katrina. Katrina spoke up.

"But senor, we are mere fishersmen. This one, he is my husband. We want no part of the drug trade. We are down here from America to make money fishing. Then we go home. Please let us go. You can tow us out into the ocean, to where the current is and we will take our chances with the sea. We know nothing about this drug business. You can check in town and the fisheries. The old man has brought many fish from us. We will pick up the man who went to town and fix our boat. With your permission, we will come back and tow the other boat away from here. It can be fixed in town. Si, you agree," she explained.

"Oh. No," he said, "you may bring the police or maybe the army back with you. No, I am afraid you all must die. We will wait until the others are back. Sorry but we must tie you up to keep you quiet," he explained.

Katrina looked over to Delbert and winked. She started slowly rising to her feet. The man with the gun did not see her as a threat and his attention was on Delbert. This he would shorty regret.

She reached her feet, nodded at Delbert and pulled the pistol from behind her. The man noticed the quick movement but reacted too late. As soon as the weapon came level with his head, Katrina shot him dead.

Delbert quickly grabbed his pistol and whirled around to confront the other two. They saw what was coming a leaped into the water on the far side of their boat. This put them out of sight, making it impossible to fire on. The did have their weapons and for a time it would be a waiting game.

Katrina grabbed the dead man by one leg and rolled him off the boat and into the water. Soon the sharks would take care of him.

"Katrina," yelled Delbert, "the other two are in the water on the far side of their boat. You cover them from the front and I'll go to the backside. Be careful. They are armed."

"Ok, got it covered," she said as she moved into place. She kept the net hoist between herself and the danger. Being metal, it afforded her some protection.

An hour passed and the two had not tried to climb aboard any of the boats. Delbert grew tired with this game and announced to Katrina.

"I'm going after the bastards. They have to be right there in the water. Cover me," he said and moved closer to the edge of the boat.

"No, don't you dare. They will kill you and that will really put the mission in jeopardy. Stay right there. Sooner or later, they have to show themselves. We'll get them then," she yelled back at him.

"Ok, ok, God don't get so cranky. We'll wait," he finally said.

Another hour went by and still no movement for the two men. Katrina went below and slapped together two sandwiches and returned with a couple bottles of beer.

She gave one of each to Delbert and kept one for herself. She tried an old stunt she had remembered hearing about.

"Hey, you two over there. We have some sandwiches and cold beer. If you toss away your guns and come on board your ship, we'll let you leave. I promise not to shoot if you drop your guns. This is the only offer you will get from us. Better, take it, now.

"Go to hell," came a voice from the other side of their boat. "We radioed headquarters before all this happened and told them we had found you here. Now we are late getting back and they will come looking for us. Soon there will be a boat or maybe two, full of armed men. When they arrive, we kill all of you. You surrender now and we may spare the woman."

Delbert and Katrina moved to the center of the boat for a quick conference.

"If he's telling the truth, we are doomed. We could swim for shore and I think we'd make it. We could then get the firepower we planted over there, but we'd lose the boats. We may need the boats to get away when Nate gets back," Delbert said.

"I know," she answered back, "but we must do something if we're to get out of this. Nate and the rangers should be back tomorrow. If others come do you think we can hold them off, Delbert?" she asked.

"No, I don't think so. I'd sure like to have that missile launcher back. With it, we could blow any incoming boat before they could get in range. I guess we jumped to quick by taking everything except small arms, to shore. Lets just wait and see what happens next. You go below and get a couple more rifles and plenty of ammo. We're not going down without a fight. We do have another advantage," Katrina blurted out.

"What's that," he asked.

"They still think we have men on shore looking for fruit. As long as they believe that, I think we'll be ok. Shoot to kill and find some cover. I think I hear a boat coming round that bend over there," she said.

Both looked and shuddered in horror. It was a speedboat, loaded with armed men.

"Quick," Delbert said. "Get the rifles and don't forget the ammo. We're going to need it"

Katrina rushed below. She hurriedly grabbed two rifles and all the boxes of ammo she could carry.

Returning to the deck, she slid three boxes of ammo to Delbert and returned to her post just as the boat loaded with men began firing. Lead was flying everywhere. The ping for slugs could be heard bouncing off metal. Katrina and Delbert would pop up once in a while and fire a couple of shots. One man on the boat fell into the ocean. Their firing was minimal because of the heavy shelling.

The two men pinned down in the water made an attempt to swim to the incoming boat. Katrina spotted them and drew a bead on one. The rifle found its mark. A dark spot appeared in the middle of his shirt. The bullet hit him right below the shoulder blades and he fell face down in the water. *At least we are cutting down the number of these bastards,* she thought.

The other man made it and the speedboat swerved and headed out to sea once he was on board.

"I wonder what they are up to," Delbert said to Katrina.

"I don't think they are leaving. They will be back. I just hope they don't put two and two together and realize we're attacking the camp. If we can keep these people busy till morning, the raid should be over and Nate on his way back. God, I hope so," Katrina as she let out a big breathes.

"Good shooting, Katrina," Delbert announced.

"Thanks, but we must be on our toes. I don't think they will try anything till dark. Then they will come. It's going to be a dark night and we have no spotlight. We must listen closely. I think they will bring canoes or something without a motor, I'll go below and fix us a big meal. You keep watch. Want another beer?" she asked him.

"Yeah, that would be good," Delbert, replied.

"I'll bring you one," she said.

While Katrina was below deck Delbert patroled the deck. He was on guard for anything that might be a threat. He was sure it would be after dark before the cartel's men came back. He looked over the two boats for a way to light up the water around them. At the same time, he wanted to keep the deck of the boat they were on, in the dark. A tall order for fishing boats. He was sure the lights would not last long. An automatic weapon would make short work of them. Hooking up lights was a problem, but fixing them so he could turn them on at the right time was the real problem.

Katrina returned with the beer and a plate loaded with French fries and a huge hamburger. She handed it to him and went back below to get her own.

A minute later, she returned.

"I'll sit to the rear of the boat and you take the bow. I don't think they will return until dark. We better stay on our toes anyway," Delbert suggested.

The took their places and chowed down. Both knew this may be their last meal until the landing party returned. This should be tomorrow if all went well. When they finished eating, Delbert took the two plates below. He washes them and put them away. Opening the small refrigerator's door, he retrieved two more beers and returned on deck.

He handed one to Katrina and opened a conversation with her.

"Help me on figuring out how I can rig lights out over the water. I think that can be done by just stripping the overheads we have an string them on the net rigging. I can extend the riggings arm. I'd like to keep the deck here as dark as possible. The real problem is how to turn them on or off at the right time.

This would be one hell of a surprise for them. During the surprise, we may be able to pick off one or two of them. They will soon shoot out the lights. However if I can rig a wire and attach a switch, I could switch them on, we'll pick off all we can and shut off the lights quick. This way they'll have nothing to shoot at till I flip them back on. What do you think?" he asked her.

"Good idea. We have to hurry. You get with the lights and I'll find a switch and rip it out. There's some extra wire on the other boat. I think it will work," she replyed.

Delbert went right to work restringing the lighting. A line was run from the hot wire, with the bulbs to the center of the deck on the far side. He was sure the invaders would come at them from the side where the other boat was. That's what he would do. Try to keep something between you and those you are attacking for as long as you could. During this process, he started up both boats. He wanted the batteries at fully charged for this operation. He moved the other boat about twenty feet from the one, they were on. He did not want anyone jumping from that boat to his or hers. They needed all the advantage they could get.

Katrina had pulled a turn switch off the wall. It was used to turn on off lights. She attached it to the wire Delbert had strung to the center of the deck. They were done and the light of day was starting to fade.

They sat down to rest, when Katrina jumped up.

"There's a lot of spare wire below deck. It's bare. Lets string it in the water along side the boat. Once the lights are gone, we rip OT the wire leading to them, and attach the other wire to the switch. When the start swimming over and are about to board us, we throw switch and give them one hell of a shock," she announced.

"Great idea, Katrina. We'll string it just out of the water so it can stay on. When they touch it, WOW," he said, "lets do it."

Meanwhile Nate and the rangers are nearing the camp. Nate has called for Jim to come over and have a chat about the attack in the morning. Brad had volunteered to sneak up to the camp and get the general layout of the camp. By doing this Nate hope to keep the loss of inocent life to a mimium. The ones being forced to work there should not suffer because of their captors. He had been gone an hour and should be returning shortly.

Nate made a call to the General for an update. He'd told him where they were. He needed to know if any changes had been made. Also how many men were in the camp compared to the last looking?

"Yes, Nate I can see you clearly. Watch out there is a man approaching you from the camp. He's moving slowly. He could be a scout. They may know you're there. He's about a hundred yards out. Better send someone to intercept this one," the General almost shouting.

"Relax General, he's ours. I sent him in to look over the camp. We attack in the morning and I wanted a look-see. He'll be reporting in very soon. Go ahead give me the rest," Nate was saying.

"The camp is the same as before. Nothing has been moved. Right now, I would say there were a dozen men, carrying guns in camp. No, wait hold it. There's three more just coming into camp. Could be they are coming back from their toilet. That's, it Nate. Anything else," he answered.

"Where is the bigest concentration of men at in the evening and early morning?" Nate asked.

"The large tent at the North end of the clearing. I believe it's there sleeping quarters. They seem to come and go to that tent a lot. The main setup for refining the dope is set out in the open, at the center of the clearing. A smaller tent, to the south of that is their storage tent. That one you really need to destroy," said the General.

"Ok, I see our man is back so I'll talk to you at 5:00 am for any information you might have. Be sure you're watching us right after that. All hell will break loose. What dope we can't destroy by explosives we'll burn with gas. Bye," Nate hung up.

"Reporting in, sir," Brad with a grin. He knew Nate hated to do anything-military style.

"Ok, report, before I kick your butt," was Nate's reply.

"I count fifteen men with arms. Inside a tent on the left side of the clearing are seven or eight Colombian farmers. I couldn't get close enough to hear any talking but I think they are being held hostage and forced to work. Other than that, it is as we thought. Your map is right in every respect. Oh, one more thing. Going away from camp, on the west side is a trail. It leads downward towards town. We might want to take a couple men in that way to block escapes. This close to the camp, that trail won't be mined. I checked it for at least one hundred yards and found none. That all, sir," and with it came another grin.

"Stick around. Jim's coming over and we will plan the attack. After that we will back away from the camp, just to be safe," Nate told him

Minutes went by and finally Jim showed. He and Nate, with Brad looking on, went over their plan. They had the Colombia Lt. Dennis also there for his imput.

A plan came together in half and hour. They would attack the camp from all sides. This would spread them thin but would confuse the enemy and they won't know what to do. With a little luck, they would knock all ressistance and procede to burn the camp. Nate advised that the people being held would be released as soon as they knew them to be innocent. The three women they had with them would help with this decision. It was settled that at daybreak they would move within striking distance. Anyone getting in close enough to silence a guard was to do it just seconds before the strike.

"I'll tell my people. We can't move before it gets light. Might be booby traps in our way," he said to all present.

"That's right," Nate said, "and we need a signal for the attack. Do your rangers have clickers like we used in Nam?"

"Yeah, we do. Those will do nicely. I'll collect half and pass them out to your men. What next?" he asked.

"Well, I'll call you on the phone to make sure you're ready. When you are, we creep to the edge of the camp. The last twenty-five yard better be on our bellies. Anyone spotting a guard they can do with a knife, will move in and I'll give the go ahead. Jim you and those with clickers will click and we rush in with guns blazing. That sound like something out of Hollywood, but it has to be. Now Jim we're going to move back aways, perhaps a couple hundred yards. No fires, no smoking. K-rations and bed. Post a guard and so will we. Have the guard relieved every couple hours. Have we got it?" he asked the small group. They all nodded yes.

Silently this attack group moved back into the jungle. It would be a long night and everyone was nervous. After all it was stressful planning this type of operation and even more so in carrying it out. Two thoughts ran though every mind. *Will this be my last night on earth? Will I survive tomorrow?*

After a few minutes, it was dark. Many of the men turned in, while others were lost in their own thoughts. Nate lies down and tried to sleep. It was always hard for him to sleep the night before an attack. In Nam, it had been the same. He prayed he had a good plan and no one on this mission would pay with his life. An uneasy sleep finally came to him.

-17-

Back at the boats, Delbert and Katrina waited for what might come to them this night. Time would tell. The night was dark with no moon. This they were glad to see. It was to their advantage. The ocean was black as sin and without the moon, they would be hard to find. In time, they would be found, but in doing so, the agressors would give away their position. If Delbert and Katrina and their lighting program worked, they should be able to cut down the odds. If they could just cut them in half, they'd have a chance.

Their eyes and ears were all straining to hear a noise of see something moving. Sound carried a long distance over water. A cough, a sneeze would tell them they were under attack.

It was nearing midnight when Katrina, whispered to Delbert.

"I hear a paddle or oar pushing against water. They're coming.

"Yes, another boat is over that way. Get ready for the lights," he whispered back.

Both had their rifles in hand and were ready. Extra rifles lie on the deck near them. This would save reloading for a while.

Katrina could barely see Delbert. She did see his arm go up and she pulled back the hammer to her weapon. All hell was about to break loose.

He dropped his arm and the lights came on, exposing the enemy. It showed four small boats with five men per boat. They began fireing. The lights blinded those in the boats as bullets whirled around them.

Men were falling overboard as slugs ripped through their flesh. As soon as they gained their eyesight back and they began returning fire, the lights went off. Much damage was done to the attackers. The two felt good about the first wave, but knew it would be difficult next time.

A moan was heard somewhere over near where the shooting occurred. A man was splashing around and going under. Perhaps a shark had him. For sure the sharks would come. Studies have shown that sharks can smell blood in the water at a distance of two miles.

Again came the sound of paddles being put to water. The next wave was about to appear. Katrina and Delbert reloaded the empty weapons and were ready. Delbert raised his arm and dropped it. The lights came on exposed a boat trying to go around behind them. Katrine cut loose on that one. Four men were in this boat and were trying to duck down low enough to escape the hail of lead coming their way. Two fell overboard and one of the other two, merely slid out of the boat and into the water. Her rifle empty, she laid it aside and picked up a fresh one. The last man in the boat was standing and firing at her. Bulets hit metal and sounded with a zing zing. Others plunged into wood with a dull thud. She took careful aim and dropped this last man. He fell with a splash.

"Get the lights, get the lights," someone in the background was yelling. It seemed everyone turned their sights on the lights and they went out all at once, as the entire string fell into the water. The advantaged was gone.

Delbert pulled the wire off the switch and quickly fastened to the other one. He flipped the switch on. They would know if it would work.

He eased over to Katrina and whispered.

"Lets move to the side they will be come to and once they touch the wire, we can hit them in the head. They'll wish they had never come this way."

"Good idea, Delbert, I'm with you," she responded.

They both moved to the far side of the boat and waited. Delbert was back where he belonged and Katrina also.

Quiet settled down for a while. Soon they would be hearing swimmers or a boat bunping theirs. In a distance, they could hear whispers, but could no make out the words. The darkness was like some evil that had come their way. Delbert was sure the other side felt the same.

An hour passed and nothing happened. The quiet was a strange new experience for Katrina. She had gotten use to the bright lights and nosie of The El Toro.

The silence was broken with a blood-curling scream at Delbert's post. Someone had grabbed or touched the hot wire. With wet hands and most of a body in water, it must have been a real shock.

Delbert leaned over the edge and saw a white face with black whiskers. Without thinking, total reflex; be hit him in the face with the butt of a rifle. The face disappeared from sight. Delbert straighten up and waited for the next one. He didn't have long to wait.

The next scream came from the center of the boat. Katrina rushed to where she heard it. Looking over see saw a figure, still holding the wire. She took her pistol and shot him between the eyes. Returning to her post, she settled in for what was to come.

The darkness and the quiet again swallowed them up like some evil demon.

Back to Nate's camp, everyone except the guards was rolled up and asleep. Each had a blanket for a cover. No sleeping bags. They had to travel light and the return trip could be a race. After all this was no Boy Scout campout. Men at war must suffer many uncomfortable situations. This was just one of them.

At last, the sky was becoming light. Sunrise would soon be upon them. Most of the sleeping men were awake. They had lit some canned heat for making coffee. Nate had given permission, feeling they were far enough away from the enemy camp, so the odor of fresh brewed coffe would not drift too far. After the entire drug, people would have their own pots on by now. That would be the aroma they would smell.

Everyone swallowed a hot cup of strong and made ready to go. From here on in, they must be very careful. The last forty yards would be on their bellies. This close to camp there should be no trip wires on booby traps.

Weapons were checked, each loaded with safety on. Soon they would be used to strike a blow against drug cartels. No time for washing. Each gulped down a K-ration, burying the containers.

Nate called the General.

"Do you have the satillite watching us?" Nate asked.

"Yes, it just came over the horizon. We count your party and I've zoomed in on the camp. The bulk of the camp is just getting up and I see three fires. Looks like three women are fussing over the fires. Cooking, I suppose. The big tent is where the enemy are and the workers are sleeping in the smaller tent. The one we talked about yesterday. You ready to push off," he asked.

"Yeah, in just a few minutes we'll be on our way. We'll surround the camp before moving in for the kill. In less that an hour we'll be on top of them. You go to watch the show, General?"

"Wouldn't miss it for the world. Good luck Armstrong. I'll go now," and he hung up the phone.

Nate dialed Jim.

"You about ready to move out?" Nate asked.

"Yes, you give the word and we're on our way," he replied.

"Set your watch with mine. It is now eight minutes till five. We move out at five. Remember work your way, looking for traps to within forty yards of their camp. The last forty yards on your bellies. Shouldn't be any traps that close in. When in position, call me. We don't want anyone jumping the gun. We all go at once. Ok."

"Got you skipper. Five o'clock and we start moving. Good luck, Nate," Jim said.

"You too," Nate answered.

Five o'clock came and the band of invaders began the tedious forward movement. They moved very slowly through the thick jungle. Inch by inch, looking for trip wires or any sort of booby traps. A couple were found and disarmed. Everyone was concentrating on that and in remembering the way, they had come. The way back was going to be a fast one and they needed to know the route of disarmed traps. Finally, they came to within forty yards of the camp.

Nate called Jim to make sure they were in place. They were.

"Ok, lets begain the attack by sneaking in close and knocking out their guards if we can. Start now," Nate gave the order.

Everyone was on their bellies and inching forward till they came into sight of the camp.

Nate spotted two guards, one at each end of the camp. The one on the south was closest to them. Nate pointed to a ranger. Then to the guard and made a quick movement across his neck with his knife. The ranger nodded and inched forward on foot. It seemed like an eternity before he saw the ranger leap from the bushes, cut the guard's throat and drag him back into the bushes. He looked towards the northern most guard just in time to witness the same. *Damn, these rangers are good,* he was thinking.

Another Ranger was creeping up on the backside of the big tent. He hesitated to view the camp. Just then, he saw a knife blade pentrate to the side of the tent. The Ranger knelt down and waited as he saw the knife slice through the canvas. The Ranger raised his rifle and aimed at the opening. A second later, a head appeared and looked to the left and the right. The mistake the man made was not looking straight ahead to where the Ranger knelt. A man's body and one leg appeared. A rifle cracked and the body slumped back into the tent. The Ranger took his first life.

A skinny man came running out of the tent where the farmers were housed. He had a pistol in each hand and was firing at anything that moved.

A Ranger had just entered the clearing and was caught by this sudden attack. He was hit square in the chest and was dead when he hit the ground.

The battle went on for no more than five minutes, but seemed like a hour. Bullets flew through the air, thick as a hive of bees. When the firing ceased, Nate sent the three women, they had freed at the shack, into the farmers tent. They were to explain what happened and that the were free to go. His recommendation was they were to go quickly and not hang around the camp.

The dead count was twelve, plus the Ranger, Nate checked him and found he was beyond help and covered him with cloth. He closed his eyes before covering him.

Jim and the Colombian Lt. met with Nate in the center of the clearing.

"Plant explosives in the equipment they were using and burn the tents. Any of the drug that is not destroyed is to have gas poured over it. There seems to be gas in the drums over there," he said pointing at ten drums stacked next to the big tent.

They assigned men to carry out the orders. Nate's crew helped.

"Jim, sorry about your Ranger. He was the only one we lost. Thank God for that. Better, get a couple men to build a stretcher for carrying him out. Don't leave a thing that would identify us as Americans. Hurry up so we can get out of here. The smoke and explosions may bring other people near by. I want to be out of here in ten minutes," Nate advised.

The three women came out of the tent with half dozen farmers and some of their families. They had a reunion and the taller of the women came over to Nate.

"God, bless you for freeing us. May God be with you always. We will go now," she said. She reached up and pulled his head down and kissed him. Nate watched as they walked off into the jungle on a path. They disappeared in seconds. One was waving as they went out of sight.

The explosives were planted and the building and tents were sent on fire.

"Everyone to this end of the clearing. The explosives are going to be sent off as soon as everyone is out of harms way. A head count was taken and Nate waved for the show to began.

Explosions went off one at a time. So the clearing was a mass of fire and the white power. A pile of dope was still in tact.

"Rangers pour gas over that pile after you open every bag and spread it around a little. Hurry now we are out of here in six minutes," Jim ordered.

Ed had taken Carl with him and had found two small trees that made a good stretcher. They took field jackets and ran the poles through the sleeves in both directions. They took strips of cloth and tied the jackets together. Once completed, they tested it. It was well built and they laid it along side the dead Ranger. They picked him up and placed him on it, face up. They tied the cloth over his head and face to keep the insects away. He was tied to the stretcher so he couldn't fall off. They trip back to the boats was going to be a fast one.

The gas was poured over the dope and the remaining drums were placed along side of the pile, now much smaller, covering more ground. A charge was placed on one of the drums and everyone moved away. It was set off and made one hell of a boom. Fire shot forty feet into the air.

The order came to move out. Nate's phone rang.

"Hello, General, did you watch the show via satellite," Nate asked as he answered the phone.

"Yes, it was a good job except for one thing. One of the drug people got away. He lit out through the jungle, heading for town. You'd better get the hell out of there. Get to the boats and move out to sea if you have to. I'll put the choppers on a ready alert. Go Nate, go," he said.

"Oh, one more thing, General. We lost one of the Rangers. Other than that, we didn't get a scratch. Just wanted you to know," Nate advised him.

"Sorry to hear that. We'll bury him with honors. I'll think how. Now get the hell out of there," yelled the general.

"Yes, sir," Nate replied.

"Let's move out. The General said one of these bastards got away. We may be hunted before long. Everyone help with the strecher along the way. Single file at a fast pace. Don't run but hurry along," Nate ordered.

Jim took the lead, closely followed by the Rangers and the Colombia Lt. Nate brought up the rear. They kept up the fast pace until they reached the shack. Jim called for a break of fifteen minutes.

"Eat now and hurry with any coffee. This will be the last break you get until we see the ocean. Fall out and rest," he ordered.

Nate came up and seated himself on a palm tree that had been uprooted by a windstorm. He torn off the K-ration and dove into its treasures. He was hungry as were the others. Canned Heat was set ablaze for quick coffee. Water was taken from the the creek and within five minutes coffee was ready. Once poured, more was put on to cook. This coffee wasn't perked. They threw grounds into boiling water and boiled it. Then they poured a little cold water in to settle the grounds. Before long, everyone had a cup. Finished with his lunch, Nate and the Colombia Lt., Dennis, walked over to the shack. Inspecting the inside, they found no sign of anyone being there since they had been.

"Get four or five concussion grenades, Dennis. We'll burn this place after spreading this poison," Nate said regarding the pile of dope.

Dennis went out to the Rangers and gathered up five concussion grenades. He carried them to Nate.

"Lets take the sacks and move them around a little so they're spread out some. The grenades will do more harm that way," Nate mentioned.

The grenades planted, they left the building. The shack was a tender box and with a wood floor should burn hot and fast.

"Everyone out of here. Start down the creek while I blow this place," Nate ordered and they push was on for the boats. Nate took another grenade, pulled the pin and tossed it into the shack. In a dead run, he headed for a high spot of land to hide behind.

Boom, boom, boom, the grenades went off, one by one and the shack was torn apart. Pieces of wood flew through the jungle. Small ones and large ones. The cocaine went forty or so feet into the air and was spred out over a good piece of ground.

Nate peeked out from behind the mound. He saw the shack was gone except for some of the floorboards and some sack material. He walked over to the mess and found nothing left that would be of use to the drug people. He pulled out a Cuban cigar, the only one he brought. He lit the cigar and a piece of paper. The cigar he put in his mouth and the paper he dropped into a pile of sawdust and paper on the floor. It immediately caught fire and soon engulfed the entire area.

Nate started down the creek after his people. *A good day's work,* he was thinking. He trotted until he caught up with the group. Everyone was feeling good about this raid. All sad they lost one of their own, but felt this job needed to be done. Hopefully this action would keep thousands of kids from become drug adicts. Useless lives to those who did. By God, at least they tried.

After five miles, they stopped to rest. This would be a short breather, then off to the boats.

"I figure we're about twelve miles from the boats," Nate was telling Jim and Dennis. "We should be there in two and a half to three hours. You both agree?"

"Yes, that's about right. The slope down to the sea is getting less and less every mile. Another five or six miles and it will be flat. That's the way I look at it. We won't be moving down hill any longer, but the jungle thins and that will be a great deal of help. The men are all scratched to hell on hands and faces. You have to admit they are a great bunch. All are feeling good about this mission and getting back home drives them on," Jim said.

"Yes, you can be proud of your unit Major. Tell then I said so. Ok?" Nate said.

"Yeah, sure, they'll be proud to have served with you," said the Major.

"Well, on your feet, the break is over. Someone exchange places with the stretcher, every half hour. Let's go," the order was given and down the creek, they went. No one aware of what awaited them at the boats.

Meanwhile back at the boats, Delbert and Katrina were waiting a full-scale attack from the cartel. Both knew the final attack would have to be before daylight. They would have the advantage once it was light and the enemy knew it.

"They are cooking up something, Katrina," Delbert said to her.

"Yeah, I know. It's now or never for them. If we can stand them off till daylight, we can hold out till Nate and them can get back. God, I hope they were successful in their attack. Anyway, I've reloaded all the rifles and the pistols I have so let the bastards come. I'm ready. Are you?"She asked.

"Right on. I've been ready for some time now. Lets quiet down and listen for the bastards. They must come soon. God I'm hungry," he said.

"Light one of those stinking cigars, that will keep your mind off it," she advised.

"Sure it will also give them a nice target. The burning tip of a ciger would be a dead giveaway. Thanks anyway," he bluted out.

"Sh, sh, I hear something. I think they're coming," she whispered.

The night was always the darkest before the dawn, they both had heard. This experience proved that point. It seemed to grow darker about now or was it just their mood. Time would tell. They stiffen, ready for the attack. They didn't have long to wait.

Katrina was standing with her back to the rail. The rail at this point of the boat was only three feet high. It was open near the deck. A pipe type railing. She was getting drowse. She would shake her head from side to side to wake herself up. She couldn't see Delbert but was confident he was awake.

Just as this throught passed through her head, a hand from the sea, grabbed her. It pulled her legs back at a fierce display of strength. This caused her to fall flat on her face with a thud. Her head struck hard and she felt dizzy. She vaguely heard some sort of a struggle at the other end of the boat as she drifted into unconsciousness.

Katrina came awake and realized her hands and feet were tied with rope. She was laying flat on her back on a bunk bed. A little dizzy yet, she turned her head wondering what had happened to Delbert. As the dizzyness cleared, she saw him laying across from her on another bunk.

"Delbert, Delbert, what happened to you?" she asked.

Her voice caused him to stir and moments later, he spoke.

"Damn if I know. I guess I fell asleep and they came out of the water. They hit me with something and out I went. You ok?" he questioned.

"Yes, I'm alright. It's light outside and Nate and the Rangers must be attacking the drug camp about now. They should make short work of it and be on their way back. I figure about five hours if all went well, they'd be back. We have to do something. These bastards could set a trap for them. God knows what they know. If they believed we had men ashore looking for fruit, they don't anymore. If we had, they'd been back before dark last night. Hopefully they believed we sent a man to town to get parts. If they did, he would be back by noon and they will wait. We killed several of them and I have a feeling they will do the same to us. We must try something," she expressing her feelings.

"I know, but what. I'm tied up and so are you. We have those hours perhaps five, to think of something. In the meantime, try to lossen your ropes. Later we can ask for water and perhaps find a way to spill some on the ropes. Wet ropes will stretch where dry ones will not. We just have to be subtle about how we do it. We can't afford to let them catch on," he told her.

They could smell coffee coming from the other boat. Soon the smell of eggs frying pasted through the cabin. Both the prisoners wondered if they would be fed.

An hour pasted and as the two worked on their ropes, Katrina would swear hers were lossening. Perhaps because she was a woman, who ever tied her up was kind to her. Delbert was having one hell of a time and little luck. Because of his size, they really tied him tight.

"Hey, on deck, can I get a drink of water," Katrina hollered.

A small man appeared at the top of the steps. He looked down and asked who was calling.

"I am. I'm thirsty. Can I have some water?"She asked. "I'm hungry too. How about some grub or are you going to starve us to death?"

The small man disappeared for a couple minutes before reappearing at the steps. He came down into the cabin. He was wary until he could see that both she and Delbert were still tied up.

"Can I sit up to drink?" asked Katrina.

Without a word, the man helped her sit up on the edge of the bunk. Her hands were tied in front of her so it wasn't difficult to sit and to hold the container she was offered. The trick was to get the knot in her rope directly under the spout. She was careful and took her time in getting it just right.

As she began to drink, she tipped the container too far forward, allowing the liquid to drip onto the knot. After taking a drink, she pulled back from the container as she looked at the man. The container was still tipped and slopped some down her front and onto the knot.

"Oh, how sloppy, I am. It's hard to drink with your hands tied. Thank you for being so kind. Can my friend have some too?" she asked nodding at Delbert.

The man said not a word, but passed the container to Delbert. Delbert had righted himself during the time Katrina was drinking and was sitting on the edge of the bunk. His hands also tied in front. He knew he had to be careful and not spill water on his ropes. This might make this person suspicious and he didn't want that. He would have to rely on her to get her ropes untied or some how slip out of them. He could wait.

"Thank you, could we have something to eat. Those eggs sure smell good," she explained.

"Why should we feed you. You will die this day. You need no food. You killed some of my friends so why would I feed you,huh?" he explained.

"Look buster, you guys attacked us. We have done nothing to you. We defended ourselves. These are dangerous waters as you know. Please feed us. We give you our word not to try to escape. After we eat and have some of that coffee, we'll tell you what you want to know. Ok?" she asked.

"Si, I will tell the boss and see. I will return in a while," he said and turned around, going back up the steps and out on deck.

A good thirty minutes later, he was back with more water and food. Another man carried the grub and sat it down on the foot of each bunk. The water was placed at the head of Katrina's bunk. The two men started away when Delbert spoke.

"Hey, how do you expect us to eat tied up like this? Can't you untie us for a few minutes while we eat. We promise not to try anything don't we?" Delbert asked Katrina.

"Yes that's right," she replied.

The second did not speak English and just shrugged his shoulders. The first one stoped and turned around. He said something in Spanish to him and he stopped. He then turned his attention to Katrina.

"The boss would kill me if you escaped. Please seniorita, nothing funny if I untie you. Si?" a question he was asking.

"Si, we try nothing. Just let us eat. We will be quick," she answered.

The first man spoke to the second in Spanish. The second sat down on the top step and drew his pistol. Apparently, they were going to untie them to eat.

The first untied Katrina and stood back as she ate. When she was finished, he tied her back the way she had been.

"Please, not so tight. It hurts my wrists," she said.

With this, the man quit tieing the knot so tight, but he double-checked it. Delbert was then untied and ate his now cold meal. After he was tied back, he asked for a drink. He was granted this and he held the container in such a way he too spilled it on his ropes.

"Damn hard to drink without spilling the water," he mentioned.

Katrina was next and also spilled some on the knot of her rope.

The two men gathered up the plates and water container and departed.

"Thank you," Katrina threw after them. But the two did not acknowledge the comment.

Back on shore, Nate's group was moving quickly through the jungle. They tried to return the same way they had come. On the way in the Rangers had broken off twigs to mark the way. This they learned in training. In their haste, they sometimes missed the markings and one or two would get off the markers. This happened to Carl.

He was hurrying through the jungle, when all at once he tripped.

"Eyeryone down, I've hit a trip wire. Down," he yelled.

No explosion occurred, but the group stayed down, hugging the earth until someone calls an all clear.

Nate worked his was up and to the left side of Carl.

"What's happened, Carl. Nothing blew," he asked.

"Damn if I know. You stay back a ways. I'll find the wire and examine the explosive. They proably set it wrong, thank God. It still could blow, so hang right there," he said.

Carl turned his head towards his feet looking for the trip wire. He certainly didn't want to pull on it. He saw it under his feet. He eased one foot over it, all the time holding his breath. This worked, so he moved the other foot over the wire and turned it away. Both feet now clear, he twisted around with his head right over the wire. This was dangerous stuff, but he felt necessary.

He followed the wire into the brush about three feet. The wire ended at an explosive device.

"Found it boss," he said.

"Did you find out why it there was no explosion," Nate asked.

"Yeah, think so. The wire leading into the device is corroded. This thing has been here a long. It could still explode. I'll mark it with my snot rag. Lets get away and we can set it off by shooting it," he advises.

"Ok, lets go," Nate said, "everyone one their feet and move away down stream."

Carl and Nate got to their feet and followed. At a distance of thirty yards they stopped.

"You found it Carl, you shoot it," Nate said with a smile.

"My pleasure," came the answer.

Carl took careful aim and fire three quick shot at his hanky. A loud explosion occurred. Bushes and dirt blew outward from the center of the explosion. Carl smiled, turned and followed the rest. Nate brought up the rear.

"Damn, there goes my last hankie," Carl expressed his loss.

A few minutes later, Nate called for a break. Everyone stopped. Those with cigarettes could smoke. They all took a drink from the creek, sat down and took it easy. Their spirits were good and every step took them closer to the way out and back to the states. In a couple of hours, they would be at the boats. Then things would move quickly and most would be in the U.S. before the cartels could find out what happened.

The fact that one got away still bothered Nate. All he could hope for was a quick retrival by choppers. He was sure the General would not let them down.

The following hour was grelling with a very thick jungle. This slowed their movement. They knew the last hour would be easy going as the jungle thined and they could make better time. All were looking forward to a good home cooked meal and no more K-rations. They contained themselves, but most felt like singing. All were up and ready to go at the end of the break. Their loads seemed lighter because the end was almost in sight.

They moved out with Nate in the lead. He was just as anxious as the others. In an hour, they would be at the boats. Nate had to smile as he noticed the pace had picked up. The men were taking longer strides and walking a little faster.

An hour later, they walked out into the clearing where the creek met the ocean. Nate put his hand up to halt the men. Something was wrong. There were three speedboats tied up to the fishing boats.

"Take covers men, until we find out what the hell is going on out there," he ordered. Dennis and Jim joined him.

"What's happening. Nate?" they both asked at the same time.

"Don't know, but something is wrong. Those other boats should not be there. God, I hope it's not the cartels baboons. Off hand, I'd say Delbert and Katrina were captive on one of the fishing boats. Our rowboats we came in on are still over there under the trees. Lets the three of us step out in the open and shout for Delbert and see what happens. Be ready to duck," was his answer.

The three stood up and walked to the edge of the water and began shouting at the boats. Nothing happened and no one showed themselves. Finally, out of desperation, Nate decided to fire a couple of shots. After all the people on the boats could be napping.

Jim took his rifle and fired it a couple times. Within seconds, fire was returned from the boats. The three dove for cover. *God, what now,* he thought.

-18-

Everyone was undercover of the trees and bushes at the edge of the jungle. Nate decided to call the General and see if the satellite was overhead. He needs more information. He dialed Brown's Realty.

"Yes, Armstrong, what can I do for you," announced the General.

"We seem to have a problem, General. Is the satellite overhead. I need information," Nate said.

"Yes, we have it for another hour. What's up," said the General.

"There are three speed boats tied up along side our fishing boats. I fear two of our people are being held captive on one of the boats. I need to know how many people are on those boats. See if you can tell what boat our people are being held on and their location on the boat. Can you do it?" Nate replied.

"Damn rights I can. Hold on," he told Nate.

"There appears two people below deck on the boat that has only one other boat tied to it. Besides that there are four men on board, all have guns. Looks like your drug dealers have caught up with you," was said when the General came back on the line. "On the other boat there seems to be six people, all men and all armed. All the arms are small and automatic. How you going to tackle this problem, Armstrong?" came the question Nate knew would come.

"May have to wait till dark and swim out to them. I sure wish I had the heavier weapons we have on board. I could blow them out of the water. If only I could blow their boats and let them escape to land for a deal to release Delbert and Katrina. Hell General, at this point, I don't know. Thanks for the info. I'll get back to you," Nate hung up.

Nate, Jim and Dennis crawled back to the safety of the trees. Nate asked all the group to move in around him. He had to tell them what was going on and ask for ideas on how they could attack the problem.

"Well, men, our mission were a success, but we need to free our two people on those boats before we can be picked up. Any ideas. I don't think they know how many of us there are, unless they beat it out of Delbert and Katrina. Nate was sure this had not happened. Those two would die before divulging information like that. Now they will expect us to wait till nightfall, so they'll be waiting for us. This chore will not be easy. I don't want to lose another man, so think about it and give me some ideas. They've only seen three of us and that's in our favor. Spread out here in the jungle and think about it. If you get an idea come see me. Rest, eat and smoke if you want too," was Nate's speech to them.

The men spread out, giving each other plenty of room. They went about cleaning their weapons as a way to kill time.Nate ate a K-ration, had a drink of water and settled back to think. He was sitting on the ground with his back against a downed tree.

"Permission to go look for fruit. That would make the rations go down a lot better," one of the three asking rangers said.

"Yeah, go ahead, but don't go far. Take one more so you'll have enough to help you carry what you find," Nate advises.

The three took off through the jungle. They walked about twenty yards apart as they went.

Nate sat and talked with Jim and Dennis.

"Those on the boat could not have been sent by the one who got away. Hell he won't be to town till this morning. He didn't have a radio or phone as far as we know. It just couldn't have been him who sent this group. If they had, Delbert and Katrina would be dead and our boats destroyed. I don't think it's possible, do either of you?" Nate asked.

"Don't see how it could be," said both Dennis and Jim agreeing.

"I think it some sort of patrol guards for the cartels. They have to keep the shoreline protected from anyone, army or police trying to sneak in like we did. The fishing boats were a nice touch. They proable never put two and two together and figured out what was going on. I know Delbert would give them a story they could believe. Damn, I don't like being pinned down like this. Fellows, we have to do something. I'm not sure what but we need to do it and get the hell out of here. The choppers can't come in until we're clear. The General doesn't want anyone seeing that American choppers are involved in this operation. Come on people think of a plan. I need help on this one.

Delbert and Katrina were working on getting loose. Their wrists were getting raw from the twisting and turning in this effort.

"Delbert, sh sh, my ropes are stretching. In another five minutes I'll be free," she said in a very low voice. Both were sure that someone was at the top of the stairs listening. They'd be damn fools if they didn't.

Minutes later, she was free. She rubbed her wrist to ease the pain. Her skin was still intact.

"Listen for someone coming and I'll untie my feet," Katrina said in a whisper.

Delbert nodded and watched her pull her feet up within reach of her hands. She worked with the knot for a couple minutes when she thought she heard someone coming. Quickly she laid down and covered her hands with a sheet.

"False alarm," Delbert said, "go ahead, it's clear."

She assumed the position and continued to work on the knot. In a couple minutes, she felt the knot give and finally came undone. She quickly jumped down and began working on the rope securing Delbert's hands. This was a harder knot to undo because it wasn't wet like her's was. After five minutes, it gave way and she untied him.

She went to the bottom of the steps and listened as Delbert freed his legs. This task completed, he jumped down from his bunk.

As his feet hit the floor, gunshots could be heard coming from shore.

"Sounds like Nate and the boys are back," Delbert speculated, "lets just stay here and see what happens."

"Yes, good idea, but we need guns. Nate and the Rangers can't attack these boats without suffering heavy casualities. We have to get out of these waters as soon as possible so the choppers can pick us up. Once the word is out about what we have done, we could have a hundred or more of thoses killers out here. Any ideas on how we can help?" she asked him.

"Yeah, we left some small arms under the bunk. These bastards have not found them so if we can lossen the screws, we'll have weapons. Keep watch and I'll try to get the screws out," he told her. He took a couple steps and was in the galley. He found a knife he could use on the screws and began the task.

"Right, but hurry, any minute now one might come below to check on us."

"I think they'll be busy trying to take whoever is on shore. Remember they don't know how many there are, nor their firepower. They still think they are anglers gathering fruit. I hope our people find the heavy stuff we stashed on shore. Hey, I think I got one of these screws loose," he told her.

"Good, how many more to go?" she asked.

Meanwhile, on shore, Nate was still studying the situation through field glasses. From time to time, he would pass the glasses to Jim and Dennis and asked for their ideas on solving this matter.

"Damn, I wish we had a couple of those ground to ground missiles we have under the bunks on those boats. We could blow a couple of their boats and make a deal to let them go in the other one. We'd tell them if they don't, we'll blow all the boats out of the water and they can walk to town. Twenty miles is not that far. They might by it?" he said, but not with much confidence.

Those gathering fruit found as much as they could carry and were headed back toward the crew, when one of them tripped over a piece of brush. Falling forward he dropped his load and put his hands out to break his fall. As he hit the ground, he rolled over, taking some brush with him. Picking himself up and brushing himself off, amidst the laugher of the other two, he noticed something shiny under the brush.

"Come on clumsy," spoke the other two," lets go. We only fifty yards from our camp."

"Wait a minute, there's something under this brush," he said as he removed some more of the brush. "My God, it's weapons. Someone stashed weapons here. Go tell the Major. I'll stand by here and uncover the rest," he sounded excited.

The two left and headed into camp. They placed the fruit they had gathered on the ground and approached the command officers.

"Major Sir, about forty to fifty yards back there we came across a cashe of weapons. They haven't been there long. No rust or anything. Come look," he addressed the Major.

"I'll go with you," Nate said and turned to Dennis. "You keep your eye on the boats and let me know if there are any changes."

The Ranger led them back to the spot where the other ranger had uncovered the weapons. When they arrived, they noticed another pile a short distance away that he had uncovered.

Nate examined the weapons. They were like new. He found a handheld missile launcher, four missiles and automatic weapons. He looked confused at this find. Then it hit him. He'd bet Delbert and Katrina had gotten rid of the weapons because they would be no need once his group was back on the boats. Thank the good lord this was done. Now they had a chance to at least scare off the thugs who held his friends prisoners.

"Hey, do we have anything we can use as a megaphone. Something we can roll up and talk through to magnify my voice. I need to talk to those people," Nate asked his little group.

"We could roll up two or three of the paper cartons that the rations come in. They are waxed and should work," Jim answered.

"Good idea, lets do it," Nate said.

Three of the boxes were slit with a knife, down the corners. Only one corner was cut on each box. A small fire was built and the waxed cardboard was warmed. It was then rolled and shaped into the needed device. As it cooled, the wax stuck the cardboard together. Nate looked at it in the completed form.

"Great, this will work," he said.

Dennis, Jim and Nate again worked their way to the clump of sand, on the beach.

"Keep your heads down, they may start shooting," Nate advise as he raised his head to speak.

"You on the boats, we need to talk," he yelled through the megaphone.

Shooting started coming from the boats. The whine of lead could be heard going over their heads. Nate ducked down and waited. They could hear the plunk of bullets into the sand around them. Little pockets appeared where each bullet landed. It stopped

As soon as it had started. Nate waited. Minutes went by before he decided to try again.

"You on the boats. We need to talk. We have you out numbered and have firepower greater than what you have. If you get on your boats and leave, we will let you. If not, we will kill you. Our people had better not be hurt. If they are that would change my offer," Nate finished and ducked back down.

Shots again were fired from the boats, raining overhead.

"Get me the tube," Nate asked one of the rangers, "and a missile. We'll teach them for sucking eggs."

Three or four minutes later, the missile launcher was handed to Nate. He peeked over the sand dune. He had to pick a boat that he could hit without damaging the fishing boats. He spotted his target. There was one of the cartels tied to the one fishing boat. This was the fishing boat Nate assumed Delbert and Katrina were on. He had to be careful and not miss.

Small waves would move the boat so that it would swing away, towards the open sea. This made it a clear shot if he moved quickly. The water would move it right back next to the fishing boat. It only stayed as an open shot, for a minute.

He stuck his head up and placed the tube (a nickname troops gave this weapon) on his right shoulder.

"Jim feed me the missile when I say so. Ok," Nate said.

"Right on. I have it in my hands. Say when," Jim answered and moved over behind Nate.

Nate waited until the water moved the speedboat out from the fishing boat. It was only minutes but felt like an hour. Then slowly the boat swung out where there was only open water behind. Nate said a little prayer and aimed the tube. When he was on target, he spoke to Jim.

"Feed me," he said and Jim pushed the missile into the tube and tapped Nate on the shoulder. The tap told Nate it was loaded. He held his fire until the boat was starting to float to the other boat and squeezed the trigger. Fire and smoke blew out the rear of the tube as the missile shot forward. It hit the speedboat broad side and blew it up. Pieces flew for hundreds of feet in all directions.

He waited for a response from the boats but none came. He picked up the magaphone and hollored through it.

"That's just a sample of our fire power. Now take your boats and get the hell out of here or we will feed you to the sharks."

Back on board the fishing boat, Delbert and Katrina, now armed was just about to take the steps up to the deck, when the speedboat exploded. The concussion pushed them back from the opening.

"God, bless'em they found where we hid the weapons. Lets go on deck and get a couple of these bastards," he whispered to Katrina.

"I'm with you, let's go," she said.

Just then, they heard voices on deck saying for someone to get the prisoners and bring them up.

"Get back in the galley and be ready to shoot. Hide your gun. I'll get the second one as he comes through the hatch, but you have to take care of the first one. Ok," Delbert explained.

"Yes," she said backing back to the little galley.

Delbert put his back against the wall next to the three steps. His hope was that the first would be in a hurry and wouldn't see him. He'd then nail the second one from behind. No more was he in place than the first set of feet started down the steps. The man passed him, seeing Katrina at the far end.

"What the hell, you little bitch," he said and lunged for her.

The second man had just came off the last step and that put Delbert behind him. Before he knew what was going on, Nate struck him over the head with the butt of his pistol. He felt the skull give and knew he'd killed him. He laid his body down and jumped over him. Katrina had the first man under her gun and he had stopped. He didn't even realize Delbert was behind him. He felt sharp pains as Delbert's pistol came smashing down over his head. He fell like a sack of potatos.

Delbert motioned to Katrina to follow him. They traversed the three steps and came out into the cabin and onto the deck. Two men were waiting for them. They were armed but had put their guns down. They were leaning agaist the bulkhead next to them. When they saw Delbert and Katrina and realized they were free, both jumped for their guns. They were a fraction too late. Delbert and Katrina both fired at the same time and the two hit the deck, dead.

Delbert stood up and yelled to Nate.

"We're free and have control of this boat. Killed four for you. Watch for others coming after us. We'll make a break for it."

Delbert went back into the wheelhouse and started the boat. Katrina shot at a couple of men on the other fishing boat as they tried to get shots off after them. She didn't hit them but they ducked back out of sight.

"Cut the anchor rope, Katrina. Use the fire ax," Delbert yelled at her.

She grabbed the ax from where it was mounted on the cabin wall and ran to the back of the boat. With two swings of the ax, they were free of the anchor.

Delbert jammed the boat in reverse and put her in full speed. They shot away from the other boats. Delbert, spun the wheel around and shifted gears, heading away towards the west. After going a few hundred yards, he circled around and landed about three hundred yards from Nate and friends.

"Katrina, you run over to Nate and report to him on how many more is left on the boats. Stay in the jungle so those on the boat can't shot you. They will try. Ask him to send a couple Rangers here to help me protect the boat," Delbert told her.

"Ok, stay safe," she said and went over the side of the boat and walked into the jungle.

In a matter of minutes, she was standing with Nate. He had moved back near the Rangers to avoid any bullets that might come flying that way.

"I'm not sure how many men are still on the boats. I think six. They are on the fishing boat. What are you going to do?" she asked him.

"I have an idea. Jim sends a couple men down to the boat and be ready to push off. We need to get the hell out of here before we get more company," Nate said to him.

"Sure, I'll go with them. See you soon. Call if you need us," he replied as he waved at a Ranger. They pushed off toward the boat.

Just then, a Ranger ran up to him and spoke.

"Sir, I found another tube in the pile, but no more missiles. We have only three left," he announced.

"Good, bring it forward and the missiles. Hurry," Nate ordered.

Nate left the security of the jungle, back to the dune. He raised his head and shouted into the megaphone.

"You on the boats, my offer stands. Get in your speedboats and get out of here or I'll blow all the boats. You have five minutes," he advised.

He dialed the phone and spoke to the General.

"Hi, General how's it going back in Washington?" Nate asked

"Fine and I see you are having a little excitement down there. What do you need from me?" asked the General.

"How many people are still on the boats, if you have the satellite. I need to know now," he explained.

"Six is all that's left. When you getting out of there. The one who got away must be in town by now. Twenty miles isn't that far. You need to move and move quickly. I don't want this to fall apart now that we're done," he inserted into the conversation.

"Just keep watching. I think we'll be out of here in minutes," Nate said and hung up.

He finished just in time. Those on the boat were yelling for him.

"Yeah, what do you want?" Nate answered just as the ranger walked up with the other tube.

"We want to leave. Do I have your word that you'll lets us go if we leave now?" the voice said.

"Yes, hell yes. Get going," he replied and waved for the Rangers to come forward.

I need someone to operate that second tube and two to feed us the missiles. Several spoke up and Nate chose three. Two to feed the tube and one to fire one.

"Listen, those guys are going for their boats. They now know we are Americans and we must kill them all. Those boats are fast so when they get away from the fishing boat, we must blow them out of the water. Any problems with that?" he asked the Rangers. They all shook their heads "no."

"Good, get ready and don't damage the fishing boat," Nate instructed.

He switched his attention back to the boats. *Three boats and four missiles,* he was thinking. The shooting must be good.

He placed the tube on his shoulder as he saw the men scurrying to get off the fishing boat. One boat pushed off and it's motor started. The other boats were filling up and the first seemed to be waiting for them. They were soon loaded and also pushed off from the fishing boat. He counted six into the three boats. They fired up their motors and began to start away.

"Feed me," Nate said and heard the Ranger say the same.

A pat came on his shoulder and he squeezed the trigger. The tube bleched smoke and fire as the missile left the tube.

In a second, the furthest boat exploded.

The second tube followered suit and fired. The second boat exploded.

"Feed me," Nate yelled.

A pat on the shoulder came and he fired. This time the missle went over the boat and exploded out to sea.

Damn, he said under his breath.

He heard the words, "Feed me," and the Ranger fired his tube again. As they all watched and prayed this would take care of the last boat. Fingers were crossed.

The boat exploded as they watched. They all gave a cheer. They were now free to go.

"Good shooting, kid," Nate said as he patted the Ranger on the back.

Nate dialed the phone that Jim carried.

"Bring that boat over here and give us a lift to the other boat," he told Delbert who was now on the phone.

"Yes, boss, coming," and the phone clicked off.

"Police your areas and don't leave a sign that would tell anyone we are Americans. Set charges in the weapons pile. Toss these tubes on the pile.

In minutes, they were on board the other fishing boat. The load was distributed. Once done and cigars passed out, they opened the engines wide open and headed out to sea.

Just passing the three-mile limit, placing them into international waters, Nate's phone rang. He was sure it was the General.

"Hello, general, we're ready for the choppers. Did you see the final curtain call on our little mission to the tropics. How soon will we see the choppers?" he asked.

"Head west towards Panama. As soon as you are within reasonable distance, I'll have them there. You need to make a few miles in that direction. You did good Armstrong. Tell your crew that deposits are being made right now for your work. A quarter million dollars each for your raid and with the money for send'em them to the deep, you are all quite well off. As soon as the choppers are in sight, set charges in the boats and sink them. That will take care of any sign this was a U.S. government operation," coming from the General.

"Can't do that General. I promised the boats to an old man fighting to keep his fish cannery open. He's getting them free of charge. I'll sign over title to him for ten thousand dollars. He won't actually pay the money but no one needs to know that. It's a good cover for him," Nate said.

"Damn it, Armstrong, I'm running the show and I say sink them. Do you hear me, sink them," yelled the General.

"Bye, General," Nate hung up.

Ed was in the wheelhouse when Nate ordered he turn west to meet the choppers. Nate called Delbert to advise him what was going on.

"Delbert, you know I'm coming back here to live and marry Loretta. These boats are a gift of the U.S. government to her uncle at the cannery. The reason I'm telling you this is that I'm not going on the choppers. I'm taking them to him and see to Loretta. I'll make my way to Panama and go out by army aircraft. Just wanted you to know. I may not get to tell your crewmembers how much I appreciate what they have done down here. We have struck a mighty blow to protect Americans for the evil of drug addiction. No one will ever know it was done, but we did it. Tell the people if I ever get to their neighborhood, I'll stop by and see them. Tell them if they ever want a great vacation to come back to Colombia and see me. They know where I'll be. Good luck to all of you and spend the money wisely. This is the last caper for me and the rest of you are getting too old for this stuff to. Hanging up now to tell my crew. Good luck Delbert, have a long and happy life," Nate said as he signed off.

Nate gathered those on board the boat. Once they were there, he passed around a bottle of whisky and a cigar for each. Katrina took a swig of the whisky, but refused the cigar.

Once the bottle had gone around and cigars were lit, Nate spoke to them.

"Here's to a job well done. We put a crimp in the drug trade in America. They will be back in business six months. They may find it hard to find willing workers. The word will spread that there is a drug war going on and no one in his right mind will go willingly. Of course, they will use forced labor, but maybe the government will curtail that pratice. I salute you all. We worked well together, but it could not have happened without Katrina who gave us the information. She endured the filth of the enemy. She had to put up with their dirty remarks and hands," he said.

Turning to her, he raised the bottle to her. "A toast to Katrina," he added and passed the bottle.

He paused to suck on the cigar as he looked over his crew. He knew he would miss everyone of them. He felt like he was losing a family. Actually these folks were closer than family. Combat, any kind of combat, makes the kind of friendships that never dims and lasts forever.

"I have an announcement. This covert operation was my last. I get too old for this stuff. It was great to see my good friends from Nam again, but now we must part. Each will go their separate way and we may not see each other again. You folks are too damn old too, so take the money we've earned and use it wisely. It will last us for life. As for me, I'm coming back to Colombia to marry Loretta an settle down. I would like the rest of you settle down and quit chasing excitement. We've all had enough," Nate was saying as the bottle came back to him. He looked around at these people, with pride shinning in his eyes. He noticed Katrina and Carl had snuggled up together. His arm around her and he felt good. He'd always worried that Carl would not find the woman of his dreams. It now appears he has. That's one wedding he likes to go to, if it comes to pass. He went on.

"In two hours the choppers will be picking you all up. I'm going to try to sneak back into town and hand over these two boats the old person at the fish cannary. I will spend a day or two with Loretta, then head to Panama. From there I'll catch a military flight to Washington. Check your bank accounts as soon as you land at home. If there's a problem call, me at a number I'll give you and I'll take care of it. Now lets have another drink, but don't get drunk. We're to close to touchdown to get silly. Someone get another bottle for below," he finished. *"Damn, I didn't mean to give a speech, "*he was thinking as he smiled to himself.

They all drank to that as they traveled outside the three miles limit. Nate's phone rang and he picked it up.

"Hi, general, what's up?" Nate asked.

"The choppers have just lifted off and will be at your location. Continue at your current speed. Dump all your arms overboard. Have everyone packed and ready to go. We don't want to stay out there long. We have a C-130 waiting in Panama to bring everyone home. How about you Nate, how will you get out of there?" asked the General with a concerned voice.

"I'll deliver the boats to our old docking place and turn them over to the old guy who helped us. I'll make it to Loretta's and spend a day and a night. I'm coming back to marry her, you know. I'll then find a way to Panama and once on the base there I'll see if your colonel will get me a plane home. I'll check in with you for a final report in three or four days. I need some time to clear up some business, then back here. Put this on the record, sir, I'm doing no more covert operations ever. I'm retired or will be as soon as I get home," Nate finished.

"I'll see you get a ride home from Panama. I'll call the colonel, myself. See you when you get home. Be careful and don't do anything I wouldn't like to do," laughing he hung up.

"Ok, everbody, dump all weapons overboard and get packed. The choppers are on their way," Nate said.

He then called Delbert and told him to ditch all the weaons in the ocean and get ready to go.

"Delbert, move your boat in behind us and throw us a line. I'll be towing that one back to port," he instructed.

"Sure you don't want some company going in there. If they know you're a part of this, they will be waiting. I'd go if you need me," Delbert told him.

"I know. So would any one of the crew. No, but thanks, I'll be fine. One of these days I'll come knocking on your door when you least expect it. Oh, tell everyone that in thirty days there will be a big wedding at Loretta's place and everyone's invited. All the food and drink you can hold. Now move into position and throw the line. We've got to hurry," Nate said.

Delbert steered to the rear of Nate's boat and had a ranger throw a line to Brad. Brad secured the rope and pulled it up short as Delbert pulled in close. He tied it off when the boats were within ten feet of each other. Nate was watching and got the high sign from Brad.

They could hear choppers coming in from the west. Their ride home. Nate waved one in over his boat. He grabbed the rope ladder and held it taunt as the crew approached to leave the boat. Katrina went first. As she grabbed the ladder, she leaned over and kissed Nate. No words were said and she climbed to the chopper and her pretty little butt disappeared inside. Next came a ranger, then two. Brad came for his turn. As he reached Nate, he held out his hand. They shook with no words spoken. Both had a lump in their throats as they said goodby. The rest of the rangers went aboard, several thanked Nate for the experience of helping out. Ed was the last to come forward. He stuck out his hand and shook Nate's. "Bye boss, see you around." Then up the ladder, he went.

Nate released the ladder and the chopper pulled it up and as Nate waved goodbye, it turned and flew into the west.

The second chopper did the same, following the first.

All at once, Nate felt lonely. This was a strange feeling for him. He shook it off, took a swig of whiskey and moved the boat slowly, heading south.

The two men in the boat moved it down to the towed boat and boarded it. They went below for the search. The two on his boat followed suit. A couple minutes later, they were back on deck. They had found nothing and were in a foul mood.

"Senor, if I find out you is with these criminals, I'll hunt you down. Understand?"

"Si," Nate said.

"We have many men and boats looking for these men. If you spot any of armed men, get on the radio. One of our boats could be here in no time," the man said.

With this, the men jumped back into their boat and pushed off, heading north.

"Well, hell," Nate thought, *"I might as well start in. Those goons know I'm here and they don't suspect me as one of the criminals.* He had to smile at this idea.

He fixed a sandwich and drank a bottle of beer. The sun was getting low in the west, so he started for Cartagena. He was not expected until after dark so he crept towards land. The sunset was more beautiful this evening for some reason. At least it was for him. In a short period of time, he'd be in the arms of his darling. *Life is good,"* he thought.

Darkness had fallen and he was not far away. As soon as it was totally dark, he pulled up to the docks and his berthing spaces. Turning off the engine, he looked around. All looked well and there was only a couple walking back and forth along the docks. He did a final check for any personal items he may have overlooked. Making sure the boats were tied securely, he again looked around. Satisfied, he walked the distance to the cannery.

The place was dark and seemed deserted. Walking up to the man door, he twisted the knob. It turned in his hand. Gentle and slowly he pushed in on it. A light came streaming out into the darkness. He quickly entered and bolted the door. Turning around he was facing the old man.

"Senor, you made it. Is all well?" he asked.

"All is fine," Nate said as he walked over and shook the old man's hand. He noticed another man standing over to one side. To this man he nodded his head then looked back at the old man.

"Did Loretta get a hold of you?" Nate asked.

"Si, she said you'd be here. The papers are on the desk for your signature, but I can't take your boats. I did nothing to deserve them," the old man stated.

"The boats were a gift to me from the U.S. Government. I now give them to you to help out. Loretta and I will marry as soon as I return from the U.S. You are her uncle, so the boats will still be in the family. Please it makes me proud to give them to you," Nate finished and walked over to the desk.

A minute later, the papers were signed and presented the keys to the old man.

"Thank you, senor, and congratulations on your coming marrage. Loretta needs a good man. Much happness to you both," the old person said.

"You'll be invited to the wedding. If you don't give her away, then you can be my best man," Nate said.

With this statement, the old man smiled and agreed.

"Oh, senor, this is Jose, he will take you to Loretta's place," he said pointing at the younger man.

Nate walked over and shook his hand.

"I'm ready to go, if you are," Nate said to him.

"Si, senor, lets walk around the corner to my car. She's waiting at her place," he told Nate.

Both men waved goodbye to the old man as the went to the car.

Minutes later, Nate was dropped off at Loretta's place. As he entered by the front door, a feeling of being home descended upon him.

The bartender saw him and waved. Nate waved back and turned to the stairs. He took the steps two at a time. The door was unlocked. He burst into the room. Loretta was just hanging up the phone. Turning and seeing him, she rushed to him.

He grabbed her with arms around her. He raised her off the floor as they kissed. A long passionate kiss. He lowered her to the floor only when they ran out of air.

"Hi, love, how my girl is," he said.

"Oh, Nate, I never thought I'd see you again," she commented as tears sneaked out from under her eyelids.

"Don't cry honey, I'm back and the job is done. We have a lifetime ahead of us." he spoke softly in her ear as he rubbed a hand over her buttocks.

They hugged as thought they'd not seen each other in years. Nate broke the silence.

"Let's have some champagne. I'm hot and sweaty and need a shower, darling," he whispered in he ear.

"Yes, lets," she agreed. Holding his hand, she led him over to the table where waited a bottle of her best champagne.

"You pop the cork, honey," she said squeezing his hand.

He let go her hand and wrapped the towel around the bottle. He peeled off the cover to the cork, twisted the wire holding the cap in place. Working the cork loose, it popped and the cork shot across the room. He filled two glasses.

"A toast to the future," he said raising his glass, she raised her's and he continued.

"To a long and happy live to us. May our love grow deeper each year," he finished. They both drank, emptying the contents of the glasses. He refilled their glasses.

"Darling, I'm going to take a shower, want to come. I'd love to soap that beautiful body. Course seeing you naked would be an extra treat," he commented.

"Shame on you," she said smiling, "this way." She led him into the bathroom.

The wine would have to wait and they sat the glasses down. He took her in his arms and kissed her was passion. With his hands, he worked the zipper in the back of her dress, downward. Finishing the kiss, she helps him get it off. It hit the floor.

He smiled as he looked over her body, she had no underclothes on.

"You naughty girl," he said, "You must have been expecting someone."

"I was," she smiled back, "and here he is. I'll turn the water on."

With her help, it only took seconds to remove his clothes and both stepped into the flowing water.

More kisses took place before the soapsuds covered their bodies. This action took place until the water was turning cold. Finally, they came back to the real world.

"Lets eat. I told the chef to prepare a very tender, thick steak for dinner. I'll ring him and have it sent up. Would you like a whisky?" Lorette was saying as he kissed her neck.

"I had something else in mind," he replied. Just rubbing his hands over he bare bottom turned him on.

"I know and I to would like to get there, but lets eat first. Once we get to the bed, we won't want to get up till morning. At least that's what I would want," she said kissing him.

"Yes, whisky would be good," he answered her question.

"Honey, look on the bed and you will find a gift for you. I put my robe on to cover up temptation, at least for now," and she left his arms and picked up her robe.

He went into the bedroom and saw a white bathrobe laying there. He'd missed seeing that when they came through the bedroom to the bathroom. He put it on and tied the belt. He walked over to the dresser and looked at himself in the mirror.

"Hey, pretty neat, thanks hon," he said, "If you keep this up you will spoil me."

"I intend to, come lets get that food up here. We'll eat on the patio and watch the lights of the city," she told him.

"Great, that would be perfect," he said.

Inside, they were both trembling. They had already entered the deepest relationship that exists between a man and woman. These two were not the least bit concerned about the future. Their only concern was in pleasing each other.

The food arrived and was placed on the patio. Once the two who had brought it left, Nate and Lorette seated themselves above the city lights.

After the meal, they just stood holding hands at the rail. They were lost in thoughts of happiness and wonder. Loretta was the first to move.

"Beat you to the bed, slow poke," she said laughing and leaving the patio running.

Nate just walked behind her. This confused her a little so she asked "Why"

He grinned before replying.

"I have a much better use for my energy than running!"

He took her in his arms and soon her robe hit the floor. His followed shortly afterwards.

The two slept in. When rising, they decided what to have for breakfast. After the meal and the dishes cleared away, they sat and talked.

"Honey, I must go to Washington and see the General. I need to go to my bank and get some money to bring here. I would like to have a big wedding right here in your establishment. I'll pay for everything. I want to invite my friends to the wedding. You, know, the ones who just went home. You invite family and friends and we'll have a great party, then settle down. What do you think? Does it sound good to you?" he said.

"Oh, yes honey that sounds great. I'll plan it while you're gone to the states. Please hurry back. I will miss you so," she explained.

"I could be back in a week, then I'll never leave you again. I do love you so," he said with emotion welling up in his heart.

"When do you think you'll go, honey?" she asked.

"Day after tomorrow I'll make my way to Panama and take a military plane from there. I do so want to spend today and tomorrow with you," he finished.

Five days later Nate was checking into a hotel room in Washington. He used his cell phone to call the General.

"What the hell you calling on this phone for. The mission is over," said the General.

"I'm at the Hilton. I can come and see you for a debriefing. Then I'm headed home for some banking business, then back to Colombia to get married," Nate spoke in firm terms.

"Married! Are you nuts. You've got it all. I sometime I wish I was single so I could come and go as I please. No honey-do lists, etc. Well ok. I'll send a car for you at nine. We'll meet at the C.I.A. building, same room as before. There will be the same group of men you met with before. Remember no names. The door guard will be expecting you. See you later," he said putting down the phone.

The day was a quiet day. Nate slept some, eats his meals and had a couple of drinks at the bar.

At nine, he was standing in front of the hotel, when a black car pulled up. It stopped for him and he entered it. A few minutes later, he was walking through the doors at the C. I. A. He had the same errie feeling as before. He was thinking, *why the hell do they always-black cars.*

The thought dissipated as he saw the guard approaching.

"You the one they are waiting for?" he asked.

"Yes," Nate answered and followered the guard downs the hall. The guard opened the door and Nate stepped into the room.

Standing there was the General.

"Hi, Nate, lets go," he said.

The wall opened and there at the table were the others. For thirty minutes they taked to Nate. There were questions and general talk. All agreed that the mission was a success. Cocaine had nearly dryed up and streets on the west coast were going through withdraws. The price had gone thru the roof and most addicts could not afford it. Nate assured them that it would take the cartels at least six months to recover. He told them exactly what his crew had done and afterwards they had but one question.

"Did you leave any evidence that Americans had been responsible for the actions," one of the men in suits asked. Nate believed this man was a senator.

"No sir, we left no sign it was us. This was proven by them searching our boats and not seizing the boats as I docked," Nate assured them.

"Oh," the other suit asked, "what happened to our boats?"

"Lost at sea. I took them out quite a ways and sank them," was the answer.

The General frowned at this answer, but said nothing. The meeting ended and all left the room except Nate and the General.

"You lied about the boats. You gave them away, didn't you?"

"Yes, but they didn't need to know that. After all this was a covert operation, wasn't it?" he grinned when he said it.

The General threw his head back and laughed.

He reached for Nate's hand and shook it.

"Thanks, Nate and have a good life," he said.

A month later, there was one hell of a party at Loretta's place. All the men came down to be there for Nate's and Loretta's wedding.

THE END

EDUCATING ANDREW
By Virginia Lanier Biasotto

The strongest bond in the animal kingdom is mother and offspring.

When something threatens, the mother instinctively acts to protect. The story of Andrew is a human example, and the enemy was one of our most revered institutions: the public school.

For most children, the beginning of school is a time of anticipation and excitement. New clothes and supplies are purchased. A preliminary visit to the classroom sets the stage for the promise, "This is where you will learn to read." For Andrew, the reading part didn't happen. For seven years solutions were sought, found and rejected. The printed page remained a mystery. The effects of his failure to read were dire. Andrew's love of life had been taken away, and his parents and teachers were helpless to do anything about it.

Paperback, 132 pages
5.5" x 8.5"
ISBN 1-4241-0171-9

When it appeared that Andrew would remain illiterate as he entered junior high school, a door opened that would change his life and that of his mother forever.

About the author:

VIRGINIA (GINGER) LANIER BIASOTTO is a native of Delaware and a graduate of the University of Delaware (1959). She is the founder of Reading ASSIST® Institute and the author of ten Reading ASSIST® text books. In 2005, Virginia received Delaware's Jefferson Award for Public Service for her contribution to literacy. She and her husband, Lawrence, are semi-retired and spend half of each year in Wilmington, Delaware, close to children, grandchildren and mothers, and the other half in Palm City, Florida.

Also available from PublishAmerica

RETURN TO THE ASHAU
By John James Kielty

A most secret plan by the U.S. Government to prepare for a pullout from Vietnam was initiated in 1968 just after the momentous Tet Offensive. The plan called for the caching of great treasure to support the expected network of spies that would stay behind. The Green Beret soldiers who unknowingly planted these treasure troves learned of its existence and now they were determined to retrieve it. The officials who directed these missions in the past were now holding higher offices and were ambitiously seeking even higher positions. The American public could not be allowed to find out about the government's plan to cut and run and the needless deaths of thousands of our young men and women who fought and died for a cause already determined to be without merit. When these government

Paperback, 358 pages
6" x 9"
ISBN 1-4241-2124-8

officials learn of the covert plans of these men to retrieve this treasure, they decide this cannot occur and the deadly decisions are made. The chase begins and with it the treachery and lies.

About the author:

John James Kielty spent twenty years as a warrior soldier, or as the Irish would call him, one of the Wild Geese. Though born in Ireland, he fought in America's wars proudly and with distinction. John James Kielty is proud of the great heritage of Irish writers with whom he shares a love of the written word. He now lives in semi-retirement in the rural mountains of southern West Virginia that are so much like his native Ireland in appearance. He spends his free time working with wood and periodically sitting at his keyboard.

Available to all bookstores nationwide.
www.publishamerica.com

Also available from PublishAmerica

THE SEED OF OMEGA
By Eugene Ettlinger

The Seed of Omega depicts the molding of rural
Palestine from the windblown nomadic land of
weeds and sand into a Mecca in the Middle East.
The land was populated by assimilation through
different cultures, which includes an ethnic
invasion after the soil had been tilled. A greater
understanding of political power through favored
in-migration status shows the melding of a select
society. The power brokers governing the land
became subservient to the will of neighboring
nations in exchange for the production of oil. The
cast is composed of variations of the Middle
Eastern Arab people, the power brokers of the
British Empire and the exiles from hostile nations
the world over.

Paperback, 511 pages
6" x 9"
ISBN 1-4137-8882-3

The diversity of characters represents different
walks of life to be filled by the shoes of the reader.
They fought for survival and a love for one another.
They were dedicated to the building of a society while struggling to implement
a diverse nation running from a past life simply to find a place in which to be.
Their fears are offset by the courage to survive in the creation of a nation.

About the author:

A native New Yorker and Fordham University graduate, Gene
Ettlinger performed graduate studies in the field of sociology.
Gene's dedication is in the development of community life.
Growing up in the mixing bowl of ethnic diversity led to his
keen interest in the alienation of unskilled workers. Gene is a
pilot, skier, skilled boating enthusiast, and an accomplished artist.
He currently resides in New York and Florida.

Available to all bookstores nationwide.
www.publishamerica.com